Ode to a Banker

Lindsey Davis was born in Birmingham but now lives in Greenwich. After an English degree at Oxford she joined the Civil Service but now writes full time. Lindsey Davis was awarded the first CWA Ellis Peters Historical Dagger for her top-ten bestseller *Two for the Lions*. She was recently voted one of the top 50 authors in the Waterstone's Reading Survey and received the 1999 Sherlock Award for Best Comic Detective for her creation, Marcus Didius Falco.

ODE TO A BANKER

Lindsey Davis

Century · London

Published by Century in 2000

1 3 5 7 9 10 8 6 4 2

Copyright © Lindsey Davis 2000

Lindsey Davis has asserted her right under the Copyright, Designs and
Patents Act, 1988 to be identified as the author of this work

First published in the United Kingdom in 2000 by Century
Random House UK Limited
20 Vauxhall Bridge Road, London SW1V 2SA

Random House Australia (Pty) Limited
20 Alfred Street, Milsons Point, Sydney,
New South Wales 2061, Australia

Random House New Zealand Limited
18 Poland Road, Glenfield
Auckland 10, New Zealand

Random House (Pty) Limited
Endulini, 5a Jubilee Road, Parktown 2193, South Africa

The Random House Group Limited Reg. No. 954009

www.randomhouse.co.uk

A CIP catalogue record for this book
is available from the British Library

Papers used by Random House
are natural, recyclable products made from wood grown in
sustainable forests. The manufacturing processes conform to
the environmental regulations of the country of origin

ISBN 0 7126 7029 7

Typeset in Bembo by SX Composing DTP, Rayleigh, Essex

Printed and bound in the United Kingdom by
Mackays of Chatham plc, Chatham, Kent

To Simon King
(another of my 'Dear Simon' notes . . .)

On your retirement from Random House.
With thanks for your friendship, patience, and loyal support for
Falco – And in memory of the smoked eel.

Author's Disclaimers

I hereby assert strenuously that the scroll-shop of Aurelius Chrysippus in the Clivus Publicius bears no relation to my publishers – who are models of editorial judgement, prompt payment, fair dealing, strong marketing, and lunch-buying. (NB: the dedication of this book is to a most excellent man, who was one of them.)

The views of M. Didius Falco on the characters and habits of authors are his views only; clearly, he has not met my delightful colleagues.

The Golden Horse is certainly not my bank.

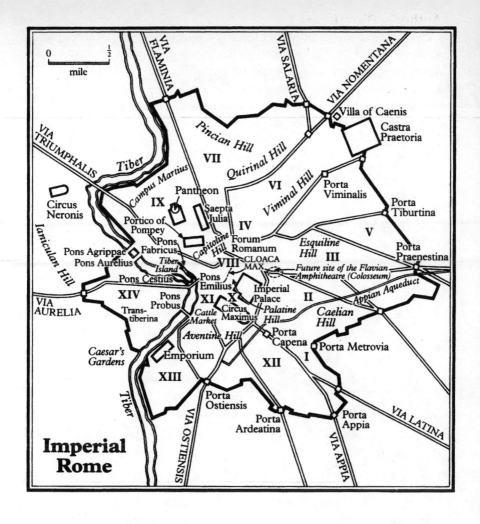

Imperial Rome

Jurisdictions of the Vigiles Cohorts in Rome:

Coh I	Regions VII & VIII (Via Lata, Forum Romanum)
Coh II	Regions III & V (Isis and Serapis, Esquiline)
Coh III	Regions IV & VI (Temple of Peace, Alta Semita)
Coh IV	Regions XII & XIII (Piscina Publica, Aventine)
Coh V	Regions I & II (Porta Capena, Caelimontium)
Coh VI	Regions X & XI (Palatine, Circus Maximus)
Coh VII	Regions IX & XIV (Circus Flaminius, Transtiberina)

PRINCIPAL CHARACTERS

Old Stagers

M. Didius Falco/Dillius Braco/ } a well-known Roman
Ditrius Basto

Helena Justina	a heroine (a loyal reader)
Ma (Junilla Tacita)	a canny depositor
Pa (Geminus)	a chipped old block
Maia Favonia (a sister)	a late-developing job-seeker
Junia (another sister)	a skilled staff manager
Rutilius Gallicus	a high profile spare time scribbler
Anacrites	a low lyer with variable interests
A. Camillus Aelianus	an ill-equipped aristocratic trainee
Gloccus and Cotta	invisible bathhouse contractors

Numerous children, dogs, pregnancies and pups

The Vigiles

Petronius Longus	a stand-in looking for a fair cop
Fusculus	an old hand with attitude
Passus	a new boy with a taste for adventure
Sergius	an official bruiser

The World of the Arts

Aurelius Chrysippus	a patron of literature (a swine)
Euschemon	a scroll-seller (a good critic) (a what?)
Avienus	a historian with writer's block
Turius	a utopian with allergies (to work)
Urbanus Trypho	the Shakespeare (Bacon?) of his day
Anna, Trypho's wife	who may have a way with her
Pacuvius (*Scrutator*)	a bad-mouthing satirist (extinct species)
Constrictus	a love poet who needs to be dumped
Blitis	from a writers' group (*not* writing at present)

From Commerce

Nothokleptes	a thieving bastard (a banker)
Aurelius Chrysippus	(him again) a secretive businessman

Lucrio	a personal banking executive (unsafe deposits)
Bos	a big man who explains bank charges
Diomedes	a very religious son with artistic hobbies
Lysa (first wife of Chrysippus)	a maker of men and their businesses (hard feelings)
Vibia (second wife of ditto)	a keen home-maker (soft furnishings)
Pisarchus	a shipping magnate who may be sunk
Philomelus	his son, a drudge with a dream

Stock Characters

Domitian	a Young Prince (a hater)
Aristagoras	an Old Man (a lover?)
An old woman	a Witness
Perella	a Dancer

ROME: MID JULY–12 AUGUST, AD74

'A book may be defined . . . as a written (or printed) message of considerable length, meant for public circulation and recorded on materials that are light yet durable enough to afford comparatively easy portability.'

Encyclopaedia Britannica

[The creditor] examines your family affairs; he meddles with your transacations. If you go forth from your chamber, he drags you along with him and carries you off; if you hide yourself inside he stands before your house and knocks at the door.

If [the debtor] sleeps, he sees the moneylender standing at his head, an evil dream . . . If a friend knocks at the door he hides under the couch. Does the dog bark? He breaks out in a sweat. The interest due increases like a hare, a wild animal which the ancients believed could not stop reproducing even while it was nourishing the offspring already produced.'

Basil of Caesarea

I

P OETRY SHOULD have been safe.

'Take your writing tablets up to our new house,' suggested Helena Justina, my elegant partner in life. I was struggling against shock and physical exhaustion, acquired during a dramatic underground rescue. Publicly, the vigiles took the credit, but I was the mad volunteer who had been lowered head first down a shaft on ropes. It had made me a hero for about a day, and I was mentioned by name (misspelled) in the *Daily Gazette*. 'Just sit and relax in the garden,' soothed Helena, after I had rampaged about our tiny Roman apartment for several weeks. 'You can supervise the bathhouse contractors.'

'I can supervise them if they bother to turn up.'

'Take the baby. I may come too – we have so many friends abroad nowadays, I ought to work on *The Collected Letters of Helena Justina*.'

'Authorship?'

What – by a senator's daughter? Most are too stupid and too busy counting their jewellery. None are ever encouraged to reveal their literary skills, assuming they have them. But then, they are not supposed to live with informers either.

'Badly needed,' she said briskly. 'Most published letters are by smug men with nothing to say.'

Was she serious? Was she privately romancing? Or was she just twisting the rope on my pulley to see when I snapped? 'Ah well,' I said mildly. 'You sit in the shade of a pine tree with your stylus and your great thoughts, fruit. I can easily run around after our darling daughter at the same time as I'm keeping a check on a bunch of slippery builders who want to destroy our new steam room. Then I can dash off my own little odes whenever there's a pause in the screaming and stone-cutting.'

Every would-be author needs solitude and tranquillity.

It would have been a wonderful way to pass the summer, escaping from the city heat to our intended new home on the Janiculan Hill – except for this: the new home was a dump; the baby had embarked on a tantrum phase; and poetry led me into a public recital, which was foolish enough. That brought me into contact with the Chrysippus organisation. Anything in commerce that looks like a safe proposition may be a step on the route to grief.

II

<hr>

I MUST HAVE been crazy. Drunk too, maybe.

Why had I received no protection from the Capitoline gods? All right, I admit Jupiter and Minerva might feel I was their most insignificant acolyte, merely slave to a sinecure, a placeman, a careerist, and a half-hearted one at that. But Juno could have helped me out. Juno really should have bestirred herself from leaning on one elbow, playing Olympian board games of hero-baiting and husband-tracking; the Queen of Heaven could have stilled the dice just long enough to notice that the new Procurator of her Sacred Geese had an unworkable glitch in his otherwise smooth-running social life. In short: I had stupidly agreed to be the warm-up act at someone else's poetry show.

My fellow author was a senator of consular rank. Disastrous. He would expect his friends and relatives to be seated on the comfortable benches while mine squashed into a few inches of standing room. He would grab most of the reading time. He would go first, while the audience was still awake. What's more, he was bound to be a bloody awful poet.

I am talking about Rutilius Gallicus. That's right. The same Rutilius Gallicus who would one day be the Urban Prefect – the Emperor's law and order chief, Domitian's strong-arm boy, that great man who is nowadays so greatly loved by the populace (as we are told by those who tell us what to think). Twenty years ago, at the time of our reading together, he was just any old ex-consul. Then, we still had Vespasian on the throne. As his legate in Tripolitania, Rutilius had recently solved a boundary dispute, for what that was worth (not much, unless you had the misfortune to live in Lepcis Magna or Oea). He had not yet become eligible to govern a province, was not yet famous for his German exploit, and nobody would ever have expected him to be the subject of heroic poetry himself. A celebrity in waiting. I thought him a pleasant mediocrity, a provincial just about holding up to wearing his senatorial purple.

5

Wrong, Falco. He was my friend, it seemed. I viewed this honour with great caution as I had gained the impression even then that he was also cosying up to Domitian, our least loveable imperial prince. Rutilius must think there was advantage in it. I chose my pals more carefully.

At home, with the matronly wife who hailed from his own town of origin – Augusta Taurinorum in northern Italy – and with whatever they possessed of a family (how should I know? I was just a newly-promoted equestrian; he might have befriended me as a fellow exile when we first met in faraway Africa, but in Rome, I would never be taken home to meet his noble kin), at home the gladsome Gallicus would be known as Gaius or whatever. I did not qualify to use his private name. He would never call me Marcus either. I was Falco; for me, he would remain 'sir'. I could not tell if he knew there was mockery clothing my respectful tone. I was never too obvious; I like to keep my record clean. Besides, if he did become Domitian's crony, you never know where toadying may lead.

Well, some of us know now. But *then* you would never have marked down Rutilius Gallicus for favour and fame.

One advantage of sharing a platform with a patrician was that he hired a grand venue. Our stage was in the Gardens of Maecenas, no less – those luxurious walkways laid out at the back of the Oppian Hill, smashing through the old republican walls, and planted on the ancient burial grounds of the poor. (Lots of manure in situ, as Helena pointed out.) Now the Gardens lurked in the lee of the more recent Golden House; they were less well hoed and watered, but they still existed, owned by the imperial family since Maecenas himself died seventy years before. There was a belvedere nearby, from which Nero had supposedly watched the Great Fire rampaging.

Maecenas had been Augustus' notorious financier: funder of emperors, friend to famous poets – and an all-round truly disgusting pervert. Still, if I could ever find an Etruscan nobleman to buy my dinner and encourage my art, I would probably stomach him finger-ing pretty boys. Presumably he bought their dinners too. All patronage is pimping of some kind. I ought to be wondering what grateful actions Rutilius would demand of me.

Well, ours was a different situation, I told myself. My patron was a well-behaved Flavian prig. But no prig is perfect, at least when viewed from the Aventine stews where character flaws proliferate like hot-room mould, doing their desperate damage in rowdy plebeian families like mine and bringing us into conflict with the pristine élite. Why am I raving? Because Gallicus' big moment in Tripolitania had been ordering the public execution of a drunk who had blasphemed against the local gods. Too late, we discovered that the luckless loudmouth being eaten by the lion was my brother-in-law. Rutilius must be funding our joint recital out of guilt towards me, his house guest at the time.

Uneasily I wondered if my sister would enliven her widowhood by attending tonight. If so, would she work out the Rutilius connection? Maia was the bright one in our family. If she realised that I was reading alongside her late husband's trial judge, what would she do to him — or to me?

Best not think about that. I had enough worries.

I had previously tried giving a public performance, but due to some misadventure in advertising, nobody came. There must have been a riotous party the same night. Everyone I invited abandoned me. Now I was dreading yet more shame, but still determined to prove to my intimate circle that the hobby they sneered at could produce good results. When Rutilius had confessed that he too wrote poetry and suggested this recitation, I had expected him perhaps to make his own garden available, for a small gathering of trusted associates, to whom we would murmur a few hexameters at twilight, accompanied by sweetmeats and well-watered wine. But he was so all-round ambitious that instead, he went out and hired Rome's most elegant hall, the Auditorium in the Gardens of Maecenas. An exquisite site, haunted by literary echoes of Horace, Ovid and Virgil. To compliment the place, I learned that my new friend's personal guest-list was topped by his other dear friend, Domitian.

I was standing on the outer threshold of the Auditorium, with a very new scroll tucked under my arm, when my associate proudly broke this news. According to him, it was even rumoured that Domitian Caesar might attend. Dear gods.

There was no escape. All the hangers-on in Rome had heard the news, and the crowd pressing in behind me blocked any chance of bunking off.

'What an honour!' sneered Helena Justina, as she propelled me forward down the prestigiously tiled entrance ramp with the flat of her hand between my suddenly sweating shoulder blades. She managed to disguise her brutality by adjusting her fine, braid-edged stole at the same time. I heard delicate music from the massed gold disks of her earrings.

'Cobnuts.' The ramp had a steep gradient. Wound like a corpse in my toga, I had no freedom of movement; once pushed, I skittered down the long slope like a descending sycamore seed as far as the huge doorway to the interior. Helena steered me straight inside. I found myself reacting nervously: 'Oh look, my love, they have erected a modesty curtain, behind which women are supposed to hide themselves. At least you can fall asleep without anybody noticing.'

'Cobnuts twice,' responded the well-brought-up senator's daughter whom I sometimes dared to call my wife. 'How old-fashioned! If I had brought a picnic, I might be in there. Since I was not warned of this abomination, Marcus, I shall sit in public smiling rapturously at your every word.'

I needed her support. But nerves aside, I was now gaping in astonishment at the beauteous location Rutilius Gallicus had bagged for our big event.

Only a stupendously rich man with a taste for mingling literature with slap-up banquets could have afforded to build this pavilion. I had never been inside it before. As a venue for two amateur poets it was ridiculous. Vastly over-scale. We would be echoing. Our handful of friends would look pitiful. We would be lucky to live this down.

The interior could have housed half a legion, complete with siege artillery. The roof soared high above a graciously proportioned hall, at the end of which was an apse, with formal, marble-clad steps. Maecenas must have run his own marble yard. The floor and walls, and the frames and ledges of numerous niches in the walls were all marble-clad. The half-round stepped area at the apsidal end had probably been intended as a regal lounging point for the patron and his intimates. It was even perhaps designed as a cascade – though if so, Rutilius' funds had not run to paying for the water to be turned on this evening.

We could manage without. There was plenty to distract our audience. The décor was entrancing. All the rectangular wall niches were painted with glorious garden scenes – knee-high cross-hatched trellises, each with a recess in which stood an urn, a fountain, or a specimen tree. There were delicate plantings, perfectly painted, amidst which birds flew or sipped from fountain bowls. The artist had an astonishing touch. His palette was based on blues, turquoise and subtle greens. He could make frescoes that looked as real as the live horticulture we could see through wide doors which had been flung open opposite the apse to reveal views over a lush terrace to the distant Alban Hills.

Helena whistled through her teeth. I felt a prickle of fear that she would want this kind of art in our own new house; sensing it, she grinned.

She had positioned me to greet guests. (Rutilius was still hovering in the outside portico, hopeful that Domitian Caesar might grace our gathering.) At least that saved me having to calm my companion. He looked cool, but Helena reckoned he was churning with terror. Some people throw up at the very thought of public speaking. Being an ex-consul did not guarantee lack of shyness. Pluck went out of the job description in the days of the Scipios. All you needed now was to be someone to whom the Emperor owed a cheap favour.

Friends of the favoured Rutilius began to arrive. I had heard their loud, high-class voices chaffing him before they ambled down here. They poured in and strolled past, ignoring me, then headed automatically for the best seats. Amongst a group of female freedwomen, came a dumpy woman whom I identified as his wife, stiffly coiffed with a crimped tower of hair and well dressed for the occasion. She seemed to be wondering if she ought to speak to me, then she decided to introduce herself to Helena. 'I am Minicia Paetina; how very nice to see you here, my dear . . .' She eyed the respectability curtain and was roundly advised by Helena to reject it. Minicia looked shocked. 'Oh, I may feel more comfortable out of the public gaze . . .'

I grinned. 'Does that mean you have heard your husband read before, and don't want people seeing what you think?'

The wife of Rutilius Gallicus gave me a look that curdled my stomach juices. These northern types always seem rather cold to those of us who are Roman-born.

Do I sound like a snob? Olympus, I do apologise.

My own friends came late, but at least this time they did come. My mother was first, a beetling, suspicious figure whose first action was to stare hard at the marble floor, which in her view could have been better swept, before she showed her affection for me, her only surviving son: 'I do hope you are not making a fool of yourself, Marcus!'

'Thanks for the confidence, Ma.'

She was accompanied by her lodger: Anacrites, my ex-partner and arch-enemy. Discreetly smart, he had treated himself to one of the snappy haircuts he favoured and now flourished a knuckle-crushing gold ring to show he had reached the middle class (my own new ring, bought for me by Helena, was merely neat).

9

'How's the snooping trade?' I sneered, knowing he preferred to pretend nobody knew he was the Palace's Chief Spy. He ignored the jibe, leading Ma to a prime seat in the midst of Rutilius' snootiest supporters. There she sat bolt upright in her best black gown, like a grim priestess allowing herself to mingle with the populace yet trying not to let them contaminate her aura. Anacrites himself failed to find space on the marble perch, so curled up at Ma's feet, looking as if he was something unsavoury she had caught on her sandal and could not shake off.

'I see your mother's brought her pet snake!' My best friend Petronius Longus had failed to wangle himself a night's leave from his duties as enquiry chief of the Fourth Cohort of Vigiles, but that had not stopped him bunking off. He arrived in his working clothes – sturdy brown tunic, brutal boots and a night-stick – as if he was investigating a rumour of trouble. That lowered the tone nicely.

'Petro, we're planning to read love poems tonight, not plot a republican coup.'

'You and your consular pal are on a secret list as potential rioters.' He grinned. Knowing him, it might even be true. Anacrites had probably supplied the list.

If the Second Cohort, who ran this sector of town, discovered him moonlighting on their ground, they would thump him. It did not worry Petro. He was capable of thumping them back good and hard.

'You need an invigilator on the doors,' he commented. He stationed himself on the threshold, unwinding his stick in a meaning-ful manner, as a flock of strangers crowded in. I had already noticed them, due to their curious mixture of unattractive haircuts and mis-shapen footwear. There were some effete vocal accents, and a whiff of bad breath. I had invited none of these odd chancers, and they did not look as though they would appeal to Rutilius Gallicus. In fact, he came scuttling after them with an annoyed expression, helpless to intervene as they gatecrashed.

Petronius blocked the way. He explained this was a private party, adding that if we had wanted the general public, we would have sold tickets. At the crude mention of money, Rutilius looked even more embarrassed; he whispered to me that he thought these men belonged to a circle of writers, who were attached to some modern patron of the arts.

'Thrills! Have they come to hear how good writing should be done, sir – or to heckle us?'

'If you're looking for free wine, you're in the wrong place,'

Petronius warned them loudly. Intellectuals were just another cudgel-target to him. He had a bleak view of literary hangers-on. He believed they were all on the cadge – like most of the crooks he dealt with. True.

The man who doled out their pocket money must be approaching, because the group started paying attention to a flurry further up the ramp. The patron they grovelled to must be the pushy type with the Greek beard who was trying to impose himself on a paunchy, disinterested young man of twenty-something, a new arrival whom I certainly did recognise.

'*Domitian Caesar!*' gasped Rutilius, absolutely thrilled.

III

HELENA KICKED me as I cursed. This was not simply because I wrote sensitive poetry that I regarded as private chamber stuff, nor because of my libellous satires. True, I did not welcome a blaze of imperial notice tonight. I would have to censor my scroll.

Domitian and I had a bad relationship. I could damn him, and he knew it. This is not a safe position with holders of supreme power.

A few years before, in the chaotic period when we were repeatedly changing emperors, many things had happened that later seemed beyond belief; after a brutal civil war, plots of the worst kind were rife. At twenty, Domitian had been badly supervised and he lacked judgement. That was putting it kindly – as his father and brother had chosen to do, even when he was rumoured to be plotting against them. His bad luck was that in the end, I was the agent called in to investigate. It was my bad luck too, of course.

I judged him on the facts alone. Fortunately for Titus Flavius Domitianus, second son of Vespasian, as a mere informer I did not count. But we both knew what I thought. During his machinations, he was responsible for the murder of a young girl towards whom I had once felt some tenderness. 'Responsible' is a diplomatic euphemism there.

Domitian knew that I held damning information, reinforced by well-stashed evidence. He had done his best to keep me down – so far only daring to delay my social promotion, though the threat of worse would always exist. So too, would a threat against him from me, of course. We both knew there was unfinished business between us.

This now promised to be a difficult evening. The uppity young Caesar had been demoted to running literary prizes. He seemed to judge them impartially – but it was unlikely that Domitian would be a friendly critic of my work.

Brushing off everyone else except Rutilius, the princeling swaggered by, in company with his glamorously tricked out wife, Domitia

Lepida – the great general Corbulo's daughter, a spectacular prize whom Domitian had blatantly carried off from her former husband. He ignored me. I was getting used to that tonight.

In the excitement, the gatecrashers managed to gain entry, but it now seemed best to allow in the largest audience we could commandeer. Among the final comers I suddenly saw Maia; she made a typically swift arrival, her dark curls and self-possessed air turning heads. Petronius Longus made a move to escort her to a seat, but she squeezed through the press, bypassed both Petro and me, boldly made her way to the best position in the room, and forced herself a niche alongside Ma. The imperial party should have been ensconced in state there at the apsidal end, but they remained to one side. Courtiers hoicked themselves up onto shoulder-high wall ledges. Domitian deigned to sit on a portable bench. I recognised – as Rutilius may not have done – that this was a courtesy visit only; the royal troupe had dropped in to be gracious, but were leaving themselves space to make a getaway as soon as they grew bored.

By now it was clear that our planned intimate evening had been hijacked. Rutilius and I had lost all control of events. The atmosphere of expectation grew. Physically, we had a very lopsided audience, for the prince and his party of flunkies loomed large on the left-hand side, encroaching on the free space we had wanted to preserve, and blocking the view for our private friends and family behind. Even Rutilius looked slightly annoyed. Total strangers were milling about in the body of the hall. Helena kissed me formally on the cheek; she and Petronius abandoned me to find seats somewhere.

We tried clearing our throats diffidently; nobody heard.

Then order somehow imposed itself. Rutilius was taking a last rattle through his scrolls, ready to start first. He had an armful, whereas I had only one, with my dubious opus copied out for me by my womenfolk; Helena and Maia believed bad handwriting would cause awkward pauses if they left me to my own devices with the original note-tablets. It was true that my efforts seemed to acquire a new dignity once they were written out in neat three-inch columns on regular papyrus. (Helena had invested in the papyrus as a gesture of support; Maia had wanted to economise by using the backs of old horse-medicine recipes, the only legacy her husband had left her.) I was twisting the copy, unwittingly tightening the roll on its roller to danger point, while pretending to grin encouragement at Rutilius. Then to our astonishment, the bearded man who was at the centre of the gatecrashers moved to the area in front of the terrace where we were intending to perform.

Now I got a better squint at him: grey hair bushing back from a square forehead, with coarse grey eyebrows too, although those looked as if they had been powdered with beanflour to make them match his silvered hair. He had a limp demeanour with knowing overtones – in personality a nobody, but a nobody who was used to getting in other people's way.

'Did you invite him?' I hissed at Rutilius.

'No! I thought you must have done –'

Then without preamble the fellow began speaking. He saluted the young prince with an oozily unctuous welcome. I thought the fellow must be a court flunkey, with pre-arranged orders to thank royalty for attending. Domitian looked unmoved, however, and his attendants were openly muttering among themselves as if they too wondered who the interloper was.

We gathered the man was a regular at literary events in the Auditorium. He was taking over, and it was too late for us to intervene. He assumed everyone knew him – a true mark of mediocrity. For some astounding reason, he had appointed himself the task of formally introducing us. At the intimate event we had planned, this was out of proportion and as relevant as a pile of muleshit. Besides, it was soon clear he had no idea who we were or what we intended to read.

A speech by this drag-anchor reeked of disaster from the first word. Since he knew nothing about us, he started with that fine insult, 'I admit I have not read their work', then followed up relentlessly, 'I hear some people enjoy what they have to say.' Evidently he was not hoping for much. Finally, with the air of a man who was just rushing off to have a good dinner in a back room while everyone else suffered, he asked folk to welcome Dillius Braco and Rusticus Germanicus.

Rutilius took it better than I did. As a member of the Senate he expected to be muddled up and misrepresented, whereas an informer wants to be derided for his real misdeeds as if he is a scoundrel who counts. While I froze and itched to reach for a dagger, tetchiness fired up Rutilius for a racing start.

He read first. In fact, he read for hours. He treated us to extracts from a very long military epic; Domitian was supposed to enjoy that type of dreariness. The main problem was the old bummer: lack of worthwhile material. Homer had snaffled all the best mythical heroes and Virgil had then grabbed the home crowd's ancestors. Rutilius therefore invented characters of his own and his fellows fatally lacked push. He was also, as I had always suspected, a far from thrilling poet.

I remember a line that started '*Lo, the Hyrcanean pard with bloodied jaws!*' This was dangerously close to the lion that ripped up my brother-in-law – and it was awful poetry. At the first hint that a *Lo* loomed, I clamped my molars tight and waited for oblivion. It was a long time coming. A competent runner could have made it from Marathon by the time my colleague drew his extracts to a close.

Domitian Caesar had been a notable in Rome for four years – long enough to learn the art of the choreographed exit. He stepped forward to congratulate Rutilius; meanwhile his whole party swirled towards us, produced complimentary smiles, then flowed out through the doors with centrifugal smoothness. The young Caesar was sucked after them like a leaf down a drain. He vanished while Rutilius was still blushing at his polite comments. We heard pattering applause from the radically thinned-out crowd. They settled down.

It was my turn, and I could sense that I had best not read for long.

By now I had decided to leave out all my love poems. Some had already been weeded out by me at home, due to the fact that my *Aglaia* sequence had been written before I met Helena Justina and was possibly too personal to recite while she sat and glared at me. One or two more of my sexually specific odes had already ended up being used by her as old fish-bone wrappers. (Accidentally, no doubt.) I now realised it would be considerate to ditch the lot.

That left my satires. Helena reckoned they were good stuff. I had heard her giggling with Maia as they copied them out for me.

As I started to read, friends of Rutilius brought wine to refresh him after his ordeal; they were more decent than I had realised and some of the drink wandered my way. That may have encouraged me to forget which passages I was meaning to censor. Instead, when the audience seemed restless I jumped over what I now saw to be the boring, respectable bits. Funny how one's editorial judgement sharpens in front of real people.

They were grateful for something scurrilous. They even called for an encore. By that point I had run out of options unless I went back to *Aglaia* and revealed myself to have once harboured philosophical feelings for a slightly trashy circus dancer whose act was all suggestive squirms. Rifling to the end of the scroll, all I could find left were a few lines that I knew my sister Maia had once penned herself. She must have cheekily written them here on my scroll to try to catch me out.

Rutilius was beaming happily; now his ordeal was finished, he had swigged even more wine than I had. This evening had been intended as a refined diversion, a soirée where we would show ourselves to be well-rounded Romans: action men who cherished moments of thoughtful intellect. An ex-consul, one with high hopes, would not thank me for inflicting on his elegant associates a rude ditty by a woman. But those very associates had plied us with a brew of startling power, so I raised my winecup and as Rutilius blearily responded, I read it anyway.

'Ladies and gentlemen, we must depart, but here's just one final epigram entitled 'No-longer-a-maiden's Prayer':

> *There are those*
> *From whom a rose*
>   *Would make me smile;*
> *And others*
> *I treated like brothers*
>   *Every once in a while.*
> *An occasional kiss*
> *Hardly came amiss*
>   *Or drove anyone wild –*
> *But the gods rot*
> *The selfish sot*
>   *Who fathered this child!*

I could see Maia laughing helplessly. It was the first time since I had told her she was widowed that she had showed pure, spontaneous mirth. Rutilius Gallicus owed her that.

By then the audience were so glad of something short that they roared applause.

It had been a long night. People were keen to disperse to winebars or worse. Rutilius was being carried off by his old-fashioned wife and his unexpectedly decent friends. We had time to assure one another that our evening had gone well, but he did not invite me to discuss our triumph at his house. That was fine, I need not invite him home to mine either.

I was preparing myself for ridicule from my own family and associates. I pointedly ignored the writers' circle as they toddled off in their battered sandals to whatever attic rooms they infused with their sour sweat. Petronius Longus pushed through them brutally. 'Who in Hades was the tedious ding-dong you two hired for the eulogy?'

'Don't blame us.' I scowled at the smug businessman's back as he meandered off in the midst of his clients. 'If I knew who he was, I'd arrange to meet him in a nice quiet place and I'd kill him!'

As an informer, I should have known that was a stupid thing to say.

IV

'STRANGE WOMAN, your sister,' mused Petronius Longus the next day.

'Aren't they all?'

Petronius was intrigued by Maia's cheeky ditty; Helena must have told him who really wrote it. At least it distracted him from abusing *my* poetic efforts. Off duty now, he was heading home for a morning's nap in the apartment we sublet to him across Fountain Court. Like a true friend, he had dropped in on our side; aggravating me would make his sleep sweeter.

'Does Maia Favonia still write poetry?' he asked curiously.

'Doubt it. She would say a mother of four has no time for scribbling.'

'Oh, she composed that one before she was married?'

'Maybe it explains why she hitched herself to Famia.'

Helena came out to join us from the inner room where she had been attempting to insert breakfast into our roaring one-year-old daughter. She looked tired. We men had been sitting on the porch, politely keeping out of the way. We made room for her. It was a squash. Worse when Nux, my dog, who was pregnant, shouldered in as well.

'So how is the happy poet this morning?' beamed Petro. He was about to enjoy himself after all. While he patrolled the streets half the night looking for muggers or gently interrogated arsonists with the helpful boot technique, he would have had ample time for dreaming up criticism. I stood up and said I had to meet a client. An old informing dodge, it fooled nobody.

'What client?' scoffed Helena. She knew how light my list was at present. Her brothers were supposed to be training as my juniors, but I had had to lay off Aelianus and I was thankful that Justinus was away getting married in Baetica.

'The client I am intending to advertise for from the steps of the Temple of Saturn.'

'While the real possibilities are searching for you in the Basilica Julia?' suggested Petro. He knew how it was. He knew the casual way I worked.

I felt as if I had known Petronius Longus all my life. He seemed part of the family. In fact, we had only been friends since we were eighteen – for fifteen years or so now. Brought up a few streets from each other, we had first met properly in the recruiting office when we joined the army as lads trying to leave home. We then served in the same dud legion, in Britain, in part during the Boudiccan Revolt. Jove help us.

We both escaped service using similar 'serious wound' pleas; lay low together for a joint miracle recovery; came home virtually bonded at the drinking arm. Petro then married. Well, that forced a slight breach, because I did not. Not for a long time, anyway. He also acquired an enviable job in the vigiles, which I did not even try to emulate. He had three children, as a Roman legally should; I was only now bestirring myself to follow suit and I might give up the idea if little Julia kept up her current screaming fits. Now Petro was estranged from his wife, which I would never be from mine. Still, he had probably thought the same of himself and Silvia once.

Petro had never been quite the upright character people believed him to be. It was rumoured that he knew my deceased sister Victorina in his early years, but then most people had known Victorina, an unavoidable blot on the Aventine. Men were aware of her anyway; she had made sure of that. Petronius only met the rest of my ghastly family later, after we came home from the army. Maia, for instance. I can remember the day I introduced him to Maia. At the time I was still getting used to the fact that while I had been a legionary in Britain, my younger sister – my favourite sister, in so far as I could tolerate any of them – had not only married without consulting me, but had produced two children and become visibly pregnant again. The first daughter subsequently died young, so that would have been with Cloelia. Cloelia was now eight.

Petro had been surprised when he met Maia, for some reason; he asked why I had never mentioned her. I might have felt worried by his interest, but Maia was obviously a decent young mother and the next thing I knew, he was marrying Silvia. At least we had avoided the awkward situation where little sister falls for elder brother's handsome friend. Who is never interested, of course.

For Maia to set herself up with Famia had seemed a desperate act, even before he really took to the drink. Still, girls have to find a way to leave home too. Always vibrant and attractive, she had been dangerously self-willed. Maia was the kind of young woman who seems to offer something special – special and mature. She was intelligent and though virtuous, she always seemed to know what good fun was. The kind that even experienced men can fall for very heavily and yearn for obsessively. Marriage and motherhood had seemed a good safe option to those of us who felt responsible for Maia.

Petronius thought her a strange woman, did he? That was rich, if he really did once flirt, or worse, with Victorina. Maia and she had been exact opposites.

While I was musing, Petronius had fallen silent, despite the glorious opportunity to rib me about the Auditorium of Maecenas last night. He must be tired after his shift. He never talked about his work much, but I knew how grim it could be.

Helena had her eyes shut, letting the sun soak into her as she tried to blot out the distant, wearing tantrum from Julia. The screams soared in volume. 'What can we do?' Helena asked Petro. He had three daughters, taken away by his wife to live with her boyfriend in Ostia; his children were all past the hysterical phase. He had lived through that, then lost them.

'It will pass. If not, you'll bloody soon get hardened to it.' His face had closed. He loved his girls. It did not help that he knew losing them had been his own fault. 'Probably a tooth.' Like all parents, he regarded himself as the expert and those of us who were new to the business as incompetent idiots.

'It's earache,' I lied. There was no visible reason for Julia to be going mad. Well, no, there was a reason. She had been a well-behaved child for far too long; we had gloated and thought parenting too easy. Now this was our punishment.

Petronius shrugged and rose to leave. Apparently he had forgotten about telling me his views on my poetry. I had no intention of reminding him.

'Go and see your client,' muttered Helena to me, knowing the client was non-existent and working herself up to be furious about being left to cope alone. She heaved herself from her stool, ready to attend to our offspring before neighbours issued writs.

'No need.' I was frowning down the street. 'I think he's found me of his own accord.'

You can usually spot them.

Fountain Court, the dirty alley where we lived, was a typical minor backstreet where deadbeats festered in dank lock-up shops. The buildings were six stories high. It managed to be gloomy right down to street level, yet even on a hot day like this the dirty tenements never provided enough shade. Between the crumbling walls surged the unpleasant smells of ink-making and over-warm corpses at the funeral parlour, while light gusts of smoke from various commercial sources (some legal) vied with humid updraughts of steam from Lenia's laundry opposite.

People walked through, about their morning business. The huge rope-twister, a man I never spoke to, had lurched past looking as if he had just come home after a long night in some oily jug. Customers visited the stall where Cassius sold slightly stale bread rolls along with even older gossip. A water-carrier slopped his way into one of the buildings; a chicken in fear of the plucker set up a racket by the poultry pens; it was the school holidays so children were out and about looking for trouble. And trouble of some other sort was looking for me.

He was a fleshy, untidy lump with his belly over his belt. Thin, untrimmed dark curls fell forwards over his brow and twisted backwards over his tunic's neck in damp-looking coils as if he had forgotten to dry off properly at the baths. Stubble patchily decorated a double chin. He came wandering along the street, clearly looking for an address. He was neither frowning enough for the funeral parlour, nor sheepish enough for the half-a-copper hag who two-timed the tailor. Besides, that woman held her horizontal at-homes in the afternoon.

Petronius passed him, not offering assistance, though he eyed up the man with deliberate vigiles suspicion. The fellow was noted. To be picked up later by a hit squad, maybe. He seemed oblivious instead of terrified. Must have lived a sheltered life. That did not necessarily mean he was respectable. He had the air of a freed slave. A secretary or abacus louse.

'Dillius Braco?'

'Didius Falco.' My teeth met grittily.

'Are you sure?' he insisted. I did not answer, lest my response should be uncouth. 'I hear you held a successful recital yesterday. Aurelius Chrysippus fancies we may be able to do something for you.'

Aurelius Chrysippus? It meant nothing, but even at that stage I had a dark feeling.

'I doubt it. I'm an informer. I thought *you* might want *me* to do something for you.'

'Olympus, no!'

'One thing you had better do is tell me who you are.'

'Euschemon. I run the Golden Horse scriptorium for Chrysippus.'

That would be some outfit where sweatshop scribes copied manu-scripts – either for their owner's personal use, or in multiple sets for commercial sale. I would have perked up, but I had guessed that Chrysippus might be the Greek-bearded irritation who had taken over our recital. The wrong label he gave me in his introduction was about to stick. So much for fame. Your name becomes well known – in some incorrect version. It only happens to some of us. Don't tell me you've ever bought a copy of Julius Castor's *Gallician Wars*.

'Am I supposed to have heard of a scriptorium at the sign of the Golden Horse?'

'Oh, it's a top business,' he told me. 'Astonished you don't know us. We have thirty scribes in full employment – Chrysippus heard your work last night, of course. He thought it might be good for a small edition.'

Somebody liked my work. Involuntarily my eyebrows raised. I invited him inside.

Helena was with Julia in the room where I interviewed clients. The child ceased her raving immediately, her interest caught by the stranger. Helena would normally have carried her into the bedroom, but since Julia was quiet she was left on her rug, absent-mindedly chewing her wooden stag while staring at Euschemon.

I introduced Helena, shamelessly mentioning her father's patrician rank in case it helped imply I was a poet to be patronised. I noticed Euschemon glancing around in astonishment. He could see this was a typical cramped lease, with one-colour painted walls, plain boarded floors, a meagre artisan's work table and lopsided stools.

'Our home is outside the city,' I said proudly. It sounded like a lie, of course. But we would be moving, if ever the bathhouse contractors managed to complete their work. 'This is just a toehold we keep in order to be near my old mother.'

I explained quickly to Helena that Euschemon had offered to prom-ulgate my work; I saw her fine brown eyes narrowing suspiciously.

'Are you visiting Rutilius too?' I asked him.

'Oh! Should I?'

'No, no; he shuns publicity.' I might be an amateur but I knew the rules. The first concern of an author is to do down his colleagues at every opportunity. 'So – what's this about?' I wanted to extract the offer, while pretending indifference.

Euschemon backed off nervously. 'As a new author you could not expect a large copy run.' He had a merry jest all ready; he must have done this before: 'The number we sell on your first publication may depend on how many friends and relatives you have!'

'Too many – and they will all expect free copies.' He looked relieved at my dry reaction. 'So what are you offering?'

'Oh, a full deal,' he assured me. I noticed his kindly tone – *leave all the details to us; we understand this business.* I was with experts; that always worries me.

'What does the deal entail?' Helena pressed him. Her tone sounded innocent, a senator's daughter, curious about this glimpse into the world of men. But she always looked after my interests. There had been a time when what I was paid – or *if* I was paid – bore a direct relation not just to what we could put on the table, but whether we ate at all.

'Oh, the usual,' muttered Euschemon off-handedly. 'We agree a price with you, then publish. It is straightforward.'

We both looked at him in silence. I was flattered, but not enough to grow stupid.

He expanded somewhat: 'Well, we shall take your manuscripts, Falco, for an appropriate price.' Would I like it, however? 'Then we make the copies and sell them from our outlet – which is attached directly to our scriptorium.'

'In the Forum?'

He looked shifty. 'Near the end of the Clivus Publicius. Right by the Circus Maximus – a prime location,' he assured me. 'Excellent passing trade.'

I knew the Clivus Publicius. It was a lonely hole, a back alley route down to the Circus from the Aventine. 'Can you give me a realistic figure?'

'No, no. Chrysippus will negotiate the price.'

I hated Chrysippus already. 'What are the options then? What kind of edition?'

'That depends on how much value we attach to the writing. Classics, as you know, are furnished with first quality papyrus and parchment title pages to protect the outer ends of the scrolls. Lesser work has a less elaborate finish, obviously, while a first-time author's work may even be prepared as a palimpsest.' Copied onto scrolls that have already been used once, with the old lines sponged out. 'Very carefully done, I may say,' murmured Euschemon winningly.

'Maybe, but I wouldn't want that for my stuff. Who decides the format?'

'Oh, we must do that!' He was shocked that I had even raised the subject. 'We choose the scroll size, finished material, decoration, type and size of the edition – all based on our long experience.'

I played dumb. 'And all I have to do is write you something, then hand it over?'

'Exactly!' He beamed.

'Can I make further copies for my own use?'

He winced. 'Afraid not. But you can buy from us at a discounted rate.' *Buy* my own work?

'Bit one-sided?' I ventured.

'A partnership,' he chided me. 'We work together for mutual benefit.' He sounded as reliable as a cheap gigolo moving in on his mark. 'Besides, we develop the markets and we carry all the risk.'

'If the work doesn't sell, you mean?'

'Quite. The house of Aurelius Chrysippus is not in business to provide kindling for bathhouse furnaces when we are forced to remainder failures. We like to get it right first time.'

'Sounds good to me.'

A harder note crept into his bland tone. 'So I assume you are interested?'

I could see Helena, who was standing behind him, shaking her head passionately, with bared teeth.

'I'm interested.' I smiled blithely. Helena had closed her eyes. 'I would like to see more of what you do, I think.' Where she might have looked relieved at my caution, Helena now acted out manic despair; she knew what I would be like if I was let loose at a scroll-seller's. She read as avidly as I did – though when it came to buying, she did not share my taste. As my taste had until recently depended upon what I could lay hands on in a limited corner of the second- or third-hand market, she was probably right to be sceptical. For most of my life I only ever had parts of scroll sets (unboxed), and I had to swap them once they were read.

'Well, you can come down and see us,' Euschemon conceded grumpily.

'I will,' I said. Helena mimed throwing a large skillet at my head. It was an excellent mime. I could smell the dumplings in the imaginary hot broth and feel the sharp-edged handle rivets dinging my skull.

'Bring your manuscripts,' replied Euschemon. He paused. 'In case you should think of writing something specially, let me give you a few tips. Even our very best works do not exceed the Greek scroll length – that's thirty-five feet, but only applies to works of high literary merit. As a rule of thumb, it's a book of Thucydides, two of Homer, or a play of fifteen hundred lines. Not many moderns rate full length. Twenty feet or even half that is a good average for a popular author.' He let me work out that my work *might* not be popular. 'So short is good – long could be penalised. And be practical in your setting-out if you want to be taken seriously. A scroll will have twenty-five to forty-five lines to a column, and eighteen to twenty-five letters to a line. Do try to accommodate our scribes. I'm sure you want to seem professional.'

'Oh yes,' I gulped.

'When you're calculating, don't forget to count the modern aids to the reader.'

'What?'

'Punctuation, spaces after words, line-end marks.'

These, presumably, had taken the place of outmoded concepts like intensity of feeling, wit, and stylistic elegance.

V

Euschemon had fallen into the old trap. He thought he had bamboozled me. Informers by repute are stupid; everyone knows that. Most of them really are – meticulous at not seeing and not hearing any valuable information, then misinterpreting what they do take in. But some of us know how to bluff.

I refrained, therefore, from rushing straight to the Chrysippus scriptorium, piteously eager to hand over my most inspired creations for a laughable fee. Not even if it came with a contractual right to buy back copies at whatever puny discount their normal cringing hacks accepted; not even if they offered me gold-leaf palmettes on their sales projection chart. Since I was an informer, I decided to check up on them. Since I had no clients (as usual), I was equipped with free time to do it. I knew the right contacts too.

My father was an auctioneer. Sometimes he dabbled in the rare scrolls market, though he was a fine art and furniture man at heart; he regarded second-hand literature as the low end of his trade. I was rarely on speaking terms with Pa. He ran off when I was seven, though he now maintained that he did give my mother financial support for bringing up the rowdy children he had sired. He may have had good reasons for leaving – better reasons than the allure of a certain redhead, anyway – but I still felt that since I grew up lacking a paternal presence, I could exist without the inconvenience of him now.

He enjoyed annoying me, so I wondered why Pa had not shown his face for my reading last night. He would not be deterred by the fact that I had failed to invite him. Once, Helena would have done so, for she had been on genial terms with the old rogue – but that was before he recommended Gloccus and Cotta, the bathhouse contractors who had made our new home uninhabitable. As their trestles and dust, and their lies and contractual wriggling, impelled her to the frustrated rage of any endlessly disappointed customer, Helena's opinion of my father had moved closer to my own; the only risk now was that she might decide that I took after him. That could finish us.

My father owned two properties that I knew of, although he was both well-off and secretive so there were probably more. His warehouse-cum-office was at the Saepta Julia, the enclosure inhabited by all sorts of double-dealing jewellers and hangdog antique frauds. It might be too early to catch him there. Auctions were held out on site, in private homes or sometimes in the Porticoes, but I had spotted no adverts for sales by Didius Geminus chalked in the Forum recently. That left his house, a tall edifice with a fine roof terrace and a damp basement down on the river frontage of the Aventine. It was the nearest place to look for him, though I always felt uneasy going there because of the redhead I mentioned. I can handle redheads, especially the elderly faded kind, but I preferred to avoid the trouble it caused with my mother if she ever heard I had met Flora. In fact I had only ever talked to the woman once, when I called in for a drink at a caupona she ran. She might have lived for twenty-five years with my father, but that gave us nothing to say to each other.

Climbing down to the river from the Aventine Hill is difficult, due to the sheer crag that faces the Transtiberina. I had a choice of descending via the Lavernal Gate to the bustle around the Emporium and then turning right, or going up past the Temple of Minerva, down a steep path towards the Probus Bridge, and walking back along the riverbank the other way. Pa's house had a view across the water roughly towards the old Naumachia, had he been interested in tantalising glimpses of mock sea battles when they were staged at festivals. For the average real-estate crook it would probably count as a selling point.

This was a noisy, bustling area with the smell of exotic cargoes and the yammer of sailors and wharfside stevedores. If the wind was in the wrong direction a faint pall of dust from the huge granaries behind the Emporium hung in the air. Being so close to the river produced its own disturbing excitement. Being down amongst the cheating whelks who worked there kept me on my guard.

I risked a strained tendon manoeuvring the doorknocker. This hunk of bronze looked like part of a horse's leg from a multiple sculpture of some tangled battle scene. The door itself had an imposing size and importance that would better suit the secret shrine of a very snobbish temple. Not so the pallid runt who eventually answered; he was a timid slave who looked as if he was expecting me to accuse him of a particularly vile incestuous crime.

'You know me. I'm Falco. Is Geminus in? Tell him his charming son is asking if he can come out to play.'

'He's not here!' squeaked the slave.

'Neptune's navel! When did he go out?' No answer. 'Buck up. I need to speak to him, and not next week.'

'We don't know where he is.'

'What? The old beggar's disappeared again? Who do you think he has run off with this time? He's getting rather ripe for fornication, though I know he does not reckon to be stopped by that –'

The slave trembled. Perhaps he thought my father's lady love was about to appear behind him and overhear my rude remarks.

I was used to being fobbed off with excuses on doorsteps. I refused to give up. 'Do you know where my dear papa has gone, or when that most excellent piece of muledung is expected back?'

Looking more frightened than ever, the fellow then whispered, 'He hasn't been here since the funeral.'

This quaking loon was determined to flummox me. Obstruction was usual in my profession, and also a regular reaction from my family. 'Who's dead?' I chivvied him cheerfully.

'Flora,' he said.

It had nothing at all to do with me, and yet I knew I would end up becoming involved, despite myself.

VI

THERE WAS no escape. I now had to trek across town to the public building complex alongside the Field of Mars where Pa kept his warehouse and office in the Saepta Julia. That was a double-storeyed edifice, set around an open area, where you could buy any kind of junk jewellery and bric-a-brac or be fleeced over furniture and so-called art by masters of the auctioneering fraternity like Pa. Unless you were desperate to acquire a fifth-hand general's fold-up throne with one leg missing, you left your arm-purse at home. On the other hand, if you hankered for a cheap reproduction *Venus of Cos* with her nose glued on crookedly, this was the place to come. They would even wrap it up for you, and not laugh at your gullibility until you had almost left the shop.

Marcus Didius Favonius, renamed Geminus after he fled from home, the paternal ancestor upon whom I ought to model my life and character, had always skulked in clutter. I picked my way through the warehouse, getting covered in dust and acquiring a large bruise from an untethered man-sized candelabrum that toppled over as I passed. I found my father slumped against the stacked parts of several dis-mantled metal bed-frames, behind a small stone Artemis (upside down in a sack of pottery oddments but you could see she was a game girl), with his feet up on a horrible Pharaonic treasure chest. Luckily he was not wearing boots. That would save the tacky turquoise and gold veneer. He was not drunk, but he had been. Probably for several days.

As they say in official despatches, the illustrious one welcomed me by name and I returned his greeting.

'Sod off, Marcus.'

'Hello, Pa.'

The sour tunic that clung to his wide, sagging frame would have been rejected even for the discards basket in a flea market. His beard had grown long enough to see that it would end up darker than his flopping grey curls. Of the famous seductive grin there was no sign.

'So you've lost her,' I said. 'Life stinks.' I sniffed the sordid air. 'And life is not the only thing that stinks around here. This, I gather, is the start of the long decline into financial ruin and personal debauchery?'

'I see you take the hard line with the bereaved in their grief,' he whined.

I had already heard from Gornia, his faithful and long-serving chief porter, that the business had suffered since Flora's unexpected demise, which had happened in her sleep a week ago. Now there were distraught buyers going hairless at non-deliveries and huffy sellers taking their custom elsewhere. The warehouse hands had not been paid. Pa had lit a fire with three months' invoices, badly singeing a batch of ivories during this gesture against life's futility. Gornia had appeared with a water-skin just in time. The ivories were damaged beyond the skill of even the most creative faker Pa employed. Gornia now looked tired; he had been loyal, but might not put up with too much more of this pathos.

'Go to the baths and the barber, Pa.'

'Sod off,' he said again, not moving. But he then roused himself to a minor flight of rhetoric: 'And don't tell me that was what Flora would have wanted, because Flora had one great advantage – she left me alone!'

'Liked to keep her hands clean, I expect. I see you're rallying,' I commented. 'That's wise, because if you don't pull yourself together I shall apply for a writ of custodial care on the grounds of your financial profligacy.'

'Will you Hades! You'll never get a magistrate to say I need a guardian.'

'Stuff you – it's the business I'll be pious about. Roman law has always taken a strict line on leaving fortunes unsupervised.' My father did have more money nowadays than I liked to contemplate. He was either a damned good auctioneer, or a complete scheming dog. The two are perfectly compatible.

It was up to him if he threw his wealth away, but a threat to take it off him was the best way to encourage more fight.

'If you are abdicating as head of the family,' I offered pleasantly, 'that puts me in charge. I could call a domestic conference in the traditional Roman way. All your affectionate descendants could flock here and discuss ways to keep you, our poor darling father, out of harm's way –'

Pa swung his feet to the floor.

'Allia and Galla would welcome some cash . . .' My eldest sisters were useless women with large families, both hitched to parasitic men. 'They both love to pry; the sensitive darlings have been perched ready to pounce on you for years. Dear sanctimonious Junia and her dry stick husband, Gaius Baebius, will be in here like ferrets down a pipe. Maia has no time for you, of course, but she can be a vengeful sort –'

'Sod off, and this time I mean it!' roared Pa.

I scowled and left him, telling Gornia to give it another day before abandoning hope. 'Hide his amphora. Now he knows that we know what is going on, you may see a sudden difference.'

I was on my way out when I remembered why I came. 'Gornia, have you had any dealings with a scroll-seller called Aurelius Chrysippus?'

'Ask the chief. He handles the dealers.'

'He's not feeling responsive to me. I just threatened to put his daughters on to him.'

Gornia shrugged. Apparently, this cruel tactic seemed fair. He did not know my sisters as I did. There ought to be a statute against letting that kind of woman loose. 'Well, Chrysippus has sold a few ex-library collections through us,' Gornia said. 'Geminus sneers at him.'

'He sneers at everyone who might be trickier than himself.'

'He hates Greek business methods.'

'What – too close to his own dirty ways?'

'Who knows? They always share the best bargains with their own people. They glue themselves together. They go off into corners to eat pastries, and it's anyone's guess if they are conspiring or just talking about their families. Geminus can cope with honest crooks, but you can't tell with Chrysippus whether he's a crook or not. Why are you interested, Falco?'

'He offered to publish some work of mine.'

'Watch your back,' advised Gornia. It was how I felt myself. On the other hand, I might have felt the same about all scroll-sellers. 'So how come he got his claws into you, Falco?'

'Heard me reading my stuff in public.'

'Oh bullock's balls!' I was astonished by the porter's fury. 'There's too much of that,' he ranted. I stepped back nervously. 'You can't move these days without some oaf unravelling a scroll at you – under the arches with some rehashed legal speech or grabbing a crowd while they are queuing for the public convenience. I was having a quiet drink the other day and a literary halfwit started disturbing the peace, reciting a crappy eulogy he had read at his grandmother's funeral as if it were high art –'

'My recital was invitation only, and Domitian Caesar attended it,' I answered in a huff.

Then I left.

VII

PA'S DISARRAY was something I needed to think about. The most satisfactory solution was to forget it by doing something else.

I decided after all that I would present myself at the Chrysippus scriptorium and size up the outfit. From Pa's place at Saepta Julia back to the Aventine could easily involve a short detour through the Forum. I could pop in at the select gymnasium I patronised and be battered in a workout with my trainer; then when Glaucus had finished toughening up my body, I could follow through with intellectual pursuits.

Afterwards, since Glaucus' gym was at the back of the Temple of Castor, I walked past the famous old establishment of the brothers Sosii, who had sold the works of Horace, to see what a decent scroll-seller looked like.

Lucky old Horace. Maecenas for patron; free gift of a Sabine farm (I owned one, but I had paid through the nose for it); reputation and readership. And when the Sosii promised Horace to sell his works from a prime position, they were talking about a corner of the Vicus Tuscus on the edge of the Forum Romanum. Abutted by the Basilica, at the heart of public life, it was a famous street packed with expensive shops, down which paraded regular festival processions as they moved from the Capitol to the Games. Their passing trade must have been real, unlike the markets that Aurelius Chrysippus was allegedly wooing on the wrong side of the Circus. The faded sign showed that the scroll-shop of the Sosii had been a fixture for generations, and a dip in the doorstep evidenced just how many buyers' feet had passed that way.

When I finally ventured on a recce to the Clivus Publicius, the only pedestrians who passed me there were an old lady struggling home with a heavy shopping basket and a group of teenage boys who were loitering on the lookout for some doddery victim they could rush, knock down, and steal from. When I appeared they vanished surreptitiously. The decrepit grandma had no idea I had saved her from a mugging; she muttered with hostility and set off again, wobbling up the street.

The Clivus Publicius starts as a tough slope leading at an angle up the north flank of the Aventine from near the end of the Circus. As it climbs and flattens out, it hooks round a couple of corners, before losing itself at a quiet summit piazza. It has always been a secluded neighbourhood – too far from the Forum to attract outsiders' interest. From one side of the street are little-known but fabulous views over the valley of the Circus Maximus. When I looked around there were a few lock-up shops, whose trade must be desultory, and beyond them I glimpsed trees in the gardens of what must be carefully discreet big houses. It was a backwater. The Clivus was a public road, yet possessed a sense of isolation that was rare.

If you live on the Aventine, the long valley of the Circus Maximus obstructs you almost every time you set out walking to some other part of Rome. I must have walked down the Clivus Publicius hundreds of times. I had passed the Chrysippus scroll-shop, but never thought it worth my notice, although I loved reading. I knew the neat, quiet frontage of old, but the staff tended to lurk on the doorstep like off-putting waiters at harbourside cauponas where the fish has been casseroling far too long. Preferring to browse at dealers (and to sneak free reads on the days when I had no money) I had only ever glanced inside this shop to where the scrolls for sale were visible in uneven piles on solid old shelves. Now when I did venture in, I found there were also boxes, presumably of better works, stored on the floor beneath the shelves. There was a tall stool and a counter on which to lean your elbows while you sampled the wares.

A decent, well-spoken sales assistant greeted me, heard I was a prospective author not a customer, then lost interest. He showed me through a doorway at the back into the scriptorium proper. It was much bigger than the outside shop suggested, a huge room full of raw materials, the clean rolls placed with evident care on banks of shelves that must have contained a small fortune in unwritten stationery alone. A large pot of mending-glue wafted unpleasantly on a brazier in one corner. There were also bins containing spare rollers to make or repair the completed scrolls, and baskets of end-knobs in various qualities. At one side table, a slave was applying gold leaf to the finials of a decorated luxury edition. I could see the papyrus was thicker and glossier than usual. Perhaps it was a special order for a wealthy client.

Another obviously experienced slave was carefully gluing a title page to a fine scroll; it bore a small portrait, presumably of the author

– a dink who looked in the painting as if he curled his hair with hot irons and had one of the coiffuring devices stuck up his back passage. I bet a new writer such as me could not expect his physiognomy to be displayed at all. I would be lucky if my work was rolled up tight and shoved into basic red or yellow papyrus jackets, like those being popped on swiftly at a long bench where completed scrolls were packed and tied in bundles by the finisher. He was gaily tossing sets into a hamper as if they were bundles of firewood.

Papyrus is notoriously fragile. Ever a collector of facts, Helena Justina had once described to me how the ten-foot reeds are harvested in Egyptian swamps, then the outer hull laboriously peeled away to reveal the white pith, which is cut into strips and spread out in two criss-crossing layers to dry in the sun, solidified by its own juices. The dry sheets are then smoothed with stones or seashells and stuck together, twenty or so to an average roll. Most of the work is carried out in Egypt, but increasingly papyrus is prepared in Rome nowadays. The disadvantage is that it dries out in transit and has to be moistened with extra paste.

'Egyptian scribes,' Helena had read out to me, delightedly devouring some encyclopaedia she had borrowed from her father's private library, 'write with the sheets in a roll stuck down right over left, because their script goes that way and as they write their reed needs to pass downhill across the joins; Greek scribes turn the roll upside down, so the joins lap the other way. Marcus, have you noticed that the grain on the inner surface of a scroll is always horizontal? That's because there is then less risk of the scroll pulling apart than if the vertical side were used –'

Here in the scriptorium specially trained slaves were bent over their rolls, feverishly following the dictation of a clear but very dull reader. He really knew how to disguise the sense. I felt sleepy straight away. The scribes were working at such a fast pace, and struggling against such vocal monotony, that I could understand how cheap editions can end up containing so many careless mistakes.

This did not bode well. Worse followed. Euschemon was out, perhaps still rounding up writing talent, but Aurelius Chrysippus happened to be on the premises. I was not allowed to hang around the scriptorium too long, but did wait a few minutes while he saw off a heavily-tanned, dissatisfied man who said little, but was obviously leaving in a bad mood. Chrysippus seemed undisturbed by whatever had caused their dissent, but the other party was biting back hard feelings, I could tell.

While Chrysippus smoothly said his farewell to this previous customer, sending him off with a free gift of honeyed dates like a true Greek, I gazed at the shelves of papyrus, with their neat labels: *Augustan*, for the highest quality, so fine it was translucent and could only be written on one side; *Amphitheatrica*, named for the arena in Alexandria where a well-known manufacturer was sited; *Saitica* and *Taniotica*, which must be made elsewhere in Egypt; then *Fanniana* and *Claudia*, which I knew were Roman improvements.

'Ah, Braco!'

I grimaced and followed him into his office. Without much preamble, I said that I wanted to discuss terms. Chrysippus managed to make me feel I was brusque and uncivilised for rushing into negotiations like an ill-mannered barbarian – yet just when I was prepared to back off and indulge in full Athenian etiquette for three-quarters of an hour, he changed tack and began haggling. I already thought the contractual conditions described by Euschemon seemed onerous. We talked for a short time before I discovered that I had mistaken the situation entirely. My main interest was the small advance for my creative efforts that I had presumed they were offering to pay.

'I enjoyed your work,' Chrysippus praised me, with that wholehearted enthusiasm authors crave. I tried to remember he was a retailer, not a disinterested critic. 'Lively and well written, with an appealing personal character. We do not have much like it in current production. I admire your special qualities.'

'So how much? What's the deal?'

He laughed. 'We are a commercial organisation,' Aurelius Chrysippus said. Then he socked me with the truth: 'We cannot subsidise complete unknowns. What would be in it for us? I do believe you show some promise. If you want a wider audience, I can help. But the deal is that you will invest in the edition by covering our production costs.'

As soon as I stopped reeling at his effrontery, I was out of there.

VIII

ANY CAREER informer learns to be adaptable. Clients change their minds. Witnesses astound you with their revelations and lies. Life, in its most ghastly configurations, appals you like some crazy distortion of the *Daily Gazette* scandal page, making most published news items seem sedate.

Me, pay *them*? I knew this went on. I just thought it only happened to sad nonentities, scribbling dull, long-winded epics while still living at home with their mothers. I did not expect some brazen vanity publisher to latch on to me.

One way that informers adapt to their setbacks is by drinking in winebars. My brother-in-law's recent death while seriously drunk had caused me to restrict my intake somewhat. Besides, I did not want to look like some over-sensitive creative type who claimed to find inspiration in the bottom of a winejug and only there. So I was a good boy. I went home.

The respectable woman I went home to could have greeted me with a welcoming smile, the offer of afternoon dalliance, and a simple Roman lunch. Instead, she gave me the traditional greeting of a Roman wife: 'Oh, it's you!'

'Dearest. Do I take it you were expecting some hunk of a lover?'

Helena Justina just smiled at me, with those mysterious dark eyes pretending to make a fool of me. I had no option but to take it as an empty threat. I would start raving with jealousy if I let my heart lurch the way it wanted to. She knew that I loved her, and trusted her – and also that I was so amazed she lived with me, any slight jolt could make me slip into maniacal insecurity.

'You do like to keep me on the hop.' I grinned.

'Do I?' murmured Helena.

She had on a flimsy stole and walking sandals; she was a girl with plans, plans that were probably devious even though there was no man involved. My presence was unlikely to delay her long. I had nothing to offer. She had already learned the gossip about Pa. She was not surprised Chrysippus was a dud. She had sent our baby out for a walk with a slave her mother had lent her, but that did not mean I stood any chance of taking her to bed.

'If I go to bed, I'll fall asleep, Marcus.'

'I won't.'

'That's what you think,' she said brutally.

The last thing she wanted was to be lumbered with me. She was going out. To a winebar, she told me. It was distinctly unlike Helena. But I knew better than to comment or to panic, let alone to object. She scowled. 'You had better come with me.'

'This is very exciting. A woman behaving like a male rascal? Let me play too! We can be lunchtime drunks together.'

'I am not intending to get drunk, Marcus.'

'What a spoilsport!'

Yet she was probably wise, for the winebar she had chosen was Flora's Caupona. Ordering a flagon there was the first step towards being sprinkled with oil on your funeral bier.

'Helena, you do love to be adventurous.'

'I wanted to see what was happening here.'

Her curiosity was soon answered: due to the death of its proprietor, Flora's was closed.

We stood for a moment on the street corner. Stringy, the caupona cat, was currently in charge of the splintery bench outside the shuttered counter; we had a long feud and he spat at me. I spat back.

Flora's, a business Pa had purchased for his girlfriend, was an eatery so unpretentious it barely rated attention from the local protection rackets. I had drunk there regularly at one time, in the days when the place sold the worst hot stews in Rome. It had perked up briefly after an extremely brutal murder occurred in a rented room on the premises; then it slumped back into a drab haunt for bankrupts and broken men.

There were points in its favour. It occupied a grand position. Goodwill had attached to the business. Its customers were doggedly loyal – sad idlers who tolerated the unwashed bowls of lukewarm broth in which lumps of animal gristle floated half submerged like supernatural monsters in a mythological tale. These stalwart daily customers could stand wine that would purple your tongue and that, working magic with the glutinous gravy, would laminate the roof of your mouth. They would never abandon their luncheon nook; for one thing, they knew there were not many others on that side of the Aventine.

Opposite stood one rival: a modest, well-scrubbed pavement foodshop called the Valerian. Nobody went there. People were afraid the cleanliness would give them hives. Besides, when nobody goes to a place there is no atmosphere. The surly clientele at Flora's wanted to sit where there were other antisocial types whom they could steadfastly ignore.

'We can still have a pleasant lunch together at the Valerian, my heart.'

'Lunch was not the point, Falco.'

Helena then decided we would visit Maia. Fine. She lived close by and it was my duty as a brother to console her in her trouble. I wanted to tell her the gossip about Flora and Pa before any of my other sisters beat me to it. She might feed us too.

To my disgust as we arrived, I saw Anacrites leave Maia's house. Perhaps he was taking some message from Ma. I skipped around a pillar and ducked down behind an oyster barrel. Helena glowered at me for my cowardice and walked by him with a cool nod, passing him before he managed to speak to her. She had always been polite to the spy, especially when he and I were working as partners on the Census, but he seemed to know he was tiptoeing on tricky ground with her. Assuming she had come alone, he let himself be bypassed and then moved off.

To see Anacrites at my sister's home was irritating. He had no real connection with my family and I wished to keep it that way. There was no reason for him to remain as my mother's lodger; he had property, he was no longer sick (the excuse for persuading Ma to look after him in the past), and he was back working in the Palace now. I did not want the Chief Spy skulking after Maia either.

Once I was sure he had vanished, I followed Helena indoors. Maia greeted me without mentioning another visitor. I kept mum. If she knew I was annoyed, that would only encourage her to encourage Anacrites. I roamed about looking for sustenance and eventually she gave us lunch, as I had hoped she might. There was less to it than there would have been once. Famia had often drunk away his salary, but at least the knowledge that she had a husband in work had allowed Maia to build up credit. Now her finances were desperately tight.

Helena told her the news about Flora and I described the state in which I had found Pa.

'The warehouse is a mess. If Marius wants to earn a few coppers, send him to help Gornia shift the stuff around.'

39

'My son is too studious to be humping furniture,' Maia retorted frigidly. 'He's not strong enough; he's delicate.'

'Time we built up his muscles then.'

'We don't need father's money.' That was untrue. Famia's pension from the Greens, who were a useless chariot faction, barely paid the rent. That left Maia with five mouths to feed. Marius, her eldest, deserved an education, and I would somehow find his school fees myself, but he had to become more worldly if he was to survive on the Aventine. Anyway, I wanted that shrewd little soul placed with Pa in the Saepta. He would tell me what was going on.

'You do need an income,' Helena said gently. Maia would take it from her. 'Are you definitely set against the tailoring plan?' This was a scheme Pa and I had concocted. We would have bought out the tailor for whom Maia had worked as a young girl, and let her manage the looms and saleroom. She would have shone at it. However, the good sense of the plan did not appeal to her.

'I can't bear it. I have moved on, Helena. It's not that I have grandiose ideas. I'll work. But I don't want to go back to what I did before – years ago, when I was unhappy, if that counts for anything.' Maia glared at me. 'Nor do I want any madcap enterprise dreamed up by someone else.'

'Choose your own then,' I groused. I had my head in a bowl of lettuce and eggs.

'I shall do that.'

'Will you let me pass on an idea?' Helena ventured as Maia screwed up her face suspiciously.

'Go ahead. I'm short of laughs.'

'Don't laugh at this. Tell Geminus that you will run Flora's.'

'You really are joking!'

'He won't want the caupona,' I agreed. 'It was the redhead's plaything.'

My sister flared up as usual. 'Marcus, you seem determined to dump some dreadful business on me!'

'Not dreadful. You would turn it around,' Helena declared.

'Maia, Pa owns the building; he has to sell up or find a new manager. If it stands there with the paint peeling and the frontage filthy, the aediles will stamp on him for urban neglect. Offer. He'll be glad to see it sorted.'

'For heaven's sake. Don't both of you gang up on me.'

'We're not doing that.' Helena shot me a reproachful look. By herself, she was implying, she could have put this plan to Maia and it might have worked.

Maia was now well het up: 'The woman has only been dead for a week. I'm not rushing in —'

'Pa needs you to do that,' I said quietly. 'He won't touch anything that reminds him of Flora — he won't even go home.'

Maia looked shocked. 'What do you mean?'

'He has not been to his house on the riverbank since Flora's funeral. The slaves are scared. They don't know where he is, or what their instructions are.'

Maia said nothing. Her mouth was pinched with disapproval. Newly widowed herself, she was the best person to tell our father that life goes on and you cannot opt out. If I knew her, she would tackle this.

Helena gathered up used dishes and carried them out to be washed later. She was lifting the pressure off Maia, at least temporarily. Even I let the subject drop.

Heading for home, we passed once again by Flora's Caupona, and had another look.

There ought to be a waiter somewhere, Apollonius. Officially he lived in a nook at the back. The previous waiter had hung himself, right by the cubbyhole where Apollonius was supposed to lurk as a watchman when the place was closed. While Helena waited in the street, I went round and shouted but failed to rouse an answer. His predecessor's suicide and the notorious murder that had happened upstairs must have made Apollonius reluctant to stay alone on the premises. People can be so sensitive.

Returning to the street, I saw a familiar figure kicking at the main door.

'Petro!'

'They're shut —' He despised Flora's, but quite often drank there; he was outraged to be thwarted by the closed door. We met a little apart from Helena and spoke in low voices.

'Flora's dead.'

'Hades!'

'Pa's a mess, and this place is out of action. We're trying to get Maia interested.'

'Surely she has enough to do?'

'Take her mind off it.'

'You're a bastard.'

'You taught me!'

We looked at each other. The jibes had been bland. Routine. Had we met earlier we could have found somewhere else to share a bench; knowing us, we could have stretched out our lunch all afternoon. Well, maybe. There was a taut look to Petronius, as if he had something on his mind.

We walked back to Helena. 'You're late on your break,' I remarked to Petro.

'Held up. Unnatural death.' He breathed in slowly. Then he exhaled, shoving his lower lip forward. He sucked his teeth. Helena was watching us, expressionless. Petro stared at me. 'Didius Falco.'

'That's me.'

'What have your movements been today?'

'Hey! What's your interest?'

'Just tell me about your day, sunshine.'

'That sounds as if I may have done something.'

'I doubt it — but I'm checking up for both our sakes.' Petronius Longus was using his official voice. It was tinged with the joky style we used together, but it would not have surprised me if he had brought out his battered set of noteboards to record my replies.

'Oh muleshit. What's this about?' I murmured. 'I've been a pious brat looking after my family all morning. Bereaved father; bereaved sister. Why?'

'I hope you can assure me this felon has been with you since noon?' Petronius demanded of Helena.

'Yes, officer.' She had a slightly sarcastic tone. She had wrapped her light-coloured stole around her darker, damson-tinted gown, and stood very still with her head up, looking down her nose like some republican statue of a painfully chaste matron. When Helena was being superior, even I felt a tremor of unease. But then one of her Indian pearl earrings trembled, and I just wanted to gnaw the trans-lucent lobe from which it hung until she squealed. She looked at me suddenly as if she knew what I was thinking. 'And with Maia Favonia,' she added coolly for Petronius.

'Then that's all right.' Petro's remote attitude softened.

Mine toughened up. 'I have an alibi, apparently. That's nice. Will anybody tell me what it's for?'

'Murder,' Petro said tersely. 'And by the way, Falco. You just lied to me.'

I was startled. 'I'll lie like a legionary — but I like to know I'm doing it! What am I supposed to have said?'

'Witnesses have listed you as one of the dead party's visitors today.'

'I don't believe it. Who is this?'

'Man called Aurelius Chrysippus,' Petro told me. He said it matter-of-factly, but he was watching me. 'Battered to death by some maniac a couple of hours ago.'

'He was perfectly alive when I left him.' I wanted to scoff, but I kept my voice level. 'There were plenty of witnesses to that. I only saw him briefly, at his scroll-shop in the Clivus Publicius.'

Petronius raised an eyebrow genteelly. 'The shop that has a scriptorium at the back of it? And behind the scriptorium, as I am sure you noticed, you can pass through a corridor into the owner's lovely house. Big spread. Nicely finished. It has all the usual luxuries. Now, Didius Falco, didn't you tell me you would like to invite Chrysippus to some quiet place and do him in?' He grinned bleakly. 'We found the body in his library.'

IX

'WOULD THAT,' enquired Helena Justina in her most refined tones, 'be his Greek or his Latin library?'

'Greek.' Petro patiently matched her irony. Her eyes narrowed slightly, approving his parry.

I butted in: 'Was the bastard really so wealthy he could afford two libraries?'

'The bastard had two,' confirmed Petro. He looked gloomy. So did I.

'He got his money from fleecing his authors then,' I growled.

Helena remained calm, full of patrician snootiness, disdainful of Petro's suggestion that her chosen partner might have soiled his hands killing a foreigner who bought and sold goods. 'You had better know, Lucius Petronius, Marcus had words with this man today. Chrysippus had tried to commission work from him – he approached us, mind. Marcus had had no thought of placing his poems before the public gaze.'

'Well, he wouldn't, would he?' agreed Petro, making it an insult on principle.

Helena ignored the jibe. 'It turned out the offer was a cheat; Marcus was expected to pay to be published. Naturally Marcus expressed his views in the strongest of terms before he left.'

'I am glad you told me that,' Petro said gravely. He had probably already known.

'Always best to be honest.' Helena smiled.

I myself would not have told Petronius anything, and he would not have expected it.

'Well, officer,' I declared instead. 'I hope you will try very hard to find out who committed this appalling crime.' I stopped simpering. My voice rasped. 'From the little I saw of the Chrysippus operation, it has the smell of a right rat's nest.'

Petronius Longus, my best friend, my army tent-mate, my drinking pal, drew himself up in a way he liked to do (it showed he was some

44

inches taller than me). He folded his bare arms on his chest, to emphasise his breadth. He grinned. 'Ah, Marcus Didius, old mucker – I was hoping you would help us out.'

'Oh no!'

'But yes!'

'I'm a suspect.'

'I just cleared you.'

'Oh Hades! What's the game, Petro?'

'The Fourth Cohort has enough to do – work up to our lugholes. Half the squad is down with summer fever and the rest are decimated by wives telling the men to bunk off and repair their roof-tiles while the sun's out. We have no manpower to deal with this.'

'The Fourth is always overworked.' I was losing this dice-game.

'We really can't cope at present,' Petronius returned placidly.

'Your tribune won't wear it.'

'It's July.'

'So?'

'Darling Rubella is on leave.'

'His villa at Neapolis?' I scoffed.

'Positanum.' Petronius beamed. 'I'm covering for him. And I say we need to buy in expertise.'

Had Helena not been there, I might have accused him of wanting free time to pursue some new woman. There was little affection between the vigiles and private informers. They saw us as devious political sneaks; we knew they were incompetent thugs. They could put out fires. It was the real reason for their existence. They had only become involved with law and order because vigiles patrols out fire-watching at night had run across so many burglars in the dark streets. We possessed more sophisticated expertise. When civil crimes occurred, victims were advised to come to us, if they wanted their affairs handled with finesse.

'Well, thanks, friend; once I would have been glad of the money,' I admitted. 'But to investigate the killing of some millionaire exploitation-magnate sticks in my craw.'

'For one thing,' Helena supported me, 'there must be thwarted authors all over the city, any one of whom was bursting to shove the slug down a drain. What happened to him anyway?' she asked, rather late in the day. As a group, we were showing the publisher little sympathy.

'The first draft was rather crude – thrusting a scroll rod up his nose. Then whoever did it developed his theme more prettily.'

45

'Nice metaphors. You mean he was battered about?' I queried. Petro nodded. 'In various violent ways. Someone was exceedingly angry with this patron of the arts.'

'Don't tell me any more. I will not take an interest. I refuse to involve myself.'

'Reconsider that, Falco. You would not want me to feel obliged to run your visit to the scriptorium past the loveable Marponius.'

'You would not!'

'Try me,' he leered.

It was blackmail. He knew perfectly well I had not crushed the life from Chrysippus – but he could make the situation difficult. Marponius, the homicide magistrate for this sector, would love a chance to get me. If I refused to assist, they might close the case in a way that was traditional for the vigiles: find a suspect; say he did it; and if he wants to get off, let him prove what really happened. Crude, but extremely efficient if they were keen on good clear-up figures and less keen on knowing who had actually bashed in a victim's brains.

Helena Justina looked at me. I sighed. 'I'm the obvious choice, love. The vigiles know me, and I'm already close to the case. I think,' I was now addressing both of them, 'this requires a drink. We need to talk about it –'

'None of your informing games.' Petronius smirked. 'I want a consultant who will solve this, not some layabout who hopes the Fourth will cover his exorbitant winebar bills.'

'So you do control a budget?'

'That's not your worry.'

'Oh, you *don't* have a budget. You're raiding the pension fund!' If Petronius was doing that – and I would not put it past him – he was vulnerable and I could apply a squeeze myself: 'Lucius, old friend, I shall need a free hand.'

'You'll take my orders.'

'Stuff that. I want my usual fees, plus expenses – plus a confession bonus if I make the killer cough.'

'Well, suit yourself – but keep a low profile.'

'Are you allowing me any back-up?'

'None to give you; that's the whole point, Falco.'

'I can bring my own support – if you can pay for it.'

'I'll pay for you; that's more than enough. I'm sure Fusculus will be happy to give you his usual tactful hints and tips, should I not be available when you require advice.'

'Don't insult my expertise!'

'Just don't get into any rucks, Falco.'

'Demand a contract,' Helena instructed me, not bothering to say it in an undertone.

X

WORD HAD spread. The crime scene was almost inaccessible behind a large crowd of Aventine dead-enders who had suddenly developed an interest in reading. Their after-lunch entertainment was to present themselves at the scroll-shop like potential customers, browsing the book baskets and keeping their eyes peeled for excitement – preferably in the form of blood.

Considering Petro's claims of undermanning, there was a commendable vigiles presence. The red tunics were here in force, mingling with the ghouls, always nosy about a new kind of location. It would not last. Once the investigation lost its novelty, it would be hard finding one of these lads for anything routine. They were mainly ex-slaves, short but wide or wiry, each handy in a fight and none of them men to cross. Joining the vigiles was a desperate measure. The work was dangerous, the community hostile, and those who escaped being fried in fires were likely to end up having their necks broken by bullyboys on the streets.

I forced a passage through the gawpers outside. Taking more interest in the layout than last time, I noticed that the scroll-shop and a shoemender's next door appeared to form the frontage of the same property. They were part of a row of small, mostly run-down-looking businesses, some no doubt with rooms at the back or on the upper floor where their proprietors lived.

'Falco.' I announced myself to the vigiles loafing in the shop. 'Assigned to this case by Petronius Longus. Round up these sightseers. Check out whether anyone saw anything; if so, I'll speak to them. Make the rest clear off.'

I heard muttering, but Petro's name carried weight.

I barged through the press in the shop and into the scriptorium. The workers were standing about looking anxious. Euschemon, the freedman who had propositioned me to sell my work, was leaning his backside against a table. It looked as if he slumped there whilst under interrogation by Fusculus, one of Petro's best men. I knew Fusculus

48

well. Seeing me, he gave a cheery wave, pressed Euschemon in the chest with the flat of his hand to warn him to stay put, and then came across.

'Falco! He nobbled you then?' The bastards must have discussed me earlier.

'I gather Marcus Rubella is sunning himself in Campania, and the rest of you have forgotten how to do any work. That's why you need me?'

'It's July. The Espartos have to douse fewer fires at night, but everyone is feeling hot and stinky and we're inundated with tunic thieves at all the public baths.'

'Well, lost underwear must be your priority! And Rubella would not want you getting bloodstains on your uniforms, while sorting out a slaying. He would hate to approve the dockets requisitioning new togs.'

'Rubella's all right, Falco.'

'Change of heart? Do I gather he's been in post long enough to stop hammering everyone because he's new? Now you all regard him as lover-boy?'

'We regard him as trouble,' Fusculus replied gently.

Tiberius Fusculus, heavy but fit, a cheery soul, was now Petro's second-in-command, having grabbed the position after Petro shunted on Martinus, the previous lazy incumbent. Fusculus was shaping up well, though his preferred element was not major crime but the thousands of elaborate fiddles and dodges that small-time crooks invented. Admiring the madness and light-fingered skill of flyboy purse-shifters and skallydiddlers, he had made an intense study of confidence tricks. Recognising Forum swindles would not help much here. As with all murders, the chances were that some obvious culprit had flared up and swiped a relative or close associate in a sudden fit of pique. Still, Fusculus would, if his services were available to me, search out clues to whoever had lost his or her temper as diligently as I could wish.

'Are you on my complement?' I asked bluntly.

'For about half a day.' Not long enough, if this turned out to be the one case in fifty that was complicated. 'What's the plan, Falco?'

'How far have you gone?'

'Corpse is still in situ. I'll introduce you when you like. He's not rushing off anywhere. This lot all claim they were together out here throughout the relevant period.'

'Which was?'

49

'After you left in a huff this morning –' He grinned; I just grinned back. 'The deceased said he was going to work on manuscripts and went into his house . . .' I glanced around while Fusculus was talking. There was, as Petro had mentioned, a doorway and a corridor which obviously led further inside the property. But if Aurelius Chrysippus was a rich man, that could hardly be the main entrance. Petro had described it as a grand abode. There must be formal access elsewhere.

'So Chrysippus was being studious. Then what?'

'A couple of hours later a slave was surprised to see the master's lunch still sitting on a salver, untouched. Somebody then found the body and the screaming started. One of our sections was just up the street, dressing down the owner of a *popina* for a food offence. Our lads heard the racket, but did not have the sense to scarper without looking. So we're landed.'

'No,' I said calmly. '*I'm* landed. Still, that should assist your clear-up figures.'

'You reckon you're the bod for it?' Fusculus chortled genially.

'A natural.'

'Right, I'll get the drinks in, ready to celebrate.'

'You're a hero. So what have you done so far without me?'

He waved at the scriptorium staff. 'I've been taking statements from this piteous bunch. Everyone who was in the main house when we arrived has been confined to quarters; there's no guarantee we collared them all, though. A couple of our lads have begun working through the house slaves for any information of interest.'

'What's the set-up domestically? Was he a family man?'

'That I've yet to find out.'

I nodded at Euschemon. 'Anything to say for himself?'

'No.' Fusculus half-turned, letting Euschemon hear him. 'Tight as a clam. But he's only had the gentle treatment so far.'

'Hear that?' I winked at the scriptorium manager, hinting at unspeakable brutality to come. 'Think about it! I'll speak to you later. I shall expect a sensible story. Mean time, stick there, where you're parked.' Euschemon frowned uncertainly. I raised my voice: 'Don't budge!'

Fusculus motioned a ranker to watch Euschemon, while he and I went into the main property to inspect the scene of death.

XI

A SHORT, DARK, undecorated corridor with a slabbed stone floor led us straight out into the library. Light flooded down from rectangular openings high above. It was very quiet. Exterior noise was muffled by thick stone walls. They would baffle interior noise too. A man being attacked here could call for help in vain.

The plain approach had done nothing to prepare us for the vast scale of this room. Three tiers of slim columns mounted to the ceiling vaults, decorously topped with white capitals in all three classical orders: Ionic, Doric, Corinthian. Between the columns were pigeon-holes, sized for complete scroll sets, rising so high that short wooden ladders stood against the walls to aid retrieval of the upper works. The pigeonholes were stuffed full with papyri. For a moment all I could take in were the quantities of scrolls, many of them huge fat things that looked of some age – collections of high-quality literature, without doubt. Unique, perhaps. Occasional busts of Greek playwrights and philosophers gazed down on the scene from niches. Poor replicas that my father would have sneered at. Too many heads of that well-known scribbler, '*Unknown Poet*'. It was words that counted here. Words, and whether they were saleable. Who wrote them came a poor second in importance.

The terrible sight on which the bald reproductions were staring down certainly gave me a chill. Once my eyes fell on the corpse, it was hard to look anywhere else. My companion, who had seen this once, stood quiet and let me take it in.

'Jupiter,' I remarked quietly. It was hardly adequate.

'He was face down. We turned him over,' Fusculus said after a while. 'I can put him back as we found him, if you like.'

'Don't bother for me.'

We both continued staring. Then Fusculus blew out his cheeks and I murmured, 'Jupiter!' again.

The open centre of the room was chaos. It should have been an area of peaceful study. A couple of high-backed, armless pedagogues' chairs must have normally served readers. They and their plush seat cushions now lay overturned on the exquisite geometric marble tiles. The floor was black and white. A pattern of great mathematical beauty, radiating outwards in meticulous arcs from a central medallion that I could not see because the body covered it. Ravishing work by a master mosaicist – now spattered with blood and soaked in pools of spilled – no, thrown, poured, deliberately *hurled* – black ink. Ink and some other substance – thick, brownish and oily, with a strong though rather pleasant scent.

Aurelius Chrysippus lay face up in this mess. I recognised the grey hair and spade-shaped beard. I tried not to look at his face. Someone had closed his eyes. One sandalled foot was bent under the other leg, probably a result of the vigiles flipping the body. The other foot was bare. Its sandal lay two strides away, dragged off, with a strap broken. That would have happened earlier.

'I'll find something to cover him.' The scene shocked even Fusculus. I had seen him before in the presence of grisly corpses, accepting them as matter-of-factly as any of the vigiles, yet here he had become uncomfortable.

I held up a hand to stop him. Before he went searching for material to drape on the remains, I tried to work out the course of events. 'Wait a moment. What do you think, Fusculus? I assume he was on the marble when found? But all this must have taken some time to achieve. He didn't give up easily.'

'I doubt if he was taken by surprise – a room this size, he must have seen whoever was coming.'

'No one heard him call for help?'

'No, Falco. Maybe he and the killer talked first. Maybe a quarrel developed. At some point they grappled. Looks as if one party at least used a chair to fence with; probably both. That was just one phase of the fight. I reckon the opponent had him on the ground by the end, and he was face down, scrabbling to escape what was being done to him. That was how it finished.'

'But before that he and the assailant – or assailants? – had been eyeballing. He knew who it was.'

'The clincher!' agreed Fusculus. 'The assailant knew there would be consequences unless this one was finished off.'

'Chrysippus. That's his name.'

'Right. Chrysippus.'

We afforded him politeness. But it was hard to think of what remained as having been a man who lived like us not long before.

I moved nearer. To do so I had to wade through a carpet of blood-spotted papyrus – scrolls that were still rolled, and others that had shot open as they fell, unravelling and then tearing as the fight progressed. These scrolls must have been out that morning, in position to be worked on in some way. There was no sign that they had been wrenched from the pigeonholes, which all looked well ordered, and anyway the wreckage lay too far from the walls of this immensely spacious room for that to have happened. They must have come from the tables that stood at intervals, one still containing a stacked pile of unboxed documents.

'You can see it was a face-to-face issue at some point,' Fusculus said. 'Some of the punches were landed from in front.' Quietly he added, 'And the other business.'

The 'other business' was both inventive and horrible.

Avoiding various viscous pools, I stepped carefully right up to the corpse. Kneeling beside it, I agreed with Fusculus. One cheek had been jellied. Fusculus waited for me to comment on the rest. 'Ouch! Very creative . . .'

Jammed up one of the dead man's nostrils was a wooden rod, the kind that scrolls are wound on. When it was shoved up his nose, the pain must have been appalling, though I did not think it would have killed him. Not unless it broke the skull bones and punctured the brain cavity. Somebody who loathed him would have felt better for doing this – but afterwards he would have been left with an opponent who was in agony and furious, yet still alive and able to identify whoever had struck him in this vicious way.

I took hold of the blood-drenched rod, with distaste, and tugged it free. Blood came with it, but no brain. No; this had not been fatal.

'This peculiar pile driving would have been most easily accomplished from the rear, Fusculus. Grab him with one arm, then ram him. Your free fist has the rod and jerks. The blow is towards you, and upwards.'

'Hard.'

'Hard!'

The end of the scroll rod now had no finial; I knew there had been one at some stage, because beneath the bright gore at the rod's tip was a short white area, its wood cleaner than the rest. The dowel had snapped, and the shorter part was tangled in the dead man's tunic folds, held by splinters on the ripped fibres of the tunic neck from which a long tear ran almost to the waist. When I laid the two broken parts side by side on the tesserae, the short end had a gilded knob in

53

the shape of a dolphin on a tiny plinth. There was no sign anywhere of the missing finial from the longer end.

'A man,' I decided, to the unspoken but inevitable question.

'Almost certainly,' said Fusculus. Working on the Aventine, he must have met some tough women. He never discounted any possibility.

'Oh, a man,' I assured him gently, looking at the bruising from the fistfight that had battered Chrysippus into oblivion. Fist, and probably boot. And elbow. And knee. Headbutts. Hands clawing at clothing, which was ripped to shreds.

I stood up, groaning. I flexed my spine. I looked around at the mess. Kicking up some of the papyrus, I saw blood under it. It seemed that at least some of the wreckage had been hurled on the floor after the man was dead. Scrolls flung everywhere. The ink thrown from its dark scriptorium-quantity flagon. The other substance furiously splashed around. Gingerly I took some up on one forefinger and sniffed.

Fusculus pulled a face. 'What in Hades is the stinky muck, Falco?'

'Cedar oil. Used to deter bookworms. They paint it over the scrolls. That's what gives them that faint yellow colouring. And the wonderful scent that rises from well-kept books. Librarians never have moths in their clothes, you know.'

'Hmm.' Fusculus was not a reader for pleasure and he rightly suspected I had made up the statement about moths. 'He may look ugly, but he's going to smell really nice on his pyre when he goes to the gods!'

Killing Chrysippus had not been enough. With the corpse at his feet, the killer had risked staying here while he threw scrolls, ink and oil all over the room. His frustration and anger had continued. Whatever he wanted had remained unaccomplished. The death solved nothing.

'One person?' asked Fusculus, watching me.

'Jove, I don't know. What do you think?'

He shrugged.

'Motive then?' I asked him.

'Primary motive: sheer bloody anger.'

'Underlying motive?'

'Business or pleasure, Falco.'

'The usual pretty excuses. Still, at this juncture, we cannot tell which.'

★

We walked around, bemused and slightly aimless.

I could see why Petronius Longus had told Helena that this was the Greek library; a room divider, formed from two huge folding doors that stood open, perhaps permanently, separated the part where Chrysippus had died from an extension in the same style which seemed to contain Latin works. Well, I recognised old Virgil amongst the dusty busts anyway.

'Can they take away the body?' Fusculus was fidgeting. The vigiles like to see scenes of crime returning to normal. That way, people imagine that something has been achieved by the law's presence.

'Once I hear what the household people say. Then they can clear the mess. Mind you, the grout in the lovely mosaic is going to hold those stains.'

'Regrouting with a wash is the answer,' said Fusculus, matching my reflective tone. 'Clean the marble pieces thoroughly, then new cement sluiced all over the lot in a thin mixture, and sponged down.'

'Expensive.'

'Oh, but worth it. They'll be looking at the fellow's gore for ever otherwise.'

'True. But, Tiberius Fusculus, whoever they are, they will probably not thank us for these careful household tips . . . So!' I was ready now for the next unpleasantness. 'Who are we talking about, I wonder? Ask your men if they have discovered anything from the household staff, will you? I'll try to find out who's who in the next of kin.'

'I gave orders that nobody here was to be allowed a change of clothing before interview. The killer would have been carrying evidence of that enforced nosebleed, Falco, if nothing else.'

'Great gods, yes; the murderer would have been covered in blood. You arranged a premises search?'

'Of course. What kind of amateurs do you take us for, Falco?'

Fusculus was well aware that murders most often happen for domestic reasons. He was right. Whoever lived here would be the first suspect or suspects, and they may not have had time or opportunity to conceal any evidence of their involvement. So I was high on the alert as I set out to discover who the dead man's domestic associates might have been.

XII

THE TWINNED library had had grandiose proportions but an austere atmosphere. Outside was a small lobby which contained a fancy wooden shelf system, displaying a half-hearted Athenian pottery collection, and an empty side table with marble supports. The far exit door was guarded by two Egyptian pink granite miniature obelisks. Right across this lobby led a wide trail of sticky footprints, in various sizes, all well smudged.

'Too many sightseers trampled the scene, Fusculus.'

'Happened before I got here,' he assured me righteously.

'Well, thanks for clearing the mob out.'

'That was the boss.'

I could imagine what Petro's full reaction to a milling crowd had been.

We emerged onto what must be the main axis of the house. The libraries and lobby had followed the line of the street outside; this suite crossed that line at right angles, coming in from the main entrance door which was to my left. An impressive set of lofty halls ran away to the right.

The style changed. We were amongst walls painted in repeating patterns, warm gold and crimson mock-tapestries, their divisions formed by trails of foliate filigree and filled with roundels or small dancing figures. Ahead and to either side stretched superb floors in assorted cutwork marbles, endless circles and triangles of elegant greys, blacks and reds. More inky footsteps marred the gorgeous stones, of course. The formal entrance to the house was nearby to the left, as I said. Prominent on the right, forming the central vista in this series of formal public spaces, was a huge hall like a private basilica.

The vigiles were finalising their staff interviews there. Slaves were holding their hands out for inspection, picking up their feet to show the soles of their sandals like horses with a farrier, quaking as they were spun on the spot by large rough men who intended to check their garments and generally terrorise them. We walked down to join this group.

'What a place!' exclaimed Fusculus.

Within the enormous dimensions of the hall, interior columns supported a canopied roof. It made a kind of mock-pavilion at the centre of the room. Decoration on the outer walls was dark and dramatic – friezes, fields and dados in formal proportions and expensive paints, depicting tense battle scenes. The colonnades made it all feel like some eastern king's audience chamber. There ought to be obsequious flunkeys moving constantly in the side aisles on slippered feet. There ought to be a throne.

'Was this where Chrysippus was intending to munch his hard-boiled eggs, Falco?' Fusculus was caught between admiration and plebeian contempt. 'Not what my granny brought me up with! It was bread rolls on a lumpy cushion in a yard at our house. First-comers got the shady bit. I always seemed to be stuck out in full sun.'

Curiously, the bronze tray with what must be the uneaten lunch was still clutched by a distraught slave. He was being closely guarded. Others, who had submitted to interview already, now clustered in frightened groups while the few last specimens were put through the vigiles' notoriously sensitive questioning technique:

'So where were you? Cut out the lies! What did you see? Nothing? Why didn't you keep an eye out? Are you fooling me, or plain stupid? Why would you want to kill your master then?' And to the weeping plea that the poor souls had no wish to do Chrysippus harm, came the harsh answer: 'Stop messing about. Slaves are the prime suspects, you know that!'

While Fusculus consulted to see what gems this sophisticated system had produced, I walked up to the slave with the tray. I signalled his guard to stand off.

'You the one who found the body?'

He was a thin, Gallic-looking scrag-end, of around fifty. He was in shock, but managed to respond to a civilised approach. I soon persuaded him to tell me it had been his daily duty to deliver a snack for Chrysippus. If Chrysippus wanted to work, he would order a tray from the kitchen, which this fellow would place on a side table in the lobby of the Latin library; the master would break off and clear the victuals, then go back to his reading. Today the tray had been untouched when the slave went to retrieve it, so he had carried it through to the Greek library to enquire if Chrysippus was so absorbed he had forgotten it. Rare, but not unheard of, I was told.

'When you saw what had happened, exactly what did you do?'

'Stood.'

'Transfixed?'

'I could not believe it. Besides, I was carrying the tray –' He blushed, aware now how irrelevant that sounded, wishing he had simply put it down. 'I backed out. Another lad took a look and rushed off shouting. People came running. Next minute they were haring about in all directions. I was in a daze. The soldiers burst in, and I was told to stay here and wait.'

Thinking about how silent the library had been, I was puzzled. Sound would never carry from indoors to the street. 'The men in red were very quickly on the scene. Someone ran out from the house?'

He looked vague. 'I think so.'

'Do you know who it was?'

'No. Once the alarm was raised, it all happened in a blur –'

'Was anybody in either area of the library when you first went in?'

'No.'

'Nobody leaving as you arrived?'

'No.'

'Anybody there the first time you went? I mean, when you first delivered the tray?'

'I only went in the lobby. I couldn't hear anyone talking.'

'Oh?' I eyed him suspiciously. 'Were you listening out for conversation?'

'Only politely.' He kept his cool at the suggestion that he eavesdropped. 'Often the master has somebody with him. That's why I leave the meal outside for him to collect when they have gone.'

'So go back a step for me: today you delivered his lunch as usual; you put down the tray on the side table, then what – did you call out or go in to tell your master it was there?'

'No. I never disturb him. He was expecting it. He normally comes out for it soon after.'

'And once you had delivered the tray, how long elapsed before you returned for the empties?'

'I had my own food, that's all.'

'What did you have?'

'Bread and *mulsum*, a little slice of goat's cheese.' He said this without much enthusiasm.

'That didn't take you long?'

'No.'

I removed the tray from his resisting fingers and laid it aside. The master's lunch had been more varied and tasty than his own, yet not enough for an epicure: salad leaves beneath a cold fish in marinade, big green olives, two eggs in wooden cups; red wine in a glass jug. 'It's over now. Try to forget what you saw.'

He started trembling. Belated shock set in. 'The soldiers say the slaves will get the blame.'

'They always say that. Did you attack your master?'

'No!'

'Do you know who did?'

'No.'

'No need to worry then.'

I was about to check with Fusculus what else had turned up, but something made me pause. The waiting slave seemed to be staring at the luncheon tray. I peered at him, querying. 'He's had one thing,' he told me.

'What do you mean?'

The slave looked slightly guilty, and certainly troubled, as though there was something he could not understand.

I waited, keeping my face neutral. He seemed intrigued. 'There was a little slice of nettle flan.' He sketched out the size with his thumb and one finger, a couple of digits of finger buffet savoury, cut as a triangle; I could imagine it. We both surveyed the food. No flan slice.

'Could it have dropped on the floor when you panicked and ran out?'

'It was not there when I went for the tray. I noticed specially.'

'How can you be sure?'

'He doesn't like pastry. I had seen it when I took the tray in. I thought he would leave it.'

'You were hoping to eat it yourself?'

'He wouldn't have minded,' he muttered defensively.

I said nothing, but that was interesting. I don't only mean that their cook served a rather eggy type of lunch. Nobody breaks off from work, investigates his tray, eats the one thing he dislikes, then abandons the rest. Somebody else must have been in that lobby. Maybe the killer himself passed that way when he left. Coolly grabbing a handful of his victim's meal? That would take nerve. Or else he was brutally callous.

Mind you, if anybody spotted him on the way out, having a fistful of pastry and a mouthful of crumbs would have made him look casual.

Fusculus approached, followed by one of his men.

'This is Passus, Falco. You probably don't know him. Joined our team recently.'

Passus looked at me with suspicion. He was a short, shock-haired, neat type with a belt he was proud of and stubby hands. He had a quiet manner and was no raw recruit; I guessed he had been seconded from some other cohort. His air was competent but not too pushy. He was carrying a set of waxed tablets, with a bone stylus bending his right ear forward, for taking notes.

'Didius Falco,' I introduced myself politely. I had always respected the men Petro gathered around him. He was a good judge and they responded well to him. 'Petronius Longus has called me in to assist on a consultancy basis.' Passus still said nothing, glancing sideways at Fusculus. He had been told, or had deduced, that I was an informer; he did not like it. 'Yes, it stinks,' I agreed. 'I'm no happier than you are. I have better things to do. But Petro knows I'm sound. I gather your squad is floundering in summer crime and needs to farm out the surplus.' I had had enough of justifying myself. 'Either that, or my dear friend Lucius has his hands full with a new girlfriend.'

Fusculus jumped. Petro's love life fascinated his men. 'He's after a new one?'

'Guesswork. He's said nix. You know how close he is. We'll only be sure when the next outraged husband comes to ask if we know why his turtledove is always tired . . . So, Passus, what's the story from the staff here?'

The new enquiry officer gave his report slightly stiffly at first, warming to the task: 'Aurelius Chrysippus had been occupying himself in his normal business. There were morning visitors; I took names. But he had been seen alive – when he asked for his lunch – after the last one is thought to have left.'

'*Thought?*' I queried. 'Are visitors not monitored?'

'The regime seems rather informal,' said Fusculus. 'There is a door porter but he doubles up as a water-carrier. If he is not at his post, people come and go as if the house was an extension of the shop.'

'Casual.'

'Greeks!' Apparently Fusculus harboured some old Roman prejudice against our cultured neighbours.

'I thought they like to protect their womenfolk?'

'No, they're just all over other peoples' women,' Fusculus sneered bitterly. A personal beef, no doubt of it. Find the female? I didn't even know that Fusculus had a girlfriend, let alone that he had had her pinched by some Piraeus skirt pirate.

'They have plenty of staff about.' Passus wanted to continue with his notes. 'It was a normal day. Chrysippus did not seem out of sorts. The alarm was raised by slaves just after midday. Most of them fled, terrified.'

'Terrified of being blamed,' commented Fusculus. Well, the vigiles, with their usual light-handed tactics, were making sure the slaves' terror was justified.

'Any of them touch the body?'

'No, Falco.' Fusculus, as senior officer present, was quick to let me know the vigiles had checked that aspect. 'They say they only looked in and then ran – well, it's pretty repellent.'

Passus took over again: 'We listened to their stories, then we carried out a hands and clothing check. No bloodstains on most of their tunics. One did have that spilt stuff from the library all up his backside, but that was because his feet had slipped from under him on the oil in there and he landed in the stuff; it's clear he has not been in a fight. Those with blood on their footwear match those who admitted they went in to gawp.'

'Arms and legs?'

'Clean.'

'Untoward bruising? Signs of a tussle?'

'Nothing new. A few bangs and cuts. All readily explained as natural wear and tear.' In most households a survey of the slaves would produce a fair set of black eyes, cuts, burns, knocks and sores.

'What do they say about the way they are handled here?'

'Routine. Smacked ears for making themselves unpopular, meagre servings in their food-bowls, hard beds, not enough women to go round.'

'So the slaves are affectionately-treated adjuncts to a normal family?'

'Model behaviour by the paterfamilias.'

'Did he extract sexual favours?'

'Probably. Nobody mentioned it.'

So far, this was not helping. 'I am still unclear how the alarm spread to the street,' I said. That niggled me. 'Who was it who ran out of the house making a noise?'

'I did!' announced a woman's voice.

We turned around and looked her up and down, which was what her rich dress and finely applied cosmetics intended us to do. Fusculus leaned one fist against his hip, considering this vision. Passus pursed his lips, not letting on whether he liked what he saw or thought the effect too flash.

'Ah! Now we're getting somewhere, boys!' I cried. It was a waggish response, which was possibly ill-mannered – but instinct told me to do it, even though this looked like the mistress of the house.

XIII

S HE WAS a good-looking piece. She knew all about it too. She did have a mouth so wide it looked as if it ran past her ears and met behind her head, but that was part of her style. The style was also extremely expensive. She wanted everyone to notice that.

The wide, red-dyed mouth was not smiling. The voice that had come from it was somehow slightly uncultured, yet I would have placed her social origins as Roman, and higher than those of Chrysippus. The dark eyes that went with the mouth and the voice were too close together for me, but men with less demanding tastes would have thought them appealing, and much had been made of them with plucked brows, deep outlines and startling tinted pastes. They had a hard expression, but so what? Women in the Thirteenth Sector were prone to that. According to the ones I knew, it was caused by men.

This was a young, confident female who had oodles of money and time on her hands. She thought that made her something special. For most people, it would have done. I was old-fashioned. I liked women with a dash of moral fibre; well, women whose flirting was honest, anyway.

'And who are you?' I kept it level, not admitting whether I was impressed by the externals. Fusculus and Passus were watching how I handled this. I could have managed better without their open curiosity, but I knew I had to show them my quality. I was up to it. Well, probably. Helena Justina would have recommended that I handle this beauty with tongs, from behind a fireproof shield.

'Vibia Merulla.'

'Lady of the house?'

'Correct. Chrysippus' wife.' Perhaps this was slightly too emphatic.

'And dear light of his life?' I made it gallant, if she chose to take my wry tone that way.

'Certainly.' The wide mouth set in a straight line.

I saw no reason to doubt her, actually. He must have been

approaching sixty; she was in her late twenties. He was an unprepossessing squit and she was a spanking little artefact. It fitted. Married for a couple of years now, and both parties still pretending to like the situation, I would guess. Standing in their luxurious home and inspecting the ranks of jewelled necklaces that burdened a fine bosom, I could imagine what might have been in it for her, while that half-revealed bust hinted at what had been in it for him.

Nevertheless, it is always worth pressing the questions. 'Were you happy together?'

'Of course we were. Ask anyone!' She may not have realised, I would do just that.

We shepherded the voluptuous Vibia to one side of the grand hall, out of earshot of the slaves who were still being processed. Her glance flickered over them anxiously, yet she made no attempt to intervene; as their mistress she would have been entitled to sit in on the questioning.

'Nice place!' commented Fusculus. Apparently this was his method of setting a wealthy householder's widow at her ease.

It worked. Vibia paid no more attention to the interrogated slaves. 'This is our Corinthian Oecus.'

'Very nice!' He smirked. 'Is that some Greek sort of thing?'

'Only in the best kind of houses.'

'But Greek?' insisted Fusculus.

He achieved his answer the second time: 'My husband's family came from Athens originally.'

'Was that recent?'

'This generation. But they are perfectly Romanised.' She, I reckoned, came straight off a true Roman trash-heap – though it might have social pretensions.

Fusculus managed not to sneer. Well, not at this stage. It was plain what he thought, and how raucous the conversation would be when the vigiles talked Vibia Merulla over later in the day.

Passus had found her a stool, so we could fuss round, ending up as if by accident in a group looming over her.

'We are very sorry for your loss.' I was examining the lady for signs of genuine grief; she knew that. She looked pale. The kohl-etched eyes were perfect and unsmudged. If she had wept, she had been neatly and expertly mopped up; still, there would be maids here employed specifically to keep her looking presentable, even in the present circumstances.

She produced a wail: 'It's horrible! Just horrible –'

'Chin up, darling,' soothed Passus. He was cruder than Fusculus. She looked annoyed, but women who carry a hint of the fish market yet lacquer themselves so expensively have to expect to be patronised.

I addressed her like a kind uncle, though I would have dumped responsibility for any niece like this. 'Forgive me for distressing you, but if we are to catch your poor husband's killer we must ascertain the full course of events today.' There were blood and oilstains on the glittering hem of her full-skirted gown, on her narrow-strapped, white leather sandals, and on the perfectly-trimmed toes visible through the dainty straps. 'You must have run in to the body when the alarm was raised?' I had let her see me inspecting her feet for evidence. Instinctively, she drew them back beneath her gown. A modest move. Embarrassed, perhaps, that they were no longer quite clean.

'I did,' she said, though for a second I thought she had to think about it.

'What you found must have been a terrible shock. I am sorry to have to remind you, but I need to be quite clear what happened next. You told us you ran into the street screaming – was that immediately after you saw what had happened?'

Vibia gazed at me. 'Do you imagine I sat down and polished my nails first?'

Her tone was fairly level. It was impossible to tell whether this was a straightforward sarcastic reaction from a wife irritated by officialdom, or the kind of fighting rejoinder I had sometimes met from culprits defending themselves.

'Why did you run outside?' I continued patiently.

'I thought whoever killed my husband might still be on the premises. I rushed out and screamed and screamed for help.'

'Excuse me, but you do have a large staff here. Were you not confident that they would protect you?' I wondered whether she was unpopular with the household slaves.

For half a breath, she did not answer. Even when she spoke, it avoided the question. 'I just wanted to get away from that horrible sight.'

'I have to ask – did it cross your mind that one of the slaves might have done it?'

'Nothing crossed my mind. I did not think.'

'Oh, quite understandable,' I assured her gently. At least this made a change from the frequent scenario where a guilty wife blames a slave to cover herself. 'Do you mind if I ask, what had you been doing that morning?'

64

'I was with my maids.'

And a mirror. And a shopful of glass powder containers. It must have taken some time just to assemble the jewellery collection, dominated by a clanking strand of gold half moons and by earrings so heavy with hard gemstones they must be torture on her lobes. You wouldn't nibble those ears. You might put an eye out, if madam tossed her head and the bank-breaking bijoux swung your way unexpectedly.

'Where's your room, lass?' growled Passus.

'On the second floor.'

'Same as your husband?' he demanded intrusively.

Vibia looked him straight in the eye. 'We are a devoted couple,' she reminded him.

'Oh, of course,' Passus returned, still being offensive as he pretended to apologise. 'But we see some terrible things in the vigiles. Some of the places we go, the first thing I'd be looking at was whether, while the husband was scribbling in his Greek library, there was a boyfriend creeping up a back stairway to visit the pretty young wife.'

Vibia Merulla seethed in silence. She may have coloured up. Under the layers of sheep-fat foundation, ochre rouge and foam of red nitre face powder, it was difficult to distinguish real effects of flesh and blood.

I took over again: 'Would you have any idea what your husband's movements were today?'

'The same as usual. He was a businessman; you must know that. He attended to his business.'

'That's rather vague, you know.' She ignored my mild reproof. Next time I would be rude like Passus. 'Part of the time he was in the scriptorium, streetside. I know that, Vibia. Then, I'm told, he came into the library. To read for his own pleasure?'

'What?'

'Reading,' I said. 'You know: words written on scrolls. Expressions of thought; depictions of action; inspiration and uplift – or for a publisher, the means to cash.' She looked offended again. Still, I knew her type; she thought plays were where you went to flirt with your girlfriends' husbands and poems were junk verses sent to you in secret packs of sweets by oily gigolos. 'He was working?' I insisted.

'Of course.'

'At what?'

'How should I know? Skipping through manuscripts, probably. We would go in and find him, scowling and grumbling – he has a stable of writers he encourages, but frankly, he does not think much of most of them.' Like the slave with the lunch tray, she still slipped into speaking as if the man were alive.

'Could you, or someone on your staff, give me these writers' names?'

'Ask Euschemon. He is –'

'Thanks. I know Euschemon. He is waiting to be interviewed.' Did a flicker of nervousness cross the lady's face? 'And did Chrysippus work on manuscripts in his Greek library like that every day?' I asked, trying to ascertain if a murderer could have planned on finding him there.

'If he was at home. He had numerous interests. He was a man of affairs. Some mornings he would be out, seeing clients or other people.'

'Where did he go?'

'The Forum, maybe.'

'Do you know anything about his clients?'

'I am afraid not.' She looked straight back at me. Was it a challenge?

'Do you know if he had any enemies?'

'Oh no. He was a much loved and respected man.'

Dear gods. Why do they never realise that informers and the vigiles have heard that claim a hundred lying times before? I managed not to look at Fusculus and Passus, lest we all three collapsed with side-splitting ridicule.

I folded my arms.

'So. You and Chrysippus lived here, blissfully married.' No reaction from the lady. Still, women rarely come straight out with complaints about men's habits at table or their mean dress allowances, not to a stranger. Well, not a stranger who has just seen the husband of the moment lying nastily dead. Women are less stupid than some investigators make out.

'Children?' put in Fusculus.

'Get away,' joshed Passus, playing a well-worn vigiles routine. 'She doesn't look old enough!'

'Child bride.' Fusculus grinned back. It might work with a dim girl, but this one was too hard-bitten. Vibia Merulla decided for herself when she wanted to be flattered. She had probably done her share of encouraging men's banter, but now there was too much at stake. She endured the joking with a face like travertine.

66

'Leave off, you two,' I intervened. I gazed at Vibia benignly. That did not fool her either, but she did not bother to react. Not until my next question: 'As the examining officer in this case, you appreciate that I need to look for a motive for your husband's murder. He was rich; somebody will inherit. Can you tell me the terms of his will?'

'You heartless bastard!' shrieked the widow.

Well, they usually do.

She had been about to leap to her feet (very nice little feet, under the bloodstains and cedar oil). Fusculus and Passus were both ready for that. One either side of her, they leaned kindly on a shoulder each, pinning her down on her stool with lugubrious expressions of completely false sympathy. If she tried to break free forcibly, the bruises would last for weeks.

'Oh, steady on, Falco!'

'Poor lady; it's just his unfortunate manner. Please don't distress yourself –'

'No offence!' I grinned heartlessly.

Vibia wept, or pretended to, into a handkerchief, quite prettily.

Fusculus went down in front of her on one knee, offering to dry the tears, which would be unfortunate if they were fake. 'Madam, Marcus Didius Falco is a notorious brute – but he is obliged to ask you these questions. A ghastly crime has been committed, and we all want to catch whoever was responsible, don't we?' Vibia nodded fervently. 'It would surprise you how many times people get themselves murdered, and we in the vigiles are then shocked to find out that their own closest relatives killed them. So just let Falco do his job: these are routine enquiries.'

'If it upsets you,' I offered helpfully, 'I can soon discover what I need to know from your husband's will.'

'Is there a will?' wondered Fusculus.

'I expect so,' Vibia fluttered, as if the thought had never occurred to her.

'And are you mentioned in it?' asked Passus, with an innocent smile.

'I have no idea!' she proclaimed rather loudly. 'I have nothing to do with matters of money; whatever other women do. It is so unfeminine.' None of us commented. The remark seemed specific, and I for one filed it in my professional memory under unfinished business. 'I expect,' she declared, as suspects tend to do when blaming someone else, 'Diomedes is the main heir.'

Fusculus, Passus, and I looked from one to another with knowing bright eyes.

'Diomedes!' said Passus to me, as if this solved a big question. Maybe he was right at that. 'Well, of course.'

'Diomedes,' I responded. 'There you are then.'

'Diomedes,' repeated Fusculus. 'Fancy us not thinking of him straight away!'

We all stopped smiling.

'Young lady,' I said – although the raw calculation in Vibia Merulla's azure-lidded eyes belonged to an efficient nymph who was as old as the cold dawn on the Sabine Hills. 'I don't want to press you unfairly, but if he is in the square for this killing, I suggest you tell us rather speedily where we might find him – and who Diomedes is.'

XIV

'DIOMEDES IS Chrysippus' son.'

Passus was already consulting a list on his waxed tablets. He whistled a little tuneless phrase through his teeth. 'If he lives here, he's not in,' he then told me in a low voice.

'He lives with his mother,' announced Vibia coldly. So she was the second wife. With the first still alive, there must have been a divorce. Another nugget to file. None of us commented. No need. Even Vibia's expression showed she understood the implications.

'This lad is an infant?' asked Fusculus, assuming that any older son would live with the father, in normal guardianship.

'He's certainly a spoilt brat who needs looking after!' Vibia snapped. The first wife's boy had definitely upset her somehow. I saw Passus glance at Fusculus, both of them convinced that Vibia 'looked after' Diomedes in some sexual way. She failed to notice the innuendo, luckily. It was too soon to harass her in that way, even if we later came to suspect a dalliance.

'He is an only child?' I kept it formal.

'Yes.' She herself had borne none then. She did not appear to be pregnant. Always a good idea to check; many a violent death has been initiated by an impending birth.

'How old is Diomedes exactly?' I had sensed what the scenario might be.

'I'm not his mother; I cannot say *exactly!*' She looked up at me and stopped playing about. She shrugged. A gauzy stole slipped from her neat little shoulders. 'Early twenties.'

'That's exact enough.' Of an age to become a suspect. 'When was the mother divorced by Chrysippus?'

'About three years ago.'

'After you came along?'

Vibia Merulla simply smiled. Oh yes; I *had* got the picture.

'So Diomedes went off to live with his mama. Did he continue to see his father?'

'Of course.'

'They are Greeks,' Fusculus reminded me. His loathing of the cultured folk from the cradle of philosophy was beginning to grate. 'Very close-knit families.'

'It's a Roman ideal too,' I rebuked him. 'Does Diomedes come to this house to see Chrysippus, Vibia?'

'Yes.'

'Has he been here today?'

'I have no idea.'

'You don't normally see your husband's visitors?'

'I do not involve myself in business.' This claim, too, was becoming repetitious.

'But Diomedes is family.'

'Not mine!'

Too crisp. She felt she was defeating our questioning too well. Time to stop it. Better to continue later, when I would know more and might have edged a step ahead of her. I told Passus to obtain details of where the first wife lived, after which I suggested Vibia Merulla might like time to come to terms with her sudden bereavement in quiet female company.

'Is there anybody we can send for, who would comfort you, my dear?'

'I can manage,' she assured me, with an impressive stab at dignity. 'Friends will no doubt rush along when they hear what has happened.'

'Oh, I'm sure you are right.'

Widows of wealthy men rarely lack for sympathy. In fact, as we left her to her own devices, Fusculus was arranging to leave a 'courtesy' vigilis guard at the house; I heard him surreptitiously give the guard instructions to note the names of people, especially men, who rushed along to console Vibia.

Before I left here, I wanted to interview Euschemon, the scriptorium manager. Meanwhile, I asked Fusculus to send a couple of men immediately to the house of the first wife and her son, to put them under close guard until I could get there. 'Prevent them changing their clothes or washing – if they have not already done so. Don't tell them what it is all about. Keep them quarantined. I'll be as quick as I can.'

I checked one final time that no useful clues had been extracted from the slaves, then I walked back through the lobby to the library. On the way, I had a close look at the side table where the lunch tray had been placed. Its two pediment feet were carved from that Phrygian marble that comes in basic white, with dark purple variegations. A couple of the wine-coloured streaks turned out to be surface only – dried bloodstains that I rubbed off with a wet finger. It confirmed that the killer might well have stopped here on his way out, in order to pinch that piece of nettle flan.

Unpleasant though it was, I had a last look at the dead man, memorising the ghastly scene in case I needed to recall some detail later. Passus brought me the address of the first wife; I would have liked to be the first to report what had happened – although I bet she would have heard of her ex-husband's death by now.

I picked up the short end of the scroll rod that had been wielded so revoltingly against the victim. 'Ask your evidence officer to label that and keep it, Passus. We may find the matching finial somewhere, if we have any real luck.'

'So, what do you think, Falco?'

'I hate cases where the first person you interview looks as guilty as all Hades.'

'The wife did not kill him?'

'Not in person. Both she and her clothes would show damage. And although I can imagine she can wind herself into quite a frenzy when she wants to, I doubt if she is strong enough to inflict this.' We forced ourselves to resurvey the corpse at our feet. 'Of course she could have hired someone.'

'She virtually fingered this son, Diomedes.'

'Too convenient. No, it's too early to accuse anyone, Passus.'

Passus looked pleased. He was curious to know the answers – but he did not want Petronius' pet private informer to be the outsider who provided them.

His hostility was a cliché, one I was well used to, yet it annoyed me. I told him to give orders for the corpse to be removed to an undertaker's. Spitefully, I added, 'Get this room cleared, not by the household slaves but by your own men, please. Keep an eye out for any clues we may have missed under the mess. And before they are flung out in a basket, I shall need a list of what all these unrolled scrolls on the floor contain, by subject and author.'

'Oh shit, Falco!'

'Sorry.' I smiled pleasantly. 'You may have to do that yourself, I suppose, if your rankers can't read. But what Chrysippus was working on today may turn out to have some relevance.'

Passus said nothing. Maybe Petronius would have wanted the

scrolls listed, had he been in charge. Maybe not.

I went back to the scriptorium, where I told the guard maintaining quarantine for Euschemon that he could be released into my custody. I could see he was not the killer; he was wearing the same clothes as when he came to see me at home this morning, with not a bloodstain on them.

There were too many scribes within earshot, and I reckoned it would inhibit him when he talked to me. I took him away for a drink. He looked relieved to be out of there.

'Think nothing of it,' I said cheerfully. After a grisly corpse and a flagrant wifelet, I was feeling dry myself.

XV

THERE WAS a *popina* on the next street corner, one of those grim stand-up foodshops with crude mock marble countertops on which to bruise your elbows. All but one of the big pots were uncovered and empty, and the other had a cloth over it to discourage orders. The grumbling proprietor took great pleasure in telling us he could not serve eatables. Apparently the vigiles had given him a bollocking for selling hot stews. The Emperor had banned them. It was dressed up as some sort of public health move; more likely a subtle plan to get workers off the streets and back in their workshops – and to deter people from sitting down and discussing the government.

'Everything's banned except pulses.'

'Ugh!' muttered I, being no lover of lentils. I had spent too much time on suveillance, gloomily leaning against a caupona counter and toying with a lukewarm bowl of pallid slush while I waited for some suspect to emerge from his comfortable lair – not to mention too many hours afterwards picking leguminous grains from my teeth.

Privately I made a note that this ban might affect business at Flora's – so Maia might not want to take on Pa's caupona after all.

'I gather you had the red tunics here, just when the alarm was raised about the death at the scriptorium?'

'Too right. The bastards put the block on today's menu right at lunchtime. I was furious, but it's an edict so I couldn't say much. A woman started screaming her head off. Then the vigiles rushed off to investigate the excitement and by the time I had finished clearing the counters, there was nothing to see. I missed all the fun. My counter-hand ran down there; he said it was gruesome –'

'That's enough!' I gave a tactful nod towards Euschemon, whom he probably knew. The popina owner subsided with a grouse. His counter-hand was absent now; perhaps sent home when the hot food was cleared away.

Euschemon had shambled after me from the house in silence. I bought him a cup of pressed fruitjuice, which seemed the only thing on offer. It was not bad, though the fruit used was debatable. The bill, written out for me with unusual formality, cancelled any pleasure in the taste. We leaned on the counter; I glared at the owner until he slunk into the back room.

'I'm Falco; you remember?' He managed half a nod. 'I called at the scriptorium this morning, Euschemon. You were out; I saw Chrysippus.' I did not mention my disagreement with him. It seemed a long time ago. 'That must have been just before he went in to work in his library. Now I have been appointed the official investigator for vigiles. I'll have to ask you some questions.'

He just held his cup. He seemed in a daze, malleable – but perhaps unreliable too.

'Let's do some scene setting – at what point did you arrive back?'

He had to search for breath to answer me. He dragged out his words: 'I came back at midday. During the fuss, but I did not realise that at first.'

I swigged some juice and tried to pep him up. 'How far had things got – were the vigiles already at the house?'

'Yes; they must have been indoors. I thought there was rather a crowd outside, but I must have been preoccupied . . .'

'With what?' I grilled him sternly.

'Oh . . . the meaning of life and the price of ink.' Sensing he might be in trouble, Euschemon woke up a bit. 'How hot was the weather, what colour olives had I chosen for my lunchpack, whose damned dog had left us a message on the pavement right outside the shop. Intellectual pursuits.' He had more of a sense of humour than I had previously realised.

'Surely your staff knew what was going on indoors?'

'No. In fact, nobody had heard any noise. They would have noticed the fracas in the street from the shop, but they were all in the scriptorium. The lads were battened down, you see, just having their lunchbreak.'

'Was the scroll-shop closed then?'

'Yes. We always pull the rolling door across and shut right down. The scribes have to concentrate so hard when they are copying, they need a complete full stop. They get their food. Some play dice, or they have a nap in the heat of the day.'

'Is the shutter actually locked in place?'

'Have to do it, or people try to force their way in even though they can see we have packed up for lunch. No consideration–'

'So nobody could have come in that way – or gone out?'

He realised I meant the killer. 'No,' he said sombrely.

'Would the shop have closed pretty early?'

'If I know the scribes, and given that I myself was not there, yes.'

'Hmm. So around the time of the death, that exit was blocked off.' If the killer made no attempt to use that route, maybe he knew the scriptorium routine. 'So how did you get indoors when you returned?'

'I banged on the shutter.'

'They unlocked again?'

'Only because it was me. I ducked in, and we jammed it back.'

'And when you arrived, the staff did not seem at all disturbed?'

'No. They were surprised when I asked if they knew what was going on in the street. I had realised the crowd was outside the master's house door –'

'Where's that?'

'Further down. Past the bootmender. You can see the portico.' I squinted round; beyond the scriptorium and another shop entrance, I noted important stonework intruding onto the pavement. 'I was going to go and speak to Chrysippus about it when one of the vigiles burst in, from the house corridor.'

'By that time he was well dead. So all the previous action had been muffled? You were out, and the scribes missed everything until after the body's discovery?' Euschemon nodded again, still like a man dreaming. 'I'll have to check that nobody came through the scriptorium after Chrysippus went indoors,' I mused.

'The vigiles asked us that,' Euschemon told me. 'The scribes all said they saw nobody.'

'You believe them?'

He nodded. 'They would have been glad to be left in peace.'

'Not happy workers?'

'Ordinary ones.' He realised why I was probing. 'They do the job, but they like it best with no supervisor on their backs. It's natural.'

'True.' I drained my cup. 'Did you go in and see the body?'

He nodded, very slowly. The horror had yet to leave him. Maybe it never would. His life had paused today, at that moment when a keyed-up vigilis rampaged down the corridor and interrupted the quiet lunchbreak. He would probably never entirely recapture the old rhythms of his existence.

He stared at me. 'I had never seen anything like it,' he said. 'I couldn't –' He gave up, waving his hands helplessly, lost for words.

I let him recover for a moment, then tackled him on more general background: 'I have to find out who did it. Give me some help, will you. Start with the business. It's doing well, apparently?'

Euschemon drew back slightly. 'I only deal with the authors and organise the copyists.'

'Man management.' I was being polite, but relentless. 'So did any of the men you managed have anything against our victim?'

'Not the scribes.'

'The authors?'

'Authors are a complaining lot, Falco.'

'Any complaints specifically?' He shrugged, and I answered for myself: 'Poor payment and dismissive critiques!' He pulled a slight face, acknowledging the truth of it. 'No grudge important enough to make a creative person kill?'

'Oh, I shouldn't think so. You don't lose your temper just because your writing is poorly received.' *Really?*

'So how were sales?' I asked lightly.

Euschemon replied in a dry tone, 'As usual: if you listen to people who commission material, they have a lively stable of writers and are expecting shortly to ruin their competitors. The competitors, however, will accuse them of teetering on the brink of bankruptcy. If you ask the scroll-shops, life is a long struggle; manuscripts are hard to come by at reasonable prices and customers don't want to know. If you look around, people are nonetheless reading – although probably not reading what the critics are praising.'

'So who wins?'

'Don't ask me. I work in a scriptorium – for a pittance.'

'Why do you do it then? Are you a freedman of Chrysippus?'

'Yes, and my patron gives me a lot of responsibility.'

'Job satisfaction is so wonderful! You're very loyal. And trust-worthy, and useful – is that all?'

'Love of literature,' he said. I bet. He could just as well have been selling anchovies or cauliflowers.

I changed elbows, giving myself a view up the Clivus Publicius instead of down it. 'So. The scroll business would appear to be doing well. Patronage pays.' Euschemon did not comment. 'I saw the house,' I pointed out. 'Very nice!'

'Taste and quality,' he agreed.

'Not so sure that applies to the wife,' I suggested.

'He thought so.'

'True love?'

'I don't want to gossip. But she would not kill him. I don't believe that.'

76

'Were they happy? Old man and his darling? Was it solid? Was it real?'

'Real enough,' said Euschemon. 'He left a wife of thirty years for Vibia. The new marriage meant everything to him – and Vibia relished what she had achieved.'

'Define it?'

'A powerful man, with money and social position, who was publicly devoted to her. He took her around and showed her off –'

'And he let her spend? All a woman could desire! So did she have a lover too?' Euschemon pulled a face, revolted by my cynicism. We would see. I smiled wryly. 'So you don't think Vibia had a reason to kill him? Not even for the money?'

He looked even more shocked. 'Oh no! That's horrible, Falco.'

'Pretty common too,' I disillusioned him.

'I don't want to discuss this.'

'Then tell me about the first wife, and the darling son.'

'Lysa,' he began carefully, 'is a tough woman.'

'The wife of thirty years? They tend to be. She kept Chrysippus in order – until Vibia snaked into his life?'

'Lysa had helped him build his business empire.'

'Aha!'

'And is, of course, the mother of his son,' Euschemon said.

'Vengeful?'

'She opposed the divorce, I heard.'

'But she had no choice. In Rome divorce is a fact, the moment one party withdraws from a marriage. So, she was cruelly abandoned after devoting her life to Chrysippus' interests. That would have enraged her. Was Lysa *sufficiently* vengeful to kill him?'

'She had a lot to say when the split happened. But I believe she had accepted the situation,' protested Euschemon. Even he could hear it sounded feeble, obviously.

'What about Diomedes? Bit of a mother's boy?'

'A decent young man.'

'Wet, you mean?'

'You're a brute, Falco.'

'Proud of it. So we have an enraged witch, now past her prime, pushing a beloved only offspring who is something of a weed, while the ageing tyrant moves on elsewhere, and the new young princess simpers . . . Like a Greek tragedy. And I do believe there is a chorus of cultivated poets, as in all the best Athenian plays – I need the names of the authors who enjoyed Chrysippus' patronage, please.'

Euschemon blenched. 'Are our authors suspects?' He seemed almost protective – but then they were an investment.

'Suspected of bad verse, probably. But that's not a civil crime. Names?'

'There is a small group we support, authors drawn from across the literary range. Avienus, the respected historian; Constrictus, an epic poet – rather dull, perhaps; Turius, who is trying to write a Utopia, though I believe he's unwell – at least, he thinks he is; then there's Urbanus Trypho, the playwright –'

I stopped him. 'I've heard of Urbanus!'

'He is very successful. A Briton, if you can believe that. Not half as provincial as people suppose. Extremely successful,' Euschemon commented, a touch sadly. 'To be honest, Chrysippus had slightly underestimated his appeal. We ought to have imposed a much more rigorous royalty structure there.'

'Tragic for you! But Urbanus is laughing all the way to his Forum bank. If he receives his deserts from the ticket office, he'll be content – and this rare human condition may put him in the clear for the killing. Have you mentioned everyone?'

'Almost. We also have the famous Pacuvius – *Scrutator*, the satirist. Something of a handful, but immensely clever – as he is all too aware. *Scrutator* is a pen name.'

'Pseudonym for what?'

'Shitbag,' said Euschemon with rare but intense bile. His loathing was so deeply ingrained he had no need to dwell on it, but reverted to an equable mood immediately afterwards.

'He's your favourite!' I commented lightly. I could pursue the reason discreetly later. 'Are all these writers employed on the same terms that Chrysippus offered me?'

Euschemon coloured up slightly. 'Well, no, Falco. These are our regulars, the mainstay of our moderns list –'

'You do pay them?' He did not reply, sensitive perhaps to my own – different – position regarding the poems the scriptorium had tried to commission. 'But do you pay them enough?'

'We pay them the going rate,' said Euschemon defensively.

'How much is that?'

'Confidential.'

'How wise. You don't want writers comparing. It could lead to them noticing discrepancies. And that might lead to jealousy.' Jealousy being the oldest and most frequent motive for murder.

The list sounded familiar. I took out Passus' written round-up of today's visitors to Chrysippus. 'Well, well. All the men you have named saw your master this morning! What can you tell me about that?' Euschemon looked shifty. 'Don't mess me about,' I warned.

'We were reviewing our future publication lists.'

'It was planned? They had appointments?'

'Informally. Chrysippus did business in the Greek way – a casual meeting, a friendly chat about family matters, politics, the social news. Then he would come to the matter in hand, almost as an afterthought. People would have known he wanted to see them, and they would have dropped in at the house.'

'So which of them likes nettle flan?'

'What?'

'Nothing. Any of these fellows have a black mark by their names?' Euschemon looked puzzled. 'Which of them, had you decided, was about to be dropped from your catalogue?'

'None.'

'No problems at all with them?'

'Oh, with authors there will always be problems! They will be only too happy to grumble. You ask them, Falco. One or two needed encouragement, let's say. Chrysippus will have handled it tactfully.'

'*Do as I tell you, or the bread supply is cut off?*'

'Please don't be crude.'

'This may seem cruder: could a disgruntled author have shoved a scroll rod up his patron's nose?'

Euschemon went rigid. 'I prefer to believe we are patrons to men of refinement.'

'If you believe that, you are deluding yourself, my friend.'

'If Chrysippus was planning changes, he had not told me. As his manager, I waited to hear what he wanted.'

'Did you have different critical standards?' I guessed.

'Different tastes sometimes.' Euschemon seemed a loyal type. 'If you want to probe into what was discussed this morning individually, only the authors know that.'

I thought of sending a runner to all the authors, commanding them to present themselves before me this evening in Fountain Court. That would perhaps allow me to tackle them at a stage when only the murderer knew Chrysippus had been killed – but it did not give me time to dissuade Helena from beating me to pieces over the intrusion. Five authors in sequence was not her idea of a family evening. Nor mine. Work has its place, but Hades, a man needs a home life.

They could wait. I would seek them out tomorrow. It was urgent (to stop them conferring), though not the most urgent thing I had to do. Before anything else now I had to interview Lysa, the aggrieved first wife.

She lived in a neat villa, large enough to have internal gardens, in a prosperous area. Unfortunately, when I found the address, I was met by two men Fusculus had sent ahead, who told me both the ex-wife and her son were out. Needless to say, no one knew where. And it was a certainty, they would both turn up at their home that evening just when I wanted to be in my own apartment having dinner myself. With prescient gloom, I told the vigiles to come and fetch me as soon as the missing relatives turned up.

So much for my home life, I thought glumly. But when I reached the apartment, the evening was ruined in any case: Helena was holding off the barbarian attack with a glint in her eyes that said I had reappeared in the nick of time. We had been invaded by my sister Junia, complete with Ajax, her untrained and unrestrainable dog, her ghastly husband Gaius Baebius, and their deaf but noisy son.

XVI

I FLASHED MY beloved a secret grin; as I had not been here when the visitors arrived, this would count as her fault. She took it with a sickly smile. Marcus Baebius Junillus, aged about three now, ran up to me as I sank wearily onto the first stool that came to hand. He flung himself on my lap, shoved his face near mine, and grinned a huge imitation of my private grimace to Helena – there was nothing wrong with his eyesight. At the same time, he growled loudly, like some horrendous wild beast. He was playing – probably. We did not see him often; when we did, we had to readjust to him.

He was named after me. That did not make him easier to handle. Junia and Gaius, with no children of their own, had adopted this scrap after his own parents abandoned him once they realised he was deaf. As I fended off his attentions, Junia grabbed him. She turned him round to face her, seized his wrist – her method of gaining his attention – then gripped him either side of his little face, squeezing his cheeks so his mouth moved to follow her saying, 'Un-cle Mar-cus!' The child calmed down very slightly, repeating her words approximately. He was a pretty boy, now showing some intelligence, and he watched Junia carefully. If anyone could do it, my sister would one day make him talk.

'She spends hours like that with him,' Gaius Baebius informed us admiringly. He had settled himself in my favourite place, holding my best beaker between both his hands. 'At home we draw pictures as well. He's learning things slowly, and he's a good little artist too.' He loved the boy (he even loved my sister, which was just as well because nobody else would); however, I guessed that as a parent he was little use. He and Junia were made for each other: narrow-minded, furiously ambitious mediocrities. That said, Junia had brains and sticking power. In fact, if she had been rather less brainy, I might have found her more bearable. She was three years older than me. She had always regarded me like a filthy blot staining a newly-scrubbed floor.

Ajax, their mad dog, now leapt on me. He was black and white, with a long snout, ferocious teeth that did occasionally sink into strangers, and a long feathered tail. He made Nux, who was a vagabond, seem well-disciplined. Just as I got a grip on him, he leapt off again. Then he kept barking and running in circles, trying to rush into the bedroom, where I guessed Helena had penned in Nux.

'You are ragging him,' Junia accused me. 'He'll never quieten down now.'

'I'm going to tie him up in the porch. Nux is expecting puppies and I don't want her to be harassed.'

'Time you thought of having another one too, Helena!' Junia knew instinctively just how to enrage Helena.

'You are turning into Ma,' I said.

'And that's another thing –' Apparently some complaint had been voiced before I arrived. 'I blame you for introducing that dreadful man to Mother.'

'If you mean Anacrites, he was dying at the time. I wish he had been finished, but that's a spy for you. When he looks as if somebody has caved half his head in and he can't last the night, he suddenly reveals that he has an iron constitution and was just fooling – then he stabs you in the back.'

'It's disgusting!' snapped Junia. Her black Cleopatra ringlets quivered and what she possessed in the way of a bosom swelled with indignation beneath the shiny material of her over-laundered gown.

'He pays Ma the rent. Stop worrying. One quiet lodger is not too much for her. Ma loves having someone to fuss over. Since Anacrites went to live with her she's looked really quite spruce.'

'You have no idea!' raged my sister. She threw an angry glance at Helena. But after the offspring hint Helena merely smiled frostily, refusing to join in Junia's rant.

I decided not to refer to Anacrites' apparent yen for Maia. Maia had enough problems. I was squinting into various bowls and jugs that were set on the table, though Gaius Baebius, who was always stolidly ravenous, seemed to have cleared out everything snackable. He saw me looking, with his usual complacence. He was a customs clerk, so I hated him even before I noticed the empty nutshell pile at his elbow and the trace of olive oil gleaming on his chin.

Little Marcus Baebius was growing frustrated. Junia wanted to berate me, so she had stopped paying attention to him. Gaius tried taking him from Junia, but this produced only paroxysms of fury. In the end, the anguished tot hurled himself face down, beating his head on the floorboards while he yelled and wept in a spectacular fashion.

Julia Junilla, our daughter, sat on Helena's lap behaving perfectly for a change. She was staring at her cousin, obviously taking tantrum lessons. I could see she was impressed.

'Ignore him,' mouthed Junia. That was rather hard to do. It was a small room, overcrowded with four adults and two children.

'I think it's time you took him home, Junia.'

'I have to talk to you.'

'Can't it wait?'

'No; it's about Father.'

'Pa as well! You seem to be wearing yourself out on family duties —'

'We saw him today, Marcus.'

Ignored, Marcus Baebius had stopped wailing and was playing dead. Junia would shriek when she noticed. Ajax went and sat on him, slobbering aimlessly. In the silence, I could now hear desperate whining from Nux in the other room.

'Leave it, Junia. Pa is in a mess, but he will sort himself out once he thinks up some new way to annoy people.'

'Well, if you lack a sense of duty, brother, I know I don't.'

'Isn't it just a question of falling on him in his grief, and pointing out that you would like to be his heirs?' I was too tired to be careful.

'Come off it, Marcus,' muttered Gaius, roused to defend the specimen of womanhood he had chosen as his prickly wife.

I had had enough. 'What do you want, Junia?'

'I came to keep you informed.'

'Of what?'

'I have volunteered to help our Father. I shall be running his caupona for him.'

It was at that moment that the party increased in numbers and the tension rose rapidly too: Maia stormed in.

She had Marius with her — her nine-year-old elder boy, whom I had recommended as a spare hand for the auction house. Maia clutched him to her skirts, with her hand tangled in his tunic as if he was in some trouble. He must have been present when Junia tackled Pa, and had let slip to his mother what he had heard. He winced at me. I mimed back a cringe.

'So!' exclaimed Maia. She definitely knew then. It was going to be rough. Ajax sprang up and was about to jump all over her, but Maia snarled herself and sent him slinking into a corner, completely cowed.

'Hello, Maia, you poor darling,' cooed Junia. They had never got on. Junia stepped over her own prone child (who had stopped holding his breath since he could see it was not working) and grappled Maia for sympathetic kissing. Maia broke free, with a shudder. I waved frantically to tell my outraged younger sister not to press charges over the caupona scam.

Ever quick, Maia belted in her wrath. She and I had always been conspiratorial, and usually allied against our elder siblings. That left Junia looking for a quarrel which failed to materialise. She assumed an expression of slight puzzlement. With years of practice, Maia and I could make her feel threatened without revealing how.

'How are you bearing up to widowhood, Maia?'

'Oh, don't you worry about me.'

'And here's poor little Marius!'

Marius sidled free of both my sisters and huddled against me where I gave him a surreptitious hug. Knowing that Maia hated her children being showered with treats, Junia insisted on donating him an *as* to buy sweetmeats. Marius accepted the coin as if it were coated with poison, deliberately forgetting to say thanks. Junia pulled him up on that, while Maia seethed.

Junia then made sure she told Maia of her own scheme to run Flora's.

'Oh really?' said Maia indifferently – then she and I set about making fun of the idea that stiff and stately Junia might ever work behind a foodshop bar.

'A caupona is hard work,' Helena joined in.

'You're all being ridiculous,' Junia assured us. 'I shall only supervise from a distance. The place is worked by waiting staff.'

We laughed openly at that. I knew Apollonius, the sole waiter, much better than she did, and I could not see him putting up with her. Anyway, Junia had a long history of quarrelling with minions. 'I don't know why you want to take on such a burden,' said Helena. Her voice was deceptively gentle. 'I thought your role in life was as Gaius' companionable partner – true Roman marriage: keeping the home, nurturing your child, and sharing your husband's intimate confidences.'

Junia looked at Helena with deep suspicion; all my wicked lass had left out of the idyllic myth was 'working your loom in the atrium', though that really would have given the game away. Not a flicker of a smile betrayed Helena.

'Junia always was an independent woman,' Gaius oozed. 'She is so capable we can't waste her talents. She will enjoy a little project of her own.'

84

'It will be the first time I ever remember our Junia holding down a job,' I scoffed. As far as I knew, she had lined up Gaius as a respectable prospect when she was about fourteen. She had sniffed out that he happened to be an orphan, left with his own apartment. He was older than Junia and already in work in the customs service – his only career. Gaius was a one-job lifer; his employer could treat him like a slave, yet his loyalty would never fade. Equally, being snaffled by my sister had been a relief to him. I doubt if he would ever have had a romantic experience otherwise. He and Junia had started saving up for ghastly furniture and an eight-bowl dinner set the minute they first held hands on a garden bench.

'Better send word to the Valerian that they'll be getting a lot of new customers from over the road,' Maia jibed acidly.

'What's the Valerian?' Junia had clearly not surveyed the market before rushing in to claim this enterprise. We told her. She still rejected all suggestions that her venture might fail due to unsuitability and inexperience. 'I just think people should rally around Pa,' she boasted. We congratulated her on her piety, making it sound as insincere as possible. She and her family left not long afterwards.

Immediately I told Maia about the Emperor's ban on hot take-aways. 'Trust me, girl. I'm quick to find you opportunities – and even quicker to get you out of mistakes.' She thought about the commercial implications, then simmered down.

I told Marius to go and rescue Nux from the bedroom; if she bore live pups, he had been half-promised one of them. He carried Nux in, then sat quietly, stroking her and talking to her in a low voice. After a while the dog suddenly reached up and licked him with her bright pink tongue. His face lit up. Maia, who had opposed the pup idea, scowled heavily at me.

She chewed her lip. 'I'm well out of that caupona. I'll have to find something else.'

'Go and see Geminus anyway,' suggested Helena. 'The caupona may not have been the only sideline Flora had.'

'That's the trouble,' said Maia. 'He is in a grand mess without her. Flora kept all the accounts at the warehouse. She managed the diary of sales, organised the bookings for Pa to view items, followed up bad debts, and virtually ran everything.'

'There you are then.' Helena grinned at my sister. 'Decide what it's worth to you, then offer to be his secretary.' She seemed to be joking, but laughed quietly. 'I'd like to be a spider in a cranny when Junia comes to split her first week's caupona takings with Geminus – then discovers that while she's scrubbing fishscales off dirty cold bowls, you are sweetly in charge of the deskwork.'

'I hate Pa,' said Maia.

'Of course you do,' I told her. 'But you want a chance to put one over on Junia.'

'Ah, some sacrifices are just begging to be made,' agreed Maia. After a while she added, 'Knowing Pa, he won't have it.'

So that was organised.

Petronius came over for a report on the Chrysippus case, and we all spent a casual evening until Maia had to leave to fetch her other children from a friend's. Petro vanished at the same time, so he missed what happened next. Helena and I were quietly clearing up, when one of the vigiles from Lysa's house turned up. But I was not required to head off into the night with him. The woman and her son had decided a better way to spoil my evening was to bring themselves to me.

XVII

CONVENTION WOULD have prophesied that Lysa, the ex-wife whom Chrysippus had rejected for a fluffy lamb, would be miserable mutton. That's not how it works. Chrysippus must have had the same taste in women thirty years ago as recently. Lysa might now be the mother of a grown man in his twenties, with half a lifetime of business experience and home-making behind her, but she also possessed a straight back and fine bone structure.

She was darker than Vibia and less prone to painting herself like a twice-a-night prostitute, but she had presence. As soon as she marched in, I prepared myself for trouble. Helena Justina was bristling even before I was, I noticed. For a small woman, Lysa could fill a room. She might have been one of my relatives; discomfort was her natural element.

The vigilis must have had a hard time from her. After a perfunctory introduction, he escaped. Helena Justina cast a swift eye over Julia, who was playing quietly while she considered how to try out the hideous behaviour she had witnessed from young Marcus Baebius. Safe from immediate interruption, Helena plonked down on a bench with her arms folded. She jerked her skirts straight and silently let it be known she was a respectable matron who did not leave her husband to the snares of strange females in her own home. Lysa pretended she had been offered a seat on the same bench and sat down as if she owned the joint. Unconsciously, both women fondled their necklaces. Declarations of status were being lined up. Helena's Baltic amber just won on exotic origin, over Lysa's expensive yet slightly pedestrian pendant emerald on a gold bobbin chain.

Diomedes and I stood. *He* had all the presence of a lamp boy. Another nobody, a copy of his father but for the beard, and I suspected that now Papa had died a beard would sprout on his descendant in the next few weeks. The son had the same ordinary face and stance, the same squared-off forehead with only slightly less wispy eyebrows and hair. About twenty-five, as Vibia Merulla had estimated, he obviously liked the fancy things in life. Multicoloured embroidery was visible around the neck of his fine-weave tunic, and on one uncovered sleeve. I could smell his pomade from six feet away. He was shaven and formally togate. I was bootless, unbelted, and decidedly unbarbered; it made me feel rough.

'You are investigating my husband's death,' began Lysa, not waiting for me to agree or not. 'Diomedes, tell him where you were today.'

The son obediently recited: 'I was engaged at the Temple of Minerva all day.'

'Thanks,' I said coolly. They waited.

'Is that all?' asked Diomedes.

'Yes. For now.' He seemed puzzled, but glanced at his mother, then shrugged and turned to go out. As Lysa made a move to follow, I held up my hand to stop her.

Her son looked back. She gestured impatiently for him to go ahead. 'Wait outside by the litter, darling.' He went, obviously used to being ordered about.

I left it until he ought to be well out of earshot, then I walked to the porch, checked, and closed the outer door.

Lysa was regarding me curiously. 'You ought to be interested in people's movements.' Gods, she was bossy.

'I am.'

'But you are not questioning my son!'

'No point, lady. You've got him far too thoroughly rehearsed.' If she flushed, it was imperceptible. 'Don't worry; I shall establish how your offspring amused himself while his father was being battered to death. Other people will be rushing to inform on him, for one thing.'

'Vibia!' she snorted. 'I'd like to know what she was doing this morning.'

'Not killing Chrysippus,' I said. 'Well, not personally. Anyway, I have been told they were a devoted pair.' At that, Lysa laughed hoarsely. 'Oh? Did the young widow have a reason to dispose of him, Lysa?' Lysa kept quiet judiciously, so I answered myself: 'She'll get the scriptorium. A nice little earner.'

Lysa looked surprised. 'Whoever told you that? There is no money in scrolls.'

This woman was supposed to have helped Chrysippus establish his business. So she would know, presumably. 'Surely your husband was a wealthy man? He must have been, if he was a major patron of the arts.'

'It never came from the scriptorium. And that's all the little cow will get. Vibia knows it too.'

I was thinking about that when Helena asked casually, 'We heard where your son has been today. What about you, Lysa?'

This affidavit sounded more real: unlike Diomedes with his one-stop temple story, Lysa produced a complicated catalogue of visiting old friends, other friends visiting her, a business meeting with a family freedman, and a trip to a dressmaker. A busy day, and if the people listed all confirmed what she had said, Lysa was accounted for. It was an intricate tapestry, with a horrible timescale and a large number of people involved. Checking would be tedious. Perhaps she was relying on that.

Helena crossed one knee over the other and leaned down to wave a doll at Julia. 'We commiserate with your loss. You and Aurelius Chrysippus were together for years, I'm told. And your support had been invaluable to him – not only in the home?'

'I made the man what he was, you mean!' growled Lysa through evidently gritted teeth. She was proud of her achievement. I for one believed in it.

'So they say,' replied Helena. 'The trouble is, crude rumour-mongers may mutter that when you lost control of the business you had helped create, that may have driven you to violence.'

'Slander.' Lysa dismissed that suggestion calmly. I wondered whether she would sue – or was she so strong-willed she would ignore that kind of gossip? Strong-willed, I decided. More harm would be done by the publicity of a court case than by silent dignity. And that way, nobody could test whether the gossip was truth or lies.

'Of course we are supposed to be a paternalist society,' Helena mused. 'But our history is written by men and perhaps they underestimate the part played by women in real life. The Empress Livia, it is well known, was a rock to Augustus throughout the decades of his reign; he even allowed her to use his seal on state papers. And in most family businesses, the husband and wife play an equal part. Even in ours, Falco!'

Helena might smile, but ours was a family business where the husband knew when to look meek.

Lysa said nothing to this philosophical speech.

'So,' Helena sprang on her in the same deceptively quiet tone, 'if Vibia inherits the scriptorium – who gets the rest?'

Lysa was well up to her. 'Oh, that will have to be confirmed when the will is read.'

'Smart get–out,' I sneered. 'I'm sure you know what it says.'

Lysa knew how to be a reed before the wind. 'Oh, there can be no need for secrecy . . . the main business will be divided. One of my husband's freedmen, a devoted servant of many, many years, whom we trusted absolutely to manage our affairs, is bequeathed a part of it.'

'I shall need his name,' I said. Lysa made a gracious gesture – though she did not volunteer it. 'Where does that leave Diomedes?' I then asked.

'My son will receive some money. Enough for him to live well.'

'By his standards?' I asked dryly. I bet they had had plenty of harsh words over his spending, but his mother looked offended that I commented. I suspected he was a wastrel, and she may have gathered what I thought. 'Is he happy with his share?'

'Diomedes has been brought up to expect the arrangements my husband has made.'

'And you, Lysa?' asked Helena.

'My contribution to the business will be recognised.'

'What happens to it now?' I pressed. Lysa was hedging and I was determined to break her reticence.

'Chrysippus has taken care of it.' The woman spoke as if for Chrysippus, the future of his business was more important than making happy heirs of people. 'It will be passed on in a way that is traditional in Greece.'

'What kind of business are we talking about?' I demanded. It must be something good, to be spoken of with the reverence Lysa used.

'The *trapeza,* of course.'

'The what?' I recognised the Greek. It sounded like something domestic. For a second its meaning escaped me.

She looked at me, wide-eyed, as if I ought to know. I had a bad feeling. When she answered, it was not dispelled.

'Why, the Aurelian Bank.'

XVIII

LATER, IN bed, I asked Helena, 'Do you ever yearn to be a "woman of independence" like Junia?'

'Running a caupona?' she chuckled. 'With the solemn approval of Gaius Baebius?'

I shifted my feet, with an effort. Nux, who was supposed to sleep in our third room guarding Julia, liked to sneak in and lie on the foot of our bed. We sometimes sent her back, but more often Julia moutaineered her way out of the cradle and came toddling after the dog so we just gave in. 'Running anything. You could certainly match Lysa and found your own bank.'

'We'll never have that much money, Marcus!'

'Ah, to quote an excellent Greek philosopher: "*Why do bankers lack money, even though they have it? − They just have other people's!*" That's Bion.'

'Naturally your favourite − Bion who said, "*All men are bad*". I'm not sure he was right about bankers lacking money . . . So − a little business of my own,' she mused. In the darkness I could not make out her expression. 'No; I have a full life with your affairs to run.'

'That makes me sound like Pa, with a female secretary constantly keeping him where he ought to be.'

'Flora ran her own caupona at the same time. And not badly. You must admit, Marcus, it has its own gruesome character. It has lasted for years. People regularly return there.'

'Dogs like peeing on the same column.'

'Don't think your father fails to notice your orderly life,' Helena said, ignoring my uncouthness as if she knew informers were not worth chastising. 'Even though you do your best to escape my efforts.'

'I'm just a lump of wet clay on your potter's wheel . . . What about Pa?'

'I went to see him today. He asked me to take over Flora's inventories and accounts. I said no − but it made me think of Maia. I didn't tell her that he had asked me first, because both of them will enjoy believing they took the initiative. Geminus won't reveal that he asked me; it's not his style. He is as devious as you are –'

'Oh thanks!'

'Maia does not want to be the second runner in anything – in so far as even she knows what she wants.'

'What is she uncertain about? That sounds as if something is going on?' Helena did not answer me. I tightened my grip on her. 'I detect a mystery. What has she told you in your girly chats?'

'Nothing.'

'Nothing, eh?' Using my stylish knowledge of women, I made a note to look out for whatever it was. 'And what do you want in life, fruit?' This was a serious question. Helena had deserted a world of senatorial luxury and ease to be with me; I never lost sight of that. 'Apart from a handsome dog with poetic sensitivities, who is very good in bed?'

Then Helena Justina, refined daughter of the most noble Camillus, gave a loud snore and pretended my efforts at marital companionship had put her to sleep.

XIX

N EXT DAY my first stop was the Forum Romanum.
Avoiding the Clivus Publicius and the scriptorium for the moment, I went down off the Aventine by the Trigeminal Gate, then through the meat market and around the bottom of the Capitol. Leading up towards the Temple of Juno Moneta – Juno of the Mint – running parallel with the overspill Forum of Julius, was the Clivus Argentarius – Silver Street. I rarely walked that way. I loathed the smell of bastards making money out of other people's needs.

The Clivus Argentarius had the exchange tables, with the hunchbacked slaves who assayed currency on hand-held balances. They would rob you, though not as mercilessly as the eastern deviants away at the Greek end of the Mediterranean. It was enough for these Roman small-change fiddlers to prey gently on dopey provincials who did not know the difference between a *dupondius* and an *as* (both brass, but on a *dupondius* the Emperor wears a radiate crown instead of a wreath – of course you knew that!) The coin-biting practitioners changing *staters* and *obols* into decent *denarii* were not my real quarries, however. I was considering the world of heavy finance; I needed to be where the big backers and brokers lurk. Those who secretly fund city enterprises at enormous interest rates during civil wars. Shipping guarantors. Investors in luxury trades. Criminals' dinner guests and Senate facilitators.

Since Chrysippus was a supporter of the arts – and supposedly rolling in money – I was surprised to discover that he did trade under the sign of the Golden Horse, right here. His Aurelian Bank, which I naturally viewed as a serious inheritance issue, appeared no more than a modest currency exchange. It had the usual lopsided table where a hangdog in a dingy tunic presided over a few battered coin boxes, gloomily swinging his creaky hand-balance from one finger as he waited for custom.

Was that all there was, though? I had noticed that all the stalls in the Clivus Argentarius, this well-placed and prestigious street, looked like one-man trinket-sellers under the cypress trees at some provincial shrine. Here, they all presented the most basic money-changing tables, apparently staffed by down-at-heel slaves. Was it a deliberate front? Bankers like to operate with bluff and secrecy. Perhaps every one had an enormous back office with marble thrones and Nubians wielding ostrich fans if you cared to sniff for it.

I presented myself at the Aurelian table and made an innocent enquiry about today's rate for Greece. 'What's that they call their coins?'

'Drachmas.' The counter-hand was brutally indifferent. Not knowing that I could have talked to him of Palmyra and Tripolitania, Britain and unconquered Germany, all from personal experience, he identified me as a lummock who had never been east of the Field of Mars. He quoted me a medium-to-high exchange rate. A bad deal, yet no worse than most of the toothy sharks here would offer.

I applied a shifty look. Well, even more embarrassed than my usual suspicious lurking act. 'Er – do you ever do loans?'

'We do loans.' He looked at me as if I were a flea on a goddess's bosom.

I told myself I had just made a pile from the Census and could look anyone in the eye. Besides, this was a professional enquiry, a legitimate test. 'What would I need to do then, to get a loan from you?'

'Agree it with the chief.'

It seemed impolite to mention that I had seen his chief yesterday lying prone and bloody, with a scroll rod up one nostril and gooey cedar oil all over him. Apparently the bank was continuing to trade as if tragedy had never struck. Had nobody told the staff yet that their proprietor had been taken out, or were they busy maintaining commercial confidence with false calm?

'Agree it?'

'Reach an accommodation.'

'How does that work?'

He sighed. 'If he likes you enough, an agreement is drawn up. *In the consulship of Blah and Blah-blah, on the Whatsit day before the Ides of March* – Let's do one – what do you call yourself?'

'Dillius Braco.'

'*I Ditrius Basto* –' Times were tough. People even messed up my aliases now – '*I certify I have received a loan from Aurelius Chrysippus, in his absence through Lucrio his freedman, and owe to him a hundred million sesterces* – that's a notional figure – *which I shall repay him when he asks. And Lucrio, freedman of Aurelius Chrysippus, has sought assurance that the hundred million sesterces mentioned is properly and rightly given* – so you are not defrauding us or using the money improperly – *and I, Ditrius Basto, give as my pledge and security* – what do you have?' He was sneering more than ever. Looking at me in my third best streaky red tunic and the boots that I hated with the frayed straps, and still unbarbered, I could not blame him.

'What is usual?' I squeaked.

'Alexandrian wheat in a public warehouse. Chickpeas, lentils and legumes, if you're a cheapskate.' I could tell which he thought applied to me.

'Arabian pepper,' I boasted. 'Bonded in the Marcellus warehouse in Nap Lane.'

'Oh yes! How much?'

'I haven't counted recently. Some has been sold, but we are hanging back so as not to flood the market . . . Enormous quantities.'

He did start to look uncertain, though disbelief still figured strongly.

'*Arabian pepper, which I own, deposited in the Marcellus warehouse, which I have maintained in a secure condition, at my risk.* Something like that,' he said politely, 'sir.'

Frauds have it easy. (The pepper had once existed, but even then it was owned by Helena, a bequest from her first husband, the loathsome Pertinax; she had long ago sold all of it.)

Believing I was wealthy, his attitude changed completely: 'Can I make you an appointment with Lucrio? When would be most convenient?'

I reckoned I would be meeting Lucrio, freedman and perhaps heir to the dead proprietor – on my own terms and in my own time.

'No, that's all right; I was just asking for a friend.'

I slipped him a half *as* I had picked up at a frontier fort in Germania Inferior, where coppers were in short supply and they had to cut them up. It was an insulting tip for anyone, even if it had been whole currency. I skipped off down the street while he was still cursing me as a mean-spirited time-waster.

I walked into the Forum.

A short hop from the end of the Clivus Argentarius and across the front of the Curia brought me to the magnificent Porticus Aemilius, one of the finest public buildings of the Augustan Age. It was fronted by and joined to the Porticus of Gaius and Lucius, a two-storey colonnade of shops which was where my own frowsty banker lurked nowadays. His gorgeous squat was probably illegal in fact, but the aediles for some reason don't move bankers on. His chained deposit chests stood in the main aisle of the Porticus on massive slabs of marble in various shades: Numidian yellow, Carystian green, Lucullan black and red, Chian pink and grey – and the purple variegated Phrygian from which the table supports at the Chrysippus house were made, and which I had seen yesterday stained with the dead man's blood. My banker's chests, along with a folding stool and an unmanned change-table, were on the lower level of the Porticus, overlooked by a frieze showing scenes from Roman history, and shaded by a larger than life-sized statue of a barbarian. Apt, if you believed money had played its sinister part in our noble past and would affect the future of the untamed areas of the world. (I was raving internally. My encounter with the Aurelian Bank's changer had left me overwrought.) The billet was also incongruous, if you believed bankers were merely men with dirty hands from shuffling coinage – that is, if you had failed to notice just how many elegant artworks most bankers own in their private homes.

I went upstairs to see Nothokleptes. If he was not in sight at his business location, he was to be found at his barber's between a couple of delicate acanthus-scrolled pillars in the upper colonnade. More beauteous décor. And the elevation gave him a good view of who was approaching.

He was seedy and suspicious, just about convincing as a Roman citizen yet by birth probably Alexandrian and originally tutored in money matters by Ptolemaic tax-collectors. A heavy man, with jowls that were designed for pegging a napkin under his chin. He spent a lot of time at his barber's, where you could find him at ease as if the shaving chair were an extension of his business premises. Since his premises downstairs were so public, and usually guarded by a very unpleasant Pisidian thug, the barber's had an advantage. While you begged to overdraw on your already empty bankbox, you could send for a cold drink and have your fingernails manicured by a sweet girl with a lisp. Although often overcommitted, as it happened I had never tried my banker for a large formal loan. That would obviously involve – as a courtesy to his associates – investment in a pumice scrape and full hair trim; the peculiar Egyptian way Nothokleptes himself was coiffed, had always put me off.

Nothokleptes was not his real name; it was given him by Petronius Longus when we two first shared a bankbox for a year after we came home from the army. Once he acquired a job in the vigiles, Petro made sure he kept his salary and his prissy wife's dowry locked out of my grasp, but the name he had stuck on our first banker had lasted, to the point that the public now used it, believing it real. Civilised bilinguists will recognise that it means approximately *thieving bastard* although, despite the strong whiff of slander, long usage would probably now bar the man from suing us.

'Nothokleptes!' I always enjoyed calling him by name.

He looked at me curiously, as he always did. I could never decide if this was because he suspected my part in renaming him, or whether he was simply amazed that anyone could survive on my income. My half-year working on the Census had eventually brought a huge upsurge in my savings, but when Vespasian allowed my name to go forward to the equestrian list, the qualification rule immediately forced me to invest cash in land. The money had flowed straight out of my box, and Nothokleptes now seemed to feel doubtful that he ever really saw it. I felt the same myself.

'Marcus Didius Falco.' His manner was quaintly formal. He knew how to make a debtor feel like a man of substance just long enough to feel safe accepting yet another loan.

I had spent years trying to avoid this character when my funds were low. We had held many conversations about whether it was even worth my while to pay the hire-fee for the bankbox that contained nothing. On these difficult occasions, Nothokleptes had impressed me with both his common sense and his ferociously unyielding attitude. Fate had always saved me with some income at the last moment. For those who were less lucky, loans might be called in with cruel detachment. Like many men who wield power over unfortunates, he looked like a soft slob who would never find the energy to come down on them. How wrong that was.

'How are you this fine day, Marcus Didius?'

'Cut the niceties!' It was my usual rebuttal. I pretended he had a secret admiration for my roguishly uncouth manner. He simply gazed at me with that air of constant wonder. 'Listen, you evil scourge –' He bravely ignored the fake affection. 'I need inside information.'

'Fiscal advice? Or investment tips?'

'Neither. I'm not here to be pillaged.'

Nothokleptes shook his head sadly. 'Marcus Didius, I long for the day you will tell me you have become a *quaestuosus.*'

'What – an upcoming new man, looking to get rich quick? I'm rich now!'

He harumphed loudly. 'Not by the world's standards.'

'You mean I should let you play dangerous games with my cash for your own profit?'

'Typical!' he groaned. 'This is Rome, of course. You are cautious men. The good Roman guards his patrimony, looking only for security, never profits.'

I squatted on the stool next to him, while his barber continued to ministrate fanatically to the oiled Pharaonic curls. 'That's about it; in Rome, the higher a man progresses up the social scale, the more commitments are thrust upon him and the less free he really is to spend his money . . . I'm promising nothing, but I do have a case with probable fees at the end of it. Have you heard of Aurelius Chrysippus?'

'I have heard that he's dead.' Nothokleptes had glanced at me sharply. He knew the kind of work I did.

'Everyone here in the Porticus is no doubt avid for details?' My banker inclined his head elegantly. At the same time, he pursed his fleshy lips as if chastising my crude insinuation. 'What can you tell me about him and his business?'

'Me, Falco? Assist you? In one of your enquiries?' When he was excited, his voice rose and he tended to speak in an affected manner that drove me mad.

'Yes. He died in a rather sensational manner. You may have heard that I am investigating?'

He waved his hand. 'This is the Forum! The very stones breathe rumour. I probably knew before you did.'

'You make me wonder if you knew Chrysippus was doomed before the man was even dead.'

'Tasteless, my friend!'

'Sorry. So what's the score?'

Nothokleptes was torn. Professional wariness warned him to clam up. But he was thrilled to be so close to a celebrated case. 'Is it true –' he began.

I cut him off. 'He had a scroll rod poked up his nose. But I never told you that.'

He hissed with dread. 'Dreadful! Was there a lot of blood?'

I gazed at him, not saying.

'Ooh, Falco! Well . . .' He lowered his voice. We had a bargain, apparently. Horror was just another banking commodity; he was prepared to trade. 'What do you want to know?' I glanced at the barber. The man was impassively snipping at a long ear lock. 'Don't worry; he does not speak Latin.'

Unlikely, but Nothokleptes would secure his silence. 'I need anything you can give me, Nothokleptes. Especially if it's scandalous.'

Nothokleptes appeared to find a new respect for my trade if it could be so much fun. 'I have never heard much that's juicy. He has been here for years. There is a fearsome wife, who has a hand in every-thing.'

'Divorced.'

His eyebrows shot up. 'You really do surprise me!'

'Another woman – half his age. Now the other is the second wife. Why are you surprised by that?'

'There were *always* other women. Stagey blondes who looked like night-moths, mostly. Lysa would find out, then sweep in and chop off the affair. Chrysippus would sob and be a chaste husband for a while. Lysa would relent and loosen the shackles. Pretty soon, he would find himself some new working girl who giggled and flattered him at how clever he was with his abacus. After they were spotted in one theatre row too many, Lysa would descend on him again with a face like Jove's thunderbolt and a similar effect.'

'Did she never threaten to leave him?'

'She was the wife. It didn't work like that.' Nothokleptes tipped his head to one side, nearly sacrificing a ringlet to curiosity. Impassive, the barber waited until he straightened up again. 'So how did the new one finally shift Lysa out?'

'Vibia Merulla is not a working hag.'

'Oh clever!'

'She is not his usual blonde either, incidentally,' I said, half-hiding a smile.

'Fascinating!'

'Well, I can untwine the tangle with the women.'

'Your favourite occupation, Falco.'

'I've had enough practice, maybe. Tell me about the bank.'

'It's Greek.'

'A *trapeza*. So they take deposits –'

'And they offer credit. What we call an *argentarius*.'

'Same as you?'

'Subtle differences,' Nothokleptes prevaricated cagily. I was not surprised. The financial world is complex, with the services offered often varying according to the status and needs of the customer. I mean, the big fish get most out of it. 'To my mind, Greek changing and lending began with temples helping out travellers at religious festivals,' Nothokleptes said. 'In Rome we were always more geared to commerce. Quayside auctions –'

'Auctions! You mean art and antiques?' I asked in surprise, thinking of Pa.

He looked disgusted. 'Commodity auctions at markets and ports.'

'Oh!' Light dawned. I had seen this in operation at Ostia and here in the Emporium. 'You mean, you hang about when cargoes are landed, to offer loans for purchasing the goods? Wholesalers obtain credit, then pay you back when they sell on at a profit? But are you saying the Aurelian Bank does *not* do that?'

'Oh, I expect they cover the range.' He seemed to be holding back.

'So who uses them?' I asked.

'The Aurelian is a family affair. Small fry may approach them, but for big deals you have to be someone they know. Otherwise, they will never explicitly refuse you, but nothing will ever happen. They work in a small circle.'

'Matter of trust?'

Nothokleptes let out a sardonic laugh. 'That's the word! It means that here, we check out strangers' solvency by posting their names on the Columnia Maena and seeing if any of our colleagues can tell us their financial state. The Greeks want to know your grandfather and fifteen uncles sailing out of Piraeus. They want to believe you are one of them. Then your credit will be good. You could run off and default and they would *still* see you as one of them – though of course, you would not dare come back, which might be inconvenient.'

'What about their own credit?' I asked dryly. 'Banks can fail.'

'Ooh! Hush; don't use such filthy language!'

'Any hint of problems with the Aurelian?'

'Not a whisper that I know of. I can listen out for you.' His eyes sharpened keenly, scenting an insider tip. Initiating doubt was not what I wanted to accomplish, but questions always carry a risk.

'Please do.' I looked at him. 'Chrysippus was very successful?' I felt Nothokleptes was ready to be more open now. 'So if he's not prowling the wharves doing commercial stuff, what is his speciality?'

'Loans with interest,' Nothokleptes told me. His tone of voice would have been more suitable for saying the man had had intercourse with a pet mule.

'Sorry – what's the difference?'

'Depends on the rates. Usury stinks.'

'What rates does the Aurelian Bank demand?'

'Twelve per cent is the legal maximum, Falco.'

'And five is more decent nowadays. You are implying they are tough?' He was implying something worse. 'So what would a Golden Horse loan run at?'

'I cannot comment.'

'Well, of course not!' I scoffed. 'Don't let me draw you into anything that seems commercially sensitive.' He insisted on stubborn silence. I let it go. 'All right. What can you tell me about the freedman who runs the loan side?'

'Nothing odd about that.' He must have thought I was querying the arrangement. 'A common ploy.'

'Ploy?'

'Well, men who are struggling to arrive socially do not touch the filthy stuff from the mint with their own soft hands, do they?' Nothokleptes was sneering at climbers with pretensions. He owned his own business, though he was low grade. As a result, so were his clients. Mind you, that did not make him poor; nor were most of the clients. He himself enjoyed handling money the way tailors fondle cloth. 'Freed slaves can trade,' he continued. 'A banker can use a slave to act for him. Many have a trusted family freedman who organises the day-to-day work of the bank, so they themselves can dine out with patricians like the respectable Roman élite.'

I whistled. 'Rather a lot of trust, if this freedman is dealing in thousands – or millions!'

'He will be rewarded.'

'With cash?'

'With respect.'

'Status? That all?'

Nothokleptes only smiled.

'What if he ever bunked off? Or simply was not up to the job? What if the agent Chrysippus used had made serious investment mistakes, or misjudgements in trusting creditors?'

'Chrysippus would go bust. And the rest of us would shiver.'

'So, do you know Lucrio?'

'Oh, I know Lucrio,' Nothokleptes remarked. 'And then, I don't know him, if you follow me.'

'No. I need a clue of thread to wander in this Cretan labyrinth.'

'I know who he is. But I would only approach Lucrio,' said my banker, who had never before appeared fastidious, 'with a heated meat skewer a yard long.' He scowled in what probably passed for a fatherly warning. 'I advise you to take the same line, Marcus Didius.'

'Thanks for the tip.' Interesting. 'What do you know about Chrysippus' son? His name is Diomedes.'

'Heard the name; never met him. Cultured hobbies, I believe. Not a player in the same game.'

Now I was surprised. 'Why not? He's twenty-five, or close; he's reached his majority. I would expect him to tread in father's sandal-marks. And presumably he inherits something now? At least, his mother told me he would have enough to live on – by their lights, so to me that's more than enough.'

'We shall have to wait and see.' Nothokleptes was holding back. This was somehow too intimate, some professional wrinkle that he would not betray.

I reckoned I had pushed it far enough. I urged the banker to keep his ears open for me, told him some horrific details of the murder as fair payment, and left him to be towelled up for his shave. His barber looked white after I described the violence. Clearly, he did understand Latin after all.

I could not bear to watch the shaving process. Nothokleptes favoured the Egyptian pumice method: his beard was scratched off forcibly – along with many layers of skin.

I had skipped down the four steps from the Porticus into the main Forum and was heading off through the rostra intending to leave on the opposite side. Then a voice hailed me, with the self-satisfied tone of somebody who knew I would have avoided him if I had spotted him first.

Hades! It was Anacrites.

XX

'**M**ARCUS, OLD friend!'

When he sounded so affable I could cheerfully have turned him upside down and placed him where the wild dogs come to pee.

'Anacrites. Here you are, standing beside the Black Stone. Well, that's an area of ill-omen, people say.' The Black Stone is an area of dark paving that marks an obviously very ancient spot, though whether it really is the grave of Romulus as some believe, who can say? Superstitions hang about the place, anyway, and seeing the Chief Spy there would set many grabbing at their amulets and muttering incantations against the evil eye.

'Same old Falco.'

I grinned nastily, acknowledging my old wish to have him dead. In the past fifteen months I had seen him twice nearly dying – and twice he had thwarted me. On at least one of those occasions, I had only had myself to blame.

He looked healthier now than for some while. An odd character. Odd, even for a Palace freedman. He could pass for someone of real consequence, or for any misshapen pebble on the track. He merged quietly into ordinary situations, yet if you looked closely his tunics verged on flash. Unusual embroidery in self-colours ran around custom-made neck-holes that were tailored to a perfect fit. He succeeded in seeming neutral and invisible, while maintaining his own, suggestively expensive, style. This subtle social double act was probably the most successful thing he did. 'Anacrites, I'm busy. What are you after?'

'Nothing particular.' He was lying, because immediately he offered, 'Fancy a drink?' So he did want something.

'I've hardly had breakfast.' I started moving off.

He stayed on my heels as far as the Golden Milestone. Well, that was a better place for him to park himself. Spies like to imagine they are the centre of the world.

'So what's the agenda these days?' he begged, desperate to be taken into my confidence.

'A patron of the arts,' I condescended to inform him. He thought I meant that I was courting one, which was not entirely off the firing trajectory, because I had done it, briefly. He made a reference that now jarred, since my poetry recital seemed an age ago: 'We enjoyed your performance the other evening.' With that 'we' he was including himself in a clutch with my relatives, Ma and Maia specifically. 'A refreshing occasion. It made me decide that I ought to go out much more. Life is not just about work, is it? Well' – he made an attempt at a joke – 'you always take that attitude yourself!'

I made no reply, leaving the conversation stranded.

'Look, Falco, I know you are very close to your family –' Wrong; if my relatives were allying themselves with Anacrites, I could not distance myself enough from them. 'I just want to clear this with you – your mother feels it would help your sister recover from her bereavement if she started to go out sometimes –'

'Oh, Maia too?'

'Can I finish?'

He had said too much already. 'What's this then?' I managed to hold down my anger and rely on a sneer. 'Are you offering to mind Maia's children while she gads off to festivals? That's extremely decent, Anacrites, though four at once is a big gang to look after. Don't get on the wrong side of Marius, is my advice – and of course you need to ensure that people don't think you have an immoral interest in little girls.'

Anacrites flushed slightly. He gave up trying to interrupt. His plan was not acting as a nursemaid but escorting Maia, I was sure of that. I stared at him, trying to make out how old he was. It had never seemed relevant before: older than me; younger than he might have been to hold such a senior position as Chief Spy; certainly older than Maia – yet not too old. His strange pale eyes held mine, annoyingly matter of fact. He thought he was one of the family. I wanted to choke.

'You'll have to take your chance,' I heard myself growl. 'Maia Favonia has her own ideas about what she will do – or not.'

'I don't want to upset you, that's all.'

Whenever he pretended to respect me, I wanted to knock him down and jump on him. 'I don't upset that easily.'

All the time we had been in confrontation, he had been weighing his purse in one hand. 'Just come from my bank,' he said, noticing my fixed stare on it (fixed on how fat his damned moneybag looked).

'Oh? Which do you use?' I asked, making it sound like a technical request for a friendly tip on which establishment was best.

'Private receivers that I've been with for years, Falco. You go to the Alexandrian in the Porticus of Gaius and Lucius, don't you?'

How did he know where my bankbox was? He had probably weaselled out this information as part of some strategy when he wanted to get at me. Even in the period when we were partners, I had kept all personal details from his prying eyes and I instinctively avoided a straight answer even now: 'Mine's a basic safe deposit man. What's yours like?'

'They charge commission on deposits, but I get real security. The service is old-fashioned, rather secretive, even.'

'Sounds a bit Greek.'

'Well, they are, as it happens.'

'Really? Would your secretive receivers lurk at the sign of the Golden Horse?' He looked startled. It was a guess, because the Aurelian Bank was on my mind, but I smiled urbanely, letting Anacrites think I had carried out some dark surveillance in his own style.

'How did you –'

'Say nothing!' I tapped the side of my nose, enjoying myself and hoping to unnerve him. We were dancing around each other well today. 'A Chief Spy needs absolute discretion, I realise.' It went with the villa in Campania that Anacrites did not like to talk about, and probably other secret hoards of treasure and properties acquired through intermediaries. As a well-placed slave at the Palace whose work involved discovering facts that people wanted to hide, he must often have come across unsought bankers' orders propped against his favourite stylus box. They might be anonymous – but he would know exactly who was asking him not to lean on them.

Well, sometimes he would be baffled; as a spy he had always been incompetent. Perhaps he had to be, to have survived in the bureaucracy. Good types are very quickly weeded out in case they corrupt the administration with dangerous methods and ideas.

'I've always been well looked after at the Golden Horse,' he bragged. 'Lucrio is an old crony –' Then the pallid eyes became suddenly wary as he wondered why I was asking. 'Is there anything I ought to be told about the Aurelian Bank, Falco?'

'Not as far as I know,' I answered breezily. Which was true at the time. If in the future his finances were threatened, I would decide then whether I had more profit in telling him as a favour – or in keeping quiet.

'Why were you interested?' Anacrites was sure he ought to be worried.

'I've just been with Nothokleptes,' I said mildly. 'That always makes me wonder what alternatives exist. Tell me; when you need to consult Lucrio, where do you get hold of him?'

'In the Janus Medius.' That was a covered passageway at the back end of the Porticus Aemilius – a haunt of financial dealers of all kinds. 'Can I assist with an introduction, Falco?'

'To the lofty Lucrio? No thanks.' No fear. I knew Anacrites wanted to overhear what I had to say to the agent.

I preferred to run suspects to earth for myself. Besides, if the Aurelian Bank's freedman had any sense of business preservation, he would soon ensure he introduced himself to me.

XXI

I CHECKED IN at the Fourth Cohort's patrol-house. The enquiry team were all out and the duty clerk reckoned I would be on my own with the Chrysippus case. Then Petronius rolled in and confirmed it.

I brought him up to date. 'So it may not be literature but banking. Want to pull it back and handle the case yourself?'

Petro flashed his teeth. 'Why should I? You're the Census tax expert. You are fully at home with money, Falco.'

'I wish I'd called in *your* Census return and audited you to Hades and back.'

'Mine was impeccable – at least, it was once I heard it might be checked by you.'

'I should have made life harder for my so-called friends,' I grumbled.

Petro shook his head sadly. 'Dream away – you're a soft touch, boy!'

'Still, I'm happy that Anacrites deposits money with Chrysippus. I'd laugh if that bank should hit the rocks, taking him with it.'

'Banks don't fail,' Petro disagreed. 'They just make money out of their customers' debts.'

'Well, I bet this bank is relevant to the murder,' I said. 'If only because of who gets to inherit the glittering reserves.'

'Assuming they have any reserves,' Petro warned. 'My banker once – when very drunk indeed – confided that it's all a myth. They rely on the appearance of solid security, but he reckoned they just trade on air.'

On our usual good terms, we gossiped some more about the dead banker, not forgetting his women. Then Petro fished out a note-tablet. 'Passus left this for you – the addresses of the writers that Chrysippus had summoned for interviews yesterday. Passus left orders that they should all be told to present themselves to you this morning. He commandeered a room there for you to use. You'll like this,' said

Petronius Longus, with a gleam, 'you will be allowed to occupy one of the libraries.'

'The Greek one?' I asked dryly.

'No; the Latin,' came Petro's riposte. 'We knew a sensitive soul like you couldn't bear to sit looking at horrible bloodstains on the floor.'

Before I made my way to the Clivus Publicius, I had a moan to him about Anacrites smooching up to Maia. Petro heard me out impassively, not saying much.

This time I did not enter the Chrysippus abode via the scriptorium, but broached the formal entrance portico as the killer must have done. It was grand architecturally, though there was a faint smell of mice. Was young Vibia Merulla a poor housewife? I could imagine what the deposed Lysa would make of that.

Today at least there was a porter sitting in a cubicle, as though after the householder's death security had been tightened up. Not much, however. The airy slave could hardly be bothered to ask my name and business. He waved me through, and let me find my own way to the library.

'I am expecting the writers whose books your master sold. Have any arrived yet?'

'No.' And I was quite late getting here myself. Bad news. Still, writers have their little routines: if I knew anything, they were either still in bed – or they had gone early for lunch. Long and leisurely, probably.

'I want to see them one at a time, so if more turn up together please make them wait. Don't let them talk to each other but put them somewhere separately.'

The house was very quiet. There were slaves padding about, though I could not decide whether they had definite errands for their mistress or were pottering by themselves. The Latin library was deserted. The inner Greek one lay even more silent. It had already lost the corpse, though cleaning up was still in hand. A couple of buckets with sponges stood against one wall. And the scrolls I had asked Passus to catalogue were now collected in a dirty heap on a table. It looked as if he had dealt with some, which he had discarded into a large rubbish hamper, though others had still to be listed. Sensibly, he had not left his list lying around – though I wouldn't have minded an advance peek myself.

Passus was not there. Nobody was.

Nobody visited the Latin library for over an hour. I dipped into Virgil's *Georgics* and put myself in pastoral mood.

Eventually, a man sidled in. 'Well, good afternoon, or should I say good evening!' I might be pastoral, but since I lacked the ameliorating influence of a warm-blooded shepherdess, I was also slightly sarcastic. 'Here to see Didius Falco? Jupiter, how prompt!'

'I am generally the first,' he said, sounding self-satisfied. I took against him immediately.

He was in his thirties or forties, moderately tall and very thin, with spindly legs and arms, and hunched shoulders. It brought out the urge to bawl like a centurion for him to straighten up. Saturnine, sallow, and dressed in shabby black. I had not been expecting high fashion from a bunch of authors, but this was the worst kind of low taste. Black fades. It also leaks at the laundry onto other people's whites. To find black on the second-hand clothes stalls you have to be in a world of your own, and a public menace.

'What's your name?'

'Avienus.'

'I am Falco. Investigating yesterday's death.' I took out a note-tablet and let him see me start a fresh waxed board in a capable manner. 'Were you the first visitor yesterday as well?'

'As far as I know.'

We discussed times briefly, and I reckoned Avienus had turned up shortly after my spat about publication terms. He was almost certainly the first to appear after Chrysippus came into the house from the scriptorium, so if the others confirmed they saw their patron alive later, it cleared him. I lost interest, but I was stuck with him in the absence of anyone else.

'What do you write, Avienus?'

'I am a historian.'

'Oho – murky doings in the past.' I was being deliberately crass.

'I confine my interests to modern times,' he said.

'New emperor, new version of events?' I suggested.

'A new perspective,' he forced himself to agree. 'Vespasian is writing his own memoirs, it is said –'

'Isn't there a rumour he brought home some tame hack from Judaea who will do the official Flavian whitewash?'

This time Avienus pulled up at my brisk interruption. He had not expected the investigating officer to crash in on his subject. 'Some limpet called Josephus has attached himself to Vespasian as the approved biographer,' he said. 'He has rather cornered the market.'

'Rebel leader.' I was brisk. 'Picked up as a prisoner. Should have been executed on the spot, or brought to Rome in shackles for the Triumph. Made a flattering prophecy or two, based on the bloody obvious, then turned traitor to his own side with commendable quick thinking.' I tried not to make this sound too insulting to professional historians in general. I like to maintain a polite veneer, at least while the suspect looks innocent. 'My brother served in Judaea,' I told Avienus amicably, to explain my knowledge. 'I heard that this flattering Judaean has been living in Vespasian's old private house.'

'That should encourage an unbiased viewpoint!' His mouth screwed up, below a hooked nose down which he could have looked quite snootily, had he possessed sufficient character. Instead, his vindictiveness was the fussy, ineffectual kind.

I smiled. 'Vespasian will charge the going rent. So – what's your own angle on our life and times?'

'I like to be impartial.'

'Oh – no viewpoint?'

Avienus looked hurt. 'I catalogue events. I do not expect renown myself – but I shall be used as a source by future authors. That will satisfy me.' He would be dead. He would know nothing about it. He was either an idiot or a hypocrite.

'Anything published? I was told you are "respected" in your field.'

'People have been kind.' The modesty was as false as a whore's golden heart.

'What are you working on at the moment for Chrysippus?' I pressed him.

'A review of fiduciary transactions since the Augustan period.' It sounded dry. That was being generous.

'Surely that has a limited appeal to a normal readership?'

'It is a small field,' Avienus boasted proudly.

'Thus allowing you to be its pre-eminent historian?' He glowed. 'Whether or not the general reader gives a *quadrans* about your subject?'

'I like to think my researches have relevance.' Nothing would put him off. I stopped wasting effort on insults.

'Was Chrysippus paying you?'

'On delivery.'

'When will that be?'

'When I finish.'

I had detected tetchiness. 'Was late delivery why he called you in yesterday?'

'We did discuss programming, yes.'

'A friendly chat?'

'Businesslike.' He was not stupid.

'Reach a decision?'

'A new date.' It sounded good.

'One you were happy with? Or one that suited him?'

'Oh, he makes all the running!'

'Well, he did,' I reminded the grumbling historian quietly. 'Until somebody battered him senseless and glued him to the tesserae of his elegant mosaic with lashings of spilt cedar oil.'

Avienus had had an unmoved expression until then; it barely changed. 'I am held up by one of my blocks,' he said, ignoring the salacious detail and returning doggedly to the point. Was that his style? The public would spurn it. Anyway, I had no truck with 'blocks'. A professional author should always be able to unearth material, then develop it usefully.

'Did you attack Chrysippus?' I sprang on him.

'No, I did not.'

'Did you have any reason to kill him?' This time he merely shook his head. 'Would any of his other authors have had such a reason?'

'Not that I could say, Falco.' Ambiguous. Are historians linguistically meticulous? Did Avienus mean he knew no reason – or he knew a reason but would not reveal it? I decided against pursuing this; he was too aware of the questioning process. Nothing would come from badgering.

'Did you see any of your colleagues while you were here?'

'No.'

I consulted my list. 'Turius, Pacuvius, Constrictus and Urbanus all visited, I have been told. Do you know them all?' He inclined his head. 'You meet them at literary functions, I presume?' Another twist of the head. He seemed too bored now, or too offended by the simplicity of the questions, to bring himself to reply aloud.

'Right. So you were first here and Chrysippus was definitely alive when you left?'

'Yes.'

I paused for a moment, as if considering, then said, 'That's it then.'

'And you will be in contact if you need anything else.' That was my line.

Apart from alienating the officer investigating him for murder, he had just lost a potential buyer. I liked history – but I would never now allow myself to read *his* work.

XXII

I HUNG AROUND quite some time longer. I was expecting five men – most of whom had apparently decided to ignore me. Since a no-show would imply guilt, this was intriguing. But I bet that when I did confront the others, they would try the old 'never got your message' trick. Maybe a heavy-handed visit from the vigiles was needed to change their minds.

Turius turned up just as I had decided to go home for lunch. He must be the infuriating one of the set.

He looked mid-twenties. An untrustworthy 'respectable' visage, with a nasty little buttoned mouth. His dress code was the opposite of the Avienus black. His tunic was vermilion, and his shoes were punched and laced. Even his skin had a bright, slightly hennaed colouring. His hair, under a shimmering oil slick, was extremely dark. The ghastly tunic was bloused over his belt in a way I loathed. While nothing about Avienus had made me consider geography, I decided at once that Turius had provincial origins. Writers tend to home in on Rome from Spain, Gaul, and other parts of Italy. I could not be bothered to ask where he came from, but found him too loud, too cocky, and probably effeminate. Hard to be sure, as I had no personal reason to enquire.

'I was starting to think nobody wanted to talk to me. Avienus is the only other person who has bothered to respond.'

'So he said.'

'You two been conspiring?' I took out the notepad, keeping my gaze fixed on him while I set it in front of me and produced a stylus. I smiled, but with unfriendly eyes.

'I happened to meet him – ' He was flustered. Perhaps he had never been interrogated before. Or perhaps it meant something.

'Where was that?'

'Just the popina at the end of the street. What's wrong with that?'

'I didn't query it.' But I *was* querying whether the writers had met to make sure their stories matched. 'A man can buy himself a snack.

Well,' I said, looking as if I disapproved, 'there are new laws against hot food stalls, but I suppose a cold bite taken at midday cannot do much harm.' Helena or Petronius would have doubled up laughing at my sanctimonious attitude. 'So! You are Turius.' Said with the right tone of distasteful surprise, that always suggests you know something.

As I hoped, he looked torn between a desire to be famous and terror that I possessed secrets. That he featured in secrets, I felt sure. Instinct only – but I trusted mine.

'Do you have a praenomen?' I was scribbling at my notes as if creating a prosecution brief for the magistrate.

'Tiberius.'

'Tiberius Turius!' That sounded good and ridiculous. 'I'm Falco.' Obviously tougher.

Before I could ask, '*What's your line, Turius?*' he told me anyway. 'I am devising rules for the ideal society.' Yes, Avienus had informed him what my questions would be. I raised my eyebrows without comment. He grew faintly embarrassed. 'Plato's *Republic* for modern times.'

'Plato,' I remarked. 'He excluded women, am I right?' Turius was trying to decide whether I approved of this fine patriarchal stance. If he could have seen the women in my life dealing with me, he would not have puzzled over the issue for long.

'There was more to it than that,' he answered cautiously.

'I bet!' Just when he thought he could engage in a critical discussion, I swept Plato aside brutishly. 'So what does your treatise have to say? Finished it yet?'

'Er – most of it is sketched out.'

'Lot of writing-up to do?'

'I have not been too well –'

'Bad back? Migraine? Face ache? Piles?' I rapped out unsympathetically. I stopped just before saying, '*Terminal desire to bore people silly?*'

'I suffer from attacks –'

'Don't tell me. I feel queasy hearing about other people's ailments.' I assessed how robust he looked, then made a swift stroke with the stylus. 'How did Chrysippus feel about your poor health, Turius?'

'He was always understanding –'

'Gave you a blast, you mean?'

'No –'

'What sort of terms were you on with him?'

'Good, always good!'

I pretended I was about to comment, then said nothing.

Turius looked down at his natty footgear. He clammed up, but I left him to it and eventually could not bear the silence. 'He could be difficult to work with.' I just listened. Turius learned fast, however. He too looked as if he was about to continue – then bit it back.

After a moment, I leaned forwards and applied my sympathetic persona. 'Tell me about Chrysippus as an artistic patron.'

His eyes met mine, warily. 'How do you mean, Falco?'

'Well – what did you do for him; what did he do for you?'

Alarm flashed. Turius thought I was hinting at immoral practices. I reckoned Chrysippus had had enough trouble with Vibia and Lysa, but it showed how Turius' mind worked.

I stuck to commercial reality: 'He possessed the money and you had the talent – does that make for an equal partnership? Will this artist/patron relationship be a feature of the ideal political state that you describe in your great work?'

'Hah!' Turius exploded with bitter mirth. 'I am not allowing slavery!'

'Enlightening – and intriguing. Give, Turius.'

'His patronage was not a partnership, just exploitation. Chrysippus treated his clients like slabs of meat.'

'Men of intellect and creativity? How could he do that?'

'We need funds to live.'

'And?'

'Can't you feel the tension around here, Falco? We hoped to obtain the freedom to carry on our intellectual work, freed from financial worry. He saw us as paid labourers.'

'So he thought giving financial support put him in complete charge? Meanwhile his writers were striving for an independence that he refused to give. What were the problems practically? Did he try to influence what you wrote?'

'Of course.' Turius had not finished his burst of rancour. 'He reckoned he published our stuff, so that was our reward. We had to do what he said. I would not have minded but Chrysippus was a lousy critic. Even his manager had better judgement of what would sell.'

He looked as if he was intending a long rant so I interrupted. 'Any other bad points?'

'You would have to ask the others.'

'Oh I will. You hated being bullied over what you could write; was that a bone of contention between you yesterday?'

'There was no contention.'

I put down my note-tablet, implying I was too annoyed even to write down his answer. 'Oh come on, Turius! I already heard a sweet little lullaby from Avienus. Don't expect me to believe that none of you was wrangling with the patron over any damned thing. Grow up. This is a murder scene and I have a killer to catch.'

'We are all watching with great interest,' he sneered.

'You could learn something.' My anger was real. 'My deadline is fixed. My contract is non-negotiable. And I shall deliver, on time, like a true professional. The masterpiece will be rolled up neatly and fastened with a twist of string. There will be supporting proofs, cogently explained in exquisitely constructed sentences. Informers don't hide behind "blocks". The guilty go before the judge.' He blinked. A clue, some say. Trouble is, you never know what clue it is. I slammed my hand on the table and roared at him: 'I think you are lying, and that alone is good enough to march you in front of the examining magistrate of the homicide court.'

Turius did not disappoint me. When I offered threats, he took the easy way out: he fingered someone else. 'Honestly, I had no difficulties with Chrysippus. Unlike Avienus with his loan.'

I folded my arms. 'Well, here we go. Do tell me about that –' Wearily, I anticipated his request: 'Yes, it can be in strict confidence.'

'I don't know the details. Only that Avienus is years behind with his supposedly erudite economic history. When he got completely stuck for money, Chrysippus gave him a loan, quite a big one.'

'A loan? I thought patrons were supposed to be more generous. What happened to literary benefactors donating free support?'

'Avienus had had as much as Chrysippus was prepared to give.'

'So what's the story on this loan at present?'

'I believe the bank asked him to repay it.'

'Avienus is asking for more time to pay?'

'Yes, but he was refused.'

'By Chrysippus?'

'I expect that agent of his did the dirty work.'

I nodded slowly. 'So Avienus is in hock, even if he completes his manuscript. Paying off the loan may still wipe him out. His project sounds a bummer to me, so it won't be expected to make much. So your theory is, he came yesterday to try to beg for time on both the loan and the delivery date. Chrysippus was adamant, probably on both counts. That does look like a motive for Avienus to run wild and kill.' I gave play to a wide and sinister grin. 'Now, Turius – when Avienus knows that my penetrating historical research with you has uncovered this startling new fact about *his* motive, he will of course fight back. So, let's save time here – what is he likely to pass on to me about you?'

That neat rejoinder really upset the utopian. He went white, and at once assumed the attitude of the betrayed – a curious mixture of hurt and vindictiveness. Then he refused to say any more about anything. I let him go, with the customary terse warning that I would speak to him again.

As he reached the door, I called him back. 'By the way, how are *your* finances?'

'Not desperate.' He could be lying – but then somebody had paid for the vermilion duds – unless he too had taken out a loan.

I had stirred some mud, and sooner than I could have hoped. Time for lunch.

When I hit the street, the baking sun had made it too humid to breathe. Nobody was about. In the Circus Maximus, just visible at the far end of the Clivus, the stinging sand on the racetrack would be hot enough to fry quail eggs.

I nearly stopped at the popina on the corner. I could see a young waiter outside, with a rag over one shoulder, counting coins into a pouch at his waist. He turned and stared at me; suddenly I lost interest. We were too close to the murder scene. He would ask about the death.

I went home for a salad with Helena instead.

I was puffed by the time I had climbed to the crest of the Aventine. Once I reached Fountain Court I would have rested and cooled off at Lenia's laundry, but nobody was about. I was too drained even to investigate the back courtyard. Besides, the mere thought of hot tubs of washing water made me feel worse. Instead, I kept my feet dragging on up the wooden stair to my own apartment – thankful that I now lived at first-storey height and not on the sixth floor. It was a mistake, though. On the sixth floor we had enjoyed some protection from menaces.

I heard voices. One in particular, a male tenor that I failed to recognise. Blowing out my cheeks, I pushed open the inner door and entered the main room. Helena was there with my sister Maia. Little Julia was standing beside Maia, messily eating a fig. Helena and Maia at once looked at me, both rather tight-lipped and ready to extract punishment for what they had been suffering.

The visitor was regaling them with some anecdote. It was not the first. I could tell that.

He was a big man, with fair swept-back hair, a loose tunic casually bunched, sturdy calves and large knobbly feet. I recognised him vaguely; he must have attended my recital. He was a writer presumably. And worse than that: he thought himself a raconteur.

XXIII

I SAW HELENA'S chin come up.

'The householder's return – Marcus! This is Pacuvius,' she broke in, heartlessly spoiling a story that the narrator would never have stopped voluntarily. I could tell it was elderly material, rich with worked-up detail yet moth-eaten too. To Maia and Helena it probably seemed endless after hours of previous monologue. I gave Helena a smile that I hoped would seem special. She did not smile back.

'Didius Falco,' I introduced myself, in a light voice. Maia glowered, convinced that I was incapable of extracting the bore. 'I was expecting you at the Chrysippus house, Pacuvius.'

'Ah! What an idiot!' He slapped his head in a way that was supposed to be comic. 'Fool of a slave never gives a clear steer –' He blundered upright from his stool, awkwardly. He wanted it to seem rude if I insisted he left. Indifferent, I walked past him and emptied a water jug into a beaker, which I tipped down my throat.

Helena then felt obliged to lighten the atmosphere: 'Pacuvius is a satirical author, known as *Scrutator* –'

He laughed diffidently. So far, I was immune to his charm. 'I have, as you gather, been entertaining your ladies with my fund of wit, Falco.' Oh yes? Neither liked men who thought themselves too witty. Both Helena and Maia were picky over how they were entertained. Once he left, I fancied they would set about dissecting him. Both could be cruel. I looked forward to listening in.

'So what's the verdict, fruit?' I asked, directly of Helena. I had no doubt she had spoken to the man with authority in my absence; he may not have believed how much I respected her judgement. He looked to me like one of those untidy single men who pretend to flirt, but who would never let a real woman come within a stadium's length.

Helena would have asked the right questions, though she would have done it slyly, as if making polite conversation. She gave her report in a quiet voice, a little too crisp to be neutral: 'Pacuvius was called in yesterday to discuss progress on his latest series of verses; he produced a new set; Chrysippus was delighted; they did not quarrel; Pacuvius left the house shortly afterwards.'

'Did he see any of the other authors?' I could have asked him that. He was now dying to answer for himself.

'He says not,' said Helena. Nice phrasing. Just the merest hint that she withheld judgement on whether the flamboyant braggart told the truth.

I smiled at her. She smiled rather wearily at me.

I bent down and picked up the baby for a fatherly greeting; Julia chose not to be used as a prop in this comedy, and she started bawling. 'Well, that sounds fine,' I said firmly to Pacuvius over the row.

The man flustered his way to the door. 'Yes, yes. I am delighted it is satisfactory. I will leave you to your domestic harmonies –' He could not resist upsetting my domesticity by returning to plonk elaborate kisses on the ladies' hands (both made very sure they had their arms stretched out ready, lest he try kissing them at closer quarters). I watched in silence. If he had dared anything else, I would have thrown him physically downstairs. I suspected Maia and Helena were secretly hoping to see it.

'If I find any holes in your story I'll want to see you again. If you can think of anyone with a reason to kill Chrysippus, you come and tell me. If you had a reason yourself, I suggest that you own up now, because I will find out. My working base is Chrysippus' Latin library.'

He bowed, as if making amends for an intrusion, and rushed off. If I was supposed to feel uncouth for my hostility, it did not work.

Julia settled down again.

'What a creep!' shrieked Maia. He may still have been within earshot. I stepped out to look. He was striding away down Fountain Court, a large man who walked too fast and caused awnings to flap as he passed. Perhaps he felt some witty verses coming on so was rushing to write them down before he forgot. He was big enough to overpower and kill Chrysippus. I classified him as too useless, though.

'We'll be in a satire, I warn you,' I said, retreating indoors again. 'I've come across his stuff. *Scrutator* is a snob. Some like to write skits on the rich. He enjoys twitting the upwardly-moving lower classes who think they have social significance. Informers have always been good material, and here's a senator's daughter who ran off to live in the gutter, together with a very pretty widow whose husband – she claims – was eaten by a lion. Gods, if I wasn't so scared of the pair of you, I would write it up myself.'

Helena flopped down on a bench. 'I thought he would never shut up.'

'So did Maia. I could see that as soon as I walked in.'

'He had no idea,' Maia chimed in – adding in her usual measured way, 'selfish, self-centred masculine monster.'

'Keep it clean in front of the baby,' I reproved her. I took out the note-tablet where Passus had prepared details of Chrysippus' visitors. 'Curious how these writers are all coming to see me in exactly the same order as their names on my list. Neat choreography. Maybe they need an editor to suggest more natural realism.' To Helena, whose determination I knew well by now, I said, 'Any pickings from that bore that I should know about?'

'It's your business,' she pretended.

I shrugged. 'I don't expect you to have wasted an opportunity.'

Since the others were exhausted, I dumped the baby on Maia and started hunting out food-bowls. 'The chopping board is under Julia's blanket,' Helena told me helpfully. I found it, and the lettuce to chop behind a pot of growing parsley. While I set about making lunch, with a competence that failed to impress anyone, my partner in life roused herself enough to tell me what she had managed to extract from the satirist. Maia threw in snippets too, while she tried to clean fig seeds off Julia.

'I think I'll spare you his life history, Marcus,' Helena decided.

'Courteous woman.'

'He has been writing for years, a regular hack with a small continuous readership, people who probably return to his work just because they have heard of him. He does have a certain blowsy style and wit. He is observant of social nuances, adept with parody, quick with cutting remarks.'

'He knows how to circulate scandal,' Maia grunted. 'All his stories were crammed with things people would rather keep quiet.' That could be a source of antipathy.

'Could you tell how he got on with Chrysippus?'

'Well . . .' Helena was dry. '*His* view was that the famous *Scrutator* is a founder member of the writing circle, without whose dogged loyalty and brilliance Chrysippus would never have survived on the literary circuit.'

'Or to put it more succinctly, *Scrutator* is a useless old fart,' said Maia.

Helena took the thoughtful approach: 'He claims that Chrysippus was thrilled by the new poems he produced yesterday, but I wonder. Could it be that Chrysippus really saw him as a dire washed-up has-been whom he wanted to drop? Now the patron is dead, who can tell? Will Pacuvius manage to have work published that might have been rejected?'

'Would he have killed to achieve publication?' I murmured, scraping salt from a block.

'Would he ever stop talking long enough?' asked Maia.

'If he really has an established market, he must want the scriptorium to continue trading as normal, without any commercial upheavals caused by the death of its proprietor.'

'Is there a sensation effect?' asked Helena. 'Might a murder increase sales?'

'Don't know – but it's presumably only temporary.' I had other priorities. 'Where's that nice matured goat's cheese?'

'Gaius Baebius ate it yesterday.'

'Jupiter, I hate that glutton! So did the talking man give you any inside patter on the others involved?'

'All cooing turtledoves, according to him,' sneered Helena.

'She does not believe it. She has met writers,' giggled Maia. 'Well, she knows you, Marcus.'

'What, no vinegar? No mean-spirited nastiness about his companions?'

'He was far too nice about them all. Not enough envy, not enough bile.' Helena's bright eyes had been dangling bait. 'But then . . .'

'Out with it!'

'What did *you* find out?'

I could play the game. I fed her one titbit. 'The historian had a large debt to the Aurelian Bank.'

'Oh, is that all?' crowed my sister, interrupting.

'I suspect he was to be dropped too – Vespasian wants his own version of history reported. Anyone who has been around during previous emperors' reigns is tainted. Chrysippus may well have been thinking he would look for someone more politically acceptable to the new régime. Waste of time trying to push the wares, otherwise.'

'Anything else?' Helena grilled me.

'The dreamer who's creating the new republic has the sniffles. An ideal society will be slow arriving, due to his funny turns.'

'What a disappointment. Which one is that?'

'Turius.'

'Ah!' Helena came alight excitedly. 'Turius has a black mark against him; *Scrutator* loved telling us this. Turius refused to include a flattering reference to Chrysippus in his work. Chrysippus put to him that if he was prepared to take the money, he ought to respond appropriately.'

'Toady up to the patron?' I grinned.

'Mention how wildly generous the patron was,' said Helena in her austere way. 'Name Chrysippus so frequently that the public learned to respect him just for being so popular – make out that Chrysippus was a man of exquisite taste and noble intention, and the next Roman world-mover.'

'Also, claim that he gives nice dinner parties,' Maia added.

'Turius foolishly prefers not to say these things?'

Helena answered with relish: 'According to Pacuvius – who may be lying for theatrical effect, of course – Turius was much more forceful than that. He proclaimed in public that Chrysippus was a devious philandering foreigner, who would have rejected Homer's manuscripts because a blind man would be a menace at public readings, and would need a costly amanuensis to take dictation.'

'A feud! I love it!' I guffawed.

Helena's eyes sought mine, brown and bright, enjoying my delight in her story. 'Then – still according to Pacuvius, who seemed rather carried away by all this – Turius raged that Chrysippus was so lacking in critical discernment he would have insisted Helen of Troy be seen constantly naked in the *Iliad*; he would have censored the love between Achilles and Patroclus in case the aediles sent him into exile for inflaming immorality; and in the *Odyssey* he would have demanded that the heart-rending death scene of Odysseus' poor old dog be cut as mere padding.'

We all winced.

I divided a small sausage between us with a sharp knife. 'Did Chrysippus know Turius had been so rude?'

'They all think so.'

'Thrills! Was there a fight? Any suggestion of violence?'

'No. Nobody thinks Turius can even find the energy to blow his nose, despite the sniffles.'

'Oh, but Chrysippus must have been furious – *he* might have picked a fight.' And Turius might have feebly run away. 'So what does Pacuvius think of Turius and his lively opinions?'

'Watery approval – but he keeps his mouth shut. As a satirist, he is a hypocrite.'

'Aren't they always? Anything else you found out?'

'Hardly anything,' Helena said offhandedly. That meant there was. 'The epic poet hits the amphora too often, and it's said that the successful playwright does not write his plays himself.'

I shook my head, then grinned at her. 'Nothing to go on at all, in fact!'

XXIV

A GOOD PICTURE of jealousies and quarrels was building. I always like a case with a crowd of seething suspects; I allowed myself to enjoy lunch.

When the conversation turned to family matters, Maia told me she had been to see Pa. Although she had investigated his situation at the warehouse, she had not come out and directly offered help. 'You tackle him. You and Helena know him better than I do. Anyway, it's you two who want me to do this . . .'

She was prevaricating. Helena and I took her back to the Saepta Julia straight after we had eaten.

We found my father frowning over a pile of what looked like bills. He was perfectly able to deal with his financial affairs; he was shrewd and snappily numerate. Once he had found a basket of odd pots and finials to keep Julia happy, I put it to him bluntly that he seemed to have lost the will to keep his daily records, and that he would be doing my sister a favour if he allowed her – and paid her – to become his secretary.

'There's nothing to it,' Pa avowed, trying to minimise the salary. 'It does not need keeping up every day –'

'I thought all business deals were supposed to be recorded in a day-book,' I said.

'That doesn't mean you have to write them up the same day they happen.' Pa looked at me as if I were simple. 'Do you write your expenses on a tablet the minute you pay out a witness bribe?'

'Of course. I am a methodical consultant.'

'Pigs' pizzle. Besides, son, just because I can, when challenged, produce a daybook looking all neat and innocent, doesn't mean it has to be correct.'

Maia shot him a look; *that* was about to change smartly around this office.

Despite this difference in ethics between them, we settled the matter easily. Like most arrangements that appear fraught with problems, once tackled, its difficulties evaporated. Straight away Maia began to explore and soon extracted a pile of accounting notes from under Pa's stool. I had seen how she kept her own household budget; I knew she would cope. She herself obviously felt nervous. While she sat down to get the hang of our father's systems, which he had devised especially to bamboozle others, Helena and I stayed to distract the suspicious proprietor from overseeing Maia so closely he would put her off.

'Who do you bank with, Pa?'

'Mind your own business!' he retorted instinctively.

'Typical!'

'Juno,' Helena muttered. 'Grow up, you two. Didius Favonius, your son has no designs on your moneychests. This is just an enquiry related to his work.'

Pa perked up, always eager to put his nose into anything technical of mine. 'What's that then?'

'A banker has been killed. Chrysippus. Ever come across his agent, Lucrio, at the Aurelian Bank?'

Pa nodded. 'I know a few people who use him.'

'Given the prices you extract at auction, I'm not surprised buyers have to get financial help.' Pa looked proud to be called an extortioner. 'I hear he specialises in loans.'

'This Aurelian outfit going down, then?' Pa demanded, ever anxious to be first with gossip.

'Not that I know.'

'I'll put the word around.'

'That's not what Marcus said,' Helena reproved him. Her senatorial background had taught her never to do or say anything that might excite a barrister. She was related to a few. It had not improved her view of the advice they gave. 'Don't slander the banker if there is nothing wrong!'

Pa wriggled and clammed up. He would be unable to resist pretending to his cronies that he knew something. That there was nothing to relate would not stop him bending ears with a sensational tale. Patter was his business; he would make it up without noticing his own invention.

I too should have kept quiet. Still, it was too late now. 'I suppose you've seen plenty of credit-brokers hanging around at auctions, ready to help out buyers with on-the-spot finance?'

'All the time. Sometimes we attract more money touts than interested purchasers to take them up. Persistent bastards too. But we don't see Lucrio.'

'No, I think the Aurelian Bank works more secretly.'

'Dodges?' asked Pa.

'No, just discreet.'

'Oh really!'

Even I smiled knowingly. 'It's the Greek style, I'm told.'

'You do mean dodges then,' sneered Pa. He and Helena chuckled together.

I felt myself looking pompous. 'No need for xenophobia.'

'The Greeks invented xenophobia,' Helena reminded me.

'The Greeks are Romans now,' I claimed.

'Not,' sneered Pa, 'that you would claim it when face to face with a Greek.'

'Sensitivity to others. Why rub Attic noses in the rich dirt of Latium? Let them believe they are superior, if that's their religion. We Romans tolerate anyone – except, of course, the Parthians. And once we persuade *them* of the advantages of joining the Empire and having their long hair cut, we may even pretend to like the Parthians.'

'You are joking,' scoffed Pa.

I let a brief silence fall. Any moment now, somebody would mention the Carthaginians. Maia, whose husband had been executed for cursing Hannibal in his home region and then blaspheming the Punic gods, looked up from her work briefly as if she sensed what I was thinking.

'So which company do you bank with?' Helena asked my father, with rather wicked insistence.

He indulged her, though not much. 'This and that. Depends.'

'On what?'

'What I want.'

'Pa never keeps much on deposit,' I told her. 'He prefers to have his capital in saleable goods – artworks and fine furniture.'

'Why pay somebody to keep my currency secure?' Pa explained. 'Or allow a halfwit who couldn't spot a good investment in a goldmine to gamble with my cash? When I want a loan to make a big unplanned purchase, I can get it. My credit's good.'

'That proves how stupid bankers are!' I joked.

'How do they know they can trust you, Geminus?' Helena asked, more reasonably.

Pa told her about the Columnia Maena, where credit merchants posted up details of clients who were looking for loans. It was the same story Nothokleptes had given me. 'Apart from that, it's all word of mouth. They consult one another; it's a big family party. Once you acquire a good reputation, you are in.'

Helena Justina turned to me. 'You could do that kind of work, Marcus – checking that people are solvent.'

'I have done, on occasion.'

'Then you ought to advertise it as a regular service. You could even specialise.'

'Make a change from being hired by the vigiles to solve cases they cannot be bothered to investigate.'

I knew why Helena was interested. I was supposed to be going into partnership with one of her brothers – Justinus, if he ever deigned to come home from Spain. Both brothers, if we could build up a large enough client base. Regular customers, such as bankers checking whether clients were creditworthy, could be useful to our agency. I pretended to be dismissive – but then winked to let her know I had heard the suggestion.

'Looking into the backgrounds of people who have not actually bludgeoned their relatives would be less dangerous too,' said Helena. I did not share her view of the business world.

'I could start with my own father's background, I suppose.'

'Get stuffed,' said Pa predictably.

This time we all laughed together.

The conversation reminded me about discovering who had poked Chrysippus with the scroll rod. I said I was going back to his house; Helena decided that first, while we were over at the Saepta Julia, it made sense to hire a litter, cross the Tiber, and visit our own new house on the Janiculan. She would come there with me. She could shout at Gloccus and Cotta, the bathhouse contractors.

By reminding him about his terrible recommendation of these two home-destruction specialists, Helena persuaded Pa to look after Julia. Maia offered to bring the baby home for us at least as far as her house. We then were able to stroll out into Rome like lovers in the mid-afternoon.

We spent a long time trying to advance things at the new house. Gloccus and Cotta packed up, rather than hear any more of our complaints. At least this time they had a good reason for leaving early. Usually it was because they could not work out how to rectify whatever had gone wrong with that morning's labour.

Even after they vanished, we did not go straight back across to the Clivus Publicius. I'm not stupid. It was far too hot to flog all the way back to the city, and during the siesta there was no hope of finding any witnesses. Besides, this was a rare chance of solitude with my girl.

XXV

THE STUPID bastards were still working their way one at a time in order down the visitors' list. The epic poet had his turn with me next.

I rather liked him. Euschemon had called him dull. Maybe his work was, but luckily I was not obliged to read it. One of life's odd quirks: authors you warm to as people somehow cannot see where their strength lies, but will insist on pouring out scroll after lifeless scroll of tedium.

It was early evening. Rome shimmering after a long hot day. People coming alive after feeling utterly drained. Smoke from the bathhouse furnaces creating a haze that mingled with scented oven fumes. Flautists practising. Men in shop doorways greeting each other with a grin that meant they had been up to no good – or were planning it for later. Women shrieking at children in upper rooms. Really old women, who no longer had children to keep in order, now standing at their windows to spy on the men who were up to no good.

I had reached the dogleg of the Clivus Publicius alone. Helena had gone to Maia's house to fetch Julia. We had been close for long enough not to want to part. But work had called.

Now I was in a quiet mood. After loving the same woman for a period of years I had gone past both the panic that she might reject me and the crass exultancy of conquest. Helena Justina was the woman whose love could still move me. Afterwards, I bathed at an establishment where I was not known, unwilling to engage in conversation. Communicating with the Chrysippus writing circle held no real charm for me either. Still, it had to be done.

It was a welcome surprise, therefore, to discover that the next of the hacks bothered to turn up for an interview, and that I took to him.

Constrictus was older than the previous group, in his late fifties at least. Still, he looked spry and bright-eyed – more so than I expected since he had been accused by *Scrutator* of draining too many amphorae.

Of course the flamboyant *Scrutator,* with his fund of off-colour stories, had carried his own traces of debauchery.

'Come in.' I decided not to complain that he should have turned up this morning. 'I'm Falco, as I'm sure you know.' If Turius and the other two had warned Constrictus that I was a bastard to deal with, he hid his terror bravely. 'You're the epic poet?'

'Oh not only epic. I'll try anything.'

'Promiscuous, eh?'

'To earn a living by writing you have to sell whatever you can.'

'What happened to *write from your own experience?*'

'Pure self-indulgence.'

'Well, I was told that the big historical pageant is your natural genre.'

'Too hackneyed. No untapped source material left,' he groaned. I had already observed this as a problem with Rutilius Gallicus and *his* heroic banalities. 'And, frankly,' confided Constrictus, 'I throw up when I'm constantly trumpeting that our ancestors were perfect pigs in an immaculate sty. They were idle shits like us.' He looked earnest. 'I really want to produce love poetry.'

'Source of contention with Chrysippus?'

'Not really. He would have loved to discover the new Catullus. The problem is, Falco, finding a suitable woman to address. It's either a prostitute — and who wants to be afflicted with helpless infatuation for any of those these days? Prostitutes are not what they were. You'll never find a modern version of sweet Ipsiphyle.'

'The whores have deteriorated just like the heroes?' I sympathised. 'Sounds a good lament!'

'Or the alternative is to fall obsessively for a highly-placed, beautiful amoral bitch who attracts scandal and has dangerous, powerful relatives.'

'Clodia's long gone.' Catullus' famous high-born hag with the dead pet sparrow was another generation's scandal. 'For the best, some would say. With special thanks that Rome is free of her brother, that rich gangster thug. Are today's senatorial families too refined to produce such a bad girl?'

'Jupiter, yes!' the poet lamented. 'Even good-time girls are not what they were. And if you do strike it lucky, the bloody women won't co-operate. I found a playmate, Melpomene by name, lovely creature; I could have devoted my all to her. We were magic in bed. Then, when I explained that she needed to dump me or it was no good for my work, she burst out wailing. What does she come out

129

with – listen to this, Falco! She said she really loved me, and couldn't bear to lose me, and why was *I* being so cruel to *her*?'

I nodded, more or less with sympathy, though I assumed he was being humorous. 'Hard to work up a metaphorical sweat over honest loyalty.'

Constrictus exploded with actual disgust. 'Jove, imagine it: an eclogue to a nymph who *wants* you, an ode about sharing your life.'

For a moment, I found myself thinking about Helena. It took me far from this hard-edged, unhappy lyricist.

'You could turn it into satire,' I suggested, trying to cheer him up. 'How's this for an epigram – *Melpomene, astonishing joy of my heart, I want to say "Don't go", but if I do, you'll die from lack of nourishment and the landlord's heavies will carve me up in the gutter for my unpaid rent. Poetry relies on misery. Leave me, please, and be quick about it – or my work won't sell.*'

He looked impressed. 'Was that extempore? You have a gift.'

'At this rate,' I said frankly, 'I'll be using my creative powers to invent a prosecution case. Would you mind giving me a motive so I can arrest you for battering your publisher? A full confession would be helpful, if you can run to it. I get a bonus fee for that.'

Constrictus became glum again. 'I did not do it. I wish I had thought of it. I freely admit that. Then I could have written a series of tragic dialogues, full of autobiographical sleaze – it always sells. Urban *Georgics*. Not a lament for those dispossessed of country land, but for those struggling against city indifference and brutality . . .'

He was off in the kind of speculative dream that could take all afternoon. When authors start imagining what they *could* have written, it is time to make a break for it.

'Look,' I said, knowing I had sounded too friendly earlier. 'I have to ask you the rubric. You came to see Chrysippus yesterday. I presume he was alive when you arrived here; can you assure me the same applied when you left?'

'If you regard being a parasitic bloodsucker as "life". If that is accepted terminology in your trade, Falco.'

I grinned. 'Informers are famous for loose definitions. Half my "clients" are walking ghosts. My "fees" tend to be insubstantial by most people's standards too. Cough up. Would a physician have diagnosed health in the man?'

'Unfortunately yes.'

'Thanks. From this I deduce you did not kill him. Mine, you see, is a simplistic art. Now! Personnel details at the scene, please: did you see anyone else here?'

'No.' He could be sensible. A pity. I really had liked him before that. If he had been a complete maniac, we might even have become friends.

'This is boring, Constrictus. So all you have to report is an amicable meeting, after which you quietly returned home?' He nodded. 'And you were subsequently shocked and amazed to learn what had transpired here?'

'Cheered,' he admitted breezily. 'Enormously encouraged to discover that someone had broken free of the chains and taken action. It was so unexpected. I saw it as revenge for all of us.'

'You are refreshingly honest,' I told him. 'So now be honest about the conditions in which you were a client of this patron, please.'

'Unendurable duress,' Constrictus boasted. 'Survival makes all of us heroes.'

'I am happy to hear it; you can use your suffering as research material.'

'He paid us too little; he worked us too hard,' Constrictus went on. 'The work was demeaning – it involved flattering him. I had a rule: get his name into the first line with at least three commendatory adjectives, then hope he would not bother to read on. Want more? I despised my colleagues. I hated the scriptorium staff. I was sick of waiting year after year for my so-called patron to give me the proverbial Sabine farm where I could eat lettuce, screw the farmer's wife, and write.'

I looked him straight in the eye. 'And you drink.'

There was a short silence. He was not intending to answer.

'I always find,' I said, trying not to sound unpleasantly pious, 'the stuff that I have written with a beaker beside me reads like rubbish once I sober up.'

'There's a simple cure for that,' Constrictus replied hoarsely. 'Never sober up!'

I said nothing. At thirty-three, I had long ago learned not to remonstrate with men who like to have their elbows always leaning on a bar. This was a very angry poet. Perhaps they all were, but Constrictus showed it. He was the oldest I had met so far; that might have something to do with it. Did he feel time was running out on him? Was he desperate to put substance into an otherwise wasted life? But often drink is an acknowledgement that nothing will ever change. A man in that mood probably would not kill – though anybody can be pushed too far by unexpected extra indignities.

I changed the subject. 'You told me you despise your colleagues. Elaborate.'

'Upstarts and mediocrities.'

'Yes, this is all confidential.' I smiled retrospectively.

'Who cares? They all know what I think.'

'I must say, the ones I have met all have potential to be dropped as no-hopers.'

'There you're wrong, Falco. Being a no-hoper is the essential criterion for getting your work copied and sold.'

'You are very bitter. Maybe you should have been the satirist.'

'Maybe I should,' Constrictus agreed shortly. 'But in this scriptorium, that bilious prick *Scrutator* holds sway –' He broke off.

'Oh do go on,' I encouraged him genially. 'It's your turn now. Each man I interview betrays the previous suspect. You get to spear the satirist. What's the dirt on *Scrutator*?'

Constrictus could not bear to waste a good suspenseful moment: 'He had a blazing row with our dear patron – surely the old bore mentioned that?'

'He was too busy confiding that Turius is not as insipid as he looks, but has insulted Chrysippus rather notably.'

'Turius had nothing to lose,' moaned Constrictus. 'He wasn't going anywhere in any case.'

'If Turius said everything Pacuvius alleges, Chrysippus had good reason to attack him, not the other way round. But what about *Scrutator*'s personal beef?'

'Chrysippus had made arrangements to send him to Praeneste.'

'Punishment? What's there – a grand Oracle of Fortune and the ghastly priests who tend it?'

'Snobs' summer villas. Chrysippus was ingratiating himself with a friend by offering to lend out the talker and his endless droll stories as a house poet for the holiday period. We were all thrilled to be rid of him – but dear bloody *Scrutator* came over all sensitive about being passed around like a slave. He refused to go.'

'Chrysippus, having promised him, was then furious?'

'It made him look a fool. A fool who could not control his own clients.'

'Who was the friend he wanted to impress?'

'Someone in shipping.'

'From the old country? A Greek tycoon?'

'I think so. Ask Lucrio.'

'The connection is through the bank?'

'You are getting the hang of this,' Constrictus said. Now he was being cheeky to me; well, I could handle that.

'I can follow a plot. I wonder which of the others I shall have to prod to be told the dirt on you? Or would you rather give me your own version?'

'It's no secret.' Once again, the poet's voice had a raw note. Despite having previously claimed that their meeting had been amicable, he now told me the truth: 'I was too old. Chrysippus wants new blood, he told me yesterday. Unless I came up with something special very quickly, he was intending to cease supporting me.'

'That's hard.'

'Fate, Falco. It was bound to happen one day. Successful poets gather together a pension, leave Rome, and retire to be famous men in their hometowns where – touched by the Golden City's magic – they will shine out among the rural dross. They go while they can still enjoy it; by my age, a successful man has left. An *un*successful one can only hope to offend the Emperor by some sexual scandal, then be exiled to prison on the edge of the Empire where they keep him alive with daily porridge just so his whimpering letters home will demonstrate the triumph of morality . . . Vespasian's womenfolk have yet to start having rampant affairs with poets.' He flexed an arthritic knuckle. 'I'll be beyond servicing the bitches if they hang about much longer.'

'I'll put the word out at the Golden House that here's a love poet who wants to be part of a salon scandal . . .' To be left without funding at his age could be no joke. 'How will your finances stand up?' I asked.

He knew why I was asking. A man plunged into sudden abject poverty could well have turned violent when the unsympathetic patron sat in his elegant Greek library telling him the news. Constrictus enjoyed informing me he was reprieved from that suspicion: 'I have a small legacy from my grandmother to live on, actually.'

'Nice.'

'Such a relief!'

'Absolves you from suspicion too.'

'And it's so convenient!' he agreed.

Too convenient?

When I pressed him about timings, he was the first person to tell me that when he left the library yesterday, he saw the lunch tray waiting for Chrysippus, in the Latin room's lobby. It seemed he might well have been the last to visit before the murderer. Honest of him to admit it. Honest – or just blatant?

I made him look at the side table with the Phrygian purple upstands. 'When did you last taste nettle flan?'

'I beg your pardon?'

'Did you go up to that buffet table, Constrictus? Did you help yourself from the tray?'

'No, I did not!' He laughed. 'I would have been afraid somebody sensible had poisoned his food. Anyway, there's a decent popina in the Clivus outside. I went out for air, and had a bite there.'

'See any of the others?'

'Not the morning he died.' He stared at me, much more daring than the rest. 'Naturally most of us met up in the afternoon, after we heard what had happened, and discussed what we would say to you!'

'Yes; I had already worked out that you did that,' I answered quietly.

I let him go. He wanted to be too clever. I had liked him, which was more than I could say for the historian, the ideal republican, or the satirist – yet I trusted none of them.

There was now only one remaining on my list of visitors, Urbanus, the dramatist. Time was running out; I couldn't wait on his convenience. I took the address Passus had obtained for me and went to his apartment. He was not in. At the theatre probably, or in some drinking-house full of actors and understudies. I could not be bothered to try searching, or to wait for him to wander home.

XXVI

THE CONVERSATION I had held earlier with Pa about keeping daybooks had stayed with me. I decided I would call in the records of the Aurelian Bank.

Big ideas! I then decided it might be asking for trouble. That did not stop me. Since I was working for the vigiles and they would be held accountable for my excesses of enthusiasm, I reckoned it could be done officially.

In July and August in Rome when you have a major project on, you must accomplish all you can in the evening. Daytime is too hot for work like mine. Even if I decided to endure the sun, nobody else would be available. So that evening, although I had every excuse to toddle home to Helena, I put in one more effort and went to see Petronius at the vigiles' patrol-house, to discuss banking.

It happened that Petro was there. When I arrived he and Sergius, the punishment man, were teasing a statement out of a recalcitrant victim by the subtle technique of bawling fast questions while flicking him insistently with the end of a hard whip. I winced, and sat out on a bench in the warm evening sun until they tired and shoved their victim into the holding-cell.

'What's he done?'

'He doesn't want to tell us.' That had been obvious.

'What do you *think* he's done?'

'Run a tunic-stealing racket at the Baths of Calliope.'

'Surely that's too routine to justify the heavy hand?'

'And he poisoned the dog Calliope had brought in to stand guard over the clothes pegs in the changing room.'

'Killed a doggie? Now that's wicked.'

'She bought the dog from my sister,' Sergius broke in angrily. 'My sister took a lot of back-chat for supplying a sick animal.' He went back inside to shout insults through the cell door. I told Petro I still thought they were being too rough on the suspect.

'No, he's lucky,' Petronius assured me. 'Being beaten by Sergius is nothing. The alternative was letting Sergius' sister get to him. She is twice as big' – that must be quite a size, I thought – 'and she's horrible.'

'Oh, fair enough.'

I discussed a plan I had for demanding sight of the banker's records, or at least the most recent. Petro raised objections initially, then his natural impulse to be awkward with financiers took charge. He agreed to make available a couple of lads in red tunics, to be my official escort, and with the provision of a suitable docket from his clerk I could approach the bank and see what happened. The vigiles clerk was a creative type. He devised a grand document, written in peculiar and extravagant language, which served as a warrant to impound the goods.

We took this to the Forum, to the Aurelian change-table. Petronius in fact came along with us. Eager for a field trip, so did the clerk. Impressed by our own bravado, we carried the day: the cashier reluctantly agreed to show us where the freedman Lucrio lived. Lucrio possessed all the relevant records, apparently. At his apartment, a discreet but obviously spacious ground-floor spread, we were told he had gone out to dinner. We could sense resistance but without their master to give orders, the household staff caved in. A slave reluctantly showed us where the records were kept, and we carried off in a handcart the tablets and sewn-together codices that looked the most up to date. We left a nice note to say we had removed them, naturally.

We towed the material back to the patrol-house. It had to be kept secure, for all sorts of reasons. Since Rubella, the tribune, was still on leave in Campania, we dumped everything in his office. Then I went out and thanked the escort. They shambled off, grinning. Ex-slaves, each doing a six-year stint in fire-fighting as a route to respectability, they were glad of some fun, especially if they could achieve it without any headbutts, bruises or burns.

'I'll have a quick squint now, then I'll be along tomorrow to start scrutiny in detail,' I said to Petro, who was himself preparing for a night out on the streets of the Thirteenth District (the patrol-house was in the Twelfth).

Having glanced quickly at the unfathomable tablets, Petronius now looked at me as though I were mad. 'Are you sure about this?'

'A doddle,' I assured him breezily.

'Whatever you say, Falco.'

'No option.' I decided on honesty: 'We're getting stuck.'

'You mean, you are.'

I ignored that. 'Once the alarm was raised after the murder, the vigiles were on the spot within minutes. We checked everyone in the household for bloodstains. His relations all have alibis. The scriptorium manager is exonerated by absence. There are no links to the literary visitors. I won't yet say for certain that the bank holds the motive, but it looks increasingly likely. I needed to swoop. We did not want chests to be cleared or items destroyed.'

'You know what you're doing,' Petronius said dryly.

Not quite, perhaps. But I was running out of leads at the Chrysippus house. The staff were in the clear. The authors all blamed each other, but none of them seemed capable of the sustained violence inflicted on the dead man. The wife and the ex-wife were too devious to assist me. Trouble at the bank was all I had left to investigate.

We gossiped for a while. I told Petro what had been happening about Maia working for Pa. He grimaced at the idea of Junia in charge of Flora's Caupona; still, plenty of wineries are run by folk who seem to loathe the notion of being hospitable. Junia could not cook; that fitted the profile of most caupona managers. Petro's one concern for Maia was how, if she needed to take herself half across Rome working at the Saepta Julia, she would manage to look after her children.

'While she's with our father, they will probably be at Ma's.'

'Oh right!' said Petronius, quick to forecast trouble. 'So every time Maia goes there to deliver or collect them, she will risk meeting Anacrites.'

'That had not escaped me. The older ones are big enough to find their way back and forth without a chaperone, but the youngest is only three or four. And you're right. Maia will not like them wandering the streets, so she will be at Ma's more now than she was before.'

We stood outside the patrol-house in silence for a moment. I had an odd feeling that Petronius was about to share a confidence. I waited, but he said nothing.

He went off on enquiries and I wandered back inside. Night was falling, so the place emptied. The clerk went off duty; he worked day shifts. 'I'll bar the main door, Falco. We have to deter maniacs with grudges from getting in while the boys are all away. You can use the side exit in the equipment store.'

The vigiles were now on active duty. Their primary role was to patrol the streets during the hours of darkness watching for fires, arresting any criminals they happened to encounter while they were out on foot patrol. Later, groups would return with their haul of naughty nightlife; until then I was sitting alone with an oil-lamp in the tribune's office, with only the man banged-up in the cell for company. He had been shouting in a desultory way, but he fell silent, pondering his fate perhaps. I had not bothered to answer him, so he probably thought he was all alone.

Rubella, the tribune whose upstairs room I had taken over, was an ex-centurion who lusted after joining the Praetorian Guard, so he kept up military neatness like a religion. I soon dealt with that, sweeping his carefully placed desk equipment to one side and moving all his furniture. He would hate it. I chuckled to myself. I had a hunt around in case he had stowed a wine flask anywhere, but he was too ascetic to indulge – or else he had taken the comforter home when he went on leave. Some tribunes are human. Being on holiday can be very stressful.

I was having trouble finding my way about the bank's figurework. Loans were hardly distinguished from deposits, and I could not tell whether interest was included in the amounts. Eventually I worked out that I had an itemised tally of day-to-day debts and credits for the bank, but no running totals for individual client accounts. Well, that was no surprise. I myself had never been sent a summary of my affairs by Nothokleptes; I relied on notes I had jotted down for myself, and had to tot up the transactions on my own waxed tablet if I wanted to be certain where I stood at any time. Similar practices seemed to be inflicted on those who had dealings at the sign of the Golden Horse.

It seemed an invitation to mislead, at best. Any of these names could have been cheated of cash. If I told them it had happened, they would be enraged. Normally, they probably never found out. In fact, the material failed to throw up a suspect. From the figures I had here, I could not really identify who should be feeling aggrieved.

Somebody was upset. I was about to find out how badly.

I had stayed later than I intended. Other people's finances are deeply absorbing. As full darkness descended and the city cooled down after the long, hot day, I came to, suddenly aware that I should be leaving. Aware also, of distant sounds from time to time. I vaguely assumed some of the vigiles were returning, or that an extremely rowdy tavern nearby must be throwing out customers. I left Rubella's office, locked it behind me and placed the cumbersome key up high on the door lintel (its place when he was absent; when he was there he guarded the key in his arm-purse, lest anyone should pinch his lunch). Everywhere was dark and felt unfamiliar to me. Unmanned, the place was eerie.

The upstairs office was an innovation Rubella devised when he was posted here, to give himself extra status. He thought discipline was best imposed by distance. Nobody argued; it kept him out of their way. The lads had always lived on the outer porch; there they could snigger about Rubella, while he could not reappear within earshot without clattering down a flight of steps. I was about to regret how noisy they were.

The lower level of the patrol-house consisted of interrogation rooms, which I knew were hung with ghastly manipulative screws and weights; it had a few cells and one barrack room, where on rare occasions the troops sheltered and slept. None of those was lit tonight. Alongside this building lay the fire-fighting equipment store, one of two run by the Fourth Cohort in each of the districts they looked after. The communicating door stood open as I loafed downstairs with my half-extinguished oil lamp. Other lamps were sometimes left flickering in the store, to aid fast access in emergencies, but tonight no one seemed to have bothered. Well, it saved the embarrassment of having the fire-fighters' building set ablaze accidentally while nobody was here.

My boots were soft on the stair treads, but by no means silent. I called goodnight to the man locked in the cell. No answer.

As soon as I turned into the store, which lay in pitch darkness, I smelt and sensed people waiting. I was alone in a strange building – tired, unarmed, and unprepared for this. Someone knocked up my arm. The lamp went out. The door slammed shut behind me. Dear gods: I was in deep trouble.

XXVII

THEY MUST have been able to see my outline in the open doorway before the lamp failed. They had certainly heard me coming. I had been careless. Nowhere was safe, not even the patrol-house of a cohort of law and order boys.

The moment my arm was jarred, I dropped to the floor and rolled. Not much use. I crashed into somebody's ankles; he shouted. Either he or someone else hauled at my tunic, found an arm, towed me one way, then kicked me in the body so I was sent in another direction.

I skewed round and crawled away crabwise, but they were on me. I grappled a torso, kneeing soft tissue. Teeth found my hand, but I was able to make it into a fist and heard the man gagging as I punched his mouth. My other hand fell on the still-warm lamp, so I flung it where I thought there was an attacker near the door; he cursed, as the pottery cracked and hot oil sprayed him. Some of them must have banged into each other, judging by their grunts of annoyance. Otherwise they did not speak. Come to that, neither did I.

The store was full of equipment; I could barely remember the layout. A pile of metal buckets had crashed over. My worst fear was the grappling hooks, but whoever these intruders were, they did not try anything so dangerous – well, not in the dark, where they might gouge the flesh or tear out the eyes of their own group. When they next found me though, at least two of them made contact at the same time. I was bucking madly; even so, I ended up pinned to what I realised was the side of the siphon wagon – the engine that could be rushed out on wheels to pump water onto large-scale fires. Metal was sticking into me painfully; I had no idea what. A hand squashed my face; I used my own teeth. Then I jerked my head away hard, knowing I would be pummelled in retaliation. I heard the fist smash into the wagon, and I bent double, despite the grip of those holding me, so the next blow went above me and missed as well.

These were determined people, but not as well trained as they could have been. Not professional heavies. Still, somebody had told them they could rough up anyone they found.

They had dragged me down on the floor. Then something scratchy and enormously heavy was thrown on top of me. Those holding me let go of my legs and arms; as they slid away, more of the scratchy stuff landed around me. Beneath it, I was unable to move and had trouble breathing. I could smell charred material. Grit and coarse strands were in my mouth and nose. Dear gods; I knew what was happening. They had dumped me under one of the esparto mats – the big thick squares of woven Spanish grass that the vigiles used for smothering fires. I was stuck under it, while my attackers had fun dancing on top, stumbling to and fro, playing at clumsy grape-pressing all over me. The esparto mat, which from the charred smell had been used a few times for its real purpose, might protect me from bruising – but at the cost of smothering me as successfully as it put out fires.

Immobile and choking, I braced myself and waited for the worst.

XXVIII

THE SITUATION changed.

The agony decreased a little. They had stopped jumping about.
For a period most went away, although one large body remained
sitting right upon my midriff, keeping me stuck securely under the
weight of the mat. I heard voices sometimes. I could feel vibrations in
the floor. People were moving about. They may have relit some
lamps, though no trace of light was reaching me through the thick
esparto matting.

I had managed to get my mouth and nose into a small air pocket.
My ribs were compressed, which constricted my breathing, but I was
alive. I could stay like this for a little while, though not for long.

At some point tonight either Petronius and his enquiry team or the
rankers would return. How soon would that be? Not soon enough,
from what I knew of them. If it was a quiet night, with few prisoners
to process, they would be tempted to drop into a caupona. Flexing my
dry tongue against the roof of my mouth, tasting old smoke and
charcoal, I blamed none of them for lingering but I prayed for them
to home in here.

Summer. Would anyone in this neighbourhood let a flaming
candelabrum topple over? A night-light catch on a curtain? A skillet
of hot oil set itself on fire? A furnace explode at a bathhouse? A log-
store smoulder? The sources of disaster in normal life were many,
though life was less dangerous in summer than in winter. Still, even if
the whole Twelfth District had eaten salad and was slumbering by
starlight, surely there was some friendly arsonist who would feel a mad
impulse to watch the vigiles racing back to their store for the
wherewithal to douse his efforts? I would stand him bail and compose
a character witness statement, if he would hurry up and kindle just a
small fire, so the alarm would be raised and I would be found . . .

Typical. Never a villain when you want one. All Rome must be
lying peaceful tonight.

I tried groaning. The ballast merchant just dug his backside into the mat above me more heavily. Whether by accident or on purpose, he moved his weight onto my head.

This was going to finish me.

Perhaps I did pass out. But eventually, some of the pain lifted. Even the mat was pulled off me, rasping roughly across my body and legs. I was dazzled by light, temporarily blinding.

I lay still. That was easy. Pretending to be dead comes naturally when you are halfway there. Around me, the air was cool, a desperately pleasant change. I breathed in gently while I could, trying to revive my strength before they tackled me again – as I knew they soon would.

Squinting through relaxed eyelids, I glimpsed various crude shoes and sandals. Dirty feet, with black, unpedicured toenails, misshapen bones and flea-bitten ankles: slaves' feet. I heard shuffling, and a silence falling, as if order was being imposed.

A man's voice asked, with only a trace of concern, 'What have you done to him?'

Someone lifted the neck of my tunic, dragging up my head. I kept my eyes shut. He let go. My head banged down on the stone floor.

Then there was a clank. Cold water brought me round, yelling. Someone had chucked a whole fire-bucket over me. This was not my favourite way to spend a balmy July night. Soaked through, I sat up, shaking my hair and wiping my eyes. I coughed up sputum. As if not caring who was here, I gripped my knees and laid my head down, gasping.

'You are Didius Falco?' enquired the same voice. I had its position now. He was the stuffed sheepgut in charge. That would be his mistake. 'Answer me!' He came nearer, so he could nudge me with his foot.

Then I rolled, and in one movement retrieved my knife from my boot. I wrenched myself upright, grabbed him, spun him with his back to me, pulled his head up by the hair, pressed an arm across his throat so he was choking, and held my knife to his throat. I backed myself into a safe position against the siphon trailer, using him as my shield.

'*Nobody move – or I kill him!*'

I yanked harder at the hair. His eyes must have been rolling, and he was no doubt grimacing. He had the sense not to struggle.

'All of you,' I told them grimly, 'go back now slowly to the wall opposite.'

When they hesitated, I made a brutal jerk with my arm on my captive's throat. He let out a wild croak of terror, trying to make them obey me. He was red in the face. They edged away. There were five. Slaves in plain tunics, unarmed of course. None seemed properly accustomed to violence. I was alone, but I knew what I was doing. Well, I thought I did.

'What's your name?' My prisoner gurgled. I wrenched at his throat viciously and shouted at the slaves, 'What's his name?'

'Lucrio.'

'*Hah!* Well, well. Is this your business practice, Lucrio? Do you beat up your clients? Extortion with menaces – that would explain a lot.'

One of the slaves made an unexpected movement. I gave Lucrio a brutal wrench, while shouting at his men to drop to the floor and lie still.

'Face down!'

When they were all prone, I moved Lucrio to a pile of ropes, unhitched a coil, tied his arms and fastened him to a wheel of the siphon wagon. I found an iron grappler lying on the floor, and grabbed it for extra protection.

I could not be bothered too much with the slaves, but I had them sit up one by one and lashed their arms to their sides. To make it difficult for them to stand up or try anything, I popped fire-buckets over all their heads. Some received full ones. Well, that would make them think twice next time they threw freezing cold water over a man who had been half suffocated.

'Right, Lucrio. I shall hear if your bother-team makes a wrong move, but let's face it – they're garbage. They should be deaf under the buckets. We'll have a private chat, shall we?'

First, I had a proper look at him.

'Hmm. Nobody is at his best with his tunic braid torn, and hanging from a cart wheel, I concede that.'

In fact he was looking more spruce than he could have done – unrepentant, anyway. He was forty, or more. He had been a slave once, but carried few signs of it. I had seen consuls who looked uglier.

His teeth were bad, but he was fit and well-fleshed, decently nourished over a long period of his life, a bathhouse frequenter and able to afford a good barber. The tunic I had damaged was of fine cloth, usually laundered to a crisp white, though I had given it an equitable scruffy look. He was dark, with a face and eyes that spoke of Thrace if you looked closely, yet he could have passed for anyone. He would not be too exotic to do business in the Forum. He was not too foreign to have prospects in Rome.

'Were you looking for me – or for what I had commandeered?'

'You had no right to take anything from my house, Falco!' He was already at ease again, despite being tied up. He had a market commerce accent. I could imagine him in some brothel-cum-bar behind the Curia, joking with his cronies about huge sums of money – mentioning tens and hundreds of thousands as casually as if they were sacks of wheat.

'Wrong. I had a warrant, and what I took was removed in the presence of the vigiles.'

'It is private material.'

'Don't give me that. Bankers are always appearing as court witnesses –' I had subpoenaed plenty myself, when working as a runner for Basilica Julia barristers.

Lucrio seemed far too sure of himself. 'Only when their evidence is called for by the specific account-holder.'

'What's that?'

'It's the law,' he told me, with some relish. 'The details of a man's finances are his personal property.'

'Not Roman law!' I was trying it on. But I sensed I had lost this. 'What I took was possible evidence in a murder case. I assume you care about what happened to Aurelius Chrysippus? He was your chief at the Aurelian. You are his freedman and his agent at the bank – and, I've been told, the heir to his fortune?'

'True.' His answer was quieter. He might be a freedman but he was bright. He understood the implications of being heir to a murdered man.

'So you, Lucrio, as heir to a man who has died in very violent circumstances, have now broken into the patrol-house of the vigiles cohort who are investigating the suspicious death? Removing evidence has to look bad!'

'It is not yours to take – nor even mine to give,' said Lucrio. He knew his rights. I was shafted. 'A magistrate has been asked to issue an injunction. I merely came to prevent any breach of confidence occurring before the order can be brought here.' He could have been in court already, pleading for me to be charged a huge fine. 'It is regrettable that before I arrived in person my staff, being eager to please me and rather excited, did perhaps overreact . . . though I suggest it was in response to provocative behaviour.'

I sighed. His threat would hold good. The vigiles were known for their tough attitude; being attacked in a patrol-house would garner me no sympathy. People would believe I had caused the trouble. Still, I answered back: 'I must get the cohort doctor to look at me. I'm stiffening up; there could be a hefty compensation claim.'

'I shall be happy to pay for any salves he recommends,' Lucrio professed hypocritically.

'I'll take that as an admission of liability.'

'No, the offer is without prejudice.'

'Am I surprised?' I was indeed feeling the pain now, and growing very tired after my ordeal under the mat. I gazed at the freedman; he gazed back, a man used to holding the power position in business discussions. 'We need to talk, Lucrio. And it's in nobody's interests for you to be tied to a pump engine.'

I had regained some kudos by reminding him he was roped up. I was doing well, in fact – until one extra slave who had, unknown to me, been secreting himself behind the spraying arms on top of the siphon engine finally found the courage to act. With a wild cry, he emerged, hurled himself off and fell on me.

He knocked my breath away. It achieved nothing, however. Because at that moment Petronius Longus entered from the street gateway. He was scowling and carrying what looked like the magistrate's injunction. Vigiles members crowded in after him. They had probably all indulged in a few quick refreshments somewhere, as I had earlier guessed they might. That would explain why they all found it quite so funny to discover a row of slaves sitting with their heads in buckets, a prisoner roped to their siphon, me on the ground not even bothering to resist attack, and one sad man who had briefly thought he was a hero, but who collapsed in fright when he saw the red tunics and had to be revived with kicks from a vigilis' boot.

Chaos ensued. I lay on my back and let them all get on with it.

Petronius, who was usually the master of a tricky situation, felt highly put out by the injunction; I could see that. (Well, his name had been on the 'warrant'.) He swiftly regained authority when his men discovered that Lucrio's slaves had set free the bathhouse thief who had been locked in the holding-cell. Instantly, Petro slammed all six slaves in the cell to replace the lost prisoner. He enjoyed himself inventing statutory punishments for what they had so foolishly done.

Lucrio was released and told he could go home. The documents would all be returned to him tomorrow, as soon as men could be spared from fire-watching to wheel the handcart to his house. Lucrio was to report to the patrol-house for formal interview when Petronius Longus returned to duty the next afternoon. We said goodbye to the freedman politely, stretching ourselves as if we were now off home for a good night's sleep.

As soon as Lucrio had gone, Petro tossed the magistrate's order in a fire-bucket, then we raced upstairs to the tribune's room. The slaves had not even found the key on the lintel, and they must have been scared to break down the door. Petronius, Fusculus, Passus, Sergius and I worked all through the night, scouring the daybooks for anything that would implicate either the freedman or one of his clients in wrongdoing. As we worked, we called out the names of any creditors we came across and Passus frantically wrote them down. Most were unfamiliar to us.

Unfortunately, we found nothing that struck us as a possible clue.

XXIX

I SLEPT IN all morning. I was alone when I woke.

Reminded of being a bachelor, in the days when I operated as a one-man informer from my dingy sixth-floor apartment on the other side of Fountain Court, I indulged in a loner's toilet. I fell out of bed, pulled off my top tunic, shook the grit and debris out of it, then put the same garment on again. I smeared my face with cold water, wiped it dry on my sleeve, found a comb, then decided not to bother with my hair. I licked my teeth: disgusting. I bared them and polished them on my other sleeve.

By now, Nux was taking an interest. This was a way of life she had never been allowed to see before; though sluggish and rotund with impending motherhood, she seemed to like the idea. She was a scruff at heart.

'Ah, sweetheart, you should have known me in my wild days!'

Nux came and lolled against my left leg, puffing slightly. Rome was too hot for a pregnant dog. I gave her a bowl of clean water, then got another for myself. She lapped messily; I did the same. After a search, I managed to find a hard bread roll where Helena had carefully hidden it in order to cause me problems.

Everything in the apartment had been left extremely neat. Helena by her absence was showing the forbearance that meant she was furious. I could remember crawling home, smelling of cinders from the esparto mat; she had squealed with disgust as I fell into bed beside her, chilled and obviously stiff after a fracas of some sort. While we worked at the patrol-house Fusculus had fetched in an offensive array of sausages and cold pies, so I probably reeked of those too. I could not help groaning as my bruises swelled. Helena had not mentioned that I had promised to refrain from fights. She had not said anything, in fact, and I was too weary to attempt to communicate. But now she was ostentatiously not here.

'We're in trouble.'

Nux looked up and licked my leg. We had tidied her up since she agreed to abandon the street life and adopt us, but her fur was not exactly washed in rosewater. She had never been a lapdog for the refined.

'Where is she, Nux?'

Nux lay down and went to sleep.

I ate my roll. Outside, I could hear Rome going about its midday business while I was the lonely late riser, proud of his relaxed style – and missing everything. Nostalgic for freedom, I pretended to be enjoying the emptiness.

Beyond the shutters, mules brayed and vegetable pallets crashed. Some considerate neighbour was smashing up used amphorae rather than wash them clean; it made a resounding racket. Far above the alley, swifts persistently screamed after midges. I could sense the heat; the sun had been burning for hours. No visitors called. I was the forgotten man. That was the bachelor's main occupation; suddenly I remembered how dreary it felt.

Eventually the silence and stillness indoors became too much for me. I put Nux on a lead, took myself to a local bathhouse, neatened up, had a decent shave, climbed into a clean white tunic, and went to look for my wife and child.

They were at Ma's house. Instinct took me straight there.

Ma had been looking after Junia's little son, so Marcus Baebius and Julia were sitting on the floor together drawing on wax tablets. Marcus, at three or whatever he was, seemed content to wield the stylus sensibly, though he did insist on running to Ma to have the wax smoothed for him every time he completed a big funny face. Julia preferred scraping up wax in wodges and sticking it to the floorboards. When they wanted to communicate they managed it by private grunts or by wildly biffing each other; Marcus had the excuse of his deafness, but I fear it was my daughter who was the more violent.

Ma and Helena were sewing. That's always a way for women to look preoccupied and superior.

'Greetings, dear females of my family circle.' They surveyed their work at arm's length and waited for me to amuse them by grovelling. 'How pleasant to find you so chastely engaged in the duties of devoted wives.'

'Look who it is,' sniffed Ma. 'And don't call me a devoted wife!'

'Yes, I know; I'm a disgrace – sorry.'

'Guilt, Falco?' Helena was being reasonable, to make me feel worse. I tipped up her chin on one finger and kissed her lightly. She shuddered. 'Do I detect breath pastilles?'

'I am always perfumed with violets.' Not to mention recent applications of tooth powder, skin toner, hair slick and body oils. A man can live well in Rome.

'You stink like an apothecary!' commented my mother.

Helena was looking particularly fresh and tidy, a dutiful matron plying the bronze needle as she helped Ma neaten tunic hems. Whoever taught her to sew? As a senator's daughter it cannot have been in her regular training. She probably asked Ma to give her a rapid lesson this morning just to make me feel bad.

Her eyes danced slightly with mockery as I inspected her. Neatly pinned gown in demure pale blue; particularly modest brooches holding together the sleeves; only a hint of gold neck chain; no finger rings, except for the silver band I once gave her as a love token. Hair in a simple bundle, with a plain republican centre parting.

'I see you're acting the injured party.'

'I don't know what you mean, Falco.'

She always knew exactly what I had in mind.

'I hope we're not quarrelling.'

'We never quarrel,' Helena said, sounding as if she meant it too.

We did, of course. Rampaging over nothing was how we acted out the daily domestic round. We both tussled for ascendancy. We both enjoyed surrendering too.

I explained quietly all that had occurred last night at the patrol-house, and was allowed to retrieve my usual status as an unsatisfactory stop-out who was probably hiding a secret life. 'Back to normal then.'

'Romancing again,' said Helena, throwing her eyes up.

Then I said I was going out to interview a suspect in the Chrysippus case. And since Julia seemed perfectly happy feeding wax to Marcus Baebius, Helena said she would leave the baby for a while and come with me. Obviously, I could not object.

Outside my mother's apartment Helena penned me in a corner of the stairwell and subjected me to a body search. I stood still and patiently let it happen. She examined each arm, scanned my legs, pulled up parts of my tunic, turned me round, twisted my head each way, and looked behind my ears.

'Caught anything with lots of legs?'

'I'm sniffing you over like Nux does.' Nux in fact was looking at her own tail in a bored manner.

'I told you where I've been.'

'And I'm making sure,' Helena said.

She touched various bruises one by one, as if counting them up. No army doctor could have been more thorough. Eventually I passed the fitness test. Then she put her arms round me and held me close. I hugged her back like a good boy, meanwhile seeing how much of the smooth republican bun I could demolish before she sensed what I was playing at and felt the hairpins being pulled out.

Good relations re-established, we set off together to find Urbanus Trypho, the playwright Chrysippus had supported, that sneak who thought he could lie low and avoid being interviewed.

XXX

Outside the apartment where I had failed to find the playwright last time, a woman was on her knees, washing the common areas. She had her back to us, and since she was being thorough, she had tucked her skirts through her legs and into her girdle – thus giving me a startling view of rump and bare legs.

Helena coughed. I looked away. Helena asked the woman if Urbanus was in, so she stood up, freeing her garments unashamedly, and took us indoors. Apparently, she lived with him.

'Anna,' she said when I asked her name.

'Like Queen Dido's sister!' I suggested, trying to interject a literary note. She gave me a level stare that I did not quite like.

Urbanus was an improvement on his colleagues. I could see that he was reasonable, sociable, not too colourful, but unlike most of the others, vividly alive. He looked like a man you could have a drink with, though not one who would annoy you by returning for a party every day.

He was writing – or at least revising a manuscript. Well, that was a new development in the unproductive Chrysippus group. When we came in, he looked up, not annoyed but intensely curious. Anna went across and cleared the scroll away protectively.

He could have been any age in the prime of life. He had an oval face with a balding forehead, and deeply intelligent eyes. The eyes watched everyone and everything.

'I'm Falco, checking witnesses in the Aurelius Chrysippus death. This is Helena Justina.'

'What do you do?' he asked her instantly.

'I check on Falco.' Her easy answer intrigued him.

'Married?'

'We call it that.'

She sat down with us. Anna, the wife, might have done the same but she had to vanish into another room whence came the cries of squalling children. It sounded like very young twins, at least, and probably another one.

'You manage to work like this?' I grinned at Urbanus. 'I thought poets ran away from domesticity to the city.'

'A dramatist needs a family life. The big plots always feature interesting families.' Fighting and breaking up, I thought, but refrained from saying it.

'Maybe you should have married a girl at home and left her there,' suggested Helena, with the merest hint of criticising males. He smiled, wide-eyed, like a man who had just been given the idea.

'And home is where?' I put to him, though Euschemon had told me.

'Britain, originally.' I raised my eyebrows, as he would expect, and he snapped in, 'Not all the good provincial writers come here from Spain.'

'I know Britain somewhat,' I answered, avoiding the natural urge to shudder. 'I can see why you left! Where are you from?'

'The centre. Nowhere any Roman has heard of.' He was right. Most Romans only know the Britons are painted blue and that they harvest good oysters on the southern coast (oysters which can be not quite so good after a long trip to Rome in a brine barrel).

'I might know it.'

'A forested place, with no Roman name.'

'So what's the local tribe? The Catuvellauni?' I was being stupid. I should not have asked.

'Further west. A nook between the Dobunni, the Cornovii, and the Corieltauvi.'

I fell silent. I knew where that was.

That central area of Britain had no desirable mineral mines to attract us, or none that we had yet discovered. But in the Great Rebellion it was somewhere not far north of Urbanus' home forest that Queen Boudicca and her burning, killing hordes were finally stopped.

'That's where the frontier runs,' I commented, trying not to sound as if I regarded it as a wild area. Trying, too, not to mention the great cross-country highway up which the rebels had streamed on their savage spree.

'Good pasture,' said Urbanus briefly. 'How do you know Britain, Falco?'

'The army.'

'There in the troubles?'

'Yes.'

'What legion?' It was the polite thing to ask. I could hardly object.

'A sensitive subject.'

'Oh the Second!' he responded instantly. I wondered if he had been hoping to get in a dig.

The Second Augusta had disgraced themselves by not taking the field in the Rebellion; it was old news, but still rankled with those of us who had suffered the ignominy imposed on us by inept officers.

Helena broke in, taking the heat off me. 'You follow politics, Urbanus?'

'Vital to my craft,' he said; he had the air of a jobbing professional who would roll up his sleeves and tackle any dirt, with the same gusto as his wife cleaned their hallway.

I took back the initiative: 'Urbanus Trypho is the name of the hour. I hardly expected such a successful playwright to let his wife scrub floors.'

'Our landlord is not lavish with services,' said Urbanus. 'We live frugally.'

'Some of your scriptorium comrades are really struggling to keep alive. I was talking yesterday to Constrictus . . .' I watched for a reaction, but he seemed indifferent to his colleagues' affairs. 'He reckons a poet needs to save up his cash so one day he can give it all up, return to his home province and enjoy his fame in retirement.'

'Sounds good.'

'Oh really! So after the excitement of Rome, you are aiming to go back to some valley among the Cornovii and live in a round hut with a few cows?'

'It will be a very large hut, and I shall own a great many cows.' The man was serious.

Admiring his candour, Helena said, 'Excuse me for asking but I too know Britain; I have relatives in diplomatic posts and I have been there. It is a relatively new province. Every governor aims to introduce Roman society and education but I was told that the tribes view all things Roman with suspicion. So how did you manage to reach Rome and become a well-known dramatist?'

Urbanus smiled. 'The wild warriors on the fringes probably believe they will lose their souls if they wash in a bathhouse. Others accept the gifts of the Empire. Since becoming Roman was inevitable, I grabbed it; my family had means, luckily. The poor are poor wherever they are born; the well-to-do, whoever they are, can choose their stamping ground. I was a lad who could have turned awkward in adolescence; instead, I saw where the good life lay. I went hotfoot for civilisation, all the way south through Gaul. I learned Latin – though Greek might have been more useful as my leaning was to drama; I joined a theatre group, came to Rome, and when I understood how plays work, I wrote them myself.'

'Self-taught?'

'I had a good acting apprenticeship.'

'But your gift for words is natural?'

'Probably,' he agreed, though modestly.

'The trick in life is to see what your gifts are,' Helena commented. 'I hope it is not rude to say this, but your background was very different. You had to learn a completely new culture. Even now you would, say, find it difficult to write a play about your homeland.'

'Intriguing thought! But it could be done,' Urbanus told her genially. 'What a joke, to dress up a set of pastoral Greeks, modernise an old theme, and say they are prancing in a British forest!'

Helena laughed, flattering him for his daring. He took it like a spoonful of Attic honey from a dripping cone. He liked women. Well, that always gives an author twice the audience. 'So you write plays of all types?' she asked.

'Tragical, comical, romantic adventure, mystical, historical.'

'Versatile! And you must really have studied the world.'

He laughed. 'Few writers bother.' Then he laughed again. 'They will never own as many cows as me.'

'Do you write for the money or the fame?' I enquired.

'Is either worth having alone?' He paused, and did not answer the question. He must have the money already, yet we knew there was public muttering about his reputation.

'So,' I put in slyly, 'what did Chrysippus have to say to you the day he died?'

Urbanus stilled. 'Nothing I wanted to hear.'

'I have to ask.'

'I realise.'

'Was your conversation amicable?'

'We had no conversation.'

'Why not?'

'I did not go.'

'You are on my list!'

'So what? I had been told that the man wanted to see me; I had no reason to see him. I stayed away.'

I consulted my notes. 'This is a list of visitors, not just people who had been invited.'

Urbanus did not blink. 'Then it is a mistake.'

I drew a long breath. 'Who can vouch for what you say?'

'Anna, my wife.'

As if responding to a cue she appeared again, nursing a baby. I wondered if she had been listening. 'Wives cannot appear in a Roman law court,' I reminded them.

Urbanus shrugged, with wide-open hands. He glanced at his wife. Her face was expressionless. 'Who wants to prosecute me?' he murmured.

'I do, if I think you are guilty. Wives don't make good alibis.'

'I thought that was all wives were for,' muttered Helena, from her stool. Urbanus and I gazed at her and allowed the jest. Anna was nuzzling her child. A woman who was used to sitting quietly and listening to what went on around her, one perhaps who could be so unobtrusive you forgot she was there . . .

'I had no reason to meet Chrysippus,' the playwright reiterated. 'He is – was – a bastard to work for. Plays do not sell well, not modern plays anyway; the Classics are always desired reading. But I manage to be marketable, unlike most of the sad mongrels Chrysippus supported. As a result, I found a new scriptorium to take my work.'

'So *you* were dumping *him*? Were you on contract?'

He humphed. 'His mistake! He had not allowed it. I did think – that is, Anna thought – he might be seeking to tie me in. That was another reason to keep out of his way.'

'And would it have been a reason to kill him?'

'No! I had nothing to gain by that and everything to lose. I earn ticket money, remember. He was no longer important to me. I deal separately with the aediles or private producers when my work is performed. When I was younger, royalties on scrolls were make or break, but now they are just incidentals. And my new scriptorium is one with a Forum outlet – much better.'

'Did Chrysippus know?'

'I doubt it.'

I wondered what happened to the heaped chests of box office money, after the family paid the bills for their frugal life. 'Do you bank with him?'

Urbanus threw back his head and roared. 'You must be joking, Falco!'

'All bankers screw their clients,' I reminded him.

'Yes, but he made enough from my plays. I saw no reason to be screwed by the same man twice over.'

While I sat thinking, Helena contributed another question: 'Falco is looking at motives, of course. You seem more fortunate than the others. Even so, there are jealous murmurs against you, Urbanus.'

'And what would those be?' If he knew, he was not showing it.

Helena looked him in the eye. 'You are suspected of not writing your plays yourself.'

It was Anna, the wife, who growled angrily at that.

Urbanus leaned back. There was no visible annoyance; he must have heard this accusation before. 'People are strange – luckily for playwrights, or we would have no inspiration.' He glanced at his wife; this time she ventured a pale half-smile. 'The charge is of the worst kind – possible to prove, if true, yet if *un*true, quite impossible to refute.'

'A matter of faith,' I said.

Urbanus showed a flash of anger now. 'Why are mad ideas taken so seriously? Oh of course! Certain types will never accept that literate and humane writing with inventive language and depth of emotion can come from the provinces – let alone from the middle of Britain.'

'You're not in the secret society. "*Oh only an educated Roman could produce this*" . . .'

'No; we are not supposed to have anything to say, or to be capable of expressing it . . . Who do they say writes for me?' he roared scornfully.

'Various improbable suggestions,' Helena said. Maybe *Scrutator* had told her; maybe she had pursued the gossip herself. 'Not all of them even alive.'

'So who am *I* – this man before you – then supposed to be?'

'The lucky dog who counts in the ticket money,' I grinned. 'While the mighty authors you are "impersonating" let you spend their royalties.'

'Well, they are missing all the fun,' Urbanus responded dryly, suddenly able to let the subject rest.

'Let's get back to my problem. It could be argued,' I put to him quietly, 'that this is a malicious rumour, which *Chrysippus* began spreading because he knew he was losing you. Say you were so affronted by the rumour you went to his house to remonstrate, then the two of you argued and you lost your cool.'

'Far too drastic. I am a working author,' the playwright protested in a mild way. 'I have nothing to prove and I would not throw away my position. And as for literary feuds – Falco, I don't have the time.'

I grinned and decided to try a literary approach: 'Help us, Urbanus. If you were writing about the death of Chrysippus, what would you say had happened? Was his money a motive? Was it sex? Is a frustrated author behind it, or a jealous woman, or the son perhaps?'

'Sons never rise to action.' Urbanus smiled. 'They live with the anger for too long.' From personal experience, I agreed with him. 'Sons brood, and fester, and permanently tolerate their indignities. Of course, *daughters* can be furies!'

Neither woman present took him up on that. His wife, Anna, had not contributed to the discussion, but Urbanus now asked her the question: whom would she accuse?

'I would have to think about it,' Anna said cautiously and with some interest. Some people say that as a put-off; she sounded as if she meant she really would mull it over. 'Of course,' she put to me, with a teasing glint, '*I* may have killed Chrysippus, for my husband's sake.' Before I could ask if she did it, she added crisply, 'However, I am too busy with my young children, as you see.'

I was satisfied that Urbanus would have been stupid to kill Chrysippus. He was in the clear, but he interested me. The conversation drifted into more general matters. I confessed to having experience as a working playwright in a theatre troupe myself. We talked about our travels. I even asked advice on *The Spook Who Spoke*, my best effort at drama. From my description, Urbanus thought this brilliant farce ought to be turned into a tragedy. That was rubbish; perhaps he was not such an incisive master of theatre after all.

While we chatted, Anna was still holding the small baby on her shoulder, smoothing its gown over its back when it grew fractious. Both Helena and I noticed that she had inky fingers. Helena told me afterwards that she thought it might be significant. 'Have the rumour-mongers picked up something genuine? Is it Anna who has the way with words?'

Nice thought. You could make a play about a woman taking on a man's identity. If it turned out to be a woman who actually wrote Urbanus' plays, now that really would be a piece of theatre!

XXXI

L AST NIGHT Petro and I had summoned Lucrio to an interview today. Although Petro had given him an hour at which to arrive, we were prepared for him not to show, or at least to turn up late. To our surprise, he was there.

We all became extremely friendly by the light of day. We had all had time to adjust our positions.

Petro and I had, in the Roman way, appropriated the only chairs as the persons in authority. Lucrio did not care. He walked about and calmly waited to be put through the grinding-mill. He was constantly masticating nuts of some sort; he chewed with his mouth open.

He was a definite type. I could imagine him in his younger days, turning the contractual tricks – cutting corners and boasting about deals with his brash friends, all belt buckles and big-bossed cloak brooches. Now he was maturing; changing from loud to subtle; from risky to absolutely dangerous; from a mere chancer to a much smoother operator, able to guide clients into lifetimes of debt.

Before I came to the patrol-house, I had been to see Nothokleptes. He had given me some interesting information about Lucrio's past. Petronius started the interview by agreeing that, since the tunic-thief had returned to jail of his own accord after he thought about the consequences, he would now release Lucrio's slaves (sending them home without letting Lucrio talk to them). Unbeknown to him, they had been well grilled. Fusculus had volunteered to come in on the day shift; after they had been starved all morning he took them bread and unwatered wine, and 'made friends' with the six of them. That had been productive too.

'Your documents have all been returned to you, Lucrio, so that's in order,' said Petro, taking charge, while I just wrote notes in an ominous manner. 'I would like to discuss the general situation and management of the Aurelian Bank. Chrysippus set it up, with the aid of his first wife, Lysa. Did he come from a financial background originally?'

'Old Athens family,' Lucrio asserted proudly. 'He was in shipping insurance; most of that business is conducted in Greece and the East, but he could see there was a gap in the market so he and Lysa moved here.'

'He specialised in loans?'

'Cargo loans mostly.'

'That's risky?'

'Yes and no. You have to exercise your judgement – is the ship sound? Is the captain competent? Is the cargo likely to fetch a profit and will there be another available for it to carry home? And then –' He paused.

Petronius, in his quiet way, was on top of the subject: 'You make a loan to a trader to cover the cost of a voyage. Insurance. If a ship founders, there is no obligation on the trader to repay the loan. You cover the loss. And if that ship returns home safely, the banker is repaid – plus an enormous profit.'

'Well, not enormous,' Lucrio demurred. He would.

'Because of the risk of miscarriage in a storm, shipping lenders are exempt from normal rules on maximum interest?' Petro went on.

'Only fair,' said Lucrio. 'We end up paying for all the voyages that come to grief.'

'Not all of them, I think. You protect yourselves as much as possible.'

'Where we can, legate.'

'Tribune,' Petro corrected him briefly, assuming Rubella's title without a blush.

'Sorry. Just a form of words.'

My friend Lucius Petronius inclined his head loftily. I hid a grin. 'This protection of yours,' he continued, worrying away, 'it can take the form of limiting the period of the loan?'

'Routine condition, tribune.'

'So a journey you are insuring must be completed within a specified number of days?'

'During good sailing weather. There will normally be a date for completion of the voyage written into the contract.'

'So if the ship sinks, you as lender do pay the costs – but only provided the journey has been undertaken in the right period? But if the ship delays sailing until after the loan's expiry date, and *then* it sinks in the drink – who is liable?'

'Not us!' exclaimed the freedman.

'You, of course, like that,' Petronius returned, rather coolly. 'But

the owner does not. He has lost his ship and its cargo – and he still has
to repay your loan.'

'He loses twice over. But that's his fault.'

'Well, his captain's.'

'Right – for dilly-dallying. These are the rules of the sea, tribune.
It's traditional. Was there some reason,' enquired Lucrio, very
politely, 'why you were interested in this aspect?'

Petronius folded his arms and leaned forwards on them. I knew this
action. He was about to bring out the gossip we had acquired. 'You
have a client at the bank called Pisarchus?'

Lucrio managed to retain his affable, unflustered dodger's attitude.
'Of course this is confidential – but I believe we do.'

'Big debtor?'

'Not too clever.'

'He lost two different ships, both sailing out of time, last winter?'

'A foolish man. Now he needs to readjust his investments rather
sharply.'

'Does he have anything left to invest, though?' asked Petronius.

'Well, you could have a point there!' chortled Lucrio, treating the
reference to big debts as a big joke.

Petro remained cool. 'Shippers are notorious for having no personal
capital. A little mouse has been squeaking to me that Pisarchus is in
severe distress over his losses, that he may not be able to repay what
he owes, and that Chrysippus and he had a quarrel.'

'My, my!' marvelled Lucrio. 'Somebody must have been pulling
really hard on this little mouse's tail. I hope no naughty members of
the vigiles have been asking questions of my slaves without clearing it
with me?'

That was when I moved in and took over. 'No, we learned about
Pisarchus from a private source.' Nothokleptes. 'It is freely available
gossip in the Janus Medius.' This must have been the first time in
history Nothokleptes had given me something for nothing. 'I hear the
odds there are on Pisarchus as the killer, in fact. My interest centres on
him too. I'm wondering if he was the man with the sour mood I myself
saw at the scriptorium, the very morning Chrysippus was killed.'

Lucrio shook his head, sorrowing. 'I'm grieved to hear that, Falco.
Pisarchus is one of our oldest clients. His family has dealt with the
Chrysippus *trapeza* for generations back in Greece.'

I flashed a smile. 'Don't fret. Maybe it's not him. Still, it has given
us a clear picture of how your *trapeza* operates.'

'Nothing illegal.'

'Nothing soft, either!'

'We have to protect our investors.'

'Oh I'm sure you do.'

I let Petronius resume the questioning. 'Let's clear up one tricky item, Lucrio . . .' Now he would definitely try out the stuff that Fusculus had squeezed from the slaves. 'I have a tip that you and Chrysippus went through a crisis once?' Lucrio looked annoyed. Petronius spelled it out: 'You have been the bank's freedman-agent for a number of years. Before that, while you were still in service as a young slave – this must have been before you reached the age of thirty, when you could be freed – you were given a portfolio to manage on your master's behalf. It was the usual situation: you were allowed to run the fund and to keep any profits, but the capital – what is called the *peculium* – still belonged to your master and had to be returned to him in due course. Now tell me – was there not a problem when you were first manumitted from slavery, and had to hand back the *peculium* and render an account of your management?'

Lucrio had stopped casually pacing the room, though he continued chewing nuts. 'It was a misunderstanding. There were queries on the figures; I was able to answer all of them.'

'What sort of queries?' insisted Petronius.

'Oh – whether I had mixed up the *peculium* float.'

'Mixed it with your own money? Had you?'

'Not intentionally. I was a lad, a bit slapdash – you know how it is. We sorted it out. Chrysippus was never bothered. It was others who made much of it – jealous, probably.'

'Yes, I assume Chrysippus ended up happy, because he went on to let you – in effect – run the bank.'

'Yes.'

'Maybe he even thought that a slight tendency to sharp practice was just what he wanted in a manager?'

'Exactly,' said Lucrio, showing us a flash of teeth.

Petronius Longus glanced through his set of note-tablets calmly. 'Well, that seems to be everything covered.' Lucrio let himself relax. Not that it was easy to tell, because he had been strikingly at ease all along. He made a move towards the door. 'Any queries on your side, Falco?' Petro asked.

'Please.' Petro sat back and I started the whole round from my viewpoint. Swapping control once Lucrio thought it was all over might unnerve him. Probably not, but it was worth a try.

'A couple of logistical questions, Lucrio: where were you at noon two days ago when Chrysippus was killed?'

'Forum. Lunching with a group of clients. I can give you their names.'

Not much point; either it was true, or by now the alibis would have been primed to lie for him. 'Were your relations with Chrysippus good? Any problems at the bank?'

'No fear. It was making money. That kept the boss happy.'

'Know any unhappy clients who bore a grudge?'

'No.'

'Apart from Pisarchus,' I corrected. 'Were there any other disappointed creditors?'

'Not in the same league.'

'Another debtor I'm looking at is one of the scriptorium authors –'

Lucrio freely supplied the name: 'Avienus.'

'That's right; the historian. He has a large loan out with the bank, I understand. Does it have an end date?'

'It did.'

'Already past?'

'Afraid so.'

'He has difficulties finding the money?'

'So he says.'

'Chrysippus was taking a hard line?'

'No, I dealt with it, in the normal way.'

'Avienus was being tricky?'

Lucrio shrugged. 'He was always appealing to Chrysippus as one of his writers, but I don't buy that. Whining and performing, the way people do. The first time, it wrings your heart.' *Lucrio*, affected by debtors' pleas? 'After that you take no notice; genuine hardship cases don't ever complain.'

'Did Avienus have any remedy?'

'Write his stuff, and deposit the scrolls so he got paid his fee and clear the debt,' sneered the freedman. He did not sound like a reading man. Then he added, 'Or he could do the usual.'

'What's that?'

'Ask another lender to buy up his loan.'

I blinked. 'How does that work?'

'The date was up. We called in the debt,' explained Lucrio, patiently. 'Someone else could advance Avienus the money to pay us.'

I followed him: 'A loan to pay off a loan? The new one covering the sum of your loan, plus the interest he owed to you, plus the new lender's profit? Jupiter!' Compound interest was illegal in Rome – but this seemed a neat way to avoid that. Bankers would support each other in this unpleasant trade. 'Spiralling down into poverty – and even slavery, perhaps?'

Lucrio showed no remorse. 'Buys him time, Falco. If Avienus ever clambers off his backside and earns something, he could cover the debt.'

Against my inclinations, I could see Lucrio's point of view. Some people with crippling debts do bestir themselves and work until they drop. 'What security has Avienus given for the original loan?'

'I would have to look that up.'

'I want you to do so, and to let me know, please. Don't tell Avienus that I'm asking. He may be your commercial client but he could also be your patron's killer.'

'I'll remember.'

'What will happen about the debt now Chrysippus is dead?'

'Oh, nothing changes. Avienus must repay the bank.'

'You're hot in pursuit, are you?'

Lucrio grinned. It was more of a grimace – not at all humorous.

Time for another shift. Petronius leaned towards me. 'Was there a query you mentioned about the will, Falco?'

'That's right.' Lucrio, I noticed, suddenly had the fixed air of a man who had been waiting for this. 'Lucrio, has the will been opened yet?' He nodded. 'Who are the main beneficiaries? Is it right that Vibia Merulla, as the current wife, was only left the scriptorium?'

'So she was.'

'And is it really worth little?'

'Better than a fish-stall at Ostia – but not much better.'

'That seems hard.'

'Her family got her dowry back.'

'Oh lovely! Who was left the bank?'

'Lysa' – he coloured very faintly – 'and myself.'

'Oh that's touching! The ex-wife who helped found the business and a loyal ex-slave.'

'A custom of our country,' Lucrio said, like a tired man who knew he would have to explain this many times to many different acquaintances. 'Greek banks have throughout history been passed jointly to Greek bankers' wives and their regular agents.'

'What,' I sneered, 'do Greek bankers' children think of that?'

'They know it has been done throughout Greek history,' Lucrio said.

'And little Greek boys are taught a love of history!' We all laughed. 'Vibia Merulla appears to have lost out heavily,' I went on. 'A Greek ex-wife takes precedence over a new Roman one? Is that traditional too?'

'Sounds good to me,' said Lucrio shamelessly. 'Lysa built the business up.'

'But in this case, the Greek banker has an only son, who has become thoroughly Romanised. Diomedes must know that in Rome, we do things differently. Here you, of course, would still have a claim to be rewarded for loyal service. Lysa would be an irrelevance, after Chrysippus remarried; Vibia would acquire a claim. And Diomedes would expect his father to acknowledge *his* importance in the family. Where does this old Greek custom leave Diomedes as a new Roman, Lucrio?'

'Whimpering!' the freedman acknowledged callously. 'Oh, it's not a disaster! He has been given a few sesterces to see him through life. It's more than most sons can expect, especially bone-idle spendthrifts with airy ideas who do nothing but cause trouble.'

'You don't sound like a follower of dear Diomedes?'

'You have met him, I believe,' Lucrio murmured – as if that answered everything.

'Well, his mother will be a grand heiress. One day, perhaps, he will be Lysa's heir?'

'Possibly.' There was a slight pause. I sensed reluctance, but the freedman despised Diomedes so strongly that he was prepared to be indiscreet for once: 'Lysa's new husband may have something to say about that,' said Lucrio.

XXXII

My next visit to Lysa, the ex-wife and lucky heiress, caught her off guard. Not expecting me, she made the mistake of being in.

Now I had gained admittance, I saw that as places go it was a desirable residence. We were sitting in a salon that was cool in the July heatwave, though lit expertly from high windows above. A series of patterned rugs was spread on the marble floor. Lush curtains tapestried the walls. Our seating was bronze-framed, with substantial padding. In a corner, on a shelf, stood a lavish wine-warmer, the kind that burns charcoal in a large chamber with a fuel store underneath, out of use at present, due to the weather no doubt. Perfect, unmottled fruit gleamed in translucent glass bowls.

'Not plying your loom like a dutiful housewife?'

It was a joke. Lysa had been reading over columns of figures while a slave who was clearly accustomed to the task took dictated notes. As I entered, I had heard the ex-wife composing messages about the bank's clients in a confident voice. She was better-spoken than Vibia, even though I guessed Lysa had humbler origins.

'Is your son around?'

'No.'

She was probably lying but I had no excuse to search the place.

'How is he bearing up to his father's loss?'

'Grief-stricken, poor boy,' sighed his mother, still lying I reckoned. 'But he tries to be brave.'

'Belonging to wealthy parents must help him cope.'

'You are a horrible cynic, Falco. Diomedes is a very sensitive soul.'

'What are his talents? What are you planning to do with him?'

'I am trying to help him decide what he wants to be in life. Once he has readjusted to his father's death, I believe he will review his ambitions. Marry soon. Settle down to building up a portfolio of property. Make something of himself in the community.'

'Public life?' I raised my eyebrows.

'Chrysippus dearly wanted him to advance in society.'

'Many a banker's descendant has done that,' I conceded. 'Our noble Emperor, for one.' Finance was a smart entrance-ticket. The descendants hit Rome well provided with money, if nothing else; all they had to acquire was social respectability. The Flavian family did that by astute marriages, as I recalled. Then civil and military positions, right up to the highest, jumped into their welcoming arms.

'Who is Diomedes marrying?'

'We have yet to decide on a suitable young woman. But I am in discussion currently with a good family.'

'One nuptial step at a time, eh?' I scoffed offensively.

Lysa knew I had reached the real subject of the interview. Already she was looking uncomfortable – though that was probably because I had not yet told her what my errand was.

'I've just been given some startling information, Lysa.'

'Really?' While seeming indifferent, she abandoned the accounts and signalled to her scribe to leave the room. No maid had appeared to chaperone her. She was a tough woman, whom I distrusted; I would have welcomed the presence of a chaperone – to protect me.

'I hear you have inherited half the *trapeza*.' Lysa inclined her head. 'Lucky woman! Did you know about your place in the will, when we discussed it previously?'

'The bequest had always been intended.'

'But you modestly kept silent?'

'There could always have been,' she said a little archly, 'some last-minute change of plan.' It would be a brave testator who would change his will after Lysa believed she was his main legatee.

'With the new wife angling to improve her own position?' I hinted. 'Had Chrysippus ever suggested that he might change the inheritance?'

'No.'

'And after the divorce, you continued to manage the affairs of the *trapeza*?'

'Women are not permitted to engage in banking,' she corrected me.

'Oh, I don't believe that ever inhibited you. Are you saying that Lucrio runs everything? Presumably, he does what you tell him?'

'No one person has ever made all the decisions. Chrysippus and I – and Lucrio too – were a joint board of management.'

'Oh, Chrysippus did come into it?'

She looked surprised. 'It was his business.'

'But you were the force running it – as you still are. And now it's in the joint hands of you and Lucrio – but I am told you are about to remarry!'

'Yes, I shall probably do that,' Lysa responded, unmoved by my fierce approach. 'Who told you?'

'Lucrio.'

I wondered if she was annoyed with the freedman, but apparently not. 'Did he name the man I am marrying?'

'Unfortunately he forgot to mention that.' He had told me coyly that I should ask her to provide the details. 'So, who is this lucky bridegroom, Lysa? Someone you have known for a long while?'

'You could say so.'

'A lover?'

'Certainly not!' That made her furious. Informers are used to it. Whatever she claimed, I would look into whether she had had an existing affair with the new husband.

'Own up. Don't you realise this places you at the top of my suspects list?'

'Why should it?'

'You and your paramour had a prize incentive to kill Chrysippus – so you could acquire the bank.'

The woman laughed gently. 'No need, Falco. I was always going to inherit the bank anyway.'

'Your new boyfriend may have wanted more direct ownership – and he may have been impatient, too.'

'You do not know what you are talking about.'

'Tell me then.'

Lysa spoke frostily. 'It has been the custom for centuries when Greek banks are inherited, to leave them jointly to the owner's widow and his trusted agent.' That was what Lucrio had told me. He had held back delicately, however, on the next peculiar Athenian joke: 'To protect the business, it is also the custom that the two heirs will subsequently join forces.' Then Lysa said, as if it were nothing extraordinary, 'I shall be marrying Lucrio.'

I gulped. Then, though it appeared not to be a love match, I wished the future bride every happiness. The couple's shared wealth presumably rendered formal best wishes for their future superfluous.

XXXIII

THIS WAS the dangerous stage, where the case could die on us. The problem with this one was not the usual lack of facts, but almost too many to co-ordinate.

The work had not ended, by any means. But there were no material clues, despite numerous loose threads. I prepared an interim report for Petro, summing up the dead ends:

- The scriptorium manager, the scribes, and the household slaves are all ruled out either by proven absence, confirmed sightings off the scene, or lack of bloodstains at the initial interrogation.
- We have yet to find the murderer's bloodstained clothes.
- The wife, ex-wife and son, and the bank's agent have all produced acceptable alibis; some of their stories are dubitable, but their movements are in theory accounted for at the time of death.
- The people who gained financially were on good terms with the victim, in funds beforehand, and in line to inherit anyway.
- The authors have motives:
  - Avienus, the historian, has a huge debt.
  - Turius, the idealist, has offended and insulted the victim.
  - *Scrutator*, the satirist, has rebelled at being loaned out like a slave.
  - Constrictus, the would-be love poet, is a drunk and in line to be dropped.
  - Urbanus, the dramatist, is flying the coop and is angry about rumours belittling him.
- There is, unfortunately, no hard evidence to link any of them to the crime.

'Any big holes?' Petro asked.

'Pisarchus, the shipper with the lost vessels and cargoes, quarrelled with the victim on the day he died. We have not yet managed to interview him; he is out of town.'

'At sea?'

'Inland; berthed at Praeneste. He has a villa there; that's where *Scrutator* was supposed to be sent to pluck a soothing lyre – perhaps to compensate for the shipper's financial grief.'

'Out of our jurisdiction,' groaned Petro; the vigiles only operated within Rome. Then he added slyly, 'But I may find I have a man travelling that way eventually. Or we'll nab him for questioning next time he comes to the city to beg for a new loan . . . Think he will?'

'They always do. He'll find new security somehow; how often does a long-haul ocean-trader cease trading?'

'Anything else I should know?'

'The big puzzle: one of the dead man's visitors. We were told Urbanus went there that day, but he denies it. I think I believe him. He had definitely been invited and the porter apparently counted him off, so was it somebody else? The régime is so vague and disorganised nobody knows for sure. If there was an extra caller, we don't know who.'

'Rats. Only Chrysippus could tell us, and he's in his funeral urn. That all?'

'I still think we ought to investigate customers from the bank.'

'And?'

'I don't trust the son.'

'You don't trust anyone!'

'True. What strikes you then, Petro?'

'I reckon the bank is at the heart of it.' He would. He was a cautious investor, suspicious of men who handled other people's savings. 'I'm going to call back Lucrio and lean on him. I'll say we don't ask for confidential information, but he must give us some names and addresses so we can interview clients ourselves. We can compare the list he gives us with the names we grabbed that night when we had access to his records. If he tries to hide a client from us, we know where to jump.'

'Lot of effort,' I commented.

My dear friend Lucius Petronius grinned wickedly. 'Just your sort of job!'

That was where I called in my junior, even though Petronius had refused to pay fees for him.

Aulus Camillus Aelianus, Helena's brother, was kicking his heels without a real career, so he had decided he wanted to play at being an investigator. Nobody thought he would stick with it, but I needed to be polite to Helena's family so I was lumbered with him until he opted out. He had no skills, but as a senator's son he did command a certain presence – enough to impress mercantile types, if I was lucky.

'What do I have to do? Lurk in alleys and spy on them?' He was keen – too keen. He had turned up in a spanking ochre tunic that would stand out a mile in the kind of alleys I normally used for surveillance. He was full of the boyish eagerness that only lasts about half a day.

'Knock on doors, my son. Learn to keep knocking for a week while bored slaves insist that your quarry is out. When you do meet the witnesses face to face, mention that we are too honourable to extract private information from their banker – but that we are conducting a murder enquiry, so they had better co-operate. Enquire gently about their deposits – they won't mind; they'll enjoy boasting of their silver reserves. When they are softened up, sternly ask what loans they have.'

'Anyone with a loan is a bad character?'

'If that were true the whole of Rome would be villains, especially your illustrious papa, who has his whole life in hock.'

'He can't help that! The moment a Roman has any status, he is compelled to spend.' I was glad to hear Aelianus defend Camillus Senior, who had already wasted hope and cash on him. At least the son sounded grateful.

'The same goes for these people, unless we learn of any debts that are –'

'Enormous?' Aulus demanded eagerly.

'No, no; their debts can be any size – just so long as they believe they can pay them back. What I'm searching for is somebody who felt under pressure.'

'Are you coming with me on this?' A faint hint of anxiety had finally struck him.

'No.' I gazed at him with what I hoped was an inscrutable expression. 'We are a two-man operation. We have to keep one man in reserve so he can go round later and apologise if you offend someone.'

'You love a joke, Falco.'

Who was joking? Camillus Aelianus was a twenty-five-year-old patrician who had never had to negotiate a delicate social situation in his life.

★

Aelianus went off alone, with a list of addresses. I had to provide him with a note-tablet; I told him to bring his own next time. At the last minute, he thought of asking me if this was likely to be dangerous. I said I did not know – then advised him to take up self-defence lessons at his gymnasium. Always one for wearing scowls, he grew even more sullen when I reminded him it was illegal to go armed in Rome.

'So what do I do if I'm in trouble?'

'Back off. If it becomes unavoidable, you can hit people – ideally, just before they hit you. But try to remember that any ugly characters you meet may be friends of mine.'

He was bound to wreak havoc. I was content to let him. Firstly, he thought he knew it all; making mistakes was the only way he would ever learn. And secondly, havoc always comes in useful when a case is stuck.

'I suppose if trouble arises, you will just blame me anyway, Falco?'

Helena's dear brother was brighter than I had feared.

I assigned my apprentice the straightforward clients. Unknown to him, I was out there myself nosing around the names I thought looked tricky.

We worked on the debtors and creditors for a few weeks. Meanwhile, Petronius had formally requested the responsible vigiles cohorts in the Forum environs to look out for Pisarchus. The month changed. That August was stifling. I had to explain to Aelianus that only honest men and career criminals stopped for holidays. In our twilight world, we kept going. At best, people would be so surprised to see us, we might catch them off guard. At worst, like the shipper Pisarchus, they would be off and unobtainable at some fern-shaded retreat.

'I don't mind a trip to Praeneste,' my junior offered hopefully. I ignored him. He was too new to be told that the jaunts were mine, while the learner minded the shop. You have to ensure that a young person, faced with life's inequalities, does not lose heart.

We had found nothing. We had to admit we had no real idea what to look for. I marked up Praeneste on a road map in a desultory way, none too keen to undertake the journey in hot weather. I knew Petro would be unable to find the cost of transport, since it lay outside his jurisdiction. Rubella would love to jump on such a breach of the rules.

Anyway, if I had to go outside the city, I would from choice be at Tibur, where I possessed a farm and needed to check on its new tenant. No chance! Informers are not supposed to have a private life.

'Is this a waste of time, Falco?'

'Most of this job is a waste of time, Aulus.'

'Why do we bother then?'

'For the tiny scrap of information that solves everything.' If and when we found it, we were unlikely even to recognise what it was.

Almost collapsing in the heat and thoroughly depressed, we were still waiting to discover any helpful clue when my dog started having her pups.

Nux had been making strange nests for a while. She had chosen me as a master; it was her mistake, but as with women, that made me feel responsible. I had been expecting the birth for some days, but we could not be sure which of her horrible suitors had fathered the pups – or when it occurred.

As soon as Helena sent me word that things were happening, I rushed back home, meeting my young nephew Marius on the stairs. After some comment from Helena that I was better at attending the dog's labour than I had been about the birth of my own daughter, Marius and I crouched alongside, while Nux struggled to deliver. She was having problems.

'Uncle Marcus, it is hopeless!' Marius was frantic. So was I, though I could not show it. He was nine; I was thirty-three. Besides, Helena was listening. 'Stuff this for a game of soldiers!' he roared. Marius had been working at Pa's warehouse. His language had deteriorated sadly. 'There's a friend of my father's who keeps dogs; I'm going to get him.'

So Marius hared off and returned with a bemused horse-vet from the Greens. This man was a typical friend of Famia's – vague, dozy and sinister. He did have more application than my departed brother-in-law; he grunted and muttered, then while Marius and I clung together unable to watch, he eventually helped Nux to whelp a single, absolutely enormous pup.

'It's a dog.'

'A boy – he's mine!' screamed Marius determinedly. The horse-vet and I surreptitiously worked on the creature, trying not to let Marius realise the imminent tragedy: the puppy was lifeless. Marius was told to look after Nux. The animal doctor sighed. My heart sank. I presumed he meant it was all over.

He faced up to the limp wet puppy, holding it between both hands, one dirty thumb propping up its flopping head and two fingers opening its pale mouth. To our astonishment, he blew air from his own lungs into it. After a moment of passive resistance, the pup could no longer bear the reek of garlic on his breath. It choked and glugged and tried to escape. It was handed to my nephew who was told to wrap it up and rub it vigorously to make it breathe by itself. I gave the vet the price of several drinks, mainly for preventing heartache for Marius; he sloped off, then when the pup had warmed up, we placed it beside Nux.

At first, she just wagged her tail at us. Noticing the bedraggled creature, she sniffed it, wearing the bemused look she had whenever Helena mentioned that Nux had let out a fart. Then her offspring moved; Nux pawed it – and decided she might as well clean it and allow it to take over her life.

'She knows she's his mother.' I felt thrilled. 'Look, he's starting to suckle. Helena, come and look at this!'

Marius tugged at my tunic. 'Come away, Uncle Marcus. We have to leave her quiet now. She must not be disturbed, or she might reject him. There must be no parade of nosy sightseers, and I think your baby had best stay in another room.' Marius, an intellectual at heart, had gone into this. I knew Helena had lent him a compendium of animal husbandry. Flushed with knowledge and ownership, he refused to entrust his precious pet to amateurs. 'I'll feed Nux for you when it is needed. You two,' he told Helena and me balefully, 'are rather too excitable, if you don't mind my saying so. By the way, Nuxie seems to have given you a problem . . .'

How right he was. Despite all my efforts to find her an attractive basket in a dark nook where she could have her grotesquely oversized pup in privacy, Nux had chosen her own spot: on my toga, in the middle of our bed.

'Let us hope,' said Helena, fairly gently, 'you are not required at any formal dress functions in the next few days, Marcus.'

Well, at least that was unlikely; August has some advantages.

XXXIV

H ELENA AND I had to make up a bed that night on my old reading
couch. This, it has to be said, was so much of a squash for two
of us that we did start behaving like infants and were without doubt
what Marius would pompously call *too excitable*.

'Does Nux having a puppy make you want another baby of your
own?' I giggled.

'You want an invitation to do something about it?'

'Is that an offer?'

That was when Helena told me she was expecting for the second
time – and when we both grew still and a good deal quieter.

All the time Helena had been pregnant with Julia, she had been
terrified the birth would be difficult. It had been. They both nearly
died. Now neither of us was able to talk about our fears for the next
baby.

The following day Marius spent most of his time with us. Sitting
cross-legged near his puppy, anyway. The presence of Helena and me
was irrelevant to him.

I was at home, writing up records for the vigiles of the debtors
Aelianus had interviewed. As a senator's son, documentation was
beneath him; if he continued to work with me, I would have to teach
him better habits. He expected me to provide a cohort of secretaries
to make sense of his notes.

Well, I would give him advice. If he ignored it, then some day
when he was in court with a client (some client I did not care for;
there were plenty of those), a barrister would demand written
evidence and the noble Aelianus would come sadly adrift.

In the afternoon Marius disappeared, but he was back again that
evening, this time carrying a rolled blanket and his personal food-
bowl.

'Joining us as a lodger? Does your mother know?'

'I told her. The puppy has to stay with Nux for several weeks.'

'Nux and the puppy are fine, Marius. You can come and see them whenever you want. You don't need to guard them all night long.'

'Arctos.'

'Who's that?'

'I'm going to call him Arctos. The Great Bear. He doesn't want a stupid name like "Nux".'

'It sounds as if you don't trust us with little Arctos,' Helena said. 'Nux will take care of him very well, Marius.'

'Oh, this is just an excuse,' Marius replied off-handedly. Helena and I were taken aback. 'I prefer to be at your house. It is such a bore going home after a long day's heavy work in the warehouse' – I knew from Pa that Marius only did light duties, and he only turned up when it suited him. As he moaned about his labours, I could hear his late father in him, different though he and Famia were – 'only to find that man Anacrites is always there.'

'Oh yes?' I said, stiffening. 'What does "always" mean?'

'Most evenings,' Marius confirmed glumly.

'Is that all?'

'He doesn't stay the night. It has not come to "*This is your nice new father*" yet,' my nephew assured me, with the astounding self-confidence Maia's children had always possessed. For nine, he was quite a person of the world. A fatherless boy has to grow up fast, but this was frightening. 'Cloelia and I would do our best to put a stop to that.'

'I recommend you not to interfere,' I told him, man to man.

'You're right! When we tried, we had Mother snivelling. It was horrible.'

'Your mother is allowed to do what she likes, you know,' I said, biting my lip and thinking, "*Not if I have any say in it.*" (Mind you, those idiots who write treatises on a Roman's patriarchal power have evidently never tried to make a woman do anything.)

'Yes, but it will go wrong, Uncle Marcus. Then he will go away, but we shall be left with the mess he has caused.'

Helena appeared to be hiding a smile; she started to prepare dinner, leaving me to cope.

I dropped my voice conspiratorially. 'So what's the score on the dice, Marius?'

'Mother says Anacrites is her *friend*. Ugh!'

'What does she want a friend for? She has you and me taking care of her.'

'Mother says she enjoys having someone to talk to – an outsider, who does not always believe he knows what she thinks and what she wants.'

Marius and I sat side by side on a bench, thinking about women and their menfolk's responsibilities. 'Thank you for telling me all this, Marius. I shall see what I can do.'

Marius gave me a look that told me to leave it to him.

I came from a family whose members saw it as life's greatest challenge to be first to interfere in any problem. I went to see my mother first. I explained the reason for my visit, becoming nervous as I did so. She was surprisingly calm. 'Has Anacrites made a move?'

'How would I know?'

'Maybe he's biding his time.'

'You are gloating over this!'

'I would never do that,' said Ma primly.

I glared at her. My mother continued pinching together the edges of little pastry parcels. She still did it dextrously. I thought of her as an old lady, but she was probably younger than Pa, who boasted of being sixty and still able to drag barmaids to bed. Mind you, the ones who agreed to it now must be a bit on the creaky side.

My mother had always been a woman who could whop three naughty children back in line while stirring a pot of tunic dye, discussing the weather, chewing a rough fingernail and passing on gossip in a thrilling undertone. And she knew how to ignore what she did not want to hear.

'I hope that's not his dinner you are making,' I muttered. 'I hope he is not receiving his starters and entrées from my sister, then coming back for dessert from you.'

'Such nice manners,' retorted Ma, obviously meaning Anacrites. She knew mine were not worth complimenting. 'Always grateful for what you do for him.'

I bet he was.

I then forced myself to visit Maia. I was dreading it.

He was there. Just as Marius had said. They were on her sun terrace, talking. I heard their low voices as I let myself in with a spare latch-lifter I had for emergencies. Anacrites was sitting in a wicker chair, leaning his head back in the last rays of sunlight that day. Maia was even more relaxed, with her legs stretched out on cushions and her sandals off.

He made no attempt to explain himself, though he soon got up to leave. I had destroyed one tryst anyway. Maia simply inclined her head and let him see himself out. They parted formally. I was not obliged to witness anything embarrassing. I could not even tell whether things had reached that stage. Were they alone, would he even have kissed her on the cheek as a goodbye?

I tried to carry on as if the Chief Spy had never been there. 'I just came to say we have acquired young Marius. He is concerned about his pup.'

Maia regarded me with a look that reminded me a little too closely of Ma. 'That is very good of you,' she commented, a stereotype remark.

'It's no trouble.'

She was waiting for me to tackle her about Anacrites. I was waiting for her to explain herself: no luck. When Maia stopped being unpredictable, she was just plain awkward.

'I'm afraid the new dog may grow rather large . . .' It would be larger than its mother before long. 'Marius is besotted. He inherits his love of animals from his father, no doubt. He's missing Famia. This might comfort him, you know –'

'I have agreed he can have the puppy,' Maia replied steadily. Of course we were not quarrelling. But I knew my sister well enough to sense her irritation simmering.

I had sat down briefly, not in the same chair that had been occupied by Anacrites. Now I rose. 'Marius is still afraid you may not agree.'

Maia was still very quiet. 'I'll come and have a look at it and tell him.'

'Right. It's cute; they always are . . . How are things with Pa?'

On neutral ground, she brightened up slightly. 'I'm getting the hang of what needs doing. Actually, I quite like the work. He hates telling me anything, but I'm interested in the antiques.'

'Ha! You'll be running the whole business soon.'

'We'll see.'

When I rose to go, Maia stayed where she was, peacefully reclining, just as she had with Anacrites. A neat, compact woman with a crown of natural curls and an equally natural stubbornness. Left to her own devices for so long while Famia hit the flagons, in her own home she had developed a powerful independent attitude. Nobody told Maia what to do. She had grown too used to deciding for herself.

Tonight, there was also a stillness about her that I found ominous. But as her male head of household, I made sure I did stoop over her and kiss her goodbye. She let me — though like most of my female relatives when treated to unaccustomed formality, she hardly appeared to notice it.

XXXV

I N THE morning, just after breakfast, I was whistled up by Petronius.
I was in the middle of whispering to Helena about Maia and
Anacrites; Marius, who had slept the night on our living-room floor
had taken his bowl of chopped fruit into the bedroom to check on the
pup.

'The spy is right in there, after her. Maia appears to go along with it.'

'What about Anacrites?' asked Helena, staying calm.

'He's playing it quietly; he looks as if he is not sure his luck will
hold,' I complained bitterly.

'Leave it; he won't last.' Helena seemed far less worried than I was.
'Maia needs to adjust. She will never stay with the first man who takes
an interest.'

Petronius had despaired of attracting my attention. He came up and
stood listening, as he waited to break in on the conversation.
Something was up; I was on my feet by then, strapping up a boot.

'Maia won't be an easy catch for anyone. Marcus, listen,' Helena
insisted, 'don't drive her to him!'

I shook myself, breaking free of my worries. 'Petro – what's the
excitement?'

'Report of a corpse, possible suicide. Hanging from the Probus
Bridge.'

'Some poor family man, no doubt . . . Am I interested?' Still
frazzled by my wrath over Anacrites, I enjoyed a hope that it might be
him strung up.

Petro nodded. 'I'm paying you to be fully involved, Falco. The
corpse may be one of the authors in the Chrysippus case.'

We walked down to the river at an even pace. Dead men wait. It was
an early hour, when it seemed natural to walk along in silence.
Otherwise, I might have thought Lucius Petronius was preoccupied.

Any other bridge in Rome would have been out of the Fourth
Cohort's remit. We were lucky, if you cared to look at it that way.

The boundary of the Thirteenth district touched the Tiber just below the Trigeminal Gate, which was the way we approached from the Aventine; the Probus lay just south of that. Beside the great wharf called the Marble Embankment and close to the bustle of the Emporium, it was a favourite spot for suicides.

Across the river we could see the Transtiberina, the lawless quarter into which only brave men ventured. Coming towards us from the far side of the bridge were red-clad members of the Seventh Cohort, in whose jurisdiction that lay. Their patrol-house stood not far from this bridge. Fusculus was also visible going to meet them, his rotund figure unmistakable.

'A confrontation?' I asked Petro.

'I'm sure the Seventh will see it our way.'

'Are they looking for work?'

'No – but if they get the idea we are keen to have this one, they may argue just to be difficult.'

'Where is the dividing line between cohorts?'

'Halfway across the river, officially.'

'Where was the corpse found?'

'Oh, about halfway,' answered Petronius sardonically.

'I see it's walked to this side!' Petro's men were clustered at the Thirteenth's end of the bridge. 'I suppose normally if a bloated jumper drifts ashore in the Emporium reaches, you would try to poke the body with an oar until it ends up on the other side and the Seventh have to deal with it?'

'What a shocking suggestion, Falco.' True, though.

The Seventh must have been bored with fishing floaters out, because before Petronius and I fetched up at the scene properly, they had already turned away. Fusculus started walking back towards us with a grin. I made no comment on these delicate issues.

The body was lying on the bridge now. A group of vigiles clustered round it casually. One was still eating his breakfast – half a fatty-looking pie.

'What have we got?' asked Petronius. He glanced at the man who was eating – who, far from feeling the reproof, instead offered him a bite. Petro took the pie from him. I assumed it was confiscated; next minute he had sunk his choppers into it and was handing on the item to Fusculus, while brushing crumbs off his chin. As I was an informer, they made sure there was nothing left when it came to my turn – but they did apologise. Nice fellows.

The vigiles discussed the event with Petro in their own terse code.

'Suicide.'

'A jumper?'

'Hung himself.'

'That straight?'

'No, chief; he made it really obvious.'

'*Too* obvious?'

'He was dangling from a noose looped over a corbel. We're just simple vigiles. Of course we rush to the obvious conclusion. That means self-hanging to us.'

'Suicide note?'

'No.'

Petronius grunted. 'I was told something about an identification clue?'

'Correspondence in a bag fastened to his belt. Addressed to Avienus. That's a name from the Chrysippus case.'

'He's a writer; he should have been able to do us a note then,' Petro scoffed.

I could do cemetery humour too: 'Avienus was not good on deadlines.'

'Well, he's one less on our suspects list,' Petro replied.

'You think he killed himself out of guilt, after murdering Chrysippus?' I wondered.

Then Fusculus laughed. The vigiles wanted to impart something more sensational. 'No – there's more to this! He's the first suicide I ever saw who climbed *under* a bridge – when most desperate people jump off the top. Then he not only tied himself to the stonework in a very awkward position, but roped a massive bundle of roof tiles to himself. Now it *could* be in case his nerve failed and he suddenly wanted to climb back up –'

'Or not!' muttered one of the others.

The men stood aside. Petro and I approached the corpse. It was Avienus all right; I identified him formally. The skinny frame and beaky face were definitely his. He was dressed in black as previously, the cloth of his tunic rumpled in awkward folds.

They had cut away the rope from around his throat as a courtesy, in case he gasped his way back to life. The vigiles normally did that with hanged bodies; I think it made them feel better. It would have been pointless in this case. Avienus had been dead for some hours when he was found by a cart-driver in the early hours.

'However did the driver see him there?'

'He had climbed off his cart to do a pee over the edge.'

'Noticing a body must have quenched the flow! Did he see anyone else lurking about?'

'No. We took a statement and let him go.'

The noose was an old-looking piece of nautical goat's hair twist, still tarry in places. It might have been found lying handy on a wharf. Suicides, in my experience, turn up at their chosen spot fully equipped.

I had seen suicides by hanging before and the results here did to some extent look right. Apart, that is, from two large bundles of shaped sun-baked pantiles which were strapped to him. They had been parcelled together in the form of a double pannier, which Fusculus said had been placed over his head with two ropes on his shoulders, and then other strands knotted each side at his waist. It would have taken some time to organise. Still, some suicides do spend hours formally preparing themselves.

'Ever picked up one of those?' asked Fusculus, indicating the tiles.

'They weigh some,' I agreed. One, falling from sufficient height, can kill a man. Plenty of spines have been ruined for ever by lifting roofers' hods.

'What do you think?'

'This is an odd one, right enough. If you don't think about it too much, it looks as though he wanted to be certain he would drop properly – making sure the weight dragged him down when he jumped, so the rope would snap his neck.'

Petronius tried waggling the historian's head to test if his neck was broken, but rigor had set in. 'Get Scythax to check that, will you?' Scythax was the cohort doctor. He examined both wounded and dead, mending whichever he could. His nature was dour and to me he seemed fonder of the dead. 'There are failed hangings sometimes; Avienus might have wanted to make sure, so he chose to take elaborate precautions.'

'But,' I said, leaning over the low wall to see the place of death, 'he could not easily have climbed over this parapet with such a weight attached to him.'

'Desperate men can amaze you. Would it be quite impossible?' asked Petro.

'Where we found him,' Fusculus replied, 'he needed to get out there first, cling on somehow, with no real foothold, yet have free hands to fasten his rope.'

'Want to leg yourself over and demonstrate?'

'No thanks! You can't reach the fixing point properly before you have climbed the parapet. But once he climbed over, so weighted down, tying his noose on the corbel would never have been feasible.'

'So he had help?' suggested Petro.

'Help – whether he wanted it or not,' I agreed sombrely.

Murdered then.

I knelt down beside the body, and detected a faint mark on his forehead, possibly a bruise left by a knockout blow. 'Put the word out that we have accepted this as suicide.'

Everyone nodded.

'What about that correspondence?'

Fusculus handed me a document. It was a letter to Avienus from his mother, obviously an elderly and frail widow, fretting about what might happen to the property she lived in. She was afraid of losing her home. I had asked Lucrio what security Avienus had offered for his bank loan, but Lucrio had never reported back to me. This told me the answer.

There was nothing else we could do. Petronius made arrangements to remove the corpse. Somebody would have to go and tell the old lady that she had even more worries now.

'Why,' I asked, still puzzled, 'did they hang him? You could make sure of killing him just as convincingly by tying on the weights, then throwing him over and letting him sink to the bottom. That too could look like a very determined suicide.'

'Somebody wanted to make sure the corpse was visible,' decided Petro. 'They wanted him found – quickly.'

'And something worse.' I was thinking it through. 'They wanted the event talked about. What happened to him is a warning to others.'

'A warning – from whom, Falco?'

I could see one possibility. It seemed to me, we might just have found another curious custom of the banking world – though whether this was the traditional punishment for defaulters, or a response to some more serious threat to solvency, I did not know.

I went to see Lucrio.

XXXVI

THE JANUS Medius is an open-ended passageway at the end of the Porticus Aemilius. This was where Anacrites had told me he would meet up with the freedman if he needed to discuss business. It was just my luck that of the two of them the first person I recognised was not Lucrio but Anacrites himself.

'Don't you own an office to plot in?' I demanded, as mildly as possible. 'You seem to be everywhere I go these days.'

'Falco!' If he called me Marcus, I think I would have throttled him. Trust him to avoid retribution. It was one of his annoying characteristics. 'I'm glad to see you.'

'It's not mutual.'

'Listen.' He was looking worried. Good. 'There are bad rumours being whispered about the Aurelian Bank.'

'What rumours?' I asked, intrigued against my will. 'Has the Golden Horse got the staggers suddenly?'

'Stirred up by your enquiries, I gather. You and Camillus have been questioning clients; people are losing confidence. Because of the work you and I did, you do have a reputation.'

'The Census? Our fame as tax terriers was never that extensive!'

Anacrites ignored my derision. 'People think you have been brought in as a specialist because the death of Chrysippus must have been related to problems with his bank.'

'Well, you can tell them I'm just sniffing for bloodstains!' I snapped.

All the same, I started looking around more keenly. The Janus Medius contained small groups of men who probably seemed more furtive than they were. Some had a foreign tinge. Most looked like gangs your mother would warn you not to play with. A couple were flanked by large ugly slaves, probably bodyguards. All could have found more congenial places to discuss the news – places where you could bathe, read, exercise, be massaged or eat fried pastries at the same time as you were gossiping. By gathering in this dead-end passage, they were consciously setting themselves aside in a private clique.

I had the distinct impression many were watching us. I felt they knew why I was there.

You can get like that on a case.

'I just want to know what's what,' Anacrites badgered me. 'I was looking for Lucrio, but he's gone to ground. Even if I corner him, he'll only pretend everything is fine – I have a large amount on deposit, Falco. Ought I to be moving it?'

'I have no information that your bank is in any trouble, Anacrites.'

'So you *are* telling me to shift my cash!' Why did he bother asking me if he was not prepared to listen? The man had taken a huge bang on the head in the past, and in his concern for his money he was growing hysterical. Never having had much cash myself, financial panic failed to grip me.

'Do what you think best, Anacrites.'

He cast a last desperate glance around and rushed off, intent on hasty action of some kind. Everyone knew who Anacrites was. At this rate, his agitation would itself start a run on the Aurelian Bank. For a wild moment, I speculated that I, by simply asking a few crass questions, might yet start an Empire-wide financial crash.

Anacrites had hardly vanished when I spotted the freedman, engaged in a hot discussion only a few yards away. He saw me, and managed to extract himself. The other party left, looking unhappy. I thought he threw back a glance at me, almost like a man seething at the source of his trouble. (I had seen enough of those to recognise the look and check that I had my dagger safely down my boot.) Lucrio recovered his composure immediately. Was that a result of regular practice?

'Didius Falco.' Unless my imagination was under too much strain, he was edging me gently to a spot where nobody could overhear us.

'Lucrio. I am afraid I bring sad news. Tell me, does a loan-contract end when one of your debtors dies?'

'No chance. We claim on the estate.'

'Why am I not surprised?'

'Which of our clients is dead?' he asked, making it seem like mere curiosity.

'Poor Avienus, the historian.'

'Zeus! He was only young. What happened to him?' Wide-eyed and startled – apparently – the freedman stared at me.

'Suicide.'

'Ah!' At once Lucrio stopped asking questions. I bet this was not the first harassed defaulter who had taken that desperate escape route.

'Don't blame yourself,' I said, two-faced as a businessman myself. (It was surely not coincidence that the bankers liked to congregate in a place named for Janus?) 'Apparently, he had secured that loan of his on his old mother's house. She will be distraught to lose both her son and her home – but I dare say it is out of the question for the bank to forget his debt?'

Then Lucrio surprised me. 'The contract was already torn up, Falco.'

'Kind-heartedness? Is there profit in that attitude?' I scoffed.

'No – but Avienus had cleared the debt.'

I was shocked. I could not believe it. I remembered what Lucrio had told me previously. If Avienus had paid up, he must have found the money through another loan. So when that fell due, his widowed mother would just be pursued by some new lender. 'Do you know who remortgaged him?'

'He maintained,' Lucrio said thoughtfully, 'that there was no covering loan. He just produced the cash. We don't quibble over that! He must have had a windfall, mustn't he?'

'Did you,' I asked, 'have a succinct personal word with him, before he paid?'

'Regularly.' Lucrio knew I was suggesting he had used threats. 'Very quiet and calm. Thoroughly professional. I hope, Falco, you are not slandering my business methods by implying harsh tactics?'

'You don't employ enforcers?'

'Not allowed,' he assured me smoothly. 'Legally in Rome, to ask a third party to collect debts, counts as passing on the loan to them. We keep ours in the family. Besides, our preference is only to deal with those we know, and know we can trust to pay.'

'Yet Avienus had great difficulty with his debt.'

'A temporary embarrassment. He did pay. That proves my point. He was a highly-valued member of our circle,' said the freedman unblushingly. 'We are very sad to lose him from among our customers.'

That settled it for me. I was now convinced this lying deviant sent Avienus to his death.

I went and saw Nothokleptes. He was at his barber's again. I was starting to think he slept there in the chair overnight. It would save paying rent. He would like that.

The barber had two customers waiting so in the traditional manner of his trade he was slowing down. Nothokleptes drew me aside and let another man take the chair.

'Have you heard,' I asked quietly, 'that a client of the Aurelian Bank committed suicide rather strangely on the Probus Bridge?'

'Word was going around the Forum first thing this morning.' Nothokleptes smiled in a sad Egyptian way. 'Suicide, was it? Very ancient traditions apply in Greek banking, Falco.'

'Apparently! You warned me about Lucrio. I had the impression you regard him as dangerous – so would he ever use enforcers?'

'Of course he does.' For once Nothokleptes actually signalled his barber to back away and leave us to talk in private.

'He pretended it's virtually illegal.'

'It virtually is.' Nothokleptes was so calm about it, I wondered if he used enforcers himself. I did not ask.

'Right! I meant, really violent ones.'

'He would call them "firm", Falco.'

'So firm they would be prepared to make ghastly examples of defaulting clients?'

'Oh, no banker ever hurts defaulting clients,' Nothokleptes reproved me. 'He wants them to come back and pay.'

I persuaded him to talk to me more generally about how bankers – or at least Greek bankers – worked. Nothokleptes painted a picture of Athenian secrecy, often involving tax avoidance, the hidden economy, and the disguising of their real wealth by the élite. As he saw it – in his self-righteous Egyptian way – his rivals had notoriously tight-knit networking relationships with clients who were treated almost as family members. Much of what he knew had come to light as a result of court cases involving fraud – significant in itself.

'Of course the biggest scandal ever was the Opisthodomos fire – the Treasurers of Athene had a clandestine arrangement where they illegally loaned sacred funds to bankers. They were planning to use the "borrowed" cash to make huge profits. They failed to realise the expected yield, could not replace the capital, and to hide the fraud, the Opisthodomos – where the money was supposed to be secured untouched – was burnt. The priests were jailed for that.'

'And the bankers?'

Nothokleptes shrugged and grinned.

'But I suppose the bankers could not entirely be blamed, Nothokleptes. The priests chose to steal the funds and to use banking confidentiality to hide their own misappropriation of the sacred treasure.'

'Right, Falco. And the poor bankers were innocents, misled by their awe for their religious clients.'

I laughed. 'And has the Aurelian ever made mistakes?'

'It would be slander to say so!'

'Would you say then,' I asked, 'that the Aurelian is straight?'

Nothokleptes hardly paused. 'It once had a rough reputation – Lysa and Chrysippus started out here as ropy old loan sharks, in essence. There has been talk. Lucrio is generally considered hard but straight.'

'How hard?'

'*Too* hard. But if Lucrio is behind this death at the Probus Bridge, if he actually wants it made public that he has rough-handled a client, then he has stepped well outside normal practice. His reason must be special too.' Nothokleptes was leading me somewhere.

'What does that cryptic pronouncement mean?'

'There is a curious whisper that the "suicide" had made threats against the bank.'

'What threats?'

That was all Nothokleptes would say. Possibly, it was all he knew. He could not say which enforcers the Aurelian Bank patronised – apparently there were debt-collecting specialists aplenty – but he thought he could find out for me. He promised to send word as soon as possible, then he scuttled back to the barber's chair.

I had a sour taste as I walked back across the Forum. I went to the baths, as I was in the area. At the gym, Glaucus commented that I was taking him through a training exercise as though I wanted to break somebody's neck. He hoped it was not his. When I said no, it was a banker's, he lowered his voice and asked me if I could confirm that one of the big deposit-takers was about to liquidate. Glaucus had heard from his customers that people in the know were withdrawing their deposits and burying their money in the corners of fields.

I said that would help thieves, wouldn't it? And did he know which fields?

He had genuine anxiety. After I limped out, I decided on an early lunch, at home. I skirted the Palatine, keeping on the flat as much as possible; Glaucus knew how to punish me for cheek. I staggered round the end of the Circus, and then walked slowly up the slope of the Clivus Publicius.

It was weeks since I had been at the Chrysippus house. I liked to keep an eye on scenes of unsolved deaths. And it was still rather early to reappear at Fountain Court, so on an impulse I went into the house. As usual, a slave on the door merely nodded when he saw me enter. He probably knew me and knew that I was being allowed to borrow the Latin library. Still, I had come without an appointment and once indoors, I could have wandered anywhere.

Without a clear idea of what I wanted, I walked through the little lobby and into the library I had used as an interview room. For a moment I stood, soaking in the atmosphere. Then, hearing a slight noise, I crossed to the room-divider, which had now been pulled across, dragged open a peeking-in space and surveyed the Greek section. I was amazed to see Passus. I had thought all the vigiles had been pulled from this case. (Was Petronius wanting somebody to spy on me?)

Passus was seated at a table, intently reading. My empty stomach must have let out a gurgle, because he looked up and flushed rather guiltily.

'Passus!'

'You made me jump, Falco. The chief just reminded me I was supposed to catalogue these scrolls for you.'

Great gods, I had forgotten all about that. 'Thanks. Found anything? You looked totally absorbed.'

He grinned shyly. 'I must admit I started reading one and found it interesting.'

'What is this great work of literature?'

'Oh, it seems to be called *Gondomon, King of Traximene* – just an adventure tale.'

'Who wrote it?'

'Well, that's what I'm struggling to find out,' Passus told me. 'I sorted out most of the scrolls, but I'm left with some that were badly mangled and messed-up. I am having to piece them together and I have not yet found the title pages of the last couple. They may have been ripped off in the fight.'

He had the furtive air of a reader who had been thoroughly hooked; he could hardly bear to break off and talk to me. Immediately I left him, he would plunge into the thrilling scroll again. An author's dream.

Grinning, I walked back quietly through the lobby. There I was in for a second surprise, one that seemed far more significant. Coming here as an unexpected visitor had certainly paid off: in the main reception area two women were taking leave of each other, embracing like sisters. One had a slight air of reserve, yet she permitted her effusive companion to kiss her, and herself returned the salutation quite naturally.

Which was odd – because the women were Vibia Merulla and Lysa, the woman she supposedly ousted from the Chrysippus marriage bed. I made a quick choice between them. Both were tricky, but one was more experienced. I always like my challenges to be as difficult as possible. When Lysa's covered litter left the house and Vibia disappeared up a staircase, I set off hotfoot to follow Lysa.

XXXVII

THE OLD lady with the shopping was out again, still trying to be knocked down by thieves; as she blundered vaguely down the hill, I had to dance around her. I caught up with my quarry near the bottom of the Clivus. Calling Lysa's name as I ran down the street persuaded the litter-bearers that I was a safe acquaintance and they set down their burden so I could speak to her. I pulled aside the modesty curtain and leaned in through the half-door.

'Lysa!' I saluted her, grinning as I got my breath. 'You're looking lovely! Are you a bride yet?'

She was richly clad, though in restrained taste. The heavy gold necklace looked like a Greek antique; it would certainly have cost enough to make Vibia jealous. Lysa coped with the summer heat by covering up – long sleeves and dark material in her gown. No trace of perspiration marred the olive skin. Her eye colours were lightly applied, so they would not run, and from within the enclosed space of the carrying chair a draught of expensive perfume rose sensually.

'What do you want, Falco?'

'I think I must be dreaming. I could swear I just saw you embracing the widow up the street.'

If she was annoyed at being under surveillance, she hid it well. 'Vibia and I have a civilised relationship.'

I whistled. I could remember Lysa calling Vibia a 'little cow'. 'I thought you hated giving up your husband to her. How come you are now cooing like love birds?'

'Hardly that!'

'Vibia is still living in your old home, I see.' This time my probing produced slightly narrowed eyes. 'Was the house included with the scriptorium in her inheritance?'

'I gave it to her as a gift,' conceded Lysa, rather reluctantly.

I whistled. 'Some gift!'

'I have a generous nature.' Even Lysa could see this was ridiculous.

She was a businesswoman with iron talons. 'Oh, it's no secret. Vibia extracted it from me.'

'How?'

'Never mind.'

'You said it was not a secret.'

'Well – it was her price for helping to arrange something . . .' When I looked sceptical, Lysa was forced to explain. 'Diomedes is to be married to a young relative of Vibia's.'

'My word, your family does love weddings! Are you planning a joint ceremony the day you hitch up with Lucrio? What thrilling news for Diomedes too – good match?'

Lysa calmly ignored my jibes. 'A charming girl. Elegant and cultured – and from a prime family. Good people, with plenty of connections.' Ah! I had thought Vibia common, but that was a response to her personal behaviour; it by no means ruled out social rank. Plenty of solid citizens have female relations who sound like scallop-sellers and who overdo the face powder. Lysa continued, 'They have been clients of the bank for years, of course; we know them very well.'

'Your son is on his way then?'

Lysa smiled contentedly. 'Oh yes,' she assured me. 'Everything is perfect now.'

I let her go. Another cameo for me to add to my curious collection.

The old dame with the shopping basket tottered up at that point and had a good stare at me. I could tell she regarded herself as a guardian of community life. Some harassed fellow's mother, no doubt. She was the kind who plies to and fro, collecting half a cabbage then returning for a sprat, hoping to brighten her day with a chance to spy on strangers.

When I retraced my footsteps, I nearly stopped at the corner popina. Again, the waiter was standing there – a tall, thin-faced young fellow in a short leather apron, keenly watching me. They were a nosy lot in this Clivus. His stare put me off. I knew the bar was the authors' meeting place. The waiter had that infallible air of wanting to chat, whether I liked it or not. Distrustful, I kept going.

I might have gone to tackle Vibia, but instead I met Euschemon, the same shaggy, shambling bundle with his usual unkempt hair and an abstracted expression. He was leaving the scriptorium but paused for a chat. I told him about the affectionate scene I had witnessed, wondering if it would affect his former loyalty. 'I don't know how they can do it!' he grumbled.

'What's that?'

'People are strange, Falco.'

'True. I was surprised to hear about this marriage. It sounded as if Vibia is being used by the Chrysippus family as Diomedes' social vaulting horse?'

'Oh, the Chrysippi obtain high interest rates from everyone,' said Euschemon cryptically. He refused to be drawn further, but I was beginning to understand what he meant. Diomedes must have had the path to social acceptance carefully mapped out for him. Did the scheme go right back to his father's own remarriage? I wondered. Was Vibia Merulla just part of the advancement plan Chrysippus worked out for his son? And if so, did Lysa know all along?

'Euschemon, I thought Vibia did not look quite as happy as Lysa was.'

He laughed under his breath. 'Well, she wouldn't.'

'Why is that?'

'I could not comment, Falco.'

His tone of voice was a clue. I took a wild guess. 'Don't tell me – Lysa has drawn Vibia into arranging Diomedes' marriage – not knowing that Diomedes, frequenting the house to see his father, had happened to catch the eye of Vibia herself?'

Euschemon corrected me on one small point: 'Lysa knows perfectly well that Vibia lusts after him.'

Wonderful. This tangle was turning into a full-blooded Greek tragedy.

'And does Diomedes return his stepmother's interest?'

'I am not interested in scandal and gossip. I have no idea.'

When people say that, it always means they know.

XXXVIII

THIS WAS too good to leave alone. I went back inside the house. Passus was still in the Greek library. He had now sorted the remnants of the tangle of papyrus recovered at the crime scene into two piles, though he was holding a few extra scrolls and looking perplexed.

'Back again?' The new man had grown more used to me. He was joshing in a mild way, as the old stagers did. 'Look, Falco, I'm having a problem with the last few of these. I think there are two different manuscripts without titles, and one of them seems to be in two different versions.'

I went right into the room this time. 'What have you found then?'

'Well, I've worked out that those scrolls on the floor with the body were all authors' draft manuscripts. The handwriting tends to be illegible and some are full of crossings out. A lot are scrawled on the backs of old stuff too – and some have insertions cross-hatched on them.'

'They are not ready for sale. Chrysippus must have been deciding which to publish. He was reviewing them – then interviewing some of the authors. Make sense?'

'Yes.' Passus consulted a note-tablet. 'I found some rejections among them. Poems by someone called Martialis had had scrawled on them, "*Who is this? No – crap!*" in red ink. And Constrictus – one of his regulars – had a submission where Chrysippus put "*Usual fluff. Small edition; reduce payment.*"'

'Any good?'

'Sex and waffle. I couldn't be bothered to read it. The poetry was straightforward and I've just listed it. Now I'm stuck. But what's left is more my taste anyway.' He gestured to the untitled scrolls he was still trying to sort out. 'Adventures; they have a romantic story, but the people spend most of their time separated and in trouble, so they never get too sloppy.'

I laughed. 'You're a fan of Greek novels!' Passus looked offended, then went red. 'No, I'm sorry. I'm not sneering, Passus. It's a change to have some culture in the vigiles. Look, Helena likes a yarn.' Helena Justina read everything. 'I want these with the missing titles to be fully evaluated. If you can carry on reading the one you've already started, I'll take the other scrolls home and get Helena to skim through – she's a very fast reader.'

Passus looked crestfallen. I told him with a smile that when Helena had finished he could have the scrolls back to read. He cheered up.

'Well, perhaps she can sort out the story that has two versions,' he suggested, quick to shed the most awkward job.

'I can try her with it . . . I'm going upstairs now for a word with the lovely Vibia.'

'I'll keep an ear out, Falco. If I hear a scream, I'll know you need rescuing.'

'Watch it. You stick with that adventure scroll. It might even tell us something useful.'

A staircase led to the upper reaches from near the main entrance door. It was curtained off; until I had seen Vibia gliding up on her glittery sandals earlier today, I had hardly noticed it.

Nobody stopped me. I walked quietly, as if I had permission. Self-confidence can take you a long way, even in a strange house.

There were various small rooms, frescoed yet not so grand as the ground-floor reception area. Most were bedrooms, some looking unoccupied as though they were kept for guests. One grand set of rooms, silent and shuttered, contained the master bedroom with the marital bed. If Vibia slept there now, she must feel like a lost little flea.

Eventually I found her in a smaller salon, propped up on a couchful of well-plumped cushions, chewing a stylus end.

'Writing! Dear gods, everyone's at it. I wish I had the ink-supply contract around here.'

Vibia flushed and put away the document. I wondered why she had been scribing it herself. 'No secretary? Don't tell me you are composing a love letter!'

'This is a formal notice asking a tenant to remove his possessions from my property,' she retorted frostily. I chanced my luck and held out my hand to look at it, but she clung on fiercely. It was her house. I was an uninvited male visitor. I knew better than to force her to do anything.

'Don't worry; I'm not going to make a grab for it. Informers avoid being accused of assaulting widows. Especially young attractive ones.'

She was naïve enough to let any kind of compliment soften her. Lysa, her rival, would never have fallen for anything so routine. 'What do you want, Falco?'

'A private conversation, please. Business, regrettably.' I had lived with Helena Justina for three years, but I could still remember how to flirt. Well, I liked to practise on Helena.

'Business?' Vibia was already giggling. She signalled to her maids, who fluttered off. They would probably listen outside the door, but Vibia did not seem to have thought of that. No hardened campaigner, apparently. Yet perhaps no innocent.

She was sitting up now, with one little foot bent under her. I joined her on the reading couch. Cushions jammed themselves into my back; their striped covers were packed hard with filling, uncomfortably reminding me how Glaucus had pummelled me; I hooked out a couple from behind me and dropped them on the floor. A lavish carpet, imported a vast distance from the East by camel-train, waited to receive these discards. My bootstuds caught slightly on the fine woollen tufts.

Vibia had perked up, now that someone handsome and masculine had come to play with her. How fortunate it was that I had bathed and shaved at Glaucus' comprehensive establishment. I would hate any hint of uncouthness to offend. And we were at close quarters now.

'What a lovely room!' I gazed around, but even Vibia cannot have supposed it was the creamy plaster covings and the painted swags of flower garland that concerned me. 'The entire house is striking – and I gather that you, lucky girl, have acquired it?'

At that she looked nervous. The smile on the wide mouth shrank a little, though the gash was still generous. 'Yes, it is mine. I have just made an arrangement with my late husband's family.'

'Why?'

'What do you mean, why, Falco?'

'I mean, why did you have to ask for it – and why ever did they agree?'

Vibia bit her lip. 'I wanted somewhere to live.'

'Ah! You are a young woman, who had been married and mistress of her household for three years. Your husband died, rather unexpectedly – well, let us assume it really was unexpected,' I said cruelly. 'And you were faced with the prospect of returning like a child to your father's house. Unpalatable?'

'I love my papa.'

'Oh of course! But tell the truth. You had loved your freedom too.

Mind you, you would not have been stuck for very long; any dutiful Roman father would soon find someone else for you. I'm sure he's surrounded by people he owes favours to who would take you off his hands. . . Don't you want to remarry?'

'Not now I have tried it!' scoffed Vibia. I noticed she did not argue with my assessment of her father's attitude.

I sucked my teeth. 'Well, you had a thirty-year age difference with Chrysippus.'

She smirked – not sweetly, but viciously. Interesting.

'Everyone else thinks you were a schemer who stole him from Lysa.'

'Everyone else? What do you think?' she demanded.

'That it was deliberately fixed. You probably had little to do with it originally. That doesn't mean you objected – any sensible girl would approve of such a rich husband.'

'What a horrid thing to say.'

'Yes, isn't it? Chrysippus probably paid your family a grand figure to get you; in return he acquired a connection with good people. His enhanced status was intended to help his son Diomedes. Then because Chrysippus gave so much to your father on your marriage –'

'You make it sound as if he bought me!' she shrieked.

'Quite.' I remained passionless. 'Because the price was so high, the bargain absolved Chrysippus from leaving you much in his will. Just the scriptorium – not a thriving concern – and not even the house attached to it. I dare say, if there had been children, other arrangements would have been made. He would have wanted children, to cement the connection with your family.'

'We were a devoted couple,' Vibia reiterated, churning out the same false-sounding claim she had presented to the vigiles and me the day her husband died.

I appraised her slim figure as we had done at her first interview. 'No luck with a pregnancy though? Juno Matrona! I hope nobody tried interfering with nature here?'

'I don't deserve this!'

'Only you know the truth of that fine declaration . . .' As I continued to be openly insulting, she said nothing. 'Devoted or not, you cannot enjoy having been purchased like a barrel of salt meat. Chrysippus treated his authors that way, but a woman prefers to be valued for her personality. I think, you were aware – or in time you became aware – of the reasons the Chrysippi – all of them, including Lysa in the interests of her beloved son – had wanted your marriage.'

Vibia no longer disputed it: 'An alliance for the improvement of all parties – such things happen frequently.'

'Discovering that Lysa had supported the idea must have been a shock though. Did you turn against your husband then? Enough, perhaps, to rid yourself of him?'

'It was not a shock. I always knew. It was no reason for me to kill my husband,' Vibia protested. 'Anyway, Lysa had a shock herself – Chrysippus soon realised that he liked being married to me.'

'I bet that pleased her! Did *she* turn against him?'

'Enough to kill him?' queried Vibia sweetly. 'Oh, I don't know – what do you think, Falco?'

I ignored the invitation to speculate. 'Let's accept that you and your husband rubbed along together happily. When Chrysippus died unexpectedly, you were threatened with losing everything you had here. That made you harden your attitude. So you persuaded Lysa to let you have the family home. Marriage for the purposes of others will never happen to you again.'

'No, it won't.' It was a simple statement, impassively made. Not, I thought, a confession of murder.

The marriage was probably complex, as all marriages are. It had not necessarily been miserable. Vibia had possessed money and independence. As I saw her when we first met, and as Euschemon had described her, she was a wife whose domestic and social place was worth having. Chrysippus had doted on her, and he loved to show her off. Expecting only a marriage of convenience, Lysa had been genuinely angry at what had been sprung on her after so many years.

'Were you happy in bed?'

'Mind your own business.'

Vibia gave me a level stare. She was no virgin. That look was too confident – and too challenging. Nor did she carry the wounds, mental even more than physical, which would have resulted from three years of sexual abuse.

'Well, I don't think you suffered. But did you hunger for better, sweetheart?'

'What does that mean?'

'The staircase to your private apartment lies unguarded and, as I found today, it's deserted. Did a lover ever stroll upstairs to visit you?'

'Stop insulting me.'

'Oh, I am full of admiration – for your courage. If Chrysippus was often working in the library, you were taking quite a risk.'

'I would have been – if I had done it,' said Vibia harshly. 'As it happens, I was a chaste and loyal wife.'

I gazed at her and murmured gently, 'Oh hard luck!'

Although she had, as they say, kept the keys of this house for three years (though in practice, I suspected Chrysippus was the kind of man who clung on to the keys), Vibia lacked experience. She was at a loss how to make me remove myself – or to summon up heavies to have me removed. She was trapped. Even when I was rude, she could only complain feebly.

'Tell me,' I challenged with a bright smile. 'Diomedes used to see his father often; was he able to come and go freely?'

'Of course. He was born and brought up here.'

'Oh! So had the loving son been allocated a room here?'

'There was a room he had always had,' Vibia replied frigidly. 'From childhood.'

'Oh how sweet! Near yours, was it?'

'No.'

'Proximity is such a fluid concept. I shall not test this with a measuring rule . . . When he visited so regularly, nobody would think much of it?'

'He was my husband's son. Of course not.'

'He could have been visiting you,' I pointed out.

'You have a dirty mind, Falco,' retorted Vibia, with that trace of coarseness that had always stopped her being entirely respectable.

'Young stepmama and idle stepson of her own age – it would not be the first time nature secretly held sway. . . Somebody told me, you wanted more to do with Diomedes than was proper.'

'That person slandered me.'

I tipped my head on one side. 'What – no secret hankering?'

'No.'

These flat little negatives were starting to fascinate me. Every time she came out with one, I felt it hid a major secret. 'You were quite rude about him when you were first interviewed.'

'I have no feelings either way,' said Vibia – with that deliberate neutrality that *always* means a lie. During all this part of my questioning, she had been looking at the oriental carpet evasively.

I changed the subject suddenly: 'So how do you feel about Diomedes marrying your relative?'

For one brief moment that wide mouth pursed. 'It is nothing to do with me.'

'Lysa said you helped arrange it.'

'Not quite.' She was scrambling to recover her composure. I sensed that Lysa had bullied her into something here. 'When I was asked what I thought, I did not raise objections.'

'And was that *failure to object*,' I demanded, 'so important to Lysa and Diomedes that they rewarded you with all this lovely property?'

At that, Vibia did look up. In fact, she became elated. 'Lysa is *so* annoyed to lose it. That's the best part for me – she is furious to see me living in what used to be her house.'

'For a matchmaker's pay-off,' I told her bluntly, 'the price is extortionate. As a banker by proxy, I am astonished that Lysa agreed.' No reaction. 'Now that you are a lone woman living without masculine protection, what, may I ask, are you doing about your stepson's childhood room?'

Vibia was well ahead of me. 'Obviously it is no longer respectable for him to come here. People might suggest something scandalous. This letter I am writing'– she produced the document she had been frowning over when I first walked in – 'says Diomedes must remove his things – and not come here again.'

'Such concern for propriety. His bride will be grateful to you, Vibia!'

She was very anxious to distract me. By chance, it seemed, the young lady had lifted her arm onto the back of the reading couch and her richly beringed hand had lolled against my left shoulder. Was it chance, or was Fortune for once looking after me? Now, with a faint jingle from a delightful silver bracelet, her small fingers began slowly moving, caressing my shoulderbone as if she were unaware of doing it. Oh very nice. She was definitely moving in on me. Feminine wiles. As if I had not encountered enough of them in my career.

I leaned back my head, like a man who was perplexed, and fell silent. Then, just as the fingertips began exploring that sensitive, rather tingly area of my neck where the tunic edge met my hairline, Passus knocked on the door. I breathed a sigh of relief – or was it regret?

'I'm just off now, Falco.' He had a scroll bundle with him. 'This is the stuff you wanted –'

'Thanks, Passus.' Both of us managed not to grin, as I jumped up from the couch and collected the scrolls from him. 'I'm finished here.' That was one way of putting it. 'I'll walk along with you. Vibia Merulla, thank you for your help.'

I bade a rapid farewell to the widow, and safely fled.

XXXIX

AGAIN, I decided against lunch at the Clivus Publicius popina.
Apart from not wanting to give Passus the idea that I dallied at
food stalls – where Petronius and the rest were bound to have told him
informers flocked like summer pests – I could now see two of the
scriptorium authors leaning on the bar. Had it been the playwright or
the love poet, Urbanus or Constrictus, I would have gone down there
and joined them but it was the gangling *Scrutator* spouting at the
flashily dressed Turius. Not in the mood for either, I went the other
way, up towards the crest of the Aventine and home. There I invited
Helena out for an early lunch at a more local eatery.

'Falco, you have a shifty look about you!'

'Certainly not.'

'What have you been doing?'

'Talking to Passus about literature.'

'Lying dog,' she said.

Even when I gave her the scrolls to read, she still looked suspicious
for some reason. She leaned over and sniffed my shoulder; my heart
pounded a little. I dragged her out to eat before the interrogation
became too drastic.

Flora's Caupona was always quiet, though not normally as tense as
we found it today. A couple of self-effacing regulars were sitting up
straight at the inside table obediently waiting for their order.
Apollonius, the waiter, walked forward to welcome us. He was a
retired teacher – in fact, he had taught me at school. We never
mentioned that. With his usual dignity, he ignored the peculiar
atmosphere, as if he had not noticed it.

'We have lentils or chickpeas today, Falco.'

'Jupiter, you're taking the pulse regulations seriously.' Most other
food stalls had probably just disguised their pots of fish and meat by
leaving them off the chalked-up menu.

'Or perhaps something cold?' he enquired.

'Something cold!' Helena gasped. It was so hot outside, we could hardly move two yards without sweat drenching us. 'Junia, just because the edict says you can only serve pulses hot, doesn't mean you are forced to provide steaming porridges even in August!'

My sister clasped her hands upon the spotless pot-counter. (Not her effort; Apollonius took a strange pride in his demeaning work.) 'We can make you a salad specially – seeing as you are family,' she condescended primly.

Her son was playing with a model ox-cart where a second table had once stood. We put Julia down with Marcus Baebius and they soon started screaming at each other noisily. I waited for the customers to leave because of the racket. They stuck it out like a bunch of stubborn thick-ribbed limpets that had been excrescences on a harbour groin for twenty years.

Helena and I took a bench outside, the only remaining seat. Junia had made Apollonius prepare the salad, so she came out to patronise us.

'How are you two getting on? When is that cradle going to be occupied again?' Helena stiffened. From now on, she would go to enormous lengths to keep her pregnancy from Junia. 'And how is that wonderful new house of yours?'

'Are you trying to make us weep?' Helena demanded, freely acknowledging that the house purchase – *her* purchase – was a bad mistake. 'Apart from the fact we are lumbered with the worst building-contractors in Rome – recommended by your father – I have now realised it is far too distant from the city for Marcus to do his work properly.'

'Father is talking about selling up,' suggested Junia. 'Why don't you do a swap with him?'

Neither of us answered her, though we both had difficulty withholding our delight at the idea of Pa having to deal with Gloccus and Cotta. Even if this had been the best solution possible – and if there was any chance Pa would agree to do it – we would still not have allowed Junia the triumph of suggesting it.

'I'll mention your interest to Pa,' she said bossily. 'By the way, did you know Maia has persuaded him to let her work at the warehouse?'

'Goodness,' murmured Helena. 'Whoever would have thought of that?'

'She won't stick it out,' Junia decided.

'Wait and see,' I replied, trying to remain calm. 'I'll remind you of that statement in ten years' time, Junia, when Maia has become a top-notch antiques expert and the Favonius auction house leads the profession under her shrewd guidance.'

'What a joker,' said Junia. Silently, I willed Mercury the god of commerce to make Flora's Caupona go broke.

Apollonius brought our food then, so Junia broke off to mention little errors he had made in seasoning the salad, and to suggest clever ways he could serve it more elegantly next time. He thanked her gravely. I caught his eye, then had to shove spring onions into my mouth quickly to cover up my grin.

'Jupiter, sister – this is a one-snatch food-bar, not a palace dining room.'

'Try not to talk with your mouth so full, Marcus. And don't tell me how to do my job.' After two weeks, she was the expert. Helena kicked me, as a signal not to upset myself arguing. Junia reassumed her regal position, leaning on the inside counter. She could not resist a final dig. 'You want to have a sharp word with Mother – about that man Anacrites.'

This time I crammed a large piece of sorrel into my mouth to annoy her deliberately, before answering: 'Ma knows what I think.'

Junia tossed her head angrily. 'She cannot know what other people are saying.'

'I don't know myself. What are you talking about?'

'Oh, don't play the innocent.'

I had a bad feeling. I tried not replying.

'Well, for one thing,' Junia enjoyed telling me, 'he has persuaded Mother to give him all her savings to invest.'

'Shush! Don't discuss our family affairs so publicly.' For once, I was happy our children were making such a racket.

This was a shock. I had been unaware Ma had any savings with which she wanted to speculate. At my side, Helena moved slightly, almost as if she had expected something else to be said. Whatever she thought, she was noticeably keeping quiet. Now she reached over me to where Apollonius had set down the breadbasket and took a roll. Then she involved herself in breaking it into very neat pieces, which she slowly ate. Flora's Caupona had always specialised in very doughy rolls. What looked like seeds on the top, usually turned out to be grit.

After chewing and swallowing my sorrel leaf to give myself reaction time, I pointed out to Junia that if Ma had been pinching back a few coppers every week from her housekeeping, it could hardly amount to much. She had brought up seven children unaided, then even after we left home she let herself be drawn into helping out the most feckless and hopeless of her offspring. Our elder brother Festus set the standard for sponging before he was killed in the East. I looked after his daughter financially, but various grandchildren were being shod, fed, and in some cases pushed through basic schooling by their devoted grandmother. She had two brothers (three if you counted the one who had sensibly run away); from them she cadged country vegetables, but otherwise our family offered few possibilities to recoup her generosity. Pa gave her a small annuity. I had always paid her rent.

Junia came outside again and whispered a huge figure that she thought our mother's nest egg might amount to. I whistled. 'How did she collect that together?'

Still, Ma always was tenacious. She bailed me out of prison once; I knew she could call on spare cash somewhere. I imagined she hid it in her mattress the way old women are supposed to do to help burglars find it easily.

'What has Anacrites done with this money, Junia?' Helena asked, looking concerned.

'He put it in some bank he uses.'

'What – the Golden Horse? The Aurelius Chrysippus outfit?' I was now horrified. I did not care where Anacrites shoved his cash, but enough questions hung over the Golden Horse to make anybody else now shun the place. 'Has Anacrites told Ma that the proprietor was recently found dead in suspicious circumstances – and that there is a suggestion of devious practice?'

'Oh Ju-no!' drawled my sister loudly. 'Well, that's Mother in trouble! I must tell her at once – she'll be devastated!'

'Just advise her quietly,' I warned. 'The bank is perfectly solvent as far as I know. Anacrites was talking to me about removing his own cash in view of these problems – but that's privileged information. I presume if he withdraws his own funds, he will do the same for Ma.'

It rankled that my mother had turned to Anacrites for investment advice. It rankled even more that he had known her financial position when I, her only son, did not.

Junia had sat down and was now posing, chin on one hand, looking thoughtful. 'Of course, maybe it would be better not to say anything to Mother after all.'

'Why ever not?' Helena's voice was sharp. She hated people acting irresponsibly. 'Somebody ought to warn Junilla Tacita. She can make up her own mind what she does about the situation – or better still, she can ask Marcus for advice.'

'No, I don't think so,' Junia decided.

'Don't be coy, Junia,' I said lazily. I hardly paid her any attention; I was intending to warn Ma about the bank myself. 'What's on your mind then?'

Being Junia, she could not bear to keep a nasty premise to herself: 'If Ma was to lose money because of Anacrites, it might put a stop to something worse.'

'Worse than Ma losing her savings?' I was coughing over a radish – not only because it was hot.

'Don't pretend you don't know,' sneered my sister. 'Everybody on the Aventine is speculating why Anacrites is living at our mother's house. Once their curiosity is aroused, people will find answers for themselves, you know.'

'What answers? And what's the damned question, anyway?'

The slow heat of indignation had already started burning before Junia told me what she believed the scandal-mongers thought: 'Oh Marcus! The gossips around every fountain are saying that Anacrites is our mother's fancy man.'

I had eaten enough of their brown-edged greenery and swallowed enough of Junia's irresponsible bile. I stood up. Without even looking at me, Helena was already collecting Julia.

As a gesture of farewell, the only one I could bear to distribute, I nodded to Apollonius for old times' sake. I set down the reckoning and left him a large tip. It would be some time before I allowed myself to visit Flora's after this.

'I am impressed by your nose for gossip, Junia. You have given me a lot to think about – and it's a long time since I heard anything so utterly ridiculous.'

'Well, let's face it, Marcus,' replied my sister callously, 'you may call yourself an informer. But when it comes to collecting information, you are absolutely useless!'

'I don't collect irresponsible chit-chat!' I retaliated, and we left.

XL

WE HAD walked nearly all the way home before I stopped dead in the street and exploded. Helena waited patiently until I stopped ranting.

'I don't believe it!'

'Well, why are you making so much fuss, Marcus?'

'I won't have my mother insulted.'

We were outside the poulterer's in Fountain Court by now. Nobody paid any attention. They were used to me. Anyway, it was midday in August. Those who could had fled to the country. Those who could not were lying prone, wishing they could go too.

Perspiration poured off me. My tunic was sticking to my back.

Helena said slowly, 'You don't know whether it is true or not. But you ought to allow the possibility that a woman of your mother's age – any age – may enjoy masculine company. With so many children, she cannot ever have had a cold disposition. She has lived without your father for a long time now, Marcus. She *might*, she just might actually want someone in her bed.'

'You're as disgusting as Junia.'

'If it was a man with a young girl, you would be thrilling with envy,' snapped Helena. She took our daughter and set off for our apartment, leaving me to do as I pleased.

I had to follow; I was raging with more furious questions. 'What do you know about all this? Is it true? What has Ma said to you? Have the pair of you been giggling over this sweet romance?'

'We have not. Look – there may be nothing in it.'

'Ma has said nothing?'

'She wouldn't.'

'Women always talk to each other.'

'About the men in their lives? Wrong on two counts, Marcus – the ones who chatter are probably discussing men they would *like* as lovers but can't get, or else men that they have lost. And some never say anything. Maia, for instance. Or me,' said Helena.

She turned back to me from our staircase.

'You never talked to other women about me?' I managed to calm down enough to find a feeble grin. 'I wasn't worth it, eh?'

Helena also relaxed. 'Too important,' she said. In case the flattery went to my head, she added, 'Who would have believed it, anyway?'

'Anyone who ever saw us together, my love.'

Then Helena suddenly tweaked my nose. 'Well, don't worry. If you run off and leave me the way your father left your mother, I shall probably replace you – but like your mother, I shall probably wait twenty years and be utterly discreet.'

It was no consolation. I could imagine Helena Justina doing just that.

I could have rushed straight off to see Ma there and then, and it would have probably been disastrous. Luckily, we were hailed cheerily from a balcony above us on the other side of the alley; to ensure our attention, Petronius Longus chucked down an old boot he kept upstairs for that purpose. Helena went indoors, while I waited. Being Petro, once he could see that I had stopped, he took his time.

'Playing the tribune still, Petronius? Come along! I don't have all day.'

'Whatever's the matter with you, Falco?'

'I'm bloody annoyed with my sister.'

'Oh, not Maia and Anacrites again?' he returned dourly.

I felt so frustrated I literally tore my hair. 'Junia!' I yelled.

'Oh.' He lost interest.

Assured that he would share my indignation, I had to tell him: 'Never mind Maia; this is a thousand times more horrible – according to Junia, Anacrites is having an affair with Ma.'

Petronius started laughing. I felt better for a moment. Then he stopped laughing sooner than he should have done. He whistled quietly. 'The rotten dog!'

'Come off it. It can't be true, Petro.'

'Oh – right!'

'I mean that.'

'Of course.'

He stared at me. I glared at him. Then he frowned. 'You don't suppose he would go so far as to dally with both your mother and your sister at the same time?'

'You're not listening to me! He has nothing to do with my mother –'

'No. You are right,' said Petronius crisply. 'I know he tried to kill you once – but not even Anacrites would want to do that to you.'

'Well, thanks, friend!'

'Not even to gain the upper hand again . . .'

Petronius Longus was no use. I changed the subject. It was the only thing to do. I asked him why he had called me, and (once he had finished sniggering over the Anacrites business) he said the shipper, Pisarchus, had turned up and was being held for questioning.

XLI

As I HAD suspected all along, Pisarchus – the shipper whom we knew had made serious losses while dealing with the Aurelian Bank – was also the man I had seen arguing with Chrysippus at the scriptorium.

He was heavily sunburned, as I had remembered, with that leathery skin and deeply ingrained colour that must have come from years of being lashed by the weather on an open deck. The solid build, once the result of hard work and regular lifting activities, had thickened up a little too much with age and a softer life. A fine-weave tunic and chunky gold finger rings said he had money – or could obtain credit, anyway. Another Greek. Both his features and his accent gave him away immediately, though he spoke that easy commercial Latin that traders use, and probably knew quite a few other languages.

Sergius, the vigiles heavy, had been delaying him until Petro and I arrived. Unsure whether he could beat people up at this stage of the enquiry, the big, handsome whip-man looked relieved to hand over. Subtle interrogation was not his skill in life. But then, it was not meant to be. Sergius was employed to thrash people – and at that he excelled.

We messed about for a while, as if Pisarchus were unimportant. 'How was he pulled in?' I heard Petronius mutter to Sergius while I pretended to be fiddling with stationery and a stylus.

'For some reason –' Sergius openly admired the man's courage – 'he volunteered to come!'

'Our punishment officer,' Petro grinned to the shipper. 'He seems to think you took a risk in coming here.'

Pisarchus, a man who must be accustomed to having command, merely raised a dark eyebrow. He sat on a stool, both feet planted apart, leaning on his knees with sturdy elbows that matched his muscled calves.

'Of course a member of the public who offers us assistance has nothing to fear from the vigiles,' stated Petronius. He managed to make it sound like a threat. 'Over to you, Falco. It's your case. Found yourself a stylus yet?'

I chewed the end of one, like a novice, glancing at a tablet Sergius had already filled in. 'Pisarchus? Shipper? Trading out of Piraeus, with a base at Ostia?'

'That's right.'

'I'm Didius Falco, on special operations here. This is Petronius Longus, acting tribune. He'll be sitting in with us for a general overview.'

'Are we likely to be long?' asked Pisarchus with horror, as if he had come here to report a stolen duck and found himself in the middle of a major crisis.

'As long as it takes,' I answered, with a slight air of surprise. 'You know what we need to talk about?'

'No.'

'Ah!' I glanced at Petro as if I found this answer highly significant. I decided not to enlighten Pisarchus yet. 'So, tell me why you came to the patrol-house, please?'

'I heard in the Forum that there had been a death.'

'Visiting Rome today? You are staying at Praeneste normally?'

Pisarchus looked surprised and disconcerted. 'How did you know?'

'Had you not told the first officer?' I made a pretence of consulting the scrawl Sergius had given me. 'No. Well, it seems you're famous around here! What did you come to report?'

He was a shrewd man. As soon as he realised the authorities had his name on a list, he backed off completely. 'You ask me what you want to know, Falco.'

I smiled. 'All right.' I felt like playing the reasonable fellow today. 'Tell me, please, about your dealings with the Aurelian Bank.'

'*My* dealings? How are they relevant?'

'We are consulting their customers about loan arrangements. It's a wide-scale exercise.'

That seemed to reassure him. 'They have given me credit a few times.'

'Marine loans, to acquire ships and to finance cargoes?'

'Yes. Normal conduct between an importer and his banker.'

'You had a couple of unfortunate voyages, I hear?'

'Two sunk. Last year.'

'You were unhappy about that?'

Pisarchus shrugged. 'Who wouldn't be? Two ships lost. Crews drowned. Cargoes and vessels gone. Customers disappointed, and no profit.'

'Sailing "out of time" by your contract terms?'

'Unfortunately.'

'So the bank called in your loans?'

'It was their right.'

'Did you quarrel?'

'No point. I didn't like it, but that is what happens.'

'So you suffered financially? The ships sailed in bad weather, uninsured, so when they sank not only did you lose the profits but also you now have to repay the Aurelian all the costs? Will it finish you?'

'Not quite,' Pisarchus replied gloomily.

'So it's a blow – but you will find the cash to start again?' He nodded. 'Another loan?' I asked.

'Obviously.'

'From whom this time? Will you go back to the Aurelian?'

A guarded look crossed Pisarchus' face. 'I might have done.' So losses did not necessarily ruin a commercial relationship. 'But I heard one or two rumours in the Forum today . . . I may try to put together another arrangement. A syndicate of family and friends. Two of my sons are in the business.'

'Shipping or banking?' queried Petro.

'Shipping!' Pisarchus clarified, slightly indignantly as if he did not regard banking as a trade. 'My sons have both done well lately, luckily for us. That's how it goes. We support one another.'

'In which case you won't need recourse to a bank.' I smiled. 'What rumours have you heard about the Golden Horse, incidentally?'

'I won't spread tittle-tattle,' Pisarchus said.

'All right. Tell me, did you have a slight altercation – over your loans, presumably – with Aurelius Chrysippus recently?'

'No,' replied the shipper. 'It is Lucrio I deal with when I need credit.'

I half-turned towards Petronius and we exchanged frankly sceptical glances. I had told him before we started that Pisarchus might be the man I had seen arguing.

'Wrong identification?' Petro suggested to me. Pisarchus frowned, wondering who had identified whom, and where.

'I don't think so!' I said firmly.

'The man sounds definite.'

'Me too. So he's definitely lying!'

I looked slowly back at Pisarchus. 'Don't mess us about, sir.'

Pisarchus looked anxious, yet he did not panic. He simply sat waiting to be told what was up. Something about him appealed to me.

He was either a clever dodger or quite straight. I found myself hoping he was innocent.

'You were seen,' I said heavily, 'at the Chrysippus scriptorium.'

He did not blink. 'That's right.'

'Well, why didn't you say so?'

'You asked me about credit. My visit to the scroll-shop was nothing to do with that.'

I took a long breath, scratching my head with the stylus. 'I think you had better explain – and make it good, for your own sake.'

He too stretched, as people do when the conversation takes a turn into a new subject. 'I had something to discuss – business for somebody else.'

'Not banking – so shipping?'

'No. Not shipping either.' This time I waited. Pisarchus coloured up gradually. He looked embarrassed. 'Sorry – I don't want to say.'

'I really think you should,' I told him quietly. I still felt that in his own way he was being honest. 'I know you were there, I saw you myself. I saw you leave, looking extremely put out.'

'Chrysippus was being difficult; he would not help my . . . friend.'

'Well, you know what happened not long after that.'

'I know nothing,' protested Pisarchus, now losing my misplaced confidence.

'Oh you do!' He had told us he did. I spelled it out angrily: 'Not long after you had your wrangle on behalf of this mysterious "friend", somebody battered Aurelius Chrysippus to death in his library. So you were one of the last people to see him – and from what the other visitors have told me, you are the last person we know for sure who had a disagreement with the dead man.'

Pisarchus lost all the colour that had swamped his face a few minutes earlier. 'I didn't know that he was dead.'

'Oh really?'

'That's the truth.'

'Well, you have been away in Praeneste!' I sneered, hardly able to believe it.

'Yes – and I deliberately made no attempt to contact Chrysippus,' Pisarchus argued hotly. 'I was annoyed with him – for several reasons!'

'Of course you were – he promised you a visiting poet, didn't he? A poet who then refused to come –'

'He blamed the poet,' Pisarchus said, still trying to play the rational type. 'I felt aggrieved, but it was hardly a mortal insult. Would I kill him over that?'

'Those I know who have been entertained by that poet, would say you were well out of it,' I conceded facetiously. I returned to my previous grim tone. 'This is serious, man! What was your other grievance, Pisarchus? What had Chrysippus refused to do for your mystery "friend" – let's hear it!'

Pisarchus sighed. When he told me the truth, I could see why a man of his kind might be reluctant to admit this. 'It was my son,' he said, now squirming on his stool. 'My youngest. He does not want to follow his brothers to sea – and for family peace I'm not arguing. He knows his own mind, and he is supporting himself as best he can while he tries to get where he wants to be . . . He has had no luck; I just tried to persuade Chrysippus he ought to give the lad a helping hand –'

'Whatever is your boy after?' I demanded, intrigued.

Then at last Pisarchus forced it out: 'He wants to be a writer,' he informed us gloomily.

XLII

I HAD MANAGED not to laugh. Petronius Longus, less sensitive to the feelings of creative artists, let out a high-pitched snort.

As soon as Pisarchus made the embarrassing admission, he relaxed somewhat. Though shame-faced, he apparently felt that now this was in the open he could return to dealing with us man-to-man.

'It happens,' Petronius Longus assured him with mock-gravity, making a sideswipe at me. 'Perfectly sane, normal types with whom you once thought you could safely go out for a drink, can suddenly turn aesthetic. You just have to hope they will see sense and grow out of it.'

'Ignore the enquiry chief,' I growled. Petro needed cutting down to size.

I was still taking the lead in this interview. I would not reveal to Pisarchus that I myself scribbled poetry. It might put him right off. Instead, with plain-spoken questions I managed to squeeze out the truth of what had happened: on the day I first saw him he had been trying to ask Chrysippus to read some of his son's work. Less high-minded than me, Pisarchus had been quite prepared in principle to shell out the production costs, just to allow the son to see his writing formally copied and sold. But at the time (with his ships stricken and the bank loans to repay), Pisarchus had been unable to afford the huge publication fee Chrysippus had demanded.

'I could have found the cash later, after my next cargoes are sold, but the fact is, my lad won't thank me. He is determined to do this by himself. When I cooled off, I knew I had better leave it right alone.'

'More to his credit. Is he any good?' I asked.

Pisarchus only shrugged. He did not know. Literature was a mystery. This was merely a whim of his youngest son's, over which he had wanted to be magnanimous. His main concern now was to clear himself. 'I was annoyed with Chrysippus. He owed me a favour or two after all the years I had banked with the Golden Horse, and all the interest he has had from me. But when he said no, I just gave up the idea, Falco. That's the truth.'

'You didn't leave any scrolls with Chrysippus, I suppose? Samples of your boy's work?'

'I had none. Philomelus keeps things close. If I had asked to borrow a scroll he would have realised I was up to something.'

'Philomelus is your son's name?'

'Yes. My youngest, as I said.'

Petronius and I thanked the proud parent for his frankness; I think we were both impressed by him. We added our polite good wishes for his son. One of us, at least, hoped the poor beggar was not forced to climb yardarms if all he wanted was to write. Maybe he had talent. Maybe he not only had talent, but might one day be a success. His papa would be surprised. Having seen how the world of literature worked, unfortunately so would I. It was a world where mediocrity flourished and genius was too often left to die.

After Pisarchus left, we called it a day. Petro and I had been on the case since early morning when the corpse was found beneath the Probus Bridge. I told him Nothokleptes was trying to find out which enforcers Lucrio used for banking business. 'Watch yourself, Falco. Those types are treacherous.'

'Right. If I finger them, I'll let you and the lads discuss with them whether they happened to hang a historian last night!'

'A nice job for Sergius,' Petronius agreed. He raised his voice: 'Fancy mixing it with debt factors?'

'Not me,' replied Sergius instantly. 'Those buggers are dangerous.'

He was normally fearless. That was worrying. Well, it would have been, if I thought *I* had to tangle with them. Instead, I braced myself for something that most people would not think twice about, though I knew it could be hazardous: I went to see my mother.

I didn't get far with that mad plan. Helena Justina had forestalled me. As I reached my mother's apartment block, I met Helena coming out. She gave me a stern look.

'Did you tackle her about this Anacrites rumour?'

'Certainly not. And she said nothing on the subject herself, Marcus. I just passed on a discreet warning about the problems with the Aurelian Bank, and said she could speak to you if she wanted advice.'

'I'll go in then.' Helena produced a freezing stare. I stayed outside. 'All right – shall I at least warn Maia? She is in a very fragile condition, and someone ought to tell her that her trusted "friend" may be a two-timing incestuous creep –'

'Don't approach either.' Helena was firm.

My half-hearted attempt at arguing was interrupted by one of Ma's tottering neighbours. They all tended to be decrepit, and this old chap must have been in his eighties. Bald and skinny, he was hooked over like a hairpin, though he clicked along on his walking stick quite spryly. Helena must have met him before because they exchanged greetings.

'Hello, young lady. Is this Junilla Tacita's son?' he croaked, seizing my hand for what passed for a shake – more of a tremble, in reality.

'Yes, this is Marcus Didius.' Helena smiled. 'Marcus, this is Aristagoras, I believe.'

'That's right. She has a good memory – wish mine was still up to it. Pleased to meet you, my boy!' He was still twitching with my paw trapped in his. 'Your mother is a fine woman,' he told me – obviously one person who did not believe Ma was cosying up to her lodger, anyway.

We managed to shed him, though he seemed to want to cling. In the confusion, Helena distracted me from my original purpose and took me on the short walk home with her. 'I need to talk to you about those scrolls, Marcus.'

'Stuff the scrolls.'

'Don't be petty. I think you will be interested. Something you told me does not fit.'

I let myself be deflected. Fortune had given me a clear sign that saving my mother from infamy was not required today. Anacrites must have bribed some bored god in the heavenly pantheon.

I growled. Helena refused to be menaced by an informer parading as a mangy bear. 'So what's up with the nutty Greek novel, fruit?'

'I thought you told me Passus was enthralled by what he was reading?'

'He could hardly tear himself away.' Except when he saw a chance to embarrass me in the clutches of Vibia . . . I kept quiet about that.

'Well, Marcus, what you gave me must be different. It's quite, quite dreadful.'

'Oho! So is Passus too easily pleased?'

Helena sounded doubtful. 'Different people like different content or writing styles. But I think he must be reading a story by some other writer than mine.'

'Mind you, some people will plod through anything . . . Passus is a

217

new boy to me. I don't know him well enough to appraise his reading tastes. But he seems sensible. Likes adventure yarns, he says. Plenty going on, and not too mushy with the love interest. Would that be too masculine for you, perhaps?'

'I can cope. Anyway, all these stories always have a very romantic view of life . . .' Helena paused. She liked to tease when I was being too serious. 'No, perhaps romance *is* more masculine. It's men who dream, and long for perfect women and ideal love affairs. Women know the opposite: that life is harsh, and mostly about clearing up the messes men create.'

'Now you sound like Ma.'

As she intended, she had managed to interest me. It was late afternoon, and we were strolling at ease now. The heat of the sun diminished as shadows lengthened, though the day was still bright. Occasional lock-up workshops started opening their shutters. Stallholders were sweeping up squashed figs and sluicing away fish-scales and scallopshells.

'So what are we talking about here, sweetheart? Poetic dramas?'

'Prose.'

'Oh! Fluff and chaff, you mean.'

'Not at all. Well-written escapism that keeps you, the reader, unrolling the scroll even when your oil-lamp is failing and you are stricken with a crick in your back.'

'Or until you nod off and set fire to your bed?'

'With the best,' Helena reproved me, 'you cannot *bear* to nod off until you finish them.'

'Are silly stories ever that gripping?'

'Oh, the silly ones are the worst in that respect . . . The stories can be daft, the plots implausible – but the human emotions will be intensely real. You know what we're talking about? *Zisimilla and Magarone,* the one I'm reading is probably called. You'll have a beautiful girl who is tougher than she looks and a handsome boy who is soppier than she thinks; they meet by chance –'

'Sounds like you and me.'

'No, this is true love.' Helena grinned. 'Not a girl losing her concentration for a moment and a man who was at a loose end.' I grinned back, as she continued, 'So – the couple may marry, or even have their first child. Then their troubles begin. A calamitous accident separates them – after which they both embark on tremendous adventures –'

'That's the part Passus likes, presumably.'

'Yes: if the pirates don't get them, the invading army will. The characters each have to spend years searching a wilderness for somebody who believes them dead. Meanwhile the pirates will be trying to rape one of them, but a resourceful slave or a faithful friend will rescue the other, the hero perhaps – though in his grief and solitude he wishes he had perished. Yet still, as he battles with monsters and enchantresses, he clings to hope –'

'Fit, but thick?' I sneered.

'The heroine will be threatened by an unscrupulous rival and doomed unjustly until she wins the respect of a noble king who has captured her, enslaved her, and naturally fallen in love with her modesty, wisdom, steadfastness and shining natural beauty. At last, with the benign care of the deities who unknown to them guard their every step, one day –'

'When the papyrus is about to run out –'

'The couple are reunited amidst tears and amazement. Then they embark on a life of endless happiness.'

'Fabulous!' I chortled. 'But the scroll I just gave you doesn't match that standard?'

Helena shook her head. 'No. Only the one Passus has, by the sound of it.'

'You've only had yours since lunchtime.'

'I am a fast reader.'

'You cheat!' I accused her. 'You skip.'

'Well, I am skipping this one. I dumped the devious brigand and the exotic female temptress – and I was not inclined to dally over the pompous chief priestess. This tale is terrible. I have better things to do.'

'Hmm. This is odd. Chrysippus was, by all accounts, a good businessman. Surely, he would have rejected anything so bad.'

Helena looked doubtful. 'Doesn't Turius say he had bad editorial judgement? Anyway, it's not that simple. You seem to have given me two different versions of *Zisimilla and Magarone*.'

'So Passus thought.'

'Parts seem to have been rewritten – by a different author, I think. To be honest, Marcus, the results are just as bad. Different, but equally awful because they are trying to be lighter and funnier. Whoever tackled the rewrites thought a lot of himself – but had no idea what was required in this genre.'

'I suppose publishers do sometimes ask for manuscripts to be improved before they accept them for copying . . . What about the scrolls Passus is reading? He seems to have a good author. Maybe he has one with a noble brigand and a devious priestess, where the rival in love turns out to be high-minded,' I scoffed.

Helena went along with it: 'While the barbarian king in whose power they end up is a complete rascal? I had better confer with Passus,' she offered. 'We can exchange stories and see what we think then.'

Fine. She would be tactful. And if he lacked judgement, she would identify the problem without offending him. If I knew Helena, she would then turn Passus into a sharp literary critic without him ever noticing that his tastes had been retrained.

It had been a long day. A corpse, suspect interviews, family shocks. I let my mind empty itself as I walked with Helena over the Aventine. At heart, it remained my favourite of the Seven Hills. Bathed in early evening sunlight and slowly cooling down, this was my favourite time of day too. People unwinding after work, and others gearing up for evening fun. The tenements echoing as daytime and night-time life began interacting on the narrow stairways and within the cramped apartments, while the odours of stale incense sank to nothing as the great temples emptied and were locked up at the approach of darkness.

We had a number of important sacred buildings around the base and on the crest of the hill. Temples to Mercury, and to the Sun and Moon fringed the lower road beside the Circus Maximus; on the crest we had that of Diana, one of the oldest in Rome, which had been built by King Servius Tullius, and the great Temple of Ceres, prominent above the Trigeminal Gate. There too was one of the many temples in Rome dedicated to Minerva.

Once, I would hardly have thought about these places. My mind would have run on shops and winebars. As an informer my interest lay in places where people might be frolicking and cheating one another; that included temples in theory, but I used to think they were just too sordid to bother with. My recent tenure as Procurator of the Sacred Geese of Juno Moneta at her state shrine on the Capitol had made me more alert to the presence of religious sites – if only out of fellow feeling for the other luckless holders of minor offices. Observation of religious duties ensnares not just priests of the seedy career type, but many a hapless dog like me who has found himself attached to some shrine in the course of his civic advancement. I knew how much they might yearn to escape – and the urge to escape is a strong human motive for all sorts of intriguing behaviour.

Ma lived near the Temple of Minerva. Minerva, goddess of reason and the arts, identified with the wisdom of Athene, and patroness of trades and craft-guilds, has a side-chapel at the monumental Temple of Jupiter Capitolinus and a great altar at the base of the Caelian Hill. And here she was, as the Aventine goddess too. It struck me belatedly that the calm, austere lady whose temple dignified Ma's district had featured in the Aurelius Chrysippus case. Her name had been given to me by one of my suspects, though I had never taken him up on it. Diomedes, son of Lysa and Chrysippus, and soon-to-be relative by marriage of Vibia, had cited her temple as his whereabouts on the day when his father had been murdered. Minerva was his as-yet-untested alibi. When Petronius had asked were there any big holes in the enquiry, I had forgotten this.

The Temple lay only a short step from Diomedes' father's house, no distance from the top end of the Clivus Publicius. It was near my own apartment too. So the Diomedes connection was something I could fruitfully investigate tomorrow, once the priests reopened for business – or whatever passed for business at a shrine to reason and the arts.

XLIII

NIGHT ON the Aventine, my favourite hill.

Stars and the mysterious steady glow of planets are piercing wisps of cloud. A persistent August temperature, with not enough air to breathe. Sleepers lying naked, or twisting unhappily on top of crumpled bed covers. Hardly a lover's cry or an owl's screech to be heard. Those few short hours when rollickers have fallen silent, slumped at unlit tables in the lowest drinking-houses as the whores give up on them in exhaustion or contempt. The dedicated partygoers are all away at the coast, splitting the Campanian darkness with their flutes, castanets and hysteria, allowing Rome some peace. The wheeled carts that flood the city in thousands at dusk all seem to be stationary at last.

The dead of night, when sometimes rain begins imperceptibly, increasing in force until thunder cracks – though not tonight. Tonight there is only the suffocating August heat, in the brief dull period when nothing stirs, a little before dawn.

Suddenly Helena Justina is shaking me awake. 'Marcus!' she hisses. Her urgency breaks through my troubled dream of being hunted by a large winged rissole dripping fishpickle sauce. Her fear shakes me into instant watchfulness. I reach for a weapon – then start fumbling after a means of light. I have lived with her for three years. I realise what the crisis is: not a sick child or a barking dog, not even the violence of Aventine low life in the streets outside. A high-pitched whine has disturbed her rest. She has heard a mosquito just above her head.

An hour later, sandal in hand, bleary-eyed and furious, I have chased the sly tormentor from ceiling to shutter, then into and sneakily out of the folds of a cloak on a doorpeg. Helena is craning her eyes, now seeing its cursed body shape in every shadow and doorframe cranny. She smacks her hand on a knot in a wooden panel that I have already tried to kill three times.

We are both naked. It is not erotic. We are friends, bound by our hatred of the devious insect. Helena is obsessive because it is her sweet skin they always seek; mosquitoes home in on her with horrific results. We both suspect, too, that they carry summer diseases that might kill our child or us. This is an essential ritual in our house. We have a pact that any mosquito is our enemy, and together we chase this one from bed to wall until at last I swat the thing successfully. The blood on the wall plaster – probably ours – is our sign of triumph.

We fall together into bed, arms and legs entwined. Our sweat mingles. We fall asleep at once, knowing we are safe.

I start awake, certain that I have heard another insistent high-pitched whine above my ear. I lie rigid, while Helena sleeps. Still believing I am listening for trouble, I too fall asleep again, and dream that I am chasing insects the size of birds.

I am on guard. I am the trained watcher, keeping the night safe for those I love. Yet I am unaware of the shadows that flit through the laundry colonnade in Fountain Court. I cannot hear the furtive feet as they creep up the stairs, nor even the crash of the monstrous boot as it kicks in a door.

The first I know of it is when Marius, my nephew and puppy-loving lodger, runs in yelling that he cannot sleep because of a row from the tenement opposite.

That is when I do grab my knife and run. Once awake, I can tell where the commotion is, and I know – with cold fear in my heart – that somebody is attacking my friend Lucius Petronius.

XLIV

I SHALL NEVER forget his face.

Dim light from a feeble wall-lamp showed the scene eerily. Petronius was being strangled. His lungs must have been bursting. He was purple, his face screwed with effort as he tried to break free. I threw my knife from the doorway; there was no time to cross the room. After racing up six long flights of stairs, I simply had no breath myself. It was a bad aim. All right, I missed. The blade sheared past the huge man's cheek. Not quite useless; he did drop Petro.

The main room was wrecked. Petronius must have roused himself when the door crashed in. I knew he had been on the balcony at some point; to attract attention he had hurled down an entire bench, tipped it right over the rocky parapet. As I had rushed here, I fell over it in the street, barking my shin badly. That was just before I stepped on the broken flowerpot and cut my foot. Petro had certainly done all he could to rouse the neighbourhood before he was overpowered. Then the giant had dragged him into the main room, and that was where I found them.

No one but me had come to help. As I pelted up the stairs, I had known that people would have been lying awake now, all petrified in the darkness, nobody willing to interfere lest they themselves were killed. Without Marius, Petro would have succumbed. Now perhaps, this gigantic assailant might kill both of us.

Milo of Croton would have nothing on him. He could have fought a rhinoceros; the betting touts would have gone crazy trying to fix the odds. He could have stepped in front of the lead quadriga in a full-pelt chariot race, and stopped it by seizing the reins, barely needing to brace his back or his enormous legs. I had seen some muscles, but he excelled all the weightlifting buttonheads I had ever had to fight before.

Petronius, no mean figure, now lay slumped at the monster's feet like a whittled doll. His face was hidden; I knew he might be dead. A pine table, so heavy it had originally taken us three days to hoist it upstairs, stood on one end with its main stretcher snapped; everything that had been on it lay in a smashed heap. With a delicate twist of his ankle, the giant kicked debris aside. Heavy potsherds skidded everywhere. It did not seem the moment to say, '*Let's talk about this sensibly . . .*'

I grabbed an amphora and heaved it at him. It bounced off his chest. As it landed, it cracked open and wine slewed everywhere. Unreasonably angered – because Petronius was a wine expert so it must be good stuff – I hurled a stool in the brute's face. He caught it, one-handed, and crushed it to a fistful of splinters. There had never been much furniture in my old office – which this was – and now there was virtually nothing in one piece.

Petronius had hooked his toga on the back of the door. Glancing down at my nudity as if shy, I grabbed the great white woollen thing. As the giant approached to crush out my life too, I swirled it once like a man who was seeking modesty in death – then flapped it in his eyes, a cloud of material that forced him to blink. Despite his flailing arm, I pancake-flipped the toga over his head. I dodged past him, trying to reach my knife. Shedding blood was my only hope. Once he grappled me, I would be lost.

He was blundering, trapped briefly in the toga's folds. I snatched the knife and since his neck was inaccessible, plunged it down between his mighty shoulder blades. My dagger had killed men in its time, but I might as well have tried to carve prime bullock steak with an ivory-handled plum-paring knife. As he spun around, with a small grunt of irritation, I did the only thing possible; I jumped on his back, temporarily out of his reach. I knew he would crash me against a wall, which with his force could be fatal. I got my arm round his neck, pegging down the toga so he could not see. One free hand was clawing behind him.

He was staggering forward. A massive foot missed the prone Petronius by an inch. The left hand had found my upper thigh and was squeezing so hard I nearly fainted. He was shaking me off, or trying to. He bucked forwards, got up speed, and by chance shot straight into the doorway to the balcony. He had wedged himself in the frame. I was still in the room behind. I slid floor-wards, leaned my shoulder and head against the slab of his waist, and pushed for all I was worth. It pinioned his arms. He was still blinded by the toga. He was stuck, but it would never last. Even my full body weight was making no impression, with raw terror to inspire me.

Material ripped; the toga had had it. I felt the brute shudder. He was

225

about to use his full strength. Either the wall would collapse, or he would burst outside. The old folding door, which had had a hard life during my tenancy, creaked in protest. I groaned with effort. Someone else groaned. My sinews were bursting. My bare feet were skidding as I pushed. I was aware of noises like Petronius complaining after a hard night. Next moment he had hauled himself upright beside me.

The giant could have resisted the two of us as easily as one, but he did not realise what was coming. Through eyes that were squinting and filled with running sweat as I struggled, I met Petro's woozy gaze. We did not need a verbal countdown. As one, we gave an unexpected heave with all our strength and shoved our assailant through the doorway.

He stumbled right out onto the parapet. It must have been stronger than I thought, because it survived his crashing weight. He was scrabbling for a grip on the stonework, but we rushed forwards. We seized a foot each. Raising them right above our heads, we leaned back, and then pushed hard again, one to each gigantic leg.

It was a hard fate, but we had no choice. It was him or us. Petro and I only had one chance, and we took it instinctively. As we lifted his legs, the huge man let out a yell; his great chest and belly bumped across the balustrade, then we had a glimpse of his bootsoles and he slid over head first.

We leaned against one another, holding each other up like drunkards, painfully gasping for breath. We tried not to listen to the instant of silence, or the heavy crunch as the faller landed. When eventually I leaned out and looked down, I did think for a second I saw him crawling, but then he lay still in the finality of death.

The rest was interesting. Dark figures suddenly materialised and bent over the body. I saw one pale face looking up, too far away to identify. Weak as I was by then, I could have been mistaken, but it seemed to me they made an attempt at dragging off the corpse. He must have been too heavy. After a moment they all rapidly walked away.

The next men to arrive had a lantern and a whistle, and were clearly a troop of vigiles.

We waited for them to notice that they were near Petro's apartment and come upstairs to us. We were both wrecked. We could have called down to them. We were too exhausted to do anything more than wave feebly.

'Who was your friend, Lucius?' I demanded wryly.

'Yours, I think, Marcus.'

'I really must notify the world that I have changed my address.'

'Good,' Petronius agreed. He was in a bad way now. As we tried to recover, failing mostly, he added in a quiet voice, 'He wanted to stop the rumours about the Aurelian Bank.'

'He told you? He didn't mind you knowing he was sent by Lucrio?'

Petro's voice rasped, due to his damaged throat. One hand was holding his neck. 'I was meant to end up dead.'

We remained silent for a while. Enjoying the moment. Both savouring the fact that Lucius Petronius Longus was alive.

'Was that,' he croaked, 'my toga you destroyed?' He hated wearing a toga, like any good Roman. Unfortunately, it was a necessary element of life.

'Afraid so.' I lolled against the outside wall, feeling slightly sick. 'Shredded, I fear. I would give you mine, but Nux whelped her pup on it.'

Petronius sat down on his haunches, unable to stay upright. He held his head between his hands. 'We can buy matching new ones, like best friends.' There was a pause. Not for the first time in our lives, we were best friends who were feeling rather ill. This time we could not even blame it on a night of debauchery. 'Thanks, Falco.'

'Don't thank me.' Petro had taken a lot of damage before I arrived. He was ready to pass out. I was too weak to help him much, but I could hear the vigiles coming up the stairs now. 'My dear Lucius, you haven't heard me confess yet what I did to your amphora.'

'Not the Chalybonium? I really wanted to try that . . .'

'Imported, isn't it? Must have cost you!'

'You damned menace,' Petronius muttered weakly. Then he keeled over. I had no strength to catch him, but I managed to get my left foot stretched out so his face — no longer that suffocated purple — landed on my foot. At least it was a better pillow than the floor.

XLV

I WOKE LATE, in my own bed again. My sister Maia was looking in at the bedroom door. 'Want a drink? I've made hot *mulsum*.'

Moving carefully, I crawled to the living room. I ached, but I had been worse. Nothing was broken or split open this time. I had no internal pain.

Nux and the puppy wagged ecstatic tails. The puppy wagged his little worm perpetually, but Nux meant a real welcome. Julia was striding about in her wheeled walking-frame; she no longer needed it, she just enjoyed the racket. Maia had been left in charge.

There was no sign of Helena. 'Do you know what she's doing?'

'*Oh yes!*' replied Maia forcefully. 'I know *exactly* what she thinks she's up to.' Cradling my beaker, I shot her an enquiring look. Her tone of voice modified. 'Changing her library book, apparently.' Swapping Greek novels with Passus. Maia was obviously not going to tell me what had caused her to sound so indignant: some girls' stuff that I was not yet old enough to know about.

'How's Petronius?' The vigiles had stretchered him over here last night and laid him on our reading couch.

'Awake.'

'Well enough to keep an eye on you two,' he rasped himself, appearing in the doorway, barefoot, bare-chested and wrapped in a sheet. Julia trundled herself over to him, bumping hard into his knee. He winced. Maia indicated the end of my bench, then unhelpfully watched Petro aim himself across the room to sit. Once he had landed, he gave her a bared-teeth grin, acknowledging that he had nearly toppled over and that she had known it would be a close thing.

Maia looked at us, from one to another. 'You're a right pair.'

'Cute little treasures?' I suggested.

'Stupid chancers,' sneered Maia.

I wondered when Helena would return. I needed to see her. My sister would forget her scorn soon enough. Helena, who never said much after I had been in trouble, would nonetheless remember this event far longer and would grieve over its danger more deeply. Every time there were bad street sounds in the night, I would have to pull her into my arms and shield her from the memory of last night's terror.

Petro was reaching to collect the beaker Maia had grudgingly poured for him. The sheet slipped, showing widespread bruising. Scythax, the vigiles doctor, had been summoned last night and had examined him for broken ribs, but thought none was damaged. He had left a painkilling draught, some of which Petro unobtrusively poured into his cup.

'Looks horrible.' Maia was right. Petronius had a good body, but the giant must have wanted to hurt him before choking out his life. It would account for some of the noise Marius had heard. Maia squinted disapprovingly at the marbled black and purple results. Petro breathed in, showing off to her how he always kept in shape; her lip curled. 'You'll have to stop chasing the women. A few well-positioned cuts might have made you look romantic – but that's just ugly.'

'I'll stop chasing when I catch the right one,' said Petronius, gazing into his hot drink. Steam, comfortingly infused with honey and watered wine, wreathed around his battered face. He looked tired and still in shock, but his brown hair stood up boyishly.

'Really?' asked Maia, with a light disbelieving inflexion.

'Really.' Petro looked up suddenly with a faint smile that implied – well, maybe nothing at all.

We were all sitting subdued and silent when we were joined by Fusculus. He gazed around as if the atmosphere made him fear the worst, then weighed up his chief's wounds with routine expertise. As a courtesy, he pulled a face. 'Nice ornaments!'

'Pretty effect, eh? It was close. Still, we're not booking a funeral. What's new?' Fusculus tossed a glance towards Maia. Suspicion mingled with masculine interest. Petronius said briefly, 'Falco's sister. You can speak.'

Now Fusculus was taking a better look at him, after noticing that Petro's throat was so sore it was limiting his speech. 'It's true? The bastard tried to strangle you . . . ?'

'I'm all right.'

'Well, chief, I do have something to report. We know who he is. The description was easy enough to put around. He was a serious heavy, known as Bos. Built like a fighting bull –'

'We know that,' I commented.

Fusculus grinned. 'Rumour says you two tossed him over a balcony?'

'Very gently.'

'Accomplished with perfect etiquette? Well, Bos had a huge reputation. Nobody but you two crazymen would have dared tackle him. If you go down to the Forum today, you'll be treated like demigods –'

'What was his status?' interrupted Petronius.

'Brute-for-hire. Leaning on people. Squashing those who refused to co-operate. Mostly he just had to arrive on the doorstep and they gave up.'

'You surprise me!'

'Who used to hire him?' I asked Fusculus intently.

'Racketeers, rent-hungry landlords – and you guessed it: defaulted-on moneymen.'

'Particular clients?'

'Often a set of debt-collectors called the Ritusii. Harsh and hard-hearted. Known for their tough methods and subtle hints of unacceptable violence.'

'Wrong side of the law?'

'No,' said Fusculus dryly. 'In their field, they make the law. They are never sued for compensation. Nobody lodges complaints.'

Petronius stretched awkwardly. 'I think I might make one.'

'Can we prove Bos was sent here by the Ritusii? Doubtful,' I reminded him. 'Neither they nor Lucrio will admit a connection; banks aren't supposed to use enforcers, for one thing. They made a bad mistake, attacking a vigiles officer – but they are unlikely to admit they sent Bos to hurt you.'

'They do know we suspect it,' Fusculus told us. 'A report had to go to the Prefect.' Petronius choked with annoyance. He had wanted to settle this in his own way. Still, he did not insist on knowing which over-hasty member of the cohort had made the report in his absence. 'The Prefect sent a detachment to pull their place apart.'

'Oh good thinking! Find anything?' I scoffed sarcastically.

'What do you think?'

Petronius said nothing. Maia removed his empty beaker, which he seemed about to drop.

'Do these Ritusii hardmen openly work for Lucrio and the Aurelian Bank?' I demanded.

'Not openly,' said Fusculus. Then an expectant grin stretched across his face. He had something to tell us and wanted to see us react. 'Anyway, Falco, less business will be coming their way from that direction now – the Aurelian Bank has been inundated with scared clients wanting to withdraw their funds. Lucrio froze all accounts this morning and called in specialist liquidators. The bank has crashed.'

I helped Petro limp back to the reading couch, where he subsided drowsily.

'Can you look after yourself?'

'I'm in the hands of a lovely nurse,' he whispered with a husky pretence at secrecy. It was the traditional male response to being trapped in a sickbed. You have to play the game.

'Helena will be back any minute,' Maia retorted, whisking out of the room with a vigorous yank at her skirts.

I covered him over. 'Stop flirting with my sister. You may be the demigod who disposed of the giant Bos – but there's a queue for Maia. Don't risk your neck with Anacrites. That man is far too dangerous.'

I meant it. It would be bad enough if the Chief Spy made any headway with my sister, but if he did and she ever decided to dump him, it would threaten all our family. He had power. He controlled sinister resources, and he made a spiteful enemy. It was time all of us remembered Anacrites had a darker side.

Of course if he was dumped by my mother at the same time as Maia saw through him, we were probably dead from the moment the letter saying, '*Darling, we've had so much fun and I really hate writing this . . .*' landed on his Palace desk. I felt sick at the thought of anyone calling Anacrites *darling*. But that was nothing to my fear of his reaction if he ever lost face by rejection as a lover – especially if he then blamed me. He had tried to have me killed once, in Nabataea. It could happen again at any time.

As I brooded, Petronius was making some quiet joke: 'Ah, I won't have any luck with Maia. I'm her brother's horrible crony – tainted goods.'

Just as well. I hated all my brothers-in-law. What a pack of irritating swine. The last thing I could have tolerated was my best friend wanting to join them. Shaking my head to be rid of this thought, I set off to the Forum – not to be greeted like a hero, but to try to see Lucrio.

As I walked, I wondered why I had not told Maia the ill-tasting gossip about Anacrites and Ma. Pure cowardice, I admitted it.

Lucrio was nowhere to be found. I was hardly surprised. When any business goes bankrupt, the executives ensure that the night before it becomes open knowledge they ride off to their personal villas a long way from Rome – taking the silverware and petty cash. The Golden

Horse change-table stood empty and unstaffed. I walked to Lucrio's home address. A fair-sized crowd had gathered, some just standing with an air of hopelessness, others flinging rocks at shutters in a desolate way. A few were probably debtors who wondered if they might escape repaying their loans now. The door stayed closed and the windows were well barred.

I felt disappointed. As a riot, it was a washout. Sightseers had started arriving just to watch for suicides among the crowd but the crowd, slightly embarrassed, all looked ready to filter off home. Those who had lost most money would stay away. They would resist accepting what had happened, pretending everything was fine. As long as they could, they would fight off despair. When it struck, nobody would see them again.

There was nothing to do here. When a sad tambourine man came to play and sing mournful drinking songs, I left before his grimy assistant reached me with the hat.

Forget Lucrio. Forget these blank loafers drifting about in the street. I did not know them and I did not care too much about their losses. But if the bank had crashed, it affected real people, people I did know. There was something I had to tackle urgently. I had to go and see Ma.

XLVI

MOTHER'S NEIGHBOUR Aristagoras, the little old fellow, was
sunning himself in the portico. Ma always kept the common
areas of her block spick and span. Over the years, she must have saved
the landlord hundreds in sweeper's fees. There were bright pots of
roses by the front entrance, which she tended too.

Aristagoras called out a greeting; I raised an arm and kept going. He
was a chatterer, I could tell.

I ran lightly up the stairs to the apartment. Most days, Ma was either
out, whirling about the Aventine on errands and causing annoyance,
or else she was in, scrubbing away at pots or chopping like fury in her
cooking area. Today I just found her sitting still in a basket armchair
that my late brother Festus had once given her (I knew, though she
did not, that the cheeky beggar won it in a game of draughts). She had
her hands folded rather tightly in her lap. As usual, her dress and hair
were scrupulously neat, though a fine aura of tragic gloom enveloped
her.

I closed the door gently. Two eyes like burnt raisins bored into me.
I pulled up a stool beside her and squatted on it with my elbows on
my knees.

'You heard about the Aurelian Bank?'

Ma nodded. 'One of the men who works for Anacrites came to see
him early this morning. Is it true?'

'Afraid so. I've just been down there – all closed up. Did Anacrites
manage to remove his cash?'

'He had notified the agent that he wanted to make a withdrawal,
but the money has not yet been paid to him.'

'Tough.' I managed to sound neutral. I gazed at Ma. Despite her
anxious stillness, her face was expressionless. 'They probably knew
they were in trouble, you know; they would have slowed up on
shelling out. I wouldn't be too concerned about him. He may have
lost a packet with the Aurelian, but he must have plenty more hoarded
away in other safe places. It goes with his job.'

'I see,' said Ma.

'Anyway,' I continued gravely, 'there are liquidators appointed. All Anacrites has to do is toddle along to see them, mention that he's the influential Chief Spy, and they will ensure he'll be top of the list of creditors who get paid in full. Only wise move they can make.'

'I'll tell him to do that!' Ma exclaimed, looking relieved on behalf of her protégé. I ground my teeth. Telling him how to bail himself out had not really been my plan.

I waited, but Ma was still keeping her worries to herself. I felt a wrench of embarrassment, as one of her youngest children talking about her finances. For one thing, we had a long-standing tussle about whether I was ever allowed to take charge of anything. For another, she was desperately secretive.

'What about your own money, Ma?'

'Oh well, never mind that.'

'Stop fooling. You had a lot on deposit with that bank, don't pretend otherwise. Had you drawn any out recently?'

'No.'

'So they had it all. Well, Anacrites is the idiot who made you put it there; you should get him to lean on them for you.'

'I don't want to bother him.'

'Right. Look, I have to deal with Lucrio on another issue. I'll ask what the situation is. If there's any chance of getting your money back, I'll do what I can.'

'There is no need to go to any trouble. You don't need to worry about me,' wailed Ma pathetically. That was typical. In fact, I would never have heard the last of it if I had left her to stew in anxiety. I said politely that it was no trouble; I was a dutiful boy who loved his mother and I would happily devote my days to sorting out her affairs. Ma humphed.

This might have been the moment to mention the rumours about Anacrites growing too close as a lodger. My nerve failed.

I could hardly imagine Mother and the spy alone together. She had nursed him when he was desperately ill; that would have involved intimate personal contact – but it was surely different from having an affair. Ma and him in bed? Never! Not just because she was a lot older than him. Perhaps I just did not want to imagine my mother in bed with anyone . . .

'What's on your mind, son?' Ma noticed me thinking, a process she always regarded as dangerous. The traditional Roman virtues specifically exclude philosophy. Good boys don't dream. Good mothers don't let them. She swiped at me. Out of long experience, I ducked just in time. I managed not to fall off my stool. Her hand sliced through my curls, missing my head. 'Own up!'

'I've heard a few rumours lately. . .'

Ma bristled. 'What rumours?'

'Just some nonsense.'

'What nonsense?'

'Not worth mentioning.'

'But worth thinking about until you get that silly grin!'

'Who's grinning?' I felt about three years old. The feeling was confirmed when my mother took hold of my ear, with a fierce grip that I knew too well.

'*What exactly are you talking about?*' demanded my mother. I wished I were fighting Bos again.

'People get the wrong idea.' I managed to writhe free. 'Look, it's none of my business –' My mother's Medusa stare told me *that* was probably true. 'I just happened to hear someone insinuate – obviously under a ridiculous misapprehension – that you might have taken up with a certain person of the male variety who sometimes frequents this place . . .'

Ma leapt out of her chair.

I sidestepped and hurried to the door, more than happy to leave in disgrace. With the door safely opened, I turned back and apologised.

Ma said rigidly, 'I'll thank you – and I'll thank whatever busybodies have been gossiping about me – to keep their noses out of my affairs.'

'Sorry, Ma. Of course, I never believed it –'

Her chin came up. She looked as if someone with his boots fresh from a cow-byre had dared to walk across a floor she had just washed. 'If I wanted a little bit of comfort in my final years, I am surely entitled to it.'

'Oh yes, Ma.' I tried not to look shocked.

'If I did have a friend I was rather fond of,' explained Ma heavily, 'assuming I dared to think I would be allowed to get away with it – then you and your high-minded sisters could rely on me to be discreet.' So she guessed it was one of my sisters spreading the story. I had better warn Junia to leave Italy.

'Sorry, Ma –'

'The least I could expect in return is a modicum of privacy!'

Dear gods. As a rebuttal, this was much weaker than I had hoped to hear. 'Yes, Ma.'

'I am not entirely decrepit, Marcus! I have had my opportunities.'

'You are a fine woman,' I assured her, unintentionally echoing Aristagoras. 'You can do what you like —'

'Oh I will!' agreed my mother, with a dangerous glint.

As I retreated slowly down to street level, I was feeling tired even though I had done hardly anything that morning. In fact, I felt as if I had been sucked down a whirlpool, then spat up stark naked on some extremely pointed rocks.

The old man in the portico had managed to fix on somebody, so I slid past unobtrusively — only to hear my name called in a loud bellow by a horribly familiar voice. I turned back in horror.

'*Pa!*' Olympus, this was turning into a family festival.

I felt astonished. I had not seen my father in this vicinity since I was seven years old. He and Ma had never met since he bunked off. For years, Ma pretended Pa did not even exist. When they were a couple, he had used his real name, Favonius. To her, the auctioneer 'Geminus' was a raffish scamp both her sons had sometimes chosen to mess about with in some masculine world she would not deign to investigate. When he wanted to communicate, even to send her money, it had to be done through an intermediary and using codes.

A mad thought struck, that when she had been talking about a new friend she might be fond of, Ma had meant that after Flora died she had made up her old fight with Pa.

No chance.

'What on earth are you doing sloping round Ma's front porch, Father? It's risking a thunderbolt.'

'Time some things were sorted.' I winced. Pa must be crazy. Interference from him was likely to bring wrath on all our heads. 'Junia just brought in the caupona takings. She told me the fine news that Junilla Tacita has acquired a follower!'

'Our Junia loves a vulgar story to spread —' With a quick glance at Aristagoras, who blinked at us from under his sunbathing hat with bright-eyed curiosity, I tipped Pa the wink that we ought to bunk off to a winebar. As one, we gave the old neighbour a farewell grin and wheeled off together, Pa's arm heavily around my shoulders in unaccustomed amity. We must have looked more like brothers than father and son.

As soon as we were out of sight, I shook myself free; I dragged Pa as far as I could — not far enough, but he soon started grumbling and wanting the drink. I reminded him that my suggestion was not really for refreshment, but saving our skins if Ma had come out and found us gossiping. 'I just tackled her, and got a sore ear – literally. That was before she told me what she thinks of people spreading rumours – a diatribe I won't dwell on.'

My father laughed. He could. It was not his ear she had twisted with her brutal digits. Well, not this time. But he looked as if he remembered the experience. We wheeled into a bar and plumped ourselves down on benches.

'Of course it must be a mistake,' I raved bitterly. It was time somebody stood up to Pa. 'We all think she's in bed with the lodger – but perhaps it's much more disgusting: she may be secretly getting back together with you.'

'Now there's an idea! Think she would wear it?' Pa never had any sense – or any tact, either. He leaned across the bar table urgently. 'So what's the real story with Anacrites?'

'Don't ask me. I've been forbidden any scandalous speculation. I'm not stupid enough to risk it now.'

'This is dreadful, son.'

I was close to agreeing, then found myself wondering – as Ma would do – what possible connection there could be with him.

'Come off it, Pa. That it's the spy is horrible enough – and it's certainly bloody dangerous – but you have a nerve interfering with Mother nowadays.'

'Don't be pious!'

'Nor you then.'

'She says she is entitled to a private life – and she's right. Maybe she's doing it just to annoy other people.'

'Me, for instance?' muttered Pa darkly.

'How did you guess? Who knows what's really going on. Mother always enjoyed a situation where everyone else was going frantic, while she just let them think whatever they liked.'

'But not if it involves that creep Anacrites!'

'Ah well.' I tried viewing it philosophically. 'He has been behaving too well lately. It was time he did something in character again.'

'Screwing your mother?' Pa sneered crudely. 'It's revolting –' He suddenly thought of a fine excuse for his own pompous attitude: 'I'm thinking about my grandchildren – especially baby Julia. She has a connection to the Senate; she cannot have her dear little reputation soiled by scandal.'

'Don't bring my daughter into it. I'll protect Julia Junilla – if it's ever needed.'

'You couldn't protect a chickpea,' said Pa, in his usual affectionate way. He craned his head, checking me over for bruises. 'I hear you were thrashed again last night?'

'You mean I saved the life of Petronius Longus, stayed alive myself, and rid Rome of a bullying piece of dirt the size of a small house.'

'Time you grew up, son.'

'Look who is talking! After walking out twenty-five years ago, and after all the floozies you have bedded before and since, coming to preach at Mother today is just grotesque.'

'I don't care what you think.' He drained his cup. I started to drain mine in a similar gesture. Then I slowed down and deliberately made the move delicate, so as not to look like him. The thoughtful, moderate one in the family. (The unbearable, good-natured bastard, my father would say.)

I stood up. 'Well, I've quarrelled with both my parents now. That's enough grief for one day. I'm off.' Pa had leapt up even faster than I did. I felt nervous. 'Now what are you up to?'

'I'm going to have it out.'

'Don't be so stupid!' The thought of him broaching Ma on this subject was so ghastly I nearly brought up the wine I had drunk. 'Have some self-respect. Well, self-preservation, anyway. She won't thank you.'

'She won't know anything about it,' came his rejoinder. 'Her boyfriend keeps office hours, presumably – well, he won't be out taking risks, not him. He'll have a nice cool nook to hide in – which is about to become hotter than he'll like. Goodbye now, son. I can't hang about here!'

When Geminus stormed off, I had no choice: I paid the bill for our drinks, then, keeping at a safe distance, hopped after him.

I thought I was the expert at Palace ceremonial. Vespasian believed he had instituted a new approachable system in his court. This Emperor allowed anyone to see him who wanted to present a petition or a crackpot idea; he had even discontinued the old practice of having all supplicants searched for weapons. Naturally, the main result of this casual attitude was that chamberlains and guards had become hysterical behind his back. To get past the supposedly relaxed operatives who now ran the Palatine could take hours.

I knew some of the people who worked there; I had also held on to various passes that I had acquired during official missions. Even so, when I reached the suite where Anacrites lurked, Pa must have got in ahead of me. The Chief Spy's office was in a dim, unpromising corridor, otherwise occupied by absentee auditors. It was a place of open doors looking onto dusty rooms with unoccupied clerks' benches and occasional stored old thrones. Anacrites usually kept his own door firmly closed, so nobody would see if he nodded off while waiting for his lackadaisical runners to bother to report in.

He had dangerous status. Officially, he worked on detachment to the Praetorian Guard, even though they never supplied him with anyone in armour to flank his office doorway. As top dog in intelligence, he might be incompetent in my eyes, yet he ranked high. Only a fool, therefore, would march in here and take him to task on a personal issue.

My heart sank as I approached. Too many observers were wandering about. There were pale-faced little slaves trotting past on errands. Other bureaucrats were sitting bored in other offices. Despite the carefree régime at the Emperor's private quarters, in these areas there were soldiers on full alert. From time to time, Anacrites' own personnel might appear. They were a seedy lot, and probably owed him favours. As a spy, the least he could do as a manager was to ensure he had bought his own team's loyalty with spare cash from the bribes fund.

From the far end of the corridor I could hear irately raised voices. My father had barged into the sanctum with his blood up. Things sounded even trickier than I had feared. I rushed down and stormed in. Anacrites looked frigid with indignation and Pa was bouncing on his heels, red-faced and roaring insults.

'Didius Geminus, get a grip,' I hissed. 'Don't be damned foolish, Pa!'

'Bugger off – don't prate at me!'

'Leave it alone, you idiot –'

'No fear! I'm going to do this bastard.'

Suddenly it was my crazed parent and me having the set-to, while Anacrites himself just stood aloof, looking bemused.

'Oh settle down, Pa! It's none of your business, and you don't even know if it's true.'

'Whether it's true doesn't matter,' roared Pa. 'People should not be saying these terrible things about your mother –'

Anacrites went white, as if he finally saw the problem. My father was now dancing like a rather flighty boxer. I grabbed at his arm. He flung me off. 'Stop it! If you calm down, you may discover the worst Anacrites has done is to lose Ma's savings in a bank that failed.'

Whoops! At that, Pa became incandescent. 'Lost her savings? That will be *my* money you're talking about! I know for sure your mother has always refused to spend what I keep sending her –'

He was right, and I should have kept quiet. He blew up. Before I could stop him, he rounded again on Anacrites, balled his fist and took a wild swing at the spy.

XLVII

A NACRITES SURPRISED me: he was ready for it and knocked Pa's arm aside. By then, I was hanging on to my father, but as I pulled down his right arm he managed to let fly with his left fist and caught the spy a mighty clip across the ear. I hauled away my maddened parent, then, as Anacrites jumped forward angrily, I drew back my own arm to hit him and protect Pa. Somebody caught hold of me.

I turned. I stopped. We all did. The person who had grabbed me with the iron grip was a woman.

'Flying phalluses, Falco! What's this brawl about?'

'Perella!' I exclaimed in shock.

She was a dancer. I mean a good one, not some twirling girl in a two-piece costume with eyes for all the men. Aged somewhere short of fifty but a long way after girlhood, Perella looked like a housewife with a headache on a bad day of the month. She was the deadliest intelligence agent I had ever met.

'Fancy running into you again.'

'No – I ran at you, Falco,' she said, letting go of me with a contemptuous flick of her wrist.

'Stay still, Pa,' I warned him grittily. 'The last person I saw upsetting Perella ended up terminally out of it. She's a rather clever lady; we worked together on a job in Baetica.'

'You stole that job from me,' Perella commented.

I grinned. Perhaps uncertainly. 'This is my father,' I introduced him, not mentioning her main occupation since Pa probably thought he was a demon at seducing dancers. 'He's a lamb normally. He just happened to hear that Anacrites has been making love to my old mother and he lost his rag.' Anacrites, who had gone red when Pa hit him, now went white again. I grabbed Pa by the scruff of his tunic. 'Come on. That's enough of us playing the fighting Didius boys. I'm taking you home.'

'Sounds as if the Didius boys – and probably your mother – had best leave town,' murmured Perella. She was implying how stupid it was to offend the Chief Spy.

'I don't think that will be necessary.' For the first time, I looked directly at Anacrites. I spoke quietly. 'You owe me one for Lepcis Magna, isn't that right?'

Perella was looking intrigued. She could obviously tell I had made a serious threat. I had done it in front of other people on purpose.

Anacrites breathed carefully. At Lepcis, he had fought as a gladiator in the arena. That meant legal infamy. If it were known, he would lose his position, and be stripped of his newly-acquired middle rank. His free citizenship would be meaningless. He would become a non-person. 'Of course, Falco.' He was standing so straight he was almost on parade at attention.

I smiled at him. It was not returned.

'So now we are on even terms again,' he pleaded.

'If you like.' Not so even as he implied. This fight with Pa would lose its importance very quickly; Anacrites would remain vulnerable to exposure for the rest of his life. No need to insist too strongly. He knew I had him. 'Take a hint, Anacrites old son – it's time to move on. My mother has loved having a lodger, but she is no longer young; she is finding it a bit much nowadays.'

'I was intending to move out,' he said, in a taut voice.

'And one other small point – she is anxious about her savings now the bank has failed.'

'I shall do what I can, Falco.' Then he asked wistfully, 'What about Maia Favonia?'

I had done enough. Never strip a man so brutally that he is left with nothing to lose. Maia would have to be the sacrifice. 'My dear fellow! That is between you and her, of course.'

He did not thank me.

'What does he mean?' demanded Pa.

'Mind your own business.' I skipped telling him that Anacrites wanted to jump generations; it would only set him off again. Or even if Pa stayed cool, if I thought too much about Anacrites making himself a 'friend' to my sister, it might be me letting fly at him.

I marched my father out of the Palace and dragged him into a closed carrying chair, away from prying eyes. I stayed with him all the way to the Saepta Julia, neither of us saying much. At the warehouse, we found Maia, writing figures neatly in the auction daybook. She appeared busy, competent, and content. At our entrance together, she looked up in surprise.

'What have you two been up to?'

'Our esteemed father just socked Anacrites.'

'You pair of fools! What for, Pa?'

'Oh . . . he gave your mother some terrible financial advice.'

Instinctively, both Pa and I decided not to mention to my sister the real subject of the disagreement.

Maia sidetracked herself, in fact: she had heard about Junia's idea that Pa and I should swap houses. While she had us together, she decided to extol the virtues of him opting for semi-retirement and moving to the Janiculan (nearer the Saepta Julia than his Aventine place, and perhaps further from the temptation to run wild and hit officials) and of me taking Pa's tall, spacious house on the riverbank (close to clients, with plenty of room for a family). Subdued, we both listened to her reasonable words. Eventually Maia found it too disconcerting.

'Oh, I can't stand any more of this! What's the matter with you two? Why are neither of you arguing?'

I had played the peacemaker quite enough today. I left Pa to calm her down.

XLVIII

I WENT HOME. Helena had returned and was talking to Petronius in our third room. She had her nose deep in a chest where my tunics were stored, lifting them out by the shoulders and subjecting each much-loved antique to a mocking survey.

'I am just checking your wardrobe. You and Lucius need to visit a tailor for new togas, so you may as well acquire some wearable tunics at the same time.' She looked up, suddenly uncomfortable, as if she had pried into my bachelor storage without my permission. 'Do you mind?'

'That's all right, love.' Seeing a washed-out wine-coloured tunic that I had forgotten I owned, I grabbed the garment and started changing into it. 'I don't keep anything in there that I don't want you to find.'

Helena went back to her inspection. After a quiet pause she asked me in an amused tone, 'So, Marcus, where *do* you hide things you are keeping secret?'

We all laughed, while I tried not to blush.

In my bankbox, was the answer – or for tricky items that passed through the home temporarily, stuffed quickly inside the slipcase of a cushion on my reading couch.

To change the subject, I told Helena and Petro what had happened earlier. 'Frankly I feel more shattered after coping with my parents than I was last night after we tackled that giant.'

Helena Justina was by then safely out in the main living room, where she had settled to her own devices and started reading a scroll. It must now be the one she had swapped with Passus that morning, when she left Maia here. She was seated in a basket chair like the one Festus had given Ma, with her feet up on a tall stool and the scroll across her knees. She had the intent air I recognised; I could hold an entire conversation with her, but afterwards she would be quite unaware of what had been said. Her mind was locked in the new

Greek novel, gallivanting about a strange landscape with Gondomon, King of Traximene, as Passus had been yesterday in the Greek library. Until she finished, she was lost to me. If I had been a jealous type like Pa, I would have been searching for that bastard Gondomon, to take a pot at him.

'Forget your darling family,' said Petro. He still sounded hoarse, though he had been given lunch and looked a little livelier than this morning. 'How about concentrating on the job I gave you? I'm anxious to see the Chrysippus case wrapped up, Falco.'

'Don't tell me – Rubella is expected back?'

'Smart boy.'

'When?'

'End of August.'

'That calls for action then. I suppose you want to present your beloved superior with a success?'

'Yes. I want this sorted – *before* he finds out how much of the slack in our budget I used up on your unconventional services,' agreed Petro, with force. 'Another reason,' he told me more mildly, 'is that I ordered Fusculus to put the bank's new owners under observation, now it's crashed. He reported back on signs that both Lucrio and Lysa are intending to pack themselves off in a hurry to Greece.'

'Oh rats. Showdown time, then.'

'Yes – results, please, Falco.'

'I have a plan, of course.'

Petro glared at me suspiciously. 'I thought you were stuck?'

'Who me?'

Until then my plan had been to eat an omelette and a bowl of wild strawberries, then snooze in bed all afternoon. Instead, I devoured the snack, lay awake on the bed – and planned out what I had to do.

'When in doubt, make a list,' snorted Petro from the doorway, craning his neck to peer at my notes.

'Stop supervising; I have Helena for that. If I may say so, you seem well enough to return to your own apartment now.'

'I'm enjoying it here . . . Anyway, my place is wrecked,' Petro groaned. Then he nagged me again: 'You come up with something, Falco – or else!'

He was worried. That suited me. When I sorted out the case, he would be relieved and grateful.

Once I was satisfied that I had covered everything, I jumped up, tucked my notes in a pouch on my belt, and strapped on my favourite boots. 'Where are you going?' Petro niggled, fretting to come with me, though he was still too pasty.

'Out!'

'Oh grow up, Falco.'

He was always bored stiff as an invalid; I took pity on him. 'Listen, tribune, I am getting somewhere –'

'Even though you don't know who killed Chrysippus, and you can't prove who strung up Avienus?'

'Pedantic swine. We may never be able to finger the Ritusii for Avienus, you know that. Professional enforcers leave no tracks, and Lucrio is clever; he knows he only has to keep his mouth permanently shut in order to get away with hiring them. If it *was* him. It could have been Lysa.'

'So what's happening?' Petronius frowned.

'I need to ask one or two more questions of almost all the suspects and witnesses. To save me running around like a crazed ant in this summer heat, I shall pull them all in together for one big enquiry session.'

'I want to be there, Falco.'

'Hush, hush, my boy! You will be in on it; I want you to see me triumphantly unmasking the villain.'

'And where are you going now?' he insisted.

'To check one last alibi.'

First, I placed one finger on Helena's scroll just when she was about to unravel the next column. She glared up at me, avid to continue reading. 'Don't, or I'll bite!'

I lifted my finger away quickly. 'Good is it, this one?'

'Yes, Passus was right. It's excellent. Quite different from the first awful thing I read for you.'

'And it looks like the author's own manuscript?'

Helena waved the papyrus impatiently, so I could see it was written in a difficult hand and littered with alterations. She was racing through it though. 'Yes, it's as blotty as a child learning the alphabet. And someone has stuck together all sorts of old documents to make a scroll to compose on – there are even a few luncheon receipts.'

'Stuffed vine leaves?'

'Chickpea mash. Are you going out, Marcus?'

'Devotions at a temple.'

Helena found time for a smile. 'Your geese on the Capitol, procurator?'

'No, the Chrysippus case.' In the background, Petronius snorted. 'I'll be back in time to cook dinner for you and the malingerer. You enjoy yourself with the zippy prose adventure. If I do any shopping for the meal, should I include Marius?'

'No. Maia took him home.'

'She wants her brood where she can see them.'

'Actually, she wants time to herself. But Junia has decided to do something nice for somebody. She is going to Ostia with Gaius Baebius.' Ostia was where Gaius worked as a supervisor of customs clerks. 'She offered to take all the children, so they can swim at the seaside.'

'Junia, on a beach? With a swarm of little ones? And they will have to stay overnight!' Doubt struck me. 'Is Maia going too?'

'I believe not,' said Helena disingenuously. I glanced at Petro and we both scowled. Helena kept her eyes fixed on the scroll. 'The whole point is to give Maia a little peace alone.'

Alone? Or sharing a few delicious moments with her admirer Anacrites?

THE TEMPLE of Minerva on the Aventine lay only a few minutes' walk away, though I cannot pretend it was one of my haunts.

Now that I had started thinking about our local temples, I came to see the Aventine as an ancient holy place. Once it had lain outside the *pomerium,* the official city boundary that had been ploughed out by Romulus. That original exclusion had allowed the positioning here of shrines that possessed for our forefathers a remote, out-of-town mystique; in the quieter squares of the modern Aventine, they still maintained their historical air of privacy. Perhaps they always would. The Aventine has a special atmosphere. The views once enjoyed from here must have been stunning. We who lived here now could still see the river and the distant hills, or in open spaces feel close to the sky and the moon.

Cacus, a god of fire who must have been a foul rapscallion, had lived in a cave at the base of the cliff; slain by Hercules, his haunt became the Cattle Market Forum. Above, we had Ceres, the great queen of agricultural growth and grain; Liberty the freed slaves' patroness in her turned-over felt cap; Bona Dea, the Good Goddess; and Luna, the moon goddess, whose temple had been one of the few buildings on the Aventine destroyed in Nero's Great Fire. Two local temples were at present working up to their annual festivals. One was Diana's majestic sanctuary in the plebeian part of the Hill, where the goddess was traditionally worshipped by working people and slaves. The other was the small shrine of Vertumnus, god of the seasons, change, and ripening plants, a fruit-wreathed garden deity of whom I had always been secretly fond.

Most classically cool was Minerva. It seemed fully appropriate that the son of a family with a Greek background would attend this temple. I could not argue with that. Diomedes was thoroughly Romanised, yet I had seen how firmly he was influenced by his mother. If Lysa loved Athene, he might well offer prayers to the armoured owl-goddess himself. A good boy – well, one who was pushed about firmly by Mama.

In the echoing sanctum, I forced a priest to speak to me. Gaining attention was so difficult I even tried citing my position as Procurator of the Sacred Geese of Juno. Hah! That got me nowhere. So I had to resort to simpler methods: threatening the shrine with a visit from the vigiles.

One of their refined operatives then deigned to take questions. I still might as well not have bothered. His answers were useless. He seemed unable to recognise my careful description of my suspect, and had no recollection of him attending the Temple on the day Chrysippus died. The priest *had* heard of Aurelius Chrysippus and Lysa. They had been benefactors of the Temple in the past. So I knew there was a link with the family. It hardly amounted to an alibi for murder.

Annoyed, I set off for Lysa's house to re-interview her son. I accepted that Diomedes had never been subjected to real interrogation before now. There could be advantages in letting him think he had escaped close scrutiny. (Not that I could think what those advantages might be.)

Outside the house, I noticed the vigilis observer that Fusculus had placed there in case the principals did a flit. He was pretending to drink at a caupona, a peaceful type of surveillance; I nodded but did not speak to him.

The place was barred and bolted as Lucrio's house had been after the bank crashed, but a porter let me in. Indoors, there were indeed signs of imminent departure. It was definitely time to act, or we would lose Lysa and the freedman. Packed bundles and chests were standing about. Since I was here before, some wall hangings and curtains had been taken down.

For once, Diomedes was in. For once, he made no attempt to seek refuge behind his mother; she did not appear at all. He had grown a beard, shaped like his father's. I told him of my inconclusive meeting with the priest, and ordered him to come back with me to the Temple, to see if he could find somebody else there who might remember him. 'If not, you may have to shave off this new face-disguise.'

As we were leaving, somebody entered the house – Lucrio, interestingly in possession of his own latch-lifter. He looked a little harassed and tired. He was also put out at seeing me – though far too astute to complain.

'Stay there.' I snapped at Diomedes. 'Lucrio, sending a thug to kill me was not a bright idea!' I would get him for that if I could.

Lucrio was too clever, or too weary to pretend. He just kicked off his outdoor shoes and filled in time shoving his feet into house slippers.

'I am sorry you had to liquidate,' I said. 'Let's get this straight though. My enquiries were never aimed against the bank maliciously – and I never suggested to people that there should be a run on deposits. Don't blame me for what has happened. I just want to identify who killed your old master.'

Lucrio made no comment on the Bos incident, but said of the bank, 'The collapse was inevitable. From the moment Chrysippus was killed, we faced a loss of public confidence.' A ghost of a smile crossed his face. 'That should be one argument against me being your killer. I foresaw this. I would never have risked it.'

'What happens now?' I asked.

'A careful and calm unwinding of our affairs in Rome. Neutral agents, experienced in such work, will pay off what they can of our debts.'

'Do something for me.' There was no question of letting him buy himself off, though if he thought he could, it might help Ma. 'Look kindly on the deposits of a little old lady called Junilla Tacita. She came to you on the recommendation of Anacrites, the spy. I expect he handled the deal.'

'He didn't,' replied the freedman, somewhat testily. 'I remember Junilla Tacita. We negotiated face to face.'

'I won't ask what arrangements you made for her. I don't expect you to break a client's confidence.'

'Good!' He was being unhelpful. It was professionally correct, though I sensed annoyance. 'What's Junilla Tacita to you, Falco?'

'My mother,' I said levelly. I wondered if Ma might have dealt with Lucrio in her inimitable style. The feeling was confirmed when I suddenly found myself exchanging wry grins with him. 'Have a look at her situation,' I instructed. 'You can tell me tomorrow – I want to finalise my enquiries. Come at noon, please, to the scriptorium. Tell Lysa, she is to be there as well.'

He nodded, then glanced curiously at Diomedes, still standing beside me with all the vigour of beached seaweed. 'Diomedes and I are just going for a nice walk, Lucrio. If his dear mother wonders what we are up to, assure the lady it is routine.'

Diomedes protested when he learned I was serious about walking up the Aventine. Apparently, he went everywhere in a carrying chair. Nonetheless, he was sufficiently nervous to let himself be dragged off on foot. I thought Lucrio, the future stepfather who had been a household slave, enjoyed seeing that.

Diomedes was useless on a route march. On the other hand, when I sized him up, his chest and arm muscles were not badly developed. He was no weakling, but I guessed he lacked real training. His mother had probably paid a fortune to a gymnasium teacher – one who let Diomedes swing too many lightweight exercise clubs and spend too long tossing little beanbags to and fro.

Money had been spent on him. He could probably read poetry and play the cithara. His clothing was expensive, of course, though his fancy boots were far too soft for tramping uneven paving stones. His tunic, soon soaked with perspiration across the shoulders, made him look like the master whilst I – in my old wine-red rag – must seem to be his slave. That would give my Aventine neighbours cause to snigger. I walked faster, striding manfully ahead of him while he trailed behind feebly.

Even before we had rounded the Circus, Diomedes was limping. I dragged him up the Clivus Publicius, towards his late father's house, at a merciless pace. He was fit enough not to get too breathless. Outside the popina where the scriptorium writers drank, I happened to see Euschemon. I stopped.

'Diomedes, you trot ahead to your temple. Try to find somebody to vouch for you at the time your father was being murdered. I'll follow in a moment.' A cunning look appeared in his dark eyes. 'Don't think of bunking off,' I told him briefly. 'Flight will brand you as the killer. I assume that even Romanised Greeks know the penalty for parricide?' This penalty was so sensational most educated people had heard of it. The details featured large whenever tourists from the provinces were hearing Roman law extolled. He must know. With a friendly smile, I told him anyway: 'Sons who kill their fathers are tied in a large sack along with a dog, a cock, a viper and an ape – then thrown into the river.'

I was not sure whether he believed me, but the son of Chrysippus scurried off in his delicate footwear, eager to establish his alibi.

Euschemon had quietly watched me despatch his ex-employer's son; he had a rather narrow expression. He had always spoken of Diomedes with restraint rather than open dislike, but they had not exchanged greetings just now.

The scriptorium manager was leaning an elbow on the popina

counter, enjoying a beaker of what looked like chilled wine and water. The waiter had been talking to him, that thin young man I had noticed several times before serving here, with a towel over one shoulder and a leather apron. I joined them and asked for a cup of fruitjuice.

'How is it going, Falco?'

'Nearly there. I want to hold some final interviews tomorrow, Euschemon. Could I trouble you to mention to Vibia Merulla that I need to use the library – and that I want her to be there? Yourself too, please.'

'Vibia is at home, if you want to speak to her.' Euschemon seemed to know I was wary of meeting her alone.

'I'm short of time, unfortunately!'

The waiter brought my drink. I dropped coppers on his tray, trying to avoid eye contact.

'Do you know this young man?' Euschemon asked me. I shook my head. 'He works here to earn spare cash. We were just discussing his prospects as a writer.' He seemed about to say more, but the waiter became embarrassed and turned away to mop around the apple press. I glanced at him. He looked ordinary enough. If he was harbouring wild dreams, the creative madness failed to show.

This was a grim place to drudge as a skivvy. Like most popinae, it served as the ante-room for meetings with low-grade prostitutes; they worked from a couple of rooms upstairs. The carved stone frieze that advertised the services available here bore the usual sad trio of a small beaker, a small dicepot – and a huge phallus. No doubt the waiter could earn extra tips by promising to fix up clients with whichever girl was youngest and perhaps least diseased.

I gave a benign smile to the young man with the optimistic hopes. Then I turned back to Euschemon. 'I want to ask you tomorrow about what's the future for the scriptorium authors. And could you arrange for the ones we interviewed about the death to be brought here for my meeting?'

'Right. But I can tell you the situation now: Vibia wants to continue the business.'

'Were you expecting that?'

'No,' he replied quietly, clearly realising I wanted to test him: did the fate of the scriptorium give him – or Vibia – some motive for Chrysippus' death? 'I always thought Vibia would sell up, to be honest. In fact, she may have surprised herself when she decided publication suited her.'

'Women make shrewd shop-owners.'

'Could be. I act as editorial adviser now. We are changing what we buy, to some extent; Vibia seems willing to take my advice. I did not always agree with Chrysippus on what made popular material.'

'He was looking at new manuscripts the morning he died.'

'Yes.' That was unexpectedly brief.

'No comment?'

'We can't find the scrolls.'

'I'm holding them for evidence.'

'That's your privilege.'

'Tell me – how do new authors normally approach you with their work?'

'Some are discovered at recitals – like you, Falco.'

I reckoned he was joking; I brushed that aside. 'And how else?'

He looked thoughtful. 'Recommendation – from individuals, or very occasionally, through the Writers' and Actors' Guild.' He paused again, still holding back.

'How,' I asked, 'does a would-be writer join the guild?'

'There is no formal requirement. He might just toddle along, for instance, and become a member of their writing circle.' Euschemon caught the eye of the waiter, who had been listening in. They both laughed and then Euschemon explained: 'Some of us have a low opinion of writers' groups, Falco.'

'Useless,' the waiter commented. It was the first time he had joined in. 'They sit around discussing how to acquire a natural style – and never produce anything. They are all intent on finding what they call their "narrative speaking tone" – but the point is, most have nothing to say.'

Euschemon chuckled in agreement. 'I have certainly found most of them a little impractical.'

I gazed at the young man. 'So, what is *your* speciality? Plays, philosophy, or poetry?'

'I like writing prose.' The waiter who wanted to be a writer looked shy again and would contribute no more. It could be modesty, or commercial discretion. Quite likely, as with many 'prospective authors', it was all a dream and he had never committed anything to papyrus. Nor ever would.

Prose was an issue. I turned back to Euschemon. 'Another technical question, please. As scriptorium manager, what would you say is the potential of Greek novels? You know, love-and-adventure yarns.'

'Critically despised of course,' the scroll-seller said. Then he smiled.

'Or to put it another way: too much fun, and far too popular. They are the next big thing. Raging best-sellers.'

I became thoughtful. 'You're buying?'

'We are!' promised Euschemon, feelingly.

As I left the popina, I could see the waiter who wanted to be a writer had gone into a private reverie. He reminded me of Helena when she was reading. He did not mind being alone. He could enter the company of his own swirling gang of vivid characters.

And unlike real people, these would do what he told them to.

L

I COULD SEE Diomedes waiting for me in the temple portico; the high square forehead he had inherited from Chrysippus was unmistakable. I quickened my steps, afraid that despite my warning he might lose his nerve and flee. Lysa had the backbone in that family.

'I found somebody!' he assured me eagerly. As if that settled everything.

'Good news, Diomedes. Let's do it properly though . . .' Before I let him take me in to see the priest, I kept him back and made him face the questioning he had so far escaped. 'I'll hear what this fellow has to say, but first I would like you to tell me in your own words what you did the morning your father died.'

Diomedes pulled up. 'I came here. I was here all morning. The priest will tell you so.' Oh, he probably would too.

'Good,' I replied gently. 'And what happened either side of your religious experience?'

Nobody had rehearsed him for this. Still, he made a go of it: 'I came straight here from my mother's house. Afterwards, I went straight home.'

'So you were not only here all *morning* – you actually stayed at the temple *all day*?'

'Yes,' he retorted defiantly.

I toughened up. 'Excuse me! Nobody loves the gods that much. Most of us walk past the local temples the same way we walk past popina brothels – without even noticing they are there. Are you wanting to become a priest?'

'I am devoted to Minerva.'

I smothered a laugh. 'Well, that's obvious! What do you want to do with your life in general, incidentally? Be an upright civic sprig as your mother intends?'

'I suppose I shall have to,' Diomedes answered, grimacing. 'She'll get her own way now.' Now what? I wondered curiously. Before I could ask him, he went on, 'I had my dreams, but there's no chance.'

'What dreams are those? I suppose you must have wanted to acquire the bank?'

'I'd rather have the scriptorium,' he surprised me by saying jealously.

'Oh? What's the attraction?'

'I am interested in literature!'

'You amaze me!' Still, everyone wanted to be a writer round here. 'Well, let's get things straight.' I decided to deal with the alibi question. 'Did you at any stage on the fatal day visit your father's house in the Clivus Publicius?'

'No, Falco.' Another haughty disclaimer that failed to ring true. I felt sure that he had done.

'So, when were you told that he had died?'

'When I reached home. Mother told me.' That was the story we had been fed before. There was nothing wrong with his memory – but was he remembering the truth, or what his stern mama dinned into him? If Diomedes had been known as a fervent patron of the Temple of Minerva, why had nobody run here to find him and tell him of his bereavement earlier? I knew what I thought was the answer to that.

'How are things between the lovely Vibia and you?'

'What do you mean?'

'I mean that frankly, I heard you and she had a backstairs romance.'

'Not true.'

'Of course she's kicked you out now – but it could be a front to allay suspicion . . . While your father was alive, I understand you were a constant visitor?'

'I went to see him, not her.'

'You were close? Devoted to your dear papa as well as to the gods? If that's true, I have to say, you are a pious prick!' Diomedes refrained from answering. Perhaps he was a normal son and shared my sentiments. Perhaps Lysa brought him up pure-minded and he was offended by my obscenity. 'How did you feel about your parents divorcing? I gather it caused no conflict of loyalty?'

'They had their reasons. I was an adult. I remained on good terms with both.'

'What were their reasons? Adding gloss to the family so you could be moved up the social scale?'

'I don't know what you mean, Falco.'

'You kept your old room at your father's house – though you lived with your mother? Why was that?'

'Mother asked me.' I waited. I was prepared to accept that the abandoned wife needed her son's support. On the other hand, I now believed quite strongly that Lysa connived at the Chrysippus remarriage with Vibia, in order to provide Diomedes with social cachet. She cannot have been as stricken as all that by a divorce that had such devious aims.

'Did your *mother* think there was an attraction between you and Vibia?'

'She did have some crazy notion that Vibia Merulla made eyes at me.'

'Olympus. How shocking! Was it true?'

Diomedes was countering my shocks quite well now. 'Possibly.'

'So how did you feel about Vibia?'

'She was my father's wife.' That really was sickeningly pious. To tone it down, he felt obliged to play the man of the world: 'Naturally, I did notice that she is very beautiful.'

'Her mouth is too wide.' I dismissed her cruelly. 'Well, did you have an affair with the beauty?'

'No.'

'Never go to bed with her? She seems ready for it!'

'I never touched her. I've said that three times now. She's a tease,' Diomedes complained. 'Once she looked as if she wanted something – then she cooled down, for no reason!'

'Did you get her letter?' I sprang on him.

'What?' This time, at an innocuous question, Diomedes flushed; was that guilt?

'She wrote and asked you to remove your property from her house, I believe?'

'Oh! Yes, she did. I had forgotten about that, I must confess . . .'

'Do it tomorrow,' I ordered him briefly. 'I want you at my meeting; you can bring slaves to pack up your stuff. How are the wedding plans, incidentally?'

Diomedes looked abashed. 'Held up, rather – because of all this trouble with the bank.'

'Tough! Of course Vibia may have gone off you once you agreed to marry a relative of hers – women can be funny about things like that.' Diomedes expressed no opinion. 'So will you be fleeing to Greece, along with your mother and Lucrio?'

'My mother thinks it would be best.'

'Don't go, if you don't want to. Rome is the place to be. What are you running away from?'

'Nothing,' said Diomedes rapidly.

I decided to stop there. I gazed at him. 'Right. Well, Greece is a Roman province; we can get you back here if we need to. But I'm hoping to settle everything tomorrow. We should know who killed your father, and you can be allowed to leave the country . . . Where is this priest of yours?'

He produced the priest, a different man from the one I questioned. This fellow, a leery, Celtic beery sort of leach, gave the son the exact cover he needed: Diomedes had been honouring Minerva from dawn to dusk, praying and offering barley cakes, the day his father died. I was surprised a temple stayed open so long. I planted the alleged devotee in front of the goddess, with her Gorgon-headed aegis, her austere helmet and her antique spear. 'Swear to me now, in the presence of this priest, and on the name of holy Minerva, that you were in this sanctum from morning to evening on the day your father died!'

Diomedes swore the oath. I refrained from calling him a lying dog.

I let him leave, only reminding him that he was wanted tomorrow for my final interview.

I held up my hand slightly, to retain the priest. Once Diomedes was out of sight, I sighed wearily. 'All right. I'm not the believing nymph Diomedes thinks. Don't mess me about. How much has he promised to the Temple, and how much is he paying you?'

'You insult the goddess!' shrieked the priest. (The heavenly goddess made no comment, a true patroness of wisdom.)

I tried both haggling and threatening, but we were deadlocked. The priest ignored the suggestive power of the vigiles, and simply laughed at my fine oration on the subject of perjury. That was depressing. I had thought my arguments were both cogent and elegantly expressed. As an informer I was most competent to speak on that unglamorous crime – having committed perjury plenty of times, on behalf of my less scrupulous clients.

As I left despondently, the priest hurried inside looking furtive. I then observed a procession, men of all ages and degrees of unkemptness, who were entering a side building of the complex. There was more variety than you would expect to see in the ceremonial gatherings of most craft guilds. Overweight or skinny; badly-dressed and pedantically meticulous; some like short-sighted auditors; some pushy, with loud laughs; some so vague they were nearly left behind by the group; occasional barrow boys. Straggly haircuts that shamed the barbering profession. Snagged fingernails. Stains. They combined the peculiarity of musicians with an aura of hunched diffidence that would be more appropriate in runaway slaves.

What caught my eye was that most of them carried waxed tablets or untidy scrolls. So did I, but mine were hidden away until needed for a practical reason.

I gripped the tunic sleeve of the last man. 'What's going on here?'

'A small gathering of amateurs, who meet regularly at the Guild.'

They were meeting for refreshment, apparently; amphorae and abundant trays of savouries were being carried in ahead of them.

'What guild is this?' I glanced in. One thing they did quite capably was to fall on and unbung amphorae.

'*Scribae et Histriones* – Scribblers and Hystericals, we say.' Authors and Actors.

The man seemed quite inclined to chat. I remembered what the young waiter had told me: all talk and no results. Conversation – and wine – was what drew them here, when they could have been head-down in their rooms actually producing work. 'We are a curious grouping, slightly eccentric, some might say . . .' he burbled, as if it was a well-worn theme.

'And what do you do here?'

'We discuss our writing with our peers.'

'Anyone famous?'

'Not yet!' It would never happen, I thought to myself. 'We have a long tradition – dates back to the marvellous Livius Andronicus. He composed a hymn to Juno Minerva that was just *so* wonderful, in return the writers' circle was allowed to meet here in perpetuity. Copyists use the accommodation by day, but when Hestia, the Evening Star, rises in majesty, the benches are given up to us –'

'Marvellous!' I enthused; my voice croaked, squeezing out such hypocrisy. But I wanted information, and this would be my last chance. 'Excuse me, I don't know your name –'

'Blitis.'

'Got a minute for a little chat, Blitis?' Inspiration struck. I pulled out my own note-tablet. 'I'm not supposed to mention this – but I'm writing up an article on modern authors for the *Daily Gazette* . . .'

It worked immediately. Well, of course it did. He proffered a cold, limp handshake. Even unpublished writers know that they should grab at publicity.

LI

PREPARATION IS the secret. Whether planning a battle campaign or creating epic verse, you need your equipment well in place and all your information docketed. For the finale of a criminal investigation, it is a good idea to invest time and care in arrangements with your catering corps. Most informers don't know that. It is why most are sad losers with only half a client list.

I bought the snacks myself. I was intending to charge them to Vibia; well, she was the distraught widow who wanted her husband avenged. (Anyway, the vigiles had a no-comestibles expenses rule for consultants; at least, that sourpuss Petronius said they did.) I enjoyed myself planning the eats: nibbles and nick-nackeroonies to sit in napkins on little trays. Olives, a few expensive shellfish, plenty of cheap stuffed vine leaves, and some diddly pastry cases, to be freshly cooked with egg fillings. Then I bought eggs. And fillings.

As a finger-buffet, it would have graced a reception given for the elderly matrons who ran a charitable orphanage. Not that I would say so. After all, Helena Justina was patron to a school for orphaned girls.

Devotion to these domestic matters took up much of that morning. (Well, you try obtaining fresh nettletips in the Market of Livia on a particular day!) Once purchased, the goodies had to be transported to the Clivus Publicius and handed over to Vibia's bemused staff, including her cook. I gave strict instructions for preparation and service. Believe me, you cannot expend too much effort on the detailing.

As I left the house, having managed to avoid ensnarement by Vibia, I asked to see the slave who took around messages. 'Seen those authors again? Are they all coming today?'

'Sure.' The household runner was a pert lad who seemed to know what he was doing.

I tried him out: 'Somebody told me you tend to give wrong instructions. "Never gives a clear steer" were his words, in fact.'

'Hah! Would that have been Pacuvius? *Scrutator?* Too bloody talkative. Never listens properly. And his mind is on other things. I have to nip carefully around that old goat – if you know what I mean.' He winked, and managed to imply he was a good-looking boy, and *Scrutator* had an eye for him. It could have been true, though it was a stock excuse among slaves.

'Any views on the other hacks Chrysippus patronised?'

'Constrictus is always trying to sponge the price of a drink off me.' To borrow cash from your own slave was one thing; cadging from somebody else's runner was probably illegal and certainly low-class. 'Turius is a waste of time; Avienus – he's dead now, isn't he? – was worse. Always wanted me to sneak on everyone else.'

'What was there to sneak?'

'How should I know?' If he did know any dirt, he was not telling me. But had he passed on scandal to Avienus? Unluckily, I had used up my vigiles allowance for bribes. (Easy; Petronius had never given me one.)

'Urbanus?'

'Urbanus is all right.'

'Yes, I liked him too. Probably means he's a villain . . .' We exchanged a grin. 'So; you were the gofer, the day your master was killed. Will you confirm the list of men he invited to the library?'

I was dreading that this would throw up a new suspect – whom I had no time to investigate. Once again the slave repeated just the old list.

'There is a problem,' I confided. 'Urbanus says he never answered the summons, but according to your door staff here, the right number of men was counted in. Any ideas?'

'Urbanus did say he wasn't going to come.'

'So who filled his space?'

'The new writer turned up.'

'What new writer?'

'I don't know his name. He came of his own accord. I met him on the doorstep. As he had never been here before, he asked me where he had to go.'

'He told you he was a writer?'

'I already knew.'

I growled. 'You just said you don't know him!'

The runner beamed triumphantly. Winding me up and then slapping me down was his best fun all week. 'I don't know what he *calls* himself – but I do know who he *is*.'

I breathed slowly. 'Right.'

'Don't you want to know, Falco?'

'No.' I could play the awkward beggar too. I had worked out who the 'new writer' probably was. 'Now you just wait in the Latin library when the meeting starts. Stay there – and try not to cheek anyone – until I ask you to come in.'

Outside the house, I stood for a moment in the column-flanked portico, clearing my mind. I enjoyed the comparative coolness under the heavy stone canopy, before I walked home to collect Helena and Petronius. I had been up just after dawn, as soon as the marketeers set up their stalls. By now, it was mid-morning. Sensible people were looking forward to going indoors for a few hours. Dogs stretched themselves out right against the walls of houses, shrinking into the last few inches of shade. Out in the streets were only those of us with desperate business in hand – and mad old ladies. The elderly woman who frequented the Clivus Publicius was wandering past now, with her basket as usual.

This time I stopped her and greeted her. 'Carry your basket, gran?'

'You get off!'

'It's all right; I work for the vigiles.'

No use: the determined dame swung at me with her shopping. The hard wickerwork was well aimed. 'Settle down,' I gasped. 'No need to be so vicious. Now, you look like a sharp-eyed, sensible woman; you remind me of my dear mother . . . I just want to ask you a few questions.'

'You're the man on that murder, aren't you?' So she had me tagged. 'It's about time!'

Keeping out of reach of the basket, I asked my questions. As I suspected, on the fatal day she had been ambling past the Chrysippus house around lunchtime. I was disappointed that she had seen nobody running out with bloodstained clothes. But she had seen the killer, I was sure of that. Rather more politely than my other requests, I begged her to join my increasing group of witnesses in an hour's time. She looked as if she thought I wanted to capture her as brothel-bait. Inquisitiveness would probably have brought her but to make sure, I told her there would be free food.

I walked down to the corner. At the popina the spindly young waiter was opening an amphora, balancing it on the point while he removed the waxed bung. He had worked here long enough to become well practised. The amphora was propped safely against his left knee while he whipped out the stopper one-handed, then he flicked his cloth around the rim to brush off stray shreds of the sealing wax. He had his back to me.

'Philomelus!'

At once, he turned round. Our eyes met. The waiter made no attempt to deny that he was Pisarchus' youngest son.

Well, why should he? He was just a would-be writer who had found a job to pay the rent while he scribbled, a job that enabled him to hang about longingly, conveniently close to the Golden Horse scriptorium.

LII

AT HOME, Petronius Longus was looking more himself today, though he seemed quiet. Helena and I dragged him with us via my sister Maia's house. I wanted Helena to be at the case confrontation, in the role of my expert witness on literature; she could hardly have our daughter toddling about there in her walking-frame. We were intending to ask Maia to look after baby Julia, but when we arrived we found her out in the street seeing off her own children for their trip to the seaside with my other sister Junia.

They were all being loaded up with bundles, prior to a long walk out to the Ostia Gate where Gaius Baebius would be waiting for them with an ox-cart. Maia's four looked surly, all rightly suspicious that this 'treat' had been arranged with an ulterior motive. Marius and Cloelia, the elder two, took Ancus and Rhea by the hand, as if assuming responsibility for poor little souls who were being sent to Ostia to be drowned, thus freeing their feckless mother for dancing and debauchery.

She was being freed for Anacrites. He knew it, and was on the spot, helping to send off her brood. The way he was fastening satchels around them almost looked competent. The spy had probably learned how to supervise children while torturing innocents into betraying their parents to Nero, but Maia and Helena seemed impressed. Petronius and I stood aside, watching the situation grimly.

'I took some leave for the festival of Vertumnus,' Anacrites told me, almost apologetically. There was no mention of Pa hitting him, but I was pleased to see his ear had swollen like a cabbage leaf. In fact, once any of us noticed, it was hard to avoid staring at his lug. I wondered how he would explain it to Maia, currently waving the children off. Marius and Cloelia stubbornly refused to wave back. Marius even refused to acknowledge me when I winked at him. I felt like a traitor, as he meant me to.

'Vertumnus? That's not until tomorrow.' Hades. It implied my sister and the spy would be spending all the intervening time together – in bed, for instance.

'I am very fond of gardening!' Maia chirruped brightly.

When we asked if it would be convenient for her to have Julia for the next few hours, she replied with unusual force, 'Not really, Marcus!'

Undoubtedly, Maia and Anacrites were not laying plans to dig out a shrubbery with hand trowels. I cursed Vertumnus. Garden festivals and regrettable behaviour have always gone together. People only have to put a prickly wreath of leaves and apples round their necks and they start to think about life surging in all the wrong places. The idea of Anacrites making offerings to the spirit of change and renewal was too ghastly to contemplate.

We had to take Julia to my mother's instead. Helena went in to beg the favour. It was too soon after I had upset Ma for me to show my face.

Petronius and I stayed out in the street, watching a group of slaves carrying out bundles from Ma's apartment and loading a short mule train. I enquired who was leaving, and they told me Anacrites. I had had enough of him today – but I could bear this. I wondered privately where they would be transporting his chattels; Petro asked straight out: to the Palatine.

'He has a house up there,' Petronius told me in a sombre voice. 'Swank place. Old republican mansion. Goes with his job.'

That was news. I only knew about Anacrites' office on the Palatine and his Campanian villa. 'How do you know?'

'He has been living on my ground,' said Petronius, like a heavy professional. His eyes narrowed with loathing. The vigiles hated the intelligence service. 'I keep an eye on local spies.'

Helena came out, this time minus the baby. She flashed me a look of relief that the arrangement had been conducted peacefully, then she too glanced at the slaves who were packing up the spy's belongings. Now it was Helena's turn to wink – at Petronius and me.

'How was Ma?' I ventured to ask nervously; I would have to go in and see her when we came back to collect the child later.

'Seemed all right.' Helena waved at someone cheerily; she had spotted the old neighbour, Aristagoras. He had joined a group of sightseers gawping at the removal gang. 'Of course,' she then told Petro and me in a strange voice, 'there is always a possibility that while Anacrites thought *he* was two-timing your mother with Maia, the excellent and spirited Junilla Tacita may have been two-timing *him*.'

Too much imagination. She read too many sensational love stories; I told her so.

Miffed, Helena chose to ignore me on the short walk to the Clivus Publicius. She tucked her arm through that of Petronius Longus. 'Lucius, I have been meaning to ask you about the other night. If you had been asleep in bed, that giant would have killed you before you could raise the alarm. But you threw the bench and the flowerpots into the street. Were you out on the balcony when he burst in?'

'With a drink!' I snorted. If so, and if he had been there until nearly dawn, I did not care to know. I had enough worries. I wanted a best friend with a casual attitude, but not one who was an outright mess.

He had definitely not been drunk, though. If he had been, he would be dead now.

'I'm on night shift this week,' he explained. 'I had only just come home.'

'So what were you doing?' Helena pried.

'Thinking. Looking at the stars.'

'Good gods,' I muttered. 'Everybody must be at it – you really have got a new woman you're mooning about.'

'Not me,' he said. We were squeezing down an alley, so he was able to concentrate on avoiding broken paving-slabs.

'Liar. Can I remind you, I told you all about it, when I fell in love.'

'Every time it happened!' he groaned. I ignored the slander.

He was still too quiet. I started to wonder if it had been a bad mistake letting him see Maia's children going off to Ostia. His own three young daughters lived there these days; his wife had taken them there with her lover, the potted salad-seller, who was trying to build up a business selling snacks on the harbour quays. Now I felt guilty. If I had finished the Chrysippus case earlier, Petronius could have gone with Junia and Gaius Baebius in their ox-cart, and could have visited his own children.

Something in his expression warned me not to mention that, not even to apologise.

Fusculus and Passus, with a few vigiles in red tunics, were waiting for us outside the house in the Clivus Publicius. Helena's brother Aelianus was talking to them. I had sent for him. This had little to do with his enquiries into the bank's clients, but it would be good experience.

We all went indoors together. Passus and Helena immediately

started conferring on the sidelines about the scrolls they had read. I checked with Fusculus that he had managed to contact the shipper, Pisarchus, and ordered him to join us here.

Petronius was walking slowly around a large handcart that was standing in the first great reception hall. Everyone was moving from their lodgings today: this, we were told as we sniffed at it like curious street mongrels, was the removal cart Diomedes had brought to take away his property. He was stripping out the room he used to have here.

Aelianus looked over the cartload with some envy. Boyhood, a spoiled adolescence, and an idle young manhood could be catalogued from this high-piled clutter. Rugs, tunics, cloaks, sandalwood boxes, half-empty wine flagons, a folding chair, a set of spears, candelabra, a double flute, a tangled horse harness, soft furnishings – and since his late father had been a rich scroll-seller, a couple of score of highly decorated silver scroll-cases. The conveyance was dangerously laden, but would probably not tip over. It was the kind of pedestrian trolley that is just too small to count as a 'wheeled vehicle' and so avoids the curfew laws. A slave would push and pull it, mounded higher than he was, at an inching pace, annoying residents all the way he went.

'Where is Diomedes?' I asked one of the slaves. He was upstairs, supervising the retrieval of his things. 'Ask him to come down right now and join me in the Greek library, please.'

I wondered too where Vibia was, though not for long: she minced downstairs in an extremely attractive summer gown of suitable flimsiness to withstand the August heat. The curtain that normally disguised the stairs had been fastened back to facilitate the removal of Diomedes' stuff. We men watched Vibia Merulla walk all the way down, while she enjoyed pretending not to notice us. Helena looked up from her discussion with Passus, and assumed a faint but obvious sneer.

'Been closeted with the boyfriend?' I asked.

'If you are referring to Diomedes,' replied Vibia coldly, 'I have not seen him or spoken to him for weeks.'

Her eyes flickered over Aelianus. Judging Vibia only by her expensive home and clothes, he smiled politely. I had my work cut out. Twenty-five, and he could not yet tell when a woman was a common piece. But she could see that *he* was young, bored, and much better bred than the vigiles.

Helena had moved towards her brother protectively. Vibia stared at Helena, not expecting a woman in our party. A brief moment of hostility passed between the two women.

I waited until Vibia made her way out of earshot, then gestured to the laden cart and murmured to Fusculus, 'That first day, you searched all the upstairs rooms, of course?'

'We did.' Fusculus looked annoyed with me for checking, but then added honestly, 'We would not have known Diomedes was significant at that stage.'

'Right. Let the slaves finish loading – then keep the handcart here, please.'

'And once we're out of the way, get this lot checked over!' Petronius quietly added. Fusculus gleamed with excitement, then signalled a ranker to lean casually against a pillar, keeping the cart well observed.

We walked through the small lobby to the Latin library. My various minor witnesses had assembled. I briefed Passus in an undertone on statements he could take now, then left him in charge of them. Helena, Aelianus, Petronius, Fusculus and I went through to the Greek library where the main suspects were self-consciously milling around.

LIII

I HAD ARRANGED the room in an open square with seats of all kinds, which I had borrowed from other rooms; they lined the four sides and faced in centrally.

Petronius, Fusculus and I clustered together at the equivalent of the throne end of this audience chamber, throwing down on spare chairs an impressive collection of note-tablets (most irrelevant, but they looked sinister). Helena positioned herself to our far right, withdrawn from us slightly in a modest way. She placed various scrolls beside her, in two large piles and a smaller set. The benches directly opposite to us had been left free, to be used later when witnesses were called in from the other library. Aelianus, in his crisp white tunic, was stationed by the dividing door, ready to tell Passus when I wanted someone sent in.

Round the corner from Helena, on the right-hand side, I sat the parties who had family connections to the dead man. Lysa and Vibia, his two wives, embraced each other with muffled sobs and clung together, ostentatiously at one in bereavement. With them were Diomedes, at his mother's side, and Lucrio, who plonked himself on the other side of Vibia as if he could not bear to sit by Lysa's tiresome son. Diomedes stared into space, as usual looking spare, like the permanent understudy at a play. At first, Lucrio sat with his arms folded grimly, but he soon relaxed and became himself, cleaning out his dental crannies surreptitiously with a gold toothpick.

Down the left-hand side were the authors: Turius, *Scrutator,* Constrictus and Urbanus. I eyed them up when they were not looking: Turius, looking flash in yet another brand new tunic and snappy sandals; *Scrutator,* at the ready to catch anyone's eye and regale them with boring stories; Constrictus, trying to avoid talking to *Scrutator* and already haunted by the need for a lunchtime drink; Urbanus, simply sitting quiet so he could take mental notes. With them sat the scroll-shop manager, Euschemon, who had just shambled in unobtrusively from the corridor that led to the scriptorium.

Even when I had managed to nudge everyone to their seats, the lofty Greek library still seemed quite empty, despite the crowd. As it started gently warming up, this cool, quiet room had probably never been so well populated. The three graded tiers of white marble columns reached high above us amidst the crammed sets of documents in their endless pigeonholes. Sunlight filtered in gently from the ceiling-height windows, motes constantly drifting in the beams of light. In the centre of the elegantly tiled floor lay the circular mosaic where Chrysippus had been found dead, its tesserae and grout still bearing faint traces of his blood after inexpert cleaning. Without comment, I fetched a striped woollen floor rug, which I flung down across the main motif, hiding the stains.

People had been talking; the murmurs abruptly died down. For a mad moment, I was reminded of the last time I addressed an invited audience – in the Auditorium of Maecenas at my recital with Rutilius Gallicus. For some reason, this time I felt much more in command. I was the professional here. Petronius, still resting his voice after Bos nearly strangled him, had given me the lead role. I did not need a script. And I dominated people's attention as soon as I was ready to speak.

'Friends, Romans, Greeks – and Briton – thank you all for coming. Sadly, I am reminded of an evening last month when I met Aurelius Chrysippus for the first time. He performed the introductions on that occasion, but today I have to do the honours. My name is Didius Falco; I am investigating Chrysippus' violent death. I am doing this as a consultant to the vigiles' – I made a polite gesture – 'in the hope of finding consolation and certainty for his desolate family.' Vibia, Lysa and Diomedes bit their lips and stared at the floor bravely. Lucrio, the dead man's freed slave, remained impassive. 'Chrysippus spent his last moments in this library. Perhaps by assembling in the same location today, we can jog someone's memory.'

'Does the killer feel his spine crawling?' asked Petronius, in a loud aside. While I continued to play the mild-mannered type, he glared around and tried to make everyone feel uncomfortable. His remark presumed the killer was already here, of course.

I took up the thread again. 'There are in fact two recent deaths in the scriptorium circle. Avienus, who was a respected historian, had the misfortune to be found hanged on the Probus Bridge. I am going to talk about that first.'

'Do we have to be here for that?' Vibia burst out, jumping to her feet. 'He is not a relation. Anyway, I was told he committed suicide.'

'Please be patient.' I raised my hand gently and waited until she sank back onto her chair again, her fingers plucking obsessively at the fancy fabric of her gown. 'I want you all here for the entire examination. One person's evidence could spark a forgotten clue from someone else. To go back to Avienus: two deaths within a small circle of acquaintances may be a coincidence. Yet they may be connected.'

'You mean, the historian killed my husband?'

I pursed my lips. 'It is a possibility.'

'Well, you can't ask Avienus to confess!' As a joke, this crack of Vibia's was not only in bad taste, but rather hysterical. Vibia Merulla seemed nicely overwrought. That was good; I had hardly started yet.

I turned to the row of authors.

'Let's talk about your unhappy colleague. When Chrysippus died, Avienus was the first person to present himself to me for interview. In my experience that can mean various things: he was innocent and wanted to get back to normal life; or he was guilty, and seeking to put up a smokescreen. Maybe he was trying to find out just how much I knew. Equally I am conscious, here in the company of writers, that he could even have wanted to experience a murder enquiry for professional reasons – because he saw it as intriguing research.'

Behind me, Fusculus let out a hollow laugh.

'Our first interview was bland,' I continued. 'I lost the chance to put further questions to him later.' If Avienus was a murder victim, that lost chance might be significant. Someone had shut him up. 'He and I talked mostly about his work. He had a "block", he told me.' I looked straight at Turius, the other fellow who had somehow extended his deadlines. 'Avienus had missed his delivery date; do you happen to know how late he was?'

Turius sniffled, unabashed, and shook his head.

I looked along to the playwright Urbanus, who replied briefly, 'Years!'

Scrutator joined in more rudely: 'Bloody years, yes!'

'I gathered these "blocks" were regular,' I commented. 'Chrysippus seems to have been generous about them. Was the same lenience extended to the rest of you, Pacuvius?'

'Never,' scoffed the big, rangy satirist. 'He expected us to hand in the goods.'

Most of the group was sitting passive but wary. Only Urbanus seemed relaxed: 'Were there some curious features of Avienus' supposed suicide, Falco?'

I glanced at Petronius Longus. 'Curious features? Noted!' he replied, as if the suggestion that these curiosities might matter was new to him.

I avoided discussing the manner of the historian's death: 'I won't go into details. I don't want to prejudice a future court case,' I said ominously. 'But why *might* Avienus commit suicide? We thought he had money worries. In truth, he had recently paid off his debt. So where did the cash come from? Not payment for finally handing in his manuscript?' I looked at Euschemon, who shook his head.

Petronius stood up and came to the centre of the room with me: 'Falco, what was the great work Avienus had been labouring at for so long?'

I pretended to consult my note-tablet. 'I quote: "fiduciary transactions since the Augustan period". Sounds rather dry. Avienus admitted his was a small field.'

'Sorry I asked!' Petro's voice rasped, as he made a show of returning to his seat.

'Was Avienus anywhere near finishing?' I asked the authors. 'Some of you used to meet him regularly at that popina down the street. Did he ever discuss his progress?'

They looked at each other vaguely, then *Scrutator* nudged Turius and hinted in a sly tone, 'You were his real crony!' Yes, the satirist really did like landing other people in it.

'We talked about his work once,' Turius confirmed, looking annoyed to be singled out. 'He was drunk at the time.'

'Were you there as well?' I jokily asked Constrictus – the poet who liked imbibing too much.

The older man shook his head. 'I have no recollection of it! Avienus was very secretive about his research. If he had been sober, Turius would never have extracted anything.'

'Some authors hate revealing details of their work until they have finished,' I put to him.

'Yes,' groused Constrictus. 'And some work never sees the light of day. *I* was never convinced Avienus had written anything at all.' Constrictus at least did turn in manuscripts; Passus had found his latest poems marked by Chrysippus, '*Usual fluff. Small edition; reduce payment . . .*'

I continued grilling Turius. 'You and Avienus must have had subject-matter in common. You want to write about the ideal political state, the future. He catalogued the past. Both of you must have ranged across the other's field. Where society might go next and where it has already been are manifestly linked. So what did Avienus have to say to you?'

That put him on the spot. He writhed awkwardly; it did no good to his smart new leather belt, as he tortured it out of shape. 'Avienus was interested in economic issues. My approach in my ideal republic is through morality.'

I laughed briefly. 'Finance and morality are *not* so closely linked – wouldn't you agree, Lucrio?'

Lucrio had been off in a dream, while we prodded at intellectual ideas. But he managed to produce a sickly grin. Some professions condemn their office holders to endless nasty jokes so he must have been used to this. I won't suggest the snide jokes about bankers have any truth in them.

Turius thought he had escaped. I whisked back again: 'What was Avienus' area of research, Turius? "*Fiduciary transactions*" – mean anything?'

He shrugged, feigning lack of interest.

I glanced back at Petro. He interpreted swiftly: '*Fiduciary* – the placing of trust: *transactions* – sounds like money, to me.'

'Bank deposits!' I whipped around to face Lucrio. 'Did Avienus investigate the Aurelian Bank?'

Lucrio sat up slightly. 'Not that I know.'

'You were the agent. The obvious person to approach.'

'Sorry; I can't help you, legate,' he avowed; discretion was part of his business mystique, so I expected nothing else.

'The bank won't help us,' I sighed, turning again to Turius. 'So let me try out my theory on you – let's suppose Avienus started to write an economic history of some sort. He put together material to illustrate aspects of the Roman social structure, perhaps how private finances have affected class movements, or some such idea. Sounds fanciful to us, the general public, but you know what historians are . . . Perhaps he looked at the ways private individuals can advance socially by improving their financial status. Or perhaps he was interested in commercial investment . . . Anyway, at some point, probably a few years ago, he must have grazed a little too close to the Golden Horse.'

There were indrawn breaths. I spun back towards the other row of seats and tackled Lucrio again: 'The word in the Forum is that your set-up has a good reputation nowadays – or did have, before you liquidated yesterday – but that was not always the case. When Chrysippus first arrived in Rome, he was a shady loan shark.'

Lucrio prepared to argue, then had second thoughts. 'Before my time, Falco.'

'Lysa?' I asked, springing it on her. She was glowering. 'Anything to contribute?'

Lucrio was dying to look at her, but Vibia sat in his way. Lysa, his dead patron's ex-wife, his own future bride, merely turned on me a formal expression of disdain.

'Saying nothing, Lysa? Another strong believer in commercial confidentiality! You won't send me a libel suit if I say, there must have been dirt, and Avienus found it. It looks as if he played it right, blackmailing Chrysippus – not too greedy – just asking for a permanent retainer. That explains why there was no pressure to produce his history. It was in the bank's interest if he *never* produced his exposé! He survived very comfortably that way. It could have lasted for years –'

'This is pure speculation, Falco,' Lysa challenged.

'Sounds convincing though!' I grinned back at her. 'When Avienus did pile on demands, he was given an enormous "loan". For some reason, Chrysippus lost patience eventually, and called it in.' I paused. 'But perhaps it was not Chrysippus who did that . . .' I turned again to Lucrio. 'You asked for the repayment, in fact?'

Lucrio had already told me so. I forced him to repeat that in the normal course of his duties as the bank's agent he had demanded repayment. He had not contacted Chrysippus first.

'So Chrysippus had no chance to stop you. You were unaware of the blackmail – Chrysippus had kept it a secret even from you, his most trusted freedman. Well, perhaps the bank's sordid history had happened while you were still a slave. Is that right, Lucrio?'

'I don't know what you are talking about, Falco.'

'My dear Lucrio, it is to your credit if Chrysippus thought you too honest to be made aware of his bank's vile past.' Lucrio looked ambivalent about being called honest; I hid a smile.

'This is quite unacceptable!' exclaimed Lysa. She made an appeal for Petronius Longus to intervene, but he only shrugged.

As a courtesy to him, my employer, I said, 'I will explore all this later.' Petronius nodded and signalled me to continue.

'Your allegations are unfounded!' insisted Lysa angrily.

'I'll justify them.'

I then said I wanted to complete my enquiry into why Avienus died. 'It may look as if the blackmail led to murder. When Lucrio pestered Avienus for the loan repayment, Avienus lost his temper. He met Chrysippus here, not to discuss his history, but to complain about Lucrio and threaten that all would be revealed. Chrysippus for some reason refused to help; perhaps by then he was tired of being blackmailed. Avienus could not stand to lose the money – so he battered Chrysippus to death.'

'Is that what you really think?' Vibia asked, eager (apparently) to have her husband's death explained that way. Lysa, on the other hand, made no comment.

I gazed at Vibia for a moment. 'What – and then Avienus killed himself at the Probus Bridge, in remorse?' I smiled derisively. 'Oh, I doubt it. There was nothing to link him to the killing; if he did it, he would probably have got away with it. But he had sustained blackmail for a number of years against a shrewd businessman – who must have tried plenty of threats and counter-measures. Avienus knew how to keep a cool head. When I saw him, he was perfectly calm about his meeting with Chrysippus. My impression was that he felt confident of his position, and satisfied with his lot.'

'So what did happen?' demanded Vibia. I suspected her of knowing more than she admitted, so she was pushing it, I thought.

'Chrysippus, who had preserved himself by paying up for years, continued doing so. It is ironical, but to keep the secret in my opinion *he* gave Avienus the money to settle with Lucrio. In effect, he paid off a loan he himself had originally granted. Well, banking is a complex business! Avienus must really have loved it.'

'This is all speculation,' grumbled Lucrio.

'That's right,' I agreed. 'So let's have a little confirmation . . .' I signalled to Aelianus who was standing by the dividing door. 'Aulus, will you ask Passus to send Pisarchus in, please? Oh, and don't let's split up a family; let's have his son here as well.'

LIV

SHUFFLING IN together, the shipper and his youngest boy were physically dissimilar. Both nervous at entering a room full of people, all of whom looked strained, they edged through the gap when the door was held open briefly. Aelianus seated them on the furthermost row of benches. They perched there, the broad, active, sunburned father and his city-pallid skinny and ascetic son. Their faces possessed the same type of bone structure, however. They sat close together, as if they were on friendly terms.

I explained quietly that we had been talking about the death of the historian Avienus, and the possibility that he was blackmailing Chrysippus.

Pisarchus and his son glanced at one another, then tried to pretend they had not. Interesting. I reckoned the blackmail was not news.

'Pisarchus, can I ask you something, please? The other day, when you came to the vigiles' patrol-house voluntarily, we – that is, the enquiry chief and I' – I nodded towards Petronius – 'assumed you wanted to give evidence in the Aurelius Chrysippus death. In fact, it transpired you had been away in Praeneste and had not even known that Chrysippus was dead.'

Pisarchus inclined his head. He was becoming more relaxed. I hoped this was due to my calm handling of the situation and reassurance. On the other hand, he had always seemed to be a self-possessed man. He was careful, yet I felt he had nothing much to hide.

'So whose death had you come to talk about?' When he did not reply, I pressed him. 'It was Avienus, wasn't it?'

Pisarchus reluctantly agreed.

'What were you going to tell us?'

Pisarchus glanced sideways at his son again. 'I can't say.'

'Then maybe you can,' I said, turning to Philomelus. 'Waiters do not have to swear a vow of confidentiality. Only doctors have a Hippocratic oath – though of course bankers' – I winked at Lucrio – 'are protected by law from giving details of clients' accounts! Priests,'

I mused, 'might make moral claims – or just as likely they might lie to protect temple benefactors.' I flicked a glance at Diomedes. 'Now, Philomelus, you are under no obligation. Avienus is dead – and let me help you here. I already know that Avienus had confided to another party that he had discovered some scandal. He was very drunk, so I assume this conversation took place over a beaker – well, several – at the popina where you work. I guess you overheard?'

Young Philomelus swallowed, neither confirming nor denying it.

'The confidant was Turius – he told us that himself.' Philomelus looked relieved. 'So, Philomelus, you heard Avienus say that Chrysippus was paying him to keep quiet?'

Philomelus had nodded before he thought about it.

'You agree? Thanks.' Looking thoughtful, I walked back slowly to the row of authors. 'Tiberius Turius! It would have saved us a lot of effort if you had told us this before.' I strode right up to him and hauled him to his feet, dragging him out into the centre of the room. 'That's a nice tunic! And I do admire your belt. Lovely tooling on the leather. Striking buckle – is that enamel northern work, or did you buy it here in Rome? Turius, let's be frank – one thing that strikes me is that you don't look as an impoverished author should. Especially one who suffers from health problems so he never produces any work.'

Turius shook off my grip from my shoulder, and straightened the sleeve of his tunic. 'Leave me alone, Falco.'

'Wasn't it more "leave me alone, *Turius*" – or so Avienus found? Didn't you decide to cash in too? Didn't you force Avienus to demand more from Chrysippus, so you could take a share?'

'Don't be ridiculous,' Turius muttered.

'Oh? Did you go directly to Chrysippus yourself?'

'No!'

'Really? Let's see; what do I know about you? You complained to me about Chrysippus treating his authors like slaves. And you had been flagrantly indiscreet: you openly refused to flatter him, and you ridiculed his critical powers.'

'He had no judgement!' snarled Turius. He turned to his colleagues. 'Well, you know all about that, Pacuvius!' It was Pacuvius, *Scrutator*, who had told Helena about Turius; I made a mental note to find out why Turius thought *Scrutator* had a special literary grievance.

But it was Turius I wanted to harry. The utopian was under extreme pressure now. He was sweating, even though the library remained pleasantly cool, and his agitation had become visible. Whatever the cause, his breaking point looked close.

'Chrysippus had at least enough judgement to keep Avienus quiet for several years! Avienus even achieved the startling coup of making Chrysippus pay off his own loan to deflect demands from his agent Lucrio. Then you rocked the boat, didn't you?' Turius looked hounded, but would not reply. 'You hated Chrysippus for his poor treatment of his authors; you thought he should be pressed as hard as possible. Is that right?' Turius was unable to look at me, desperately unhappy now. 'What happened then? You knew the secret too – or at least you knew a secret existed. Did Avienus fear he had lost everything because you interfered? Is that what made the poor beggar kill himself?'

'All right!' Turius cracked, even more easily than I expected. 'Don't keep on. I can't bear any more – I am responsible. I killed him!'

Around us a hum of thrilled conversation rose, then died again. I marched Turius back to his former place and sat him down again.

I shook my head sadly. 'I hope you feel better for telling us that. Now, in your own interests, say nothing else. This is a rather disturbing development – so, listen everyone.' Raising my voice to command their attention, I nodded to Aelianus to open the doors. 'We could all benefit from a short pause. Let's have some refreshments, and then start again.'

The dividing door to the Latin library was then pulled right aside and a flock of slaves marched in, carrying my prepared buffet trays.

LV

PEOPLE LOOKED startled, but a snack never comes amiss. It broke the tension. The slaves mingled, courteously offering titbits and savouries, then little cups of drink. Turius slumped, trembling and covering his face, while the others shrank away from him. Small groups muttered in low voices and occasionally glanced in my direction. I went and sat beside Helena.

'You were wonderful, darling,' she cooed. She always knew how to undermine me if I looked overconfident.

Lucrio strolled up, finishing a mouthful of giant prawn. 'How's your mother, Falco?'

'Depressed about her savings, you know that.'

'No need to be.' He had come over on purpose. 'Can't mention the amount — but she had it all on sealed deposit.'

I scooped up olives from a passing tray. 'What does that mean?'

He sneered at my ignorance. 'Sealed or "regular" deposits are literally that: the coins or other valuables are placed in sacks that are formally secured with tags. They have to remain untouched. Irregular deposits are when the banker has the right to use the money in search of profits — invest it in suitable schemes to provide income.'

'For the depositor or for you?' I sneered back.

He ignored that. 'Sealed ones remain entirely the property of the depositor, and must be handed back untampered with, on demand. Frankly, the Aurelian believed that was a waste of resources. I tried hard to change Junilla Tacita's mind so her principal would earn for her, but she remained determined.'

This was cheering news. Helena was smiling. 'She just wanted to put the money in a safe place, and not take any risks? That's your mother, Marcus! I can just imagine her deciding that nobody else would gamble with her cash!'

Lucrio looked wry. 'Seems a very shrewd lady. When we assayed the coins, there was the fewest number of counterfeits and copper "souls" that our changer had ever seen in a single batch.'

I chortled. 'My mother doesn't just bite all her change to check it – she scares all Hades out of anyone who looks likely to slip her a fake! . . . What's the position for her, now the bank has failed?'

'The liquidators can't touch her money,' Lucrio admitted off-handedly. Would he have told Ma, had I not asked? 'If she wants it back, she should ask.'

'I'll come and get it.'

'She has to appear in person, Falco. Normal procedure,' Lucrio snarled. How sensible. You don't want wicked sons stealing from their poor old mothers.

I had been keeping an eye on the others. The assembly had been given time to relax; now they were looking for seconds from the drinks trays. It was time I unsettled them by calling a halt.

'Thanks, everyone. Could you now please return to your seats?'

I then spent a few moments consulting the head waiter, making sure I was seen making notes of what he told me.

'Sorry to keep you. By the way, that was a little test I ran. When Chrysippus died, we know that his killer stopped outside in the lobby and pinched some nettle flan from his lunch tray.' People shifted uneasily, the bright ones already catching on. 'As you may have noticed, the salvers today were quite large. We placed the most expensive and tasty snacks around the rim, within easy reach, while at the centre, where you had to stretch, were portions of nettle flan. I was just checking who took the flan –'

'Oh for heavens sake!' Lysa was absolutely furious. 'You are surely not intending to use that kind of evidence to accuse anyone!'

I smiled. 'Hardly. I do know how badly that would be received by Marponius, the homicide magistrate – and what scorn a defending barrister would pour on it. Anyway,' I added light-heartedly, 'if the nettle flan was enough to convict, from the number of bits he scoffed, I would be arresting the enquiry chief, Lucius Petronius!'

Petro pretended to look embarrassed. I deliberately passed him the list of who else had eaten the flan. He read it, without changing expression, while I continued.

'Right then, Turius; you made a startling confession.' I tutted. 'I wonder why you did that?'

Turius had remained hunched on his seat during the break, not partaking of the refreshments. Now he flushed painfully. He was deeply regretting his outburst. He was a fool, and it would serve him right if I arrested him – but I was convinced the bank's enforcers were to blame for the historian's death.

'Anyone help you with this alleged killing?'

'No –'

Once again, I dragged him to the centre of the room. It took little effort. Standing there, his head hung and he tried to avoid my eye. 'How strong are you, Turius? Could a sickly man, working alone, have knocked out Avienus, then shunted him over a parapet and held him there, while stuffing his head through a noose?'

'I –'

'Let's say you did kill him, Turius. Whatever was your motive? Avienus refused to press Chrysippus for more money? Perhaps. So you killed him, to take over as sole blackmailer? At some point there must have been pay-offs to you – it would explain your fancy outfits, wouldn't it, Turius?' He said nothing, perhaps confirming that he did receive payment. 'But to put pressure on Chrysippus direct, you had to know *exactly* what Avienus had discovered against the bank. Had he told you that?'

'No!' Turius wailed, by now distraught. 'That time he was drunk he held back the full evidence. Afterwards he refused to say anything more.'

'So you never took over as the blackmailer?'

'No.'

'Stick to that line,' I warned him. 'Because if anyone thinks you *do* know the details, you too may be obliterated by violent heavies called the Ritusii. They had a strongman called Bos, who probably helped Avienus to his death, and who tried to strangle Petronius.' I noticed Lucrio lean forward slightly as if to look curiously at Lysa. Did that mean *she* hired the Ritusii and he had only just found out? 'Bos is dead' – Lucrio sat back, pulling an amazed face – 'but the Ritusii are still at large – I suggest you get out of their reach, Turius.'

'Thank you,' he gasped.

'Don't thank me. The vigiles and I like good urban hygiene – we don't want stinking corpses in this heat. I'd hate to see an idealist like you dangling from a rope with a purple face.'

'Oh Hades . . .' Way out of his depth, Turius once more buried his head in his hands.

I spoke more kindly: 'Now cut out the nonsense: tell me, why did you say you had killed the historian?'

He looked up, his glistening hair ploughed into furrows by his fingers. 'I should never have urged him to ask for extra money. That brought about his death. I feel responsible.'

He did bear responsibility, but he can never have imagined a fatality would happen. What was the point in pressing it? Those who decided to wipe Avienus out, bore far more guilt than this pathetic creature. 'That sounds like regret,' I suggested.

'Of course I regret it, bitterly.'

'Then I suggest you make amends to his old mother, if you can.' I paused. 'And I would like you to explain how you can afford the fancy wardrobe, when you are not making money from writing. Where do the smart tunics come from, Turius?'

Turius hated having to answer, but he understood he was still vulnerable to suspicion. He had to come clean. He closed his eyes and announced clearly: 'Chrysippus never paid me enough to live on. I moonlight as a private poetry-reader to rich women. I have done it for years.'

He meant more than reading aloud eclogues. The clients who wheezed, '*Ooh Turius, you have such a lovely voice!*' would be buying his body. I had thought him effeminate, but he was really a widows' pretty boy.

His nerve failed. He crumpled. He whispered pitifully, 'I have said that in confidence, of course . . .'

Despite the flash clothes, he was not even good-looking. The wealthy old hags who slavered over him must be loathsome. I shuddered, and let him slink back to his seat.

I gazed at the Chrysippus family. Time to get tough.

'So, who sent the Ritusii to nail Avienus? Chrysippus was dead, but who else wanted to be rid of the blackmailer? You, Lysa. You inherited the bank – after you had been closely involved in its early years. You told me, no one person ever made decisions. That means you knew what went on. What were the historian's threats? Extortionate commission? Making debtors with a doubtful credit-record pay annual interest above the legal maximum? Or was it misuse of funds? You're a Greek – I know that notorious story about the Opisthodomos fire, when a temple treasury in Athens was burnt down because a sealed deposit had been used for speculation – and lost – illegally. Sound like anything you and your husband used to do?'

'You won't prove anything against us,' Lysa replied calmly.

'We can check the bank's records.'

Her composure remained immaculate. 'You will find nothing discreditable. Loans from years ago have all been repaid. It is a tradition of Greek banking that whenever a loan is cancelled, the contract is destroyed.'

Oh very neat! 'The vigiles will find witnesses somewhere.'

Lysa glared at me. It gave me an odd feeling to be discussing such matters with a woman. Lysa herself seemed perfectly at ease; her very competence implicated her in what the bank had done wrong. She could have pleaded female ignorance of its practices, but the thought never occurred to her.

'The Golden Horse is known for its hungry interest rates,' I continued. 'Petronius Longus hopes to nail you on a usury charge. I myself want to trace those "fiduciary transactions" that Avienus had tracked and used to help his personal liquidity. My suspicion is that when you started out in Rome, Lysa, sealed deposits – regular deposits, as they are known – were used for speculation in irregular ways.'

'Prove it!' She was angry enough – without even knowing that it was Lucrio who inadvertently gave me this lead a few minutes ago. Lucrio realised, and looked sick.

'I'll do my best,' I promised. Lysa fixed me again. I was impervious to seething women. 'So did you have Avienus destroyed, Lysa? When Chrysippus died, Avienus must have thought he had lost his milch cow and what's more, he had Turius nagging him. Did he try you? I imagine you resisted blackmail far more strongly than Chrysippus!'

'I don't stand for sneaks,' Lysa agreed, showing a rare flash of deep anger. She knew the admission proved nothing against her. I decided to leave that. The vigiles were finding it hard to prove a direct link in the killing between Lysa (or Lucrio) and the Ritusii. The pair might yet get away with eradicating Avienus, especially if they left for Greece. Even if Rubella, on his return, thought it was worth enquiry time, only with a cast-iron case would Petro be allowed to haul the villains back from overseas. If Rubella did press the issue, however, I reckoned the truth would out eventually.

I returned to the bank's agent. 'Lucrio – a word. Even if you knew nothing about the blackmail before Chrysippus died, by the time we commandeered your records, you must have twigged.' It was conceivable he had just wanted to get the records back quickly in order to see if his late master had overstepped the line. More likely, he knew all too well what had occurred. 'You tried to snatch the records back at night by force – a crazy overreaction. You could have played it cool and claimed the law. Why was the situation so urgent that you raided the patrol-house? You put us on the alert. Foolish, Lucrio.'

I could make no impression on the sanguine Lucrio. It was clear he and Lysa had made a pact of silence. Lysa even seemed to be glad that I was questioning them about the bank.

There could be a reason for that: it kept the heat off another subject.

I changed my line of approach. 'I want to wind this up. Let us now consider Chrysippus and what happened to him.'

I took several deep breaths and paced around the square, gazing at each suspect.

'What kind of man was he? A shrewd businessman, who had built up an empire from nothing when he came to Rome as a foreigner. If his initial methods involved sharp practice, that is true of thousands like him. By the time he died, he had become a respectable figure, involved in several areas of commerce, a patron of the arts, with a son – Diomedes – who was entrenching himself in Roman society, and due one day to marry well.'

Diomedes woke up sleepily from an apparent trance. He had probably been given some sort of education, but he did not look particularly bright. To follow an involved series of arguments had been beyond him. He had perked up earlier when the food trays came, but mostly he had slumped beside his mother looking bored stiff, as if he were still ten years old. He enjoyed hearing his name mentioned in public, though.

If he really had followed my methods today, he might now have feared I was about to jump on him.

I smiled, first at Diomedes, then at Lysa. She knew what I was doing. I could see fear in her eyes for her son.

'Concentrate on events the day he died. Chrysippus was here in the library.' We all looked around. Those of us who had been here after the body was discovered relived the silence that terrible day: the long tables stacked with scrolls, the overturned chairs, the corpse, the mess, the blood.

'Diomedes,' I commanded. 'You look rather like your father, especially now you've acquired that beard. Come here, will you. And let's have Philomelus – I am choosing him at random, by the way.'

The two young men approached, both looking apprehensive.

'Thanks, you two. Now help me re-enact what happened, in case it jogs a memory. Helena, could I trouble you?' I gave Philomelus, the thin waiter, an empty scroll rod she had been keeping ready for me. 'Take this. Now both pretend you are having a shouting match.' They were poor or nervous actors, but I shoved them about a bit. Diomedes wanted to resist, which was perhaps understandable. Philomelus had no meat on him, and lacked any gymnasium training, though he was a more intelligent mover. 'Now. Philomelus, you are the killer: stab Chrysippus with the rod.' He made a feeble gesture towards Diomedes' chest. 'You fight a bit more, exchanging blows – now you're dead, Diomedes. You fall on the floor – here, where I put the rug.'

Diomedes knelt and then lay full length, assuming his position rather decorously. He had entered the spirit to some extent, however, and was stretched out face down, crossways across the rug. I helped him up, thanked them both, then let them go back to their seats.

I looked at Diomedes with my head on one side. 'Interesting! You lay face down. According to your alibi, you never saw the corpse. But you lay down – as it happens – exactly how your father was first found. Later, the vigiles turned him over.' To stop Diomedes offering excuses, I went on quickly, 'Of course, you probably talked to the slaves and perhaps to Vibia about your father's death. That would be entirely natural.'

Having mentioned Vibia, I turned swiftly to her. 'Vibia Merulla, Diomedes has an alibi; he was at the Temple of Minerva – a priest, honest no doubt, will vouch for him. Tell me, did you know he was there?'

'Yes,' she answered, flushing as attention turned on her. 'Yes, I did. He often goes there.'

'Tell me then – when you found Chrysippus lying here, why did you not send to the Temple, which is only a few steps away, to let Diomedes know his dear papa was dead?'

'I never thought about it,' Vibia declared, a little too boldly. 'I was very shocked.'

'Understandable. Now – you used to like Diomedes once, but your feelings have changed. Do you want to tell us about that?'

'No!' she squeaked indignantly.

'He's very interested in literature, he told me. Did you decide he was only after you because you would inherit the scriptorium?'

'I was never interested in him, nor he in me.'

'Well, you certainly don't like him now. You won't speak to him and you want his possessions removed from your house. Did something happen to make you feel so strongly? Did he *do* something?'

Vibia shook her head in silence.

'I need to know this, Vibia. Why didn't you tell Diomedes about his poor father dying? A harsh person might wonder: *Maybe she thought he already knew.*' Vibia still stubbornly refused to be drawn. 'Of course, he was being religious all day, wasn't he? Be warned, Vibia – if I could prove Diomedes was *not* at the Temple when he says, I would look at him very closely as a suspect, and I would look at you as well!'

Under the layers of face decoration, Vibia may have gone pale. She made no further protest; I reckoned she wanted to defend herself, but something held her back.

I walked back across the room, crossing the rug that lay where the body was found. I bent down and replaced the rug to lie the way Diomedes had done. 'Diomedes, I noticed you lay down in an east-west direction. You followed the real line of the body, of course.' I paused for a second theatrically, as if honouring the corpse. 'Anyone would think you knew.'

Diomedes made as if to speak, but his mother gripped him tightly by the arm.

'Now then!' I tackled the authors and Euschemon. 'Chrysippus spent that morning reading new manuscripts. My first thought was that he might have been killed by a disgruntled author. Avienus and Turius both needed him alive so he could pay blackmail demands. Were there advantages or disadvantages in his death for the rest of you? What has been the result? Euschemon, have you kept the status quo?'

Euschemon looked reluctant, though he piped up: 'We are, actually, dropping all this group from our list. I am sure they understand. They were Chrysippus' personal clients, a close circle he supported as artistic patron. Once the scriptorium fell into new hands – whether Vibia had sold it or kept it herself – these authors became candidates for dismissal. They are all bright men, Falco,' he commented. 'They would have known the risks.'

'So they owed their patronage and publication to Chrysippus, and they knew they might lose both if he died.' I ran my eyes along the line. 'Except for you, Urbanus. You were leaving him anyway.'

'And I never came here that day,' he reminded me.

'I believe you. One extra person did visit him in your place,' I said. Then I signalled Passus to send in the slave who ran errands.

He marched in confidently, then quailed when he saw how many people were here. I was brisk with him.

'Just one question. The day your master died, you saw a would-be author who was not on the visiting list coming to the house. Will you now point out that man?'

'That's him!' squeaked the slave, his voice breaking. As I expected, he pointed straight at Philomelus.

LVI

'D ID YOU come here that day, Philomelus?'
The young waiter stood up again. 'Yes, Falco.' He spoke
quietly. Though he looked nervous – and behind him his father
looked nearly frantic – the young man met my gaze without
wavering.

'You saw Chrysippus?'

'Yes.'

'Alone?'

'Yes.'

'Tell us what you talked about.'

'I have written a story,' Philomelus said, this time flushing shyly. 'I
wanted him to publish it. He had seen a copy ages ago, and had not
returned the scrolls. I came to beg him to take it for publication –
though I had made up my mind to retrieve the scrolls, if he did not
want it.'

'What happened that day? Did he agree to buy your work?'

'No.'

'Did he perhaps ask you to pay him a fee to publish it?'

'No.'

'So what happened?'

'Chrysippus was very evasive. Eventually he told me it was just not
good enough.'

'Did you get it back?'

Philomelus looked thoroughly downcast. He made a heartbroken
gesture. 'No, Falco. Chrysippus confessed that he had lost the scrolls.'

I looked around the library. 'Well, there are certainly a great many
documents here; he could well have mislaid one. Careless, though. He
should have looked for your manuscript. It was your property –
physically and creatively. To you, it represented months of work and
all your hopes. How did you react?'

'I was devastated.' Clearly, Philomelus was still deeply affected.

'Angry?'

'Yes,' admitted the youth honestly.

'Did you threaten him?'

He hesitated. 'Yes.'

'With what?' Philomelus did not answer. 'Violence?' I asked sharply.

'No, I never thought of that,' Philomelus sighed, conceding ruefully that he lacked both aggression and physique. 'I told him that I would tell my father what had happened, and our family would never do business with him again. Oh, I know it sounds feeble!' he quavered. 'I was in anguish. But it was all I could think of to say.'

Pisarchus stood up and put a heavy arm around his shoulders. The threat about withdrawing their business would have been carried out – though I was not sure Chrysippus would have cared.

'Then what?' I asked.

'I went back to the popina,' Philomelus replied. 'Then I was sent home early because the vigiles had complained about the hotpots; we partly closed down until they tired of checking us.'

'You did not come back here?'

'No. I went straight to my lodgings, faced up to what had happened, and started to write out the whole story again.'

'Very professional!' I applauded. Now I turned nasty: 'Quite cool-headed too – if you had battered Chrysippus to a pulp before you left this library!'

Philomelus wanted to protest, but I stopped him defending himself.

'Don't despair,' I told him in a charitable tone. 'Your manuscript may not have disappeared.'

I signalled Aelianus to send in Passus, and I myself brought forward Helena Justina. Fusculus by prior arrangement went out to take up Passus' post with the witnesses. As he walked by, I muttered in his ear a reminder about a search Petronius had ordered.

I resumed the debate.

'Manuscripts are important in this case. My associates have been cataloguing the scrolls that were found here after Chrysippus died. Passus, you first. Will you tell us about the majority – the scrolls with title pages – please?'

Passus reiterated what he had told me: that apparently Chrysippus had been making marketing decisions, mainly in the negative. Passus gave the report competently, though was more nervous in front of the large audience than I had expected. I indicated that he could sit with Petronius.

Now it was Helena's turn. Unafraid of the crowd, she waited quietly for me to give the lead. She looked neat in blue, not extravagantly dressed or bejewelled. Her hair was turned up in a simpler style than usual, while unlike Lysa and Vibia who were bare-armed and brazen, she had sleeves to the elbow and kept a modest stole over one shoulder. She could have been my correspondence secretary, but for her refined voice and confidence.

'Helena Justina, I asked you to read an adventure tale.' I nodded to the seats behind us, where the scrolls were lying. Philomelus looked as though he wanted to rush over there and search for his beloved manuscript. 'Can we have your comments, please?'

I had not rehearsed her in detail, but Helena knew I wanted her to talk first about the one we thought was called *Zisimilla and Magarone*, the awful yarn she could not bear to finish. Now I knew Philomelus had been told his story was not good enough to publish, I thought perhaps he had written this. Mind you, it presumed that in turning him down, Chrysippus had had enough critical judgement to recognise a dud. Turius had libelled the arts patron as a know-nothing. None of the others, including his scriptorium manager Euschemon, had ever suggested that Turius libelled him.

'I hope it is in order for me to speak,' demurred Helena.

'You are in the presence of some excellent businesswomen,' I joked, indicating Lysa and Vibia.

Helena would have been debarred from giving evidence in a law court, but this was in essence a private gathering. Behind us, the vigiles representatives were looking glum about her coming here, but it was my show, so they said nothing. Petronius Longus would divorce a wife who thought she could do this. (Helena would contend that his old-fashioned moral attitude might explain why Arria Silvia was divorcing him.)

'Just speak at me, if the situation worries you,' I offered. It was unnecessary. Helena smiled, looked around the room, and firmly addressed everyone.

'Passus and I were asked to examine various scrolls which had lost their title pages during the struggle when Chrysippus was killed. We managed to reconstruct the sets. One manuscript was an author's copy of a very long adventure in the style of a Greek novel. The subject matter was poorly developed, and the author had overreached himself.' Philomelus was hanging his head gloomily. 'I would like to stress,' Helena said, sending him a kind glance, 'these are personal opinions – though I'm afraid Passus and I were in full agreement.'

'Was the quality up to publication standard?'

'I would say no, Marcus Didius.'

'Close?'

'Nowhere near.'

'Helena Justina is being polite,' muttered Passus from the vigiles row. 'It absolutely stank.'

'Thanks, Passus; I know you are a connoisseur.' He looked pleased with himself. 'Helena Justina, was there anything else you should tell us about this particular manuscript?'

'Yes. This may be important. There were extra scrolls, written in another hand and a different style. Someone had clearly attempted revisions.'

'Trying to improve the original draft?'

'Trying,' said Helena, in her restrained way.

'Succeeding?'

'I fear not.'

I sensed a mood change among the authors' seats. I turned to them. 'Any of you know about this ghostwriting?' Nobody answered.

'They may call it editing,' Helena suggested. I knew her dry tone; she was being very rude. People sniggered.

'I would like to know who did this trial revision,' I fretted.

'From the style,' said Helena crisply, 'I would think it was Pacuvius.'

'Hello! Going into prose, *Scrutator*?' We gave the big man a chance to reply but he shrugged and looked indifferent. 'What made you think of him?' I asked Helena. 'You are familiar with his work, no doubt. Did it have meticulous social satire, topicality, biting shafts of wit, and eloquent poetry?'

'No,' she said. 'Well, since nobody owns up to the revisions, I can be frank. The new version was long-winded, mediocre, and ham-fisted. The characters were lifeless, the narrative was tedious, the attempts at humour were misplaced and the total effect was even more muddled than the first draft.'

'*Oh, steady on!*' Pacuvius roared, stung at last into admitting he had been involved. 'You can't blame me – I was sculpting a middenheap of crap!'

The ensuing hubbub stilled somewhat eventually. To mollify him I assured him that Helena had only been trying to inspire his admission. Helena remained demure. Pacuvius probably realised her ferocious critique was real. I asked him to explain his role.

'Look, it's no real secret,' he blustered. 'Chrysippus used me sometimes to tidy up ragged work by amateurs. This, for some reason, was a project he was keen on at one time. I told him all along it was hopeless. He showed it to some of the others and they refused to touch the thing.' The others were grinning, all relieved they had no responsibility. 'The plot was shapeless; it lacked a decent premise anyway. Helena Justina is fairly astute about the faults.'

Pacuvius was patronising, but Helena let it pass.

'Are manuscripts frequently rewritten in detail, prior to formal copying?' I queried, looking shocked.

Most of the authors laughed. Euschemon coughed helplessly. After a moment, he explained. 'There are works, Falco, sometimes by very famous people, which have been through numerous redrafts. Some, in their published form, are almost entirely by somebody else.'

'Jupiter! Do you approve?'

'Personally, no.'

'And your late master?'

'Chrysippus took the line that if the finished set was readable and saleable, what did it matter who actually wrote the words?'

'What do you think, Euschemon?'

'Since enhancing his reputation is one reason for an author to publish, I regard major reworking by others as hypocrisy.'

'Did you and Chrysippus have disagreements?'

'Not violent ones.' Euschemon smiled, aware of my reasoning.

'There are more sinister crimes,' I decided, though I did agree with him. 'The public might feel cheated, if they knew.'

'Misled they may be sometimes,' Euschemon said. 'But we can't accuse the disappointed reading public of killing a publisher for it.'

I felt the joke was out of place. 'While you're helping me, Euschemon, can you tell me – does a copying house receive large quantities of unpublishable work?'

Euschemon threw up his hands. 'Cartloads. We could build a new Alp for Hannibal from our slush pile – complete with several model elephants.'

'Your "slush pile" is mainly rejects – how do the authors generally take it?'

'They either slink off silently – or they protest at enormous length.'

'No point in that, presumably?'

'Decisions are rarely reversed.'

'What *could* change a publisher's attitude?'

Euschemon was wearing his satirical expression now. 'Hearing that a rival business was interested would bring about a rapid rethink.'

I smiled, equally dryly. 'Or?'

'I suppose for the right author, acceptance could be bought.'

'*Io!* Do publishers sell works in which they don't believe?'

'Hah! All the time, Falco. A bad book by a known name, or a book by a personal friend, for instance.'

'Does it ever work the other way? Discouraging a good author, who might otherwise be a rival to some dud they do choose to patronise?'

Euschemon smiled wryly.

I tackled Pacuvius again. 'Back to these scrolls – when you came here that fateful day, was the revised effort a subject you and Chrysippus discussed?'

'Yes. First, I had the usual sordid tussle about whether he would pay a fee for my wasted work. He wanted me to continue the rewrites; I insisted it was worthless to try. At last we agreed that I had done all I could with the material, which he would be using for oven fuel. He should have burnt it before involving me. He was a temperamental idiot. With no taste, as Turius has always said. I simply could not understand why Chrysippus was so determined to make something of this yarn.'

'Did you know who had written it?'

Scrutator looked uneasy. 'I was never told directly.'

'But you had your own idea? One last question. Pacuvius, why were you so reluctant to be sent to Pisarchus' villa as a poet in residence? Was it only because you resented the brutal way you were ordered to go?'

'I knew Pisarchus' son wrote adventures. He had mentioned it at the popina. I had a feeling this unfortunate story might be by him.' *Scrutator* looked at the shipper and Philomelus apologetically. 'I thought Chrysippus was sending me to Praeneste so I could be nagged into more editing. I couldn't face that, I'm afraid.'

'Thanks,' I said. To Aelianus on the dividing doors, I then called, 'Will you bring in the witness from the Temple of Minerva, Aulus, please?'

LVII

IF ANYBODY was surprised to see my witness, nobody gave a sign of
it.

'Thank you for attending. I apologise for the long wait. We are
in the final stages of a murder enquiry, but please don't be alarmed.
I would like you to confine yourself to answering the exact
questions I ask. You are a member of the Scribes' and Actors'
Guild?'

'Yes,' answered Blitis, my contact from last night.

'Do you recognise any other members here?'

'Yes, and –'

'Thank you!' I stepped in quickly. 'Just answer the questions,
please. I understand that a writers' group meets regularly at the
Temple of Minerva to discuss their work-in-progress. The member
whom you recognise here has done that?'

'Yes.'

'Often?'

'Yes.'

'Has the group ever discussed an adventure tale called something
like *Zisimilla and Magarone*?'

'Er – yes.' Blitis looked slightly embarrassed.

'Relax,' I grinned. 'I shall not ask for an unfettered review of it.' He
looked relieved. 'We have already had that.' He looked embarrassed
again. 'It is by someone in this room, am I right?'

'Yes, Falco.'

'A technical detail – when you heard this poor work being read at
the Temple, did you see the scrolls? I am wondering specifically if it
had a title page?'

'I seem to remember that it did.'

'Thanks. Just sit on the bench at the back, will you?' There was
room next to the vigiles. All my witnesses would be put safely there
now.

I paced down the floor, crossing the rug on the centre mosaic, like a barrister thinking up his concluding remarks as the last water clock ran out and his talk-time expired.

'In any murder enquiry, what we need is actual evidence. One of the first problems in this case was that nobody seems to have seen the killer straight after the crime. We know he must have been heavily blood-stained, yet we never found his clothes. Other items from the scene were missing too: part of the scroll rod that was a murder weapon and, of course, the title page of the manuscript Chrysippus had been reading.'

I turned to Helena, who had remained standing patiently nearby. 'What about that manuscript? Helena Justina, although you did not enjoy it, you read most of it. Can you give us some idea of the person who wrote it?'

Helena pondered, then said slowly, 'A reader. Someone who has devoured plenty of similar novels, without properly digesting what makes them grip. It is too derivative; the ingredients are rather clichéd and it lacks originality. It's by someone unskilled, but someone who has plenty of time to write. I imagine the project meant a very great deal to the author.'

I turned back to Blitis. 'When *Zisimilla and Magarone* was discussed at your writers' group, there were unfavourable comments. What was the author's reaction?'

'He refused to listen. Our remarks were well-meant discussion points. He threw a tantrum and stormed out.'

'Is that usual?'

'It has happened,' Blitis conceded.

'With the same degree of violence?'

'Not in my experience.'

I asked Helena, 'Would this fit your assessment?'

She nodded. 'Marcus Didius, I can envisage a scene here where Chrysippus was approached by the author of *Zisimilla and Magarone*, who obviously had a wild yearning to be published. Chrysippus explained – perhaps not tactfully – that the work was unacceptable, although attempts had been made to improve it using a successful and well-known redrafter. The author became distraught and probably hysterical; tempers flared, the scroll rod came into play, and Aurelius Chrysippus was violently killed.'

'We know that the killer then continued in his rage, throwing ink, oil, and various scrolls around the room.'

'I imagine that was when he ripped the title pages from the scrolls,' said Helena.

'From more than one?'

'Yes,' she said gently. Helena paused for emphasis. 'There is a second story, Marcus Didius. It is one of fine quality. Both Passus and I enjoyed it tremendously. I would imagine that if Chrysippus read the second, he knew that was the one he must take.'

Euschemon sat up keenly. No doubt he wanted to quiz Helena on this tempting sales prospect.

'I suppose Chrysippus may have told the disappointed author that he had been pipped by someone else?'

'If Chrysippus was unkind,' said Helena.

'And it would fuel the reject's disappointment?'

'His grief and frustration must have been intense.'

'Thank you.'

Helena sat down, putting her hand protectively over the pile of scrolls beside her, which we now knew included a probable best-seller.

I fetched Blitis and led him in front of Philomelus. I positioned myself carefully to intervene if there was trouble. 'Do you know this young man?'

'I have met him,' said Blitis.

'Among your group at the Temple?'

'I saw him there once.'

'Thanks. Sit over there with the vigiles again, please.' I myself led Blitis back. I was not expecting trouble, but it was a moment to take care.

'Philomelus.' Philomelus was rigid. 'You are a pleasant young man, working hard to support your dream. You come from a good family, with a loving, supportive father. He believes in you even though you have abandoned the family trade and want a most insecure career. Unknown to you, your father even tried to influence Chrysippus in your favour. Pisarchus would actually have paid for your work to be published – however, he knew you would find that untenable. Your father sees you as an upright character, whereas I am now faced with the opposite thought. You are a would-be writer of adventure tales who visited Chrysippus just before he died. You admit you became angry and you threatened him. It appears I have no alternative but to arrest you for his murder.'

Philomelus stood up. I gave him room, and stayed alert. His eyes met mine, harder than I had seen them. His father wanted to leap up beside him, but I gestured Pisarchus to let the lad handle this. The father's chin jutted, as though he was clinging on stubbornly to his faith in his son.

Philomelus was so angry, he could hardly bring words out. Yet the anger was controlled. 'Yes, I came here. Some of it happened as you say. Chrysippus did tell me my story was rubbish, and he said it was not worth copying. *But I did not believe him!*' Those eyes were blazing now. I let him go on. 'I knew it was good. I felt something odd was happening. I am starting to understand it now, Falco – I was being cheated. He never *lost* my manuscript; the man intended to steal it and say it was written by somebody else –'

I held up my hand. 'Are these the ravings of a complete madman? Or have you something significant to say in your defence?'

'Yes!' Philomelus roared. 'I have something to tell you, Falco: my story is not *Zisimilla and Magarone* – I would never call a character Zisimilla; it is almost unpronounceable. "Magarone" sounds like a stomach powder too. My novel is entitled *Gondomon, King of Traximene!*'

I turned to the benches behind me and found Helena Justina beaming with delight. I pushed Philomelus down to his seat with one hand on his shoulder. 'Stop shouting,' I said gently. I glanced over to Helena. 'What's the verdict?'

She was thrilled for the young man. 'A shining new talent. A breathtaking story, written with mystical intensity. An author who will sell and sell.'

I grinned briefly at the shipper and his startled son. 'Sit quiet, and contemplate your talent and your good fortune: Philomelus, my assessors reckon you are good.'

LVIII

THERE WAS a certain amount of extraneous activity. The room was humming with noise like a banquet when they let in the naked dancers. As I walked back to the centre of the room, Euschemon scuttled past me. He ensconced himself alongside Philomelus and they started muttering in undertones. Then Helena gathered up part of her scroll collection and beetled down the row to return his lost manuscript to the excited young author. She sat down with him and Euschemon and I saw her shaking her finger. If I knew her, she was advising Philomelus to obtain a reliable business adviser before he signed away his contractual rights.

Fusculus appeared through the dividing door, looking pleased with himself. He gave me a vigiles nod. I interpreted as best I could. With the vigiles it might only mean a take-out lunch box had arrived. I mimed that he was to bring in the old lady who walked about the Clivus Publicius. Fusculus winced. She must have given him the hard basket treatment.

Lysa was head-to-head with Diomedes. Time to stop her little games.

'Attention, please – and *quiet!*' I shouted in a commanding tone.

Fusculus brought in the grandma, leading her gingerly by one arm. He walked her slowly around the room for me. I asked her to point out anyone she remembered seeing the day of the murder.

Enjoying her role at the centre of things, the aged dame fastidiously stared at everyone, while they looked back in a state of nervous tension – even those who I was certain had nothing to fear. My star witness then indicated all the authors except Urbanus (a good test of reliability), followed in turn by Philomelus, and even Fusculus, Passus, Petronius, and me. Really thorough – and useless for my purposes.

Taking her free arm, I made her stand in front of Diomedes. 'Did you leave one out?'

'Oh, I have seen him such a lot of times . . . I'm sorry, Falco, I really can't say.'

Diomedes laughed; it was brittle and overconfident. Fusculus caught my eye above the old lady's head, and I could sense his hostility. All his antipathy to Greeks was now focussed on this one. He grinned nastily at Diomedes and Lysa, then guided the nosy old woman to a seat among the vigiles, so she could watch the fun.

'Worth a try,' I said ruefully. 'You're a lucky fellow!' I told Diomedes. 'I really was convinced you were lying. I thought you had been here. The way I saw it, you killed your father, Vibia discovered you at the scene covered in blood, then she helped you cover up your tracks – literally in the case of some bloody footprints. It might even have been the lady who thought of sending you on your way casually chewing nettle flan. Once you were cleaned up and had left the house, she rushed outside screaming as though she had only that moment found the body . . .'

People heard me out in hushed silence. They could see how well the story fitted the facts. Vibia Merulla remained expressionless.

'In return for Vibia's silence about your guilt – I thought – your mother gave up this house to her. Vibia herself was so horrified by finding you at the crime scene, Diomedes, she started avoiding you . . . And that was why she disliked the thought of you marrying one of her relatives. Still!' I exclaimed brightly. 'How wrong can I be?'

I spun round to the resolute widow.

'Nothing to say, Vibia? If you're hiding your husband's murderer to get it, you really do hunger for possession of this house! Still, a Corinthian Oecus is a rare feature. And of course, the property came fully furnished – the furnishings are beautiful, aren't they? So lush. Every cushion stuffed to bursting point.'

I faced Diomedes.

'I am not intending to call that priest of yours as a witness. I believe he lied about you making offerings all day. You do go to the Temple of Minerva, but you don't go there to pray. There are other reasons for hanging about there on a regular basis – the writers' group, primarily. Tell us: do you write, Diomedes?'

He looked shifty, but he sat tight and glared at me. His mother's face was also blank.

'Blitis!' I called out. 'Does Diomedes write?'

'Yes,' said Blitis. 'He wrote *Zisimilla and Magarone*.'

'Truly! A secret scribbler?' I went on relentlessly. 'Do you lurk in your room dreaming up and honing your creative masterpiece, young fellow? And, Diomedes, do you persist with it, even when all around you describe it as no good?'

I spun back towards the vigiles. I asked Petronius swiftly, 'Did he have the flan?'

'Yes,' answered Petro immediately, not needing to consult his notes. 'He grabbed the last piece when I was trying to get my hands on it.' I saw Helena resisting a giggle, while the vigiles grinned at one another.

I strode over and bent down to the old dame. 'Can I make a suggestion? I think Diomedes came here around lunch time and then breezed back later, heading towards the Temple of Minerva, looking a little too innocent?'

'Oh, I remember now.' She too grinned through toothless gums. She was a game old duck, thoroughly enjoying this. 'I did see him go in when I was fetching some lentils for my dinner. When I was getting a bit of onion later, I watched him come out again. I thought it was peculiar because he was wearing different clothes.'

'*Aha!* Why was that?' I demanded of Diomedes. 'Was there blood on the first set?'

'She's got it wrong,' he scowled.

I signalled to Aelianus. He moved those who were seated on the furthermost bench; Fusculus went to help him kick the seating aside, fling the doors open, and wheel in the great trolley that bore Diomedes' property.

I crossed the room towards the heaped baggage. First, I pulled out a scroll from a chased silver container. 'Helena, glance at this, please. Tell me if you recognise the handwriting from the tale you and Passus hated so much.' She nodded almost immediately. Fusculus came up behind me, probably intending to hint at where I ought to look in the cart, but I managed without any help from him. 'Diomedes, you agree that all this is your personal property?'

Shoved roughly inside a knee-high boot I could see papyrus. 'What have we here? An interesting boot-shaper. Two very crumpled sheets that purport to be – let's see: the title pages to *Zisimilla and Magarone* and also *Gondomon, King of Traximene*. What's that about, Diomedes?' I dragged him to his feet. 'Looks like proof of who wrote *Gondomon* – this title page is written on the back of a used popina drinks bill.'

'Mine!' Diomedes blustered recklessly. 'I often drink there –'

'Urbanus, it says.'

Urbanus looked unfazed then told me, 'I leave the bills behind. Philomelus tucks them in his pouch. He has no money for equipment and I'm happy for him to reuse them for writing.'

Lysa, resplendent in maternal wrath, swept to her son's side. 'Foolish boy,' she reproved her son. 'Now tell the truth!' She turned to me. 'These prove nothing!' she snorted at me. 'Blame Chrysippus. He wanted to exchange the title page on the scrolls he stole from the shipper's son. He was planning to publish the story under our son's name. Diomedes was far too sensitive and honest to agree . . . In fact, Diomedes removed and kept the original, so he could prove what had happened if his father went ahead —'

Oh, she was good!

'Very generous!' Among the swathes of rich brocaded curtaining, pillows and floor rugs, lay one cushion that looked extremely lumpy, ill-stuffed and quite untypical of this house. It was nothing like the smooth, fat items I had thrown on the floor from Vibia's couch that time. I dragged it from the pile. 'This is from your room too?' Deeply perturbed, Diomedes gave a brief nod.

Wrenching open some loose and amateur stitchery that cobbled one seam on the slipcase, I flung the innards across the floor at his feet. People gasped.

'One heavily bloodstained tunic. A pair of bloody shoes. A scroll rod finial, with a dolphin riding on a gilded plinth — the exact match of the finial on the rod you forced so crudely up your father's nose.'

Diomedes leaned across me and grabbed a spear from his pile of belongings. Helena cried out.

'Jupiter!' I muttered, as I grabbed the shaft. I went hand-over-hand up it in a couple of swift moves, until I was leaning on Diomedes' chest. 'Where exactly were you planning to shove that?' I demanded sarcastically.

We were inches away from each other, but he hung on to the spear. Petronius had reached us. He and Fusculus grabbed Diomedes. I wrenched the spear from his grasp. They twisted his arms up his back.

I took hold of his fancy tunic, either side of his miserable neck. 'I want to hear you confess.'

'All right,' he admitted coldly. Lysa burst into uncontrollable and hysterical wails.

'Thank you,' I said in a polite tone. It was worth a fee bonus to me. 'Details would be useful.'

'He refused to take my work, although I was his only son. Mine was as good as anyone else's — but he said he had found something wonderful. He was going to pretend Philomelus' story was worthless so he could pay nothing for it. He would even make Pisarchus pay the production costs, and then take all the profits. He was beside himself with excitement. Then he said that as the publisher of a high-class work, he could not afford to soil his name by selling mine alongside it.'

'So you killed him?'

'I never meant to do it. Once we started to fight, it just happened.'

His hysterical mother was now battering me, as she tried to fling her arms protectively around her boy. I let go of him and pulled her away.

'Leave it, Lysa. You can't help him. It's all over.'

That was true for her too. She collapsed, sobbing. 'I can't bear it. I have lost everything –'

'Chrysippus, the bank, this house, the scriptorium, and your crazy son – then of course without the bank, you have probably seen the last of Lucrio. . .' I tried wheedling encouragement: 'Admit to us that you had Avienus killed, and we can lock you up as well.'

Some women fight it all the way. 'Never!' she spat. So much for my wild hope of claiming not one but two confession bonuses.

As the vigiles logged the evidence and prepared to take their prisoner away, Diomedes remained surprisingly calm. Like many who confess to ghastly crimes, ending his silence seemed to bring him relief. He was very pale. 'What will happen now?'

Fusculus reminded him tersely: 'Just like your evidence.' He kicked at the empty cushion case. 'It's the Tiber for you. You'll be sewn in the parricide sack!'

Fusculus refrained from adding that the wretched man would share his dark death-by-drowning with the dog, the cock, the viper, and the ape. Still, I had told him yesterday. From his terrified eyes, Diomedes was all too aware of his fate.

LIX

I T SEEMED to take hours to conclude the formalities. The vigiles are hard, but even they dislike taking in parricides. The dire punishment strikes horror into everyone involved.

Petronius left the patrol-house with me. We went home via my mother's, where Helena had gone to fetch Julia. I told Ma what Lucrio had said about her money being safe. Naturally, Ma replied that she had been well aware of that. If it was any of my business, she informed me, she had already reclaimed her cash. I mentioned that Nothokleptes seemed a good bet as a banker to me, and Ma proclaimed that what she did with her precious sacks of cash was private. I gave up.

When she asked if I knew anything about stories that my father had been involved in an altercation with Anacrites the other day, I grabbed Julia and we all went home.

By chance, as we crossed the end of the street nearby where my sister lived, who should we see but Anacrites himself.

Petronius spotted him first and caught my arm. We watched him. He was leaving Maia's house, unexpectedly. He was walking along with both hands in his belt, his shoulders hunched up, and his head down. If he saw us, he pretended not to. Actually, I don't think he noticed us. He was in his own world. It did not appear to be a happy place.

Helena invited Petronius to dine with us that evening, but he said he wanted to set his apartment straight after the fight with Bos. After she and I had eaten, I sat out on the porch for some time, unwinding. I could hear Petro crashing about opposite. From time to time he tipped trash off the balcony in the traditional Aventine manner: making sure he shouted warnings, and sometimes even allowing long enough for pedestrians to scuttle out of danger in the street below.

Eventually, with Helena's approval, I sauntered off alone. I went to see Maia.

She let me in, and we went out onto her sun terrace. She had been having a drink, which she shared with me; it turned out to be nothing stronger than the goatsmilk she normally kept for the children. 'What do you want, Marcus?' She was always abrupt.

We had been too close for too long for me to mess about being delicate. 'Came to check you were all right. I saw Anacrites, looking grim. I thought you and he had had plans?'

'He had the plans. Far too many.'

'And too soon? You were not ready?'

'I was ready to dump him, anyway.'

She might have been crying earlier; it was impossible to tell. If so, she had gone past needing to shed her woes and was now calm. She looked sad, but unrepentant. There were no visible doubts. I wondered when she had made up her mind. Somehow, I did not think that Maia had ever heard the rumours about Anacrites and our mother. But she might know he had given Ma stupid advice financially. That would count against him with my sister, to a degree he might never have realised.

'I'm sorry if you have lost a friend.' I found that I really meant that.

'So am I,' said Maia quietly.

I scratched my ear. 'I see him around town. He is bound to ask me, when he can face me, whether I think you mean it.'

'Then tell him what you think,' she said, being her old awkward self. I shrugged, then drank my milk.

We heard someone knocking at her door. Maia went to answer, leaving me relaxing in the sun. If it was another close associate, she would bring them out here; if it was door-to-door lupin-sellers, she would see them off and come back cursing.

Low voices were talking. Far be it from me to eavesdrop, but I was an informer; the new visitor sounded familiar. I leaned back, tucked the toe of my boot under the handle, and inched open the sun terrace door.

'My brother is here,' I heard Maia say, in an amused tone.

'Nice!' replied Petronius Longus, my supposed best friend, with what sounded like a sneaky grin. 'Family conference?'

'Why, what sort of conference were *you* planning?' quipped Maia in a slightly lower voice. Surely she must have known I could over-hear them. 'What's this you've brought?' she demanded suspiciously.

I heard the squeak of the front door hinge, as if it was opening wider. There was a rustling noise. 'A garland of Vertumnus. It's his festival, you know –'

Maia laughed raucously. 'Oh don't say it's my turn to be backed into a corner by Lucius Petronius, the Aventine seduction king, and enticed into a night of festival fun?' Maia was my favourite sister and a model of chaste Roman motherhood – but she gave me the impression that in the absence of action from Petro, *she* would consider cornering *him*. The innuendo was flagrant. He must have thought the same.

'Don't talk like that,' begged Petro, in a strange tone. 'Maia Favonia, you will break my heart.'

'You're serious!' Maia sounded surprised. Not as surprised as me.

'I don't want to be passing festival fun,' he bragged. What a fraud.

'I won't ask what you *do* want then.' Something was going on, something sufficiently intriguing to stop me calling out a ribald joke. 'So?' asked Maia.

Then Petronius answered gravely in a formal tone, 'I am reconstructing my apartment. I want to buy some replacement pots and foliage to put on the balcony . . .'

Maia laughed again, more quietly this time. 'My dear Lucius, so that's how you do it! You murmur, *"Don't touch me, I'm too honourable!"* Then you talk about potted plants.'

Petronius carried on patiently as if she had not interrupted. 'They seem to have some good stuff at that stall below the cliff. Will you come and help me choose?'

There was a pause. Then Maia said suddenly: 'Good idea. I like that stall. I saw they are selling watering pots. You dunk them in a bucket of water, then you can rain a gentle shower onto your special plants . . .' She stopped, sounding wistful, remembering she could no longer afford treats.

'Let me buy you one,' offered Petronius.

'Wait there,' said Maia cheerfully.

My sister poked her head around the door and smiled brightly at me. Around her neck, she was wearing a ludicrous garland of leaves, twigs and fruit. I refused to remark on it.

'I'm just going on an expedition with a friend for a few horticultural sundries,' she told me in a sweet, inconsequential way. I loved gardening too, but there was no offer to include me. 'You can finish your milk. Make sure you pull the door closed when you go, please.'

I felt as if Anacrites was not the only person my sister Maia had dumped that day.

★

I went home, through streets full of slightly threatening revellers who were preparing for the festivals of Vertumnus and Diana. There were people jumping out from behind pillars, wearing animal skins. I could faintly smell smoke – perhaps singed fur. Others had bows and arrows and were targeting hapless passers-by. On the Aventine, nobody needed moonlight to behave crazily. Unpleasant mimes were enacted with horns, while phallic garden gods were everywhere. Mounds of greenery made alleyways impassable, street hawkers were flogging trays of congealed snacks, and drink was being consumed in fabulous quantities. Where the two happy festivals collided, rival groups were squaring up for a good fight. It was time to huddle safely indoors.

Back home, I told Helena that my sister was shamelessly leading on my friend, and that he was encouraging her.

'Dear gods. I never thought I would see Maia and Petronius canoodling over a balcony fern and a watering pot.'

'Don't watch then,' scoffed Helena, chewing the end of a pen. She had a codex spread open on her knee, a double pot of red and black ink, and was updating our accounts. 'Think nothing of it, you dear sentimentalist. They may be giggling over propagation pots tonight – but tomorrow is another day.'

'Sounds like some daft girl in a romance, trying to console herself.' I reached for a wine flagon and a good scroll to read. As I gripped the scroll rod and pulled out the first columns of words on the faintly yellowed papyrus, wafts of writing ink and cedar oil assailed me with nostalgia.

Helena Justina folded her arms and said nothing for a long time. As she did when she was letting her imagination roam. I stopped reading and gazed at her. Her eyes met mine, dark brown, intelligent, perturbingly deep with love and other mysteries.

I smiled at her, showing my own devotion honestly, then immersed myself in my scroll again. You never know with secretive, imaginative women what surprises they are dreaming up.